THE GLASS SHADOW

ALAYNA COOPER

[BOOK TITLE] The Glass Shadow

Cooper, Alayna, Author
The Glass Shadow
Alayna Cooper

ISBN: 9781790972906

[Category] NOVEL

QUANTITY PURCHASES: Schools, companies, professional groups, clubs, and other organizations may qualify for special terms when ordering quantities of this title. For information, email alayna.a.cooper@gmail.com.

This is dedicated to…

My wonderful family; thanks for being there all the way.

My friends in Chicago; you left me with some great memories.

My friends in Colorado; there are some new memories to make!

And to anyone who buys this novel; I sincerely hope you enjoy.

For all of your support and encouragement,

Thank you.

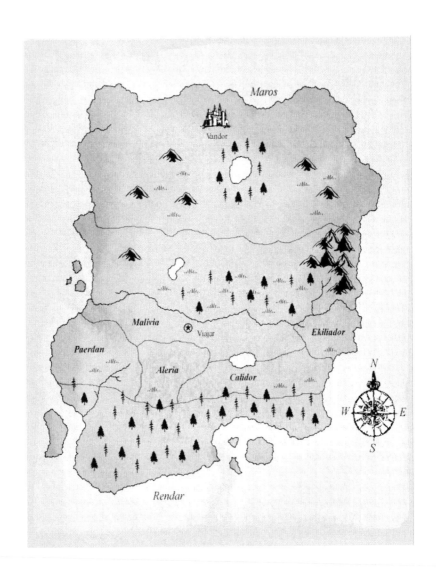

The dusk is dawning, it's time to go!
Before the land is filled with snow
We set off shore, onto the sea
Oh, come along, along with me!
The night is coming, the cold is near
The dark and death bring much to fear
So come along, we can't be late!
The dusk is dawning on our fate.

CHAPTER 1
ALICE BRINK ~ MARIS STILLIAN
THE BARREN

It was a wasteland that lay out before them.

A cruel, unforgiving wasteland that seemed to have no end, and no beginning. The last light of day shone dimly on the black, sharp stones and rocks that made up the landscape. A breeze cut through the air, bitter and cold, a breath of forgotten dreams and approaching nightmares. Silence filled the emptiness, a silence so dominating that one couldn't help but be overwhelmed by the sound of their own breathing. It was a dead land. A broken land.

Wearily, a man and woman, both covered in dried blood, stumbled forward towards the endless horizon. Dirt-stained packs that seemed much too light were slung over their shoulders. They were travelers.

"Maris, *we need to stop.*" Panted the woman known as Alice Brink, pausing to catch her breath. "We need to rest." Sweat lined her brow, her face flushed and hands shaking.

The other, Maris Stillian, shook his head. "It's just past noon. We can't, not now."

The sun was pale, strained, and let on little light straight above them in the sky. Though Maris's instincts told him it was not so, the rest of him thought it to be much later. They both looked exhausted, the pain lined clearly on their faces.

"The days are getting darker." Alice noted a few moments later, when he did not elaborate, and Maris nodded in agreement.

"That doesn't mean we can rest sooner, hun. When did the Alice Brink I know become the first to quit?" He asked, helping her over a boulder.

Alice remained silent; it may have been that she did not have the strength to argue. Her hair tangled with the wind, her skin deathly pale, pouring sweat. Maris had dark skin, burly and strong, with a shaved head and a slight beard. He wore a silver chain around his neck, the only thing the could be considered remotely good-looking about him. They both bore countless scratches, wounds, and scars. Unshaven skin and thin stomachs portrayed them as what would be considered commoners of the street, but anyone who knew them would say otherwise. In fact, they looked much better than some who dared wander in such places as this. The Barren was a formidable place, far from home and poisoned by war and a twisted radiation. The pair continued to stumble onward, the multiple sharp, jutting rocks just begging to be tripped over.

"Any shelter in sight, then?" Alice asked, looking hopefully past his shoulder. She knew that should they come upon such, they would not pass it by. Alice didn't think she could last another night out in the open; they knew all too well what lurked in the dark when light fell.

Maris shook his head, now annoyed. "If there was, it's long behind us." His eyes didn't even glance up to the distance. God knew how many times he had already checked.

They fell into a moment of silence, the only sound being the occasional grunt, the clatter and scraping of rocks, and the depressing call of crows in the distance. Not but seconds later, Alice felt a disturbance; a strange disturbance within the earth below. She stopped and knelt, putting her ear to the ground. It vibrated, creating a trembling sound just barely heard. A rumbling beneath the earth. Maris had felt it too. Just as he opened his mouth to question it, the ground beneath them began to shake. They both stopped, worried. There had been quakes like this during their journey in the Barren, few and scarce, but this one was stronger, faster… closer.

Suddenly, with a crack like the sound of a gun, the ground split open like a gaping maw, revealing the world below to the world above. Stones flew, dust rose. More cracks broke into the surface, causing them to get over their shock and stumble out of the way.

There was a loud roar, one that must have been the land changing, sliding, shifting.

"Alice! Run!" Maris tripped over a rock and scrambled away from a slithering crack, back in the direction they had come. "Run, goddamnit!"

Alice was waiting for him, eyes wide, full of terror. Danger was clearly upon them. However, Alice didn't run, from either shock or fear or wanting to help. Maris got to his feet and dashed forward, trying to pull Alice along with him. Unfortunately, Alice's muscles didn't seem to want to move. The dust and rubble slowed them down even more, and Maris looked back at the collapsing land behind them. Alice blinked, and seemed to finally come to her senses. Seeing that she did not need to be dragged, Maris ran full speed, having no intention of being caught in the storm. He tripped and hit his face hard on the rocks, splattering blood.

Alice passed him, not able to see through the dust. Without hesitation he ignored the pain and the hot blood running down his face and kept running, running. But it wasn't enough. By the time he looked though dark to notice Alice was far ahead, it was too late. Maris's clothes billowed in the rush of wind as he called out. The sun had faded, the light was gone; so was his hope.

"*Alice!*"

He could see her horrified face as he ran, the ground falling into the depths just behind his heels. Alice backed up, pure panic gripping her stomach. Even at full sprint Maris couldn't outrun it. Just as the ground came to a rest, just as the thundering beneath the earth came to a halt, he slipped over the edge, gripping on by just his fingers. Even running her fastest, Alice knew she would never reach him in time.

Maris tried to yell, but his throat was constricted, his terror overwhelming. Tears flowed from his mangled, exhausted face as he made one last effort to get his other hand onto the small, jagged edge. Fire ran through his arms, his bare feet scrambling for a nonexistent foothold. The ground under him, the land that they were supposed to cross was all but gone, crumbling down into the dark abyss of a ravine below. And as the last light faded, as the last streaks of yellow and orange flashed on the rocks through the clouds, Maris Stillian's hand slipped, and he fell into the bottomless pit with one last, desperate scream. Alice dashed to the edge, tears dripping down her dirty, bloodied face. She sank to her knees and managed to choke out a sob in her grief.

The traveler winced at the harsh wind, the dry taste of ash and dust in her mouth, the starless sky, the faint roars, and most of all the scream that was bitterly cut off in the deepening night.

LIROS DAYLAN
THE BARREN

Liros Daylan, known as Lee to the family he had left behind, sat resting on the edge of the brook, a cold sweat dripping down his pale forehead. His disheveled hair was coated in dirt, his clothes comparable to the likeness of rags. All in the grey forest was calm, but still he glanced over his shoulder, frightened, muttering to himself. Lee probably had been traveling for many days, months, even. He didn't know. What he did know was that Rendar was far, far away from here... and that *here* was a very bad place. Lee had no bags, no supplies, no nothing. His eyes had glazed over; he was clearly starving. A small waterfall splashed down onto the rocks below, creating the distinguished sound of clattering hooves. Dead, withering trees surrounded him and the river, the ground littered with gray leaves, dying grass, and black, sharp weeds.

Breathing hard, Lee leaned forward and scooped muddy water into his already dirt-smeared hands. The water was bitter and cold, like the wind, and the dark grit and dirt made him flinch as it drained down his parched throat. He could tell it was fresh water, that he was sure of, yet there was still something off about it. Something wasn't quite right. But no matter how much he wanted to, he couldn't have the luxury of worrying about that right now.

Lee took a small book out of his satchel and opened it, hands shaking from hunger. *Lost again,* he thought, scolding himself. How was he ever going to get back? *You aren't, little Lee, you're never going to get back, you're never going home.* His thoughts had turned dark, had twisted and worked against him, as they so liked to do.

The land had changed so much, the old maps were almost useless. All he had was this, the guide to Maros, written by a man who for some reason loved to speak in riddles and rhymes. The guide to the Barren; the only guide. The only anything about anything to do with this place that there was. Sighing, Lee squinted and looked under the section he was looking for. The ink was fading, but still legible.

Along the river, the river of black
When you go in, you don't ever come back
When you follow its path, you die of thirst
Unless you drink, and forever be cursed
So don't get close! Don't go near!
A darkness dwells forever here
Along the river, the river of black
When you go in, you don't ever come back.

Great. That's... that's fucking great. Lee glanced down at the river, looking through the mud. He couldn't see the bottom; a darkness seemed to swirl in the depths. Instead of despairing, a small grin overtook him. *Well, shit,* he thought, now spitting back into the water. *So much for taking a bath.* He laughed at the idea. The laughing quickly turned to a cough, and he started hacking up blood, dark and phlegm-like. Lee hoped the rhyme was just a figment of the author's imagination, but deep down he knew he wouldn't be so lucky. A sickness was most likely upon him; he had lived long enough in the Barren to know that luck didn't exist.

You're dead, little Leeeeeee, you're a dead man. With despair, he thought about Rendar, now so far away. He missed his home, missed the hills and his friends, missed the local bar with the highest-quality scotch he'd ever tasted; missed his son, his farm in southern Paerdan. All the states of Rendar, despite their various political and economic conflicts, were better places to live than here. This was a rotting, dead wasteland. Lee knew better than to think that just the war had caused all this. Something more had caused the sickness of this land. *And the sickness is what'll get you, it'll get you soon and you're never going home, never ever going back.*

11

The blurry sun slowly sank down towards the forest lined horizon, causing him to stagger to his feet and try hopelessly to brush off the dirt on his pants. Better make good use of the daylight he had left. *What daylight? There is no light in hell, little Lee.* He was driving himself to the edge. His scratched hands left lines of blood along his worn jeans, only making it worse. With a sigh, he gave up. There were more important things to focus on.

They never stopped to rest. They would be close. Lee could already feel their presence. The savages were everywhere, lurking in the unseen shadows. Lurking behind the trees, in the bushes... in the river. He was never safe. Trees blurred past as he ran, as he ran as if his life depended on it. Of course, in a way, it did.

After what seemed like miles, Lee came to a stop. Night was arriving sooner than he had expected. Taking a deep breath, he knew he couldn't waste anymore time. Just as he took a few short steps, he heard a sound he had imagined, feared, and dreaded for nights on end. Hooves. A sharp memory of fear filled his mind, and he shook away the panic. He had to go. *There's nowhere to go, little Lee. It's just me and you, you and me,* the voice taunted him. There was a slight pause. *And them.* He just had time to look up at the glazing sunset before the darkness covered the sky, shadows crawling.

Crows cawed, wolves howled, the sound of horses came closer, closer, closer. The freezing, bitter wind rushed past him, as if even it were trying to escape from what came.

As fast as it has begun, it was over. A black-tipped arrow pierced his back, his eyes filled with shock, pain flooding his body. And as he fell onto the ground, into the black chasm, into the arms of death, the dark men and horses stampeded over him, as if Liros Daylan had never even been there at all.

RILEY CANSON
THE BARREN

The soft moonlight of an ending night splashed across the swaying gray grass, shimmered on the black rocks, and gleamed on the dead, sickening fields. Riley Canson, a young woman, pushed through the tangles of thorns and plants as she further journeyed into the Barren. The brisk, somehow pleasing cool wind brushed the landscape, whisking away the lingering smell of rot and the feeling of sickness.

Her hands brushed the dry, fragile grass, her shoulders shifting and adjusting to the heavy weight of her pack. This was one of the rare early mornings that she experienced here; Riley had the intention of enjoying it. Before long the sun was rubbing its eyes and sighing before wearily rising up to another morning. Dapples of light flowed along the ground, giving her hope that she would be able to renew the Barren, if not just explore it.

However, good times could not last. Clouds gathered ahead, and she knew rain would be upon her. Luckily, (if there was such thing as luck in the Barren) she spotted a cave. Rubble surrounded it, and Riley took great care to ignore the shapes that vaguely resembled bones. She felt a drop on her face, and brushed it away with her hand. She was *not* spending another night out in the rain. There was something wrong with it, the rain. It was poison.

Impatiently brushing stray strands of red hair out of her eyes, Riley walked gingerly into the cave, careful not to misplace her steps. She remembered bits and pieces from the notes in her pack, written by a person who had once lived here... a guide. It was one that had been written when this land was still known as Maros, and the three kingdoms, Vandor, Vinia, and Valca still flourished. At least, before they fell. They had once been like the cities from the past, metal and glass and rising into the sky. She recalled Illius, the king of Vandor at the time, having found a secret passage from a cave that led right into his castle. Perhaps she had come upon it.

Just as the thought appeared, Riley stepped on something hard- something metal? She knelt down and brushed off the black sand and rocks that covered up an old, rusted steel helmet. On it, the insignia of Maros- a bull's head, facing forward. If this was really the cave... she would have a straight passage to Vandor, a straight passage to her goal, and certainly with less dark-radiation. She hoped. The sickness of it inside her had started to spread.

Letting out a sigh of relief, she got back to her feet, filled with new hope. Her visions of the strange orb could stop, and if the stories were true... The orb might still be in Vandor. Riley could get to it, do something to make her dreams stop. Do something that mattered. If there was an orb, of course. The Glass Shadow was only legend, after all. In the past, such an idea would have been considered ridiculous; but times had changed. Life had changed. She stepped forward, curious. A tune of a song from her childhood repeated itself in her mind, and, setting aside her fear of the darkness, started to sing.

She struggled to remember the words as she walked into the cave, feeling along the walls, keeping herself from panicking and running back outside. The rain had started to splatter on the rocks. It was a song she had learned long ago, and she felt comforted by it. Her voice was shaky, her eyes darting back and forth into the darkness. The sound echoed through the tunnel, but it was too late to stop. If she did, she would be consumed in darkness, panic, and silence. Her foot hit a rock and she stumbled, but kept on singing.

The world faded back out to the entrance of the cave, and her singing became fainter and fainter. Her words dimmed out, and there were moments of silence, all quiet but the rustle of grass and the breath of the wind. The sun disappeared behind the clouds and the drizzle of rain watered the earth.

She was never seen again.

CHAPTER 2

ROVAS MCHENRY
VIAJAR, MALIVIA

"These are dark days."

Rovas Mchenry stood in front of the Rendarian council, a serious look on his worn face. In the room, there was a long table, seating the leaders of each of Rendar's states. Sophia Henderson, for Paerdan. Brias Falimer, for Calidor. John Keller, for Aleria. Natalie Denroe, for Ekiliador... And finally Rovas Mchenry himself, for the honored state of Malivia. *Though most of them can't tell a fox from a hare, much less rule a country,* he thought, smirking. Rovas may have grown up without a mother, but he had at least been raised by proper men of the sea and the docks in Eastern Calidor. From there, he had risen to the top... to here. These others, he didn't trust them. He didn't think he ever would.

They had been placed in their positions of power for no other reason other than their wealth, and their family names. Granted, he was a part of the Malivian family currently in charge, but he was different. Rovas had worked hard to get here. He *deserved* to be here. But now was not the time for that. *Now is the time for my revenge, the time for the hearts of the men I hate to know what it's like to suffer.*

A window was behind him, showing a high view of the Malivian Capital, Viajar. Brick towers and houses and even what looked like castles made up the landscape, banners bearing the Rendarian symbol hanging from windows and markets and flags. Old metal buildings, rusted and crumbling, were inhabited by the homeless huddled around trash can fires. The busy streets were wide;

some people rode horseback, some climbed onto buses choking out exhaust, others had bikes. Most were walking.

It was a busy day. Traders sold artifacts from the old world, watches, rusted nails, light bulbs, even some jewelry. Anything they could scavenge. The gunsmiths repaired their old guns, while the marketers and vendors sold food from the farms in Aleria and Paerdan. One shop was even auctioning working motorcycles in a garage. It was a broken city, put together with the scraps of what had been left behind.

A Rat played a broken guitar on the corner, his beard long and his skin dirty. His hat lay beside him, the few silver coins glittering inside it. Rats were the homeless of the streets, the criminals, and the poor. They lurked everywhere in the shadows. It was a messy sight, but a sight *he* had power over. The thought filled Rovas with pride. And now here he stood in the heart of the Castle, in the heart of the democracy of their world.

The weather was chilly, the trees along the roads alight with fall colors. Fall had lasted longer than expected, five months already. Long or short, harsh or slight, it always changed. The seasons were always unpredictable. They always had been, since the rebirth of the world. In the room, a decorative carpet lay under the table, while paintings hung on the walls. A radio crackled in the corner, playing one of the few stations there was to offer. Leaders were dressed in light furs over their suits, for winter was coming early. Their eyes were focused on Mchenry, waiting. The politicians were in a discussion of the Castle, the government of Rendar; it was clearly an important meeting.

Rovas continued to speak. "Dark days indeed. And dark days... require action." He paused to slick back his dark hair, and to scratch at his stubble. "The Barren is spreading into the Ashen Desert. Freelanders move south, into the grasslands. If we don't act, soon they'll be in our land. Scavengers, thieves... murderers. The sick, the poor, and the lost."

The others nodded in agreement.

16

Rovas fingered the gold-engraved hilt of the dagger at his side as he talked. It was still stained with blood from the day before. Public execution was never pretty, but it was satisfying. If his recollection was correct, the body now hung from a lamppost on the edge of the city. Rovas grinned at the thought. Everyone did their best to avoid and ignore places like that, due to the blood on the streets, splattered in every which way. It had become one of the most common places to display those who had defied the Castle. It was empty for the most part, but for the crows. And... the hungry ones. The hungry Rats. Both the real ones, and the men.

"The spreading of the Barren is also causing storms, the unusual weather. The air is tense, like the smell of fear before the battle. Do you not feel it?" He looked each one of them in the eye, inducing them, setting fear into their hearts. "*Do you not feel it?*"

The others could feel it, he knew, but he needed the sense of urgency. Manipulation was a hard task, but in the end, the control was his and his alone.

Rovas continued. "Small quakes disturb us every other week or so, but there are more, and they are stronger every time. Many dismiss it, the quakes are so small, but my council and I... well, we agree it's more. The Barren, the past land of Maros, is spreading, and if we do not act the dark-radiation will come. My scouts have reported it, and even they are too afraid to venture out again." He *was* starting to sweat, despite his inner confidence. Malivia would be the first to become one with the Barren. They were closest to the border, to the grasslands. However, he had a plan already, one the other leaders didn't know; his revenge. Truthfully he cared little for the fate of his country, and focused more so on settling the last of his debts before the end. The other rulers were deep in thought, worried.

Mchenry continued after a brief silence. "I... think I may have a solution."

Brias Falimer, Calidor's leader, looked up at him. "And what might that be? War on earth itself?"

Mchenry looked frustrated, but was too worried and ignored the comment. *One day he'll learn to treat me with more respect,* he thought, frowning with distaste. *Once he learns ruling isn't as simple as he may think. Maybe he'll be the next one left dead for the crows.* Rovas quickly dismissed the thought from his mind; that was for another time.

"There is rumor of an orb. A Glass Shadow. Some have tried to obtain it before. One that might be powerful enough to stop the Barren. From the legend, the orb washed up on shore, where a fisherman found it. He brought it to Vinia, where Harrison showed it to the other kings- Ilius and Amor. They supposedly kept it in Vandor, where Illius swore to watch over it. After the war, after the land died... we don't know what happened to it. Everyone left Maros... No one could live in such conditions. After our ancestors sailed here, to the last bit of land on earth, we exploited the mysteries of the new world the unstable core had created. The mysteries we still remain oblivious to-"

"What has this got to do with a solution? We don't need a history lesson." Sophia stood up. "What else can we do but wait? The Barren is far, far away. It has lain dormant for hundreds of years, why should it not do the same today? We have plenty of time to work out a reasonable solution, just finish up for now. I have a meeting at noon and am not too eager to miss it."

Rovas cleared his throat and again nervously scratched the stubble on his beard, which was, as he'd recently noticed, spotted with grey hairs despite his younger age.

"Just trying to help you make the connection, I hope you can understand." His voice was thin and bitter. Sophia tapped her watch expectantly, though warily flinched at his cold gaze.

"Yes, well..." Rovas gathered his bearings and continued. "Getting to the solution. I propose we send out... travelers. To retrieve the orb."

There was a moment of silence. He'd said it so quietly that it was possible some of them hadn't even heard it.

Brias scowled, looking unimpressed. "Really? Come on! Are you serious? You have a whole council at your back and that's the best you can come up with? This is ridiculous." He shook his head, scoffing.

John looked shocked. "Rovas....you can't be serious. What would that even do? How would that even help? No one has dared go into the Barren for years."

He was a soft soul, John, bless him. *Can't see an inch out his window, much less his own lands.* Rovas doubted the man even knew what *really* went on beyond his front door. He himself had an ongoing drug business in southern Aleria.

Natalie entered the conversation, bearing a quite irritated demeanor. "All of you! Listen to him! It's not like any of you came up with something better. This isn't the time for an argument!" She glared at Brias, who gave her an exasperated look and turned back to Mchenry.

John now had the look of a parent disapproving a child. "I do have to admit... I am a bit disappointed." He glanced up at the Malivian leader. "Past experiences... Stillian... Daylan ... Canson... none of their ventures ended well. Only Brink made it back alive, but even then she didn't make it very far into the Barren. You must have a good reason."

Brias forced a smile through gritted teeth. "So, then tell us. Enlighten us on this wonderful solution. What would meager travelers do to stop the spreading of an irreversible, destructive disease?

Mchenry shifted nervously, biting his lip, exaggerating his actions. They needed to believe him, after all. "I have been... having visions."

"Well, that's never good." Brias joked, yet a glint of fear hid in his eyes.

"What about?" Sophia pushed, seeming to have forgotten all about her meeting. It was three minutes past noon. The notion of visions, for some reason, did not seem to surprise them; perhaps they were simply too afraid to test Mchenry's patience, or question his sanity.

"Something is there. In Vandor. I- I've seen the orb. The Glass Shadow. It's real, and well, *not* broken." Rovas was rushing now, his voice shaking, as if some panicked commoner from the city had taken him over and was trying to convince an audience of his insane reasonings. The others were taking in every word. He really was quite convincing... yet he was an actor. That was his talent. The man had been an actor since he'd learned he could lie. The visions were true, but Rovas wasn't the least bit afraid of them. Along with the dreams, he had been hearing voices in his head, strange voices, mixed and muddled, and in his gut he knew they were connected. The voices were faint and barely legible, though he could hear them nonetheless. As if on cue, it started happening again.

(Help us freeusfree us Rovas we're blind we're blind we're blind) He couldn't seem to be rid of them. But what could he do about it? Nothing, yet. This was much bigger than him. He knew what he would do, though, if time allowed. He knew his plan would succeed. And if worse came to worse, he knew he would survive. He had a ship. *That only is, if worse comes to worse.*

"There's something other than the orb, though. Something *alive*. It's rage, it's power... It, or they, may be using the orb to cause the spreading. We need to act before they decide they may want to speed things up."

He didn't really know this. Half of what he was saying was utter bullshit- *but they'll believe it.* Yes, he would make sure of that. Something bigger than himself was happening, this he was sure of, no matter what lies he told; and he would make sure he got what he wanted done before it was out of his hands.

Natalie interrupted John, who had opened his mouth to speak. "So, the quakes are just a reaction to the earth changing?"

"That's the most likely scenario, yes."

They sat in silence for a moment, Rovas having taken his seat at the head of the table.

"Tell us more about... these travelers." Brias looked slightly ashamed, but determined. "Will them retrieving the orb keep the dark-radiation at bay? Will it give us peace?"

20

Mchenry nodded. "Yes, I'm sure of it. The Glass Shadow holds immense power, this you must understand. We cannot let it fall into the wrong hands."

Rovas refrained from mentioning that his visions filled him with an aching hunger. Whatever was sending him these dreams and whispering in his head, it was hungry.

The politicians did not question his decision. Rovas had read of such quests for greater powers in several stories, and though he highly doubted it would work, he would not pass up the chance to give the revenge his enemies deserved. Four men, four unlucky men would be sent out to their doom; for Rovas Mchenry did not give up his grudges easily. Whether they brought home the orb or not, they would suffer; this was all he wanted.

"And who are these travelers you plan to send out? Who's strong enough to face something like this?"

Rovas crossed his arms, certain in his statement. "Jacob Fortemer, who lives right here in this city. Marion Armais, a criminal from the south. Oliver Monterose, yes, the journalist. And Louis Willson, a farmer in Paerdan."

"Are you positive? Do you trust them?"

Not in the slightest. "With my life."

"And are they capable?" Brias asked critically.

"Without a doubt."

The leaders nodded, respecting his decision.

Sophia looked worried. "How will the public deal with this? I see it's a... if you could even call it a decent option. Our only option. A trial and error, giving we know almost nothing about this situation... but they'll certainly protest this. They'll know something is wrong, that they're in danger."

Rovas only smiled sweetly at her ignorance, shaking his head. "You think we would tell the city? It would be all over the papers, word would spread in every inn and bar and home and fear would grip the hearts of all. Chaos would reign, not us. The public *will not know.* In fact, I have had these men in mind for a while. People I know that deserve a little... ah, penance. For their crimes.

21

We snatch them up, offer them something they can't refuse for a good hearted cause, and send them on their way. Tell them to retrieve this Glass Shadow and bring it back. It's a win either way for us. If they die, or if they actually succeed. Though I..."

Rovas paused, chuckling. "Highly doubt that. They may be reluctant at first, so I have connections... they will not be able to return after they have set foot past our border. And if by chance they decide to come back and make it into Rendar without the orb, well, that's where my hired friend comes in. He is well paid, I assure you, and easily trusted. He will deliver them to the Barren and leave them in the night. By then it will be too late for them to turn back."

The politicians seemed confused by his lack of concern for the travelers' survival, but said nothing. Their fear of Rovas Mchenry would forever trump their instinct to oppose him.

"So what do we tell them? If they have no interest in this, why push?" John asked. "I doubt they will stand for it, I-"

Rovas interrupted. "I feel I explained that already. *Money*, my friend. People will do anything for it. What is it with you all and telling the truth? This game is one to be played carefully, like chess. With men, however, you do not force your pawn into place. You must know what will make it move itself."

There was silence. *Soon they will learn the way of the world. Not everyone tells the truth.* "We will tell them they are to retrieve the orb and bring it back here, so we might use it's power to stop the spreading of the Barren. That is the truth, I assure you. And do not worry, if they survive and return with the orb, we will know what's out there and use the Glass Shadow to stop it. We'll promise them whatever they ask... more, even. They will be more than willing to go for the right price, if they still are the people I think they are."

It was all so clever, so planned out and precise that he had started to grin. This wasn't really for Rendar. He was almost certain they were all doomed. No, this was for himself. This was for revenge, for the people of his past that had no idea what was coming. Checkmate.

"Oh, and it will all be for the greater good."

John nodded, convinced. "A quest for the orb, a chance for the unfortunate to rise to the top..."

Sophia, too, was deep in thought. "And if they succeed..."

Rovas Mchenry finished the sentence in his head. *No one ever need know they were meant to die.*

CHAPTER 3

JACOB FORTEMER

VIAJAR, MALIVIA

Jacob Fortemer, a young man with twenty-six years of age upon him, sat on a couch, trying to muddle through a book titled The History of Rendar. History was one of his favorite things, and though many preferred to ignore it, it was quite interesting.

Jacob's dark blue eyes darted across the pages, immersed. The couch was a dull, scratchy brown; his sister's choosing, matching the bland stone walls, the old, worn carpets, and the scratched wooden floor. The only decor was a faded many-colored rug and a black and white picture of the old world- with towers high as the clouds... a city. It had cost him much more than he ever dared tell his sister. The windows were open, letting in a slight autumn breeze, diminishing the smell of oldness. In Viajar, you couldn't get the fanciest things. Their radio played a quiet song, and he found himself humming it as he read.

Jacob looked up to see his daughter flipping a coin. She wasn't really his daughter. He had found her on the streets when he was a Rat, long after his time as a lawyer; but that didn't matter to him. They were family in other ways than blood. Her curly blond hair bounced up and down as she moved to grab the coin each time. Jacob started to go back to his book, but freezed what he realized what he was seeing.

"Emilia!" She squeezed the shining coin in her hand, smiling mischievously.

"I told you not to get into the money again!"

"So? It's one. You've got a lot." She started flipping the coin again. He ran a hand through his tousled black hair.

24

"Yeah, one coin that could pay for your dinner!"

He had a right to be angry, yes, but she was only twelve. She had to learn. And he knew Emilia loved the coins. When they had been on the streets, before he had landed his new job, they had to steal to survive. She was tough. Streetsmart. Observant, even. But she was still a child, and because of her time without a home she lacked the social skills that she now needed. Grimly Jacob remembered back to only months ago.

The sky was dark, the stars alight. The windows flickered with light, candles and electric both. Electricity was not something rare, though it was old and did not often work. Many did not bother with it. But that didn't matter just now. Now the summer air blew, the cotton of his jacket itched his neck, and Emilia's golden curls disappeared and she crawled through the lower window embedded into the brick wall. He sighed and paced back and forth, worried. He didn't like her stealing alone. Or stealing at all.

After a few minutes he knelt down to the window and whispered. There was no response. Jacob whispered again, this time louder. Nothing. His heart racing he slid down into the darkness, looking around in the dim candlelight. It was a cellar, storage for the inn above them, barrels of wine and herbs and frozen meat- though there was no sign of his daughter. He took one step forward, shivering, and almost screamed when she came from behind him, her finger to her lips. She pointed. In the corner was a dog, on its side, blood trickling from it's slashed throat. He looked at Emilia in horror, and heard her whisper.

"He barked. He barked, Papa, he wasn't supposed to do that. He would have caught us." Her eyes were red, scared; Jacob knew she was fond of animals. "I'm sorry. Papa, I'm sorry."

The memory pained him. He wouldn't have been able to do that. He would have run and starved. But she did what she did, and they ate. Thinking back on this, Jacob didn't notice the jangle of keys out front that meant Rachel Fortemer, his sister was home from the market. Or work. To be honest, he didn't really care. And yes, his sister. The only one he could go to, once he'd found where she lived.

His new work as an mechanic's assistant did not pay much, and only just enough to pay the tax. Rachel paid for most everything else. *She worked for the Castle.* Emilia tossed him the coin as the door opened and ran to her room.

He went back to his book. *The Core had become dangerously unstable, and soon enough many parts of the earth sank beneath the sea...*

Jacob pretended to be immersed in his reading as Rachel looked over at him, setting down her bag.

Society fled to the ocean, but many perished in the chaos. There was only one piece of land left on the surface, as far as we know, the land on which we have constructed our civilization...

"Jacob, home already? How was your day?" She glanced at his book. "Oh! I won't bother you, but where's Emilia? I need help with dinner."

Rendar, the world we turned into a well functioning society, consisting of the lands Malivia, Aleria...

"In the bedroom." Jacob said, wishing she would go and get his daughter before she could ask him any more questions. The time with his sibling had been long and dragging, the same every day. Her constant chatter and cheerful tone made him want to yell, while a long day at work only made him more likely to give in to his frustration. She didn't understand what he and Emilia had been through. She didn't know anything, and others with secrets would know how hard it would be to live with someone like that. Jacob was growing sick of her, the hope that she could become family again having only been a dream. He would never forgive her for what she had done.

Each day he could tell she was trying to make up for it, but it would take much longer than a month to redeem herself. She was why Jacob had been on the streets in the first place. She had left him, her little brother, to the mercy of the orphanage. She had left him because *he* was the burden on her hopes for prosperity. He read without understanding, immersed in his thoughts.

...Paerdan, Ekiliador, and Calidor. Our government, the Castle, formed on the date 393, the 21st of Summer. Maros, our neighboring continent, had already been there for hundreds of years, since the old world had collapsed around them. We were the most people they had seen of yet, as they informed us, to travel the sea still after so long a time...

Rachel walked into the kitchen. "Emilia! I need you in here for a bit."

He heard her coming in, not reluctantly and without complaint. He was proud of his daughter- she knew, despite her age, the hardships of life and that now they were well. The sound of chopping vegetables and boiling water was pushed to the back of his mind as he tried to finish the chapter.

We had thrived off the sea for centuries, and had finally come to a place to call home. Maros had three kingdoms, Vandor, Vinia, and Valca, each ruled by a king. Harrison ruled Vinia, Amor had Valca, and Illius controlled Vandor, the center city. We were at peace until... The sound of knocking filled his head, distracting, and he looked up.

"Someone's at the door," Jacob said, annoyed. He went back to his book.

... the Lost War. Rendar had sent a messenger to Vandor, who got into a fight with an official and ignited rivalries between the various political unions and gangs...

Rachel set down the bundle of herbs she was about to put into the pot and wiped her hands on a towel. She wore a rather uncertain expression; the Fortemer family rarely got any visitors. Mostly they kept to themselves, as some families in the city did. Nevertheless she put on a bright smile as she opened the door, the rusty bronze bell jingling in welcome.

Which then started a war with Maros. For more information, go to chapter six. The next chapter, chapter four, was titled *The New & Strange Chemical Releases of the Earth's Core.* It was Jacob's favorite subject- how the earth's core had become unstable and released chemicals and gases resulting in things never before possible. It was unprecedented, though destructive.

Setting the book down, he got up to watch Emilia in the kitchen. Sometimes she forgot how dangerous the stove was. He heard Rachel's voice as he helped Emilia twist the knobs to turn down the flame. The soup was almost done.

"Sir, there isn't a single reason why any Enforcer should be at my door." His sister said, using the condescending tone she was so fond of. *Enforcer? What the hell else can go wrong today?* For just once he wanted to feel in control of his damned life. Was that too much to ask? Jacob told Emilia to watch the soup.

"But-"

"Just wait here."

She glared, but turned back to the flames, knowing he would tell her the situation later. He would, if it was something that concerned her.

Jacob walked up behind his sister, confused. A man in a maroon uniform and black breeches stood in the doorway; a badge, combed hair, and black boots. His cloak was black as well, with a thin salt-and-pepper fur lining, though it hardly looked as if it provided much warmth. The symbol of Rendar was stitched in gold in the top right of his chest. The head of a wolf was their sigil, while Maros's had been the head of a bull. It was funny, Jacob thought, how many strange, fantastical aspects they had added into their new world. *It was a fresh start, I guess.*

The man's coffee-brown eyes were intimidating and stern, with a coldness that sent a shiver down Jacob's spine. A gun was at his side, a dagger at his other. Jacob backed away warily. Few people in Rendar had guns... one or two in every ten. The gunsmiths were the richest, he thought, perhaps even more so than those who ruled in the Castle. They thrived off the need to shoot; and hell, there was more than enough pent-up anger to go around nowadays. Rachel looked puzzled, even frightened. Never had she gotten in trouble with the Castle before. Never. It was something she prided herself

28

on. The man did a quick scan of the room, causing Jacob to think he was looking for something- or someone.

"Can we help you, sir?" His sister asked with a now trembling voice. She had a right to be fearful. Enforcers were highly trained and unforgiving. He himself had been silent. *What a coward.* A knot seemed to have formed in Jacob's throat. They were looking for him. Slowly he backed away.

Had they found out it was him who had stolen the necklace? They needed the money that time, there was no choice. Or was it the man he had pickpocketed on the street? Or the bread he had snuck from the market? His heart fluttered nervously. The Enforcer slowly walked towards the kitchen.

"You are Rachel Fortemer, I assume?" He turned his back to Jacob. Letting out a sigh of relief, he walked over to Emilia, taking her in his arms and carrying her to the bedrooms before they could be brought to a higher notice. It wasn't about him. The Enforcer's voice rang through the house.

"Sister to Jacob Fortemer?"

He froze in his tracks, barely daring to breathe. A stone dropped in his gut, filling him with dread.

Rachel answered in a confused voice. "Yes, but why-"

The Enforcer interrupted. "Have you seen him lately? Is he here, now? You don't have a husband, another brother or cousin?" Jacob could imagine the stern glare the Enforcer was giving her.

"No, that was him, just now-"

She was cut off; there were footsteps. They had to get out. He'd done too much theft to be kept out of jail. Jacob hesitated. He couldn't do that to Emilia. He couldn't take her back out there. She... she would be safe here. It was him they were looking for. Jacob gave her a quick kiss on the forehead, and avoiding looking into her confused, terrified eyes. Quickly he locked the door to the bedroom and moved to open the window when he heard the Enforcer's voice again, louder this time.

Jacob fumbled with the window lock, starting to slip into the arms of his memories, thinking about how Rachel would say windows should always be locked, as the family's lifetime savings were kept in the house. *Her* lifetime savings. Rachel didn't trust the banks; though, honestly, Jacob could understand that. It might have been the one thing they both agreed on.

The window unlocked with a click and he started to climb out. The wind was loud and raging in his ears, the coldness in the air burning his bare skin. He had forgotten a jacket. Forgotten to grab anything of importance. *Dammit, Jacob!* He thought to himself as he pulled himself out above the empty alley below. *Get something right, for once.* But there was no turning back. He urged himself to hurry, the sounds from behind the door growing louder and louder.

"Where is he? Where did he go?" The Enforcer yelled something else, and the stomping of boots crashed through the house. Jacob winced. Why were they searching for him? How had they found him? More voices flooded into the room.

"Wait! What're you doing?" Rachel. "He hasn't done anything!" Her voice was shaky, confused. Guilty. Jacob could hear another Enforcer speak.

"He'll be coming with us."

A crash. Footsteps. In a panic he pushed himself farther through the window, just as the door shook and was pounded upon. Leaves blew past him as he tried, shaking, to make his way down the stone wall. The sky was clouded over, the city around him busy and humming with tension. Normally, Jacob would have enjoyed the view of the city, but not now. Now there was nothing below him but the hard cold ground many feet down.

Suddenly, a loud crash came from behind him, and Jacob couldn't help but turn and look. Three Enforcers stood in the doorway, including the one he had seen before. The one to the left was familiar, but only because she had been patrolling the market by their house. And then the third, whom he didn't recognize.

"There!" They grabbed him before he could even think to leap out, and by then it was too late.

"Where's your daughter?" At first he thought he'd misunderstood, but he asked it again and his gut was gripped with fear. Jacob shut his eyes and internally screamed. *Why, why, why couldn't I just have gone faster?* And what did they mean where was his daughter? He had left her outside the room. She didn't seem of great importance to them, though, because he motioned to the others.

"Wait! Where is she? Where is she?" Jacob yelled. He had left her. Where had she gone? *"EMILIA!"* She would be taken, or-or starve, or something else, why oh why had she gone-

They tied his hands in rough, thin rope, and the third pulled out his gun, rusted and old. A gun? *Wait, no, no, nonononono-*

"Wait!" Jacob started to struggle. "Let me go!"

The Enforcer raised the gun, bashing the side of Jacob Fortemer's head with brute force. There was a sharp pain, dizziness, and all went black.

LOUIS WILLSON
THE FARMLANDS, PAERDAN

Louis Willson looked up at the rising sun, contemplating the day ahead. Paerdan was a poor land, but their farms kept them going. This light-skinned, twenty year old man was among the many who worked days on end, though he had nothing past his knee. His left, if it mattered. *Not that it does,* Louis thought. *It's still a leg gone, in everyone's eyes.* A pair of wooden crutches had served him well for many years, but had broken just yesterday. Now, he sat on the porch of his home, where he lived with his ailing sister and brothers.

Their mother had died ages ago, their father never quite an influential part of their lives. Louis had known him, of course, but only because the man had needed help with his ship on the far-away docks. His brothers... they never got along with Louis. Henry and Kendrick did not bother him. They were older, and too respectable for behavior like that. However, Wrenn, Caios, and Faylon seemed to make it a priority to ridicule him. Louis was used to it by now. May, his sister, was the only one he really loved.

His siblings now worked in the fields, but Louis had left them to construct a new pair of crutches. He called them crutches, but they weren't more than sticks, really.

Louis's deep, kind green eyes moved over the calm land, and he hoped he could be of use to his siblings by the afternoon. It was the least he could do for them.

With all the weather changes, Louis hoped the cold would stay away, but he knew they would not be so lucky. The ground was cold, the sky pale. Chilly wind would bite their skin, the dying leaves coloring the grass. They would buy crops from the other farms, and hunt food to store in the basement. Their own fields would freeze and die, as would their pipes, unfortunately. He was thankful they had running water in the first place. Today, a colder day, just reminded him of the work ahead.

Suddenly, his older sister, May, rode in on the path, her motorcycle dropping to the dirt as she dismounted.

"Louis!"

She was holding a package. A smile shone on her face, her blouse waving in the wind. It had been a long time since he had seen his sister smile. She wore a wool jacket and boots that were splattered with mud. Despite so, she looked better than she had in a while, and he hoped her strange sickness was a thing of the past.

"May? What're you doing?" He noticed, despite her smile, that she looked exhausted. Concern filled him immediately. "Where were you?" She picked up the package, wrapped in leather, and walked up the porch steps to his side.

"In the town." She slumped into the chair beside him, and handed over the package. However, Louis wasn't interested in it. It took two hours to get to the town on the bike, and two hours back. He glanced up at the sun. Early morning. She would have had to have left before dawn, perhaps earlier, depending on how much time she spent there.

"You never thought to tell us?" Louis said, concerned. He straightened up.

"I had to go early. For this." She motioned to the package in his lap. Confused, Louis unwrapped the leather and, to his delighted surprise, removed gleaming wooden crutches. They were stained, shiny and smooth, the surface carved with designs and patterns; not to mention strong and sturdy, as well as comfortable as he stood up to test them out.

"Do you like them? You know the woodworker, Melner, works only at night. He's old, drinking until he can't see two feet in front of his face, waking up at five in the evening and wondering where the day went. That's why I had to go early. They should last a while."

Louis smiled, but could only imagine what it had cost. "How... how much did you pay, May?" His voice was weary with sadness, with a hint of dread. He loved the gift, and they had instantly become his most prized possessions, but it had to have cost a fortune. Whiskey wasn't cheap, and Melner wasn't a cheap man. He looked at her, and she turned away.

"How much?" Louis was dreading the answer, but he needed to know.

"Six coins, three ten dollars."

He gaped at his sister, eyes wide. He had expected a few dollars at most, but thirty? Paerdan was not wealthy like Malivia or Ekiliador, so the value of the coin was much higher. She looked a little guilty, but recovered quickly.

"It'll be worth it. You need a new set so often, and you're always hurting, and we can't spare the time to gather the right wood. This'll save you a lot of pain."

He looked at the crutches, as if deciding whether or not it would be wrong to use them. "I'm taking from the family. We could have bought a week's worth of crops with those coins."

This'll be what his siblings glare at while they go hungry to their beds. Louis looked over at her, but she was fast asleep. She was older than him by few years, twenty four going on twenty five, if he remembered right; but she was sick, with something even the doctors in the village knew nothing about, and should not have even been out of the house. The sickness inside her was starting to show, show like a bruise on an apple, a dead tree in a summer forest.

"Thank you, May."

He spread a blanket over her and hobbled off the porch, with intentions to feed and brush the horses. *You will never stop being a burden,* he told himself. *You will never be what they want you to be, no matter how hard you try.* The feeling of guilt dug itself deep into his heart, he glanced at the fields again, watching his other brothers hard at work. Thanks to his crutches, he would be able to work longer. Harder. Faster. *But at what cost?* He would never be as valued as his brothers.

Louis continued slowly over to the stables, tucking his less than shoulder-length red-blonde hair behind his ear. The sun had just begun to peek over the trees in the distance when the loud stomping of hooves thundered up the path. Louis looked up from the sight of hay and horses to find a black cloaked man ride up on an even darker steed. He was wearing an Enforcer's uniform underneath, the badge assigning him to Paerdan tucked away, hidden. Or perhaps the man wasn't assigned to Paerdan at all. He clearly wanted to blend in as much as he could, though not many people wore maroon and black other than the Enforcement.

Louis shivered, and wrapped his jacket around himself. He wasn't expecting it to get this cold. He stepped onto the road and raised his hand, a clear, peaceful symbol of stop. The Enforcer didn't slow down, and Louis tried to dart out of the way, hoping to run as well as he could and fetch his brothers. However, the officer rode off the road and cornered him, cutting him off. Louis looked for a gun on him, but there was none to be found. It was most likely hidden in his cloak. Only the highest trained, most deserving Enforcers were presented with such weapons. No one else but those with enough coin to buy them from the Castle or the gunsmiths.

"Sir, what's your purpose here?" Louis yelled, wary, annoyed. He hated dealing with Enforcers. There was a moment of silence. "Sir?"

The man did not speak, however, but drew a dagger and motioned with his head to mount the horse.

Louis sighed, rolling his eyes. "God, what've I done now, run too far away from town? Did I kill some poor bastard?" Louis could hear his own voice, hear it like an echo in his head. He tried to sound irritated, but it shook. Most tried not to show it, but all feared the Enforcers. He quickly regained his confidence. Why should he care? "Oh that's right! I didn't do anything, *because I'm a fucking cripple.*"

The horse approached him, the dagger gleaming, shining in the sun. He put the tip to Louis's throat. A voice came from under the hood, laced with controlled anger. "And yet I wonder what it would look like covered in your blood."

35

It was a threatening, almost irresistible voice, deep and orderly. Louis felt it impossible to deny his command. And what would he do otherwise? Run? He couldn't. Even if he had two legs he could not outrun that beast of a horse. Refuse? The hooded man had made it clear enough.

His mind and body screamed out in protest as he mounted, gripping his crutches as if they might try to escape him. They turned around and bolted down the path, away from his home. Louis kept silent, wanting to scream out but knowing no one would hear. The rider paid him no attention. All Louis could do was grab onto his cloak to keep from falling. He thought about jumping off, but the road was rocky, and it was dangerous at this speed.

Trying to fight the rider would surely not end well for him, and even if he tried pushing the man off, well, he feared that he wasn't physically able to do so while staying mounted. Instead, Louis Willson looked back towards his home, disappearing in a haze of fog.

MARION ARMAIS
REISE, CALIDOR

The clouds gathered overhead, casting a chilly feel over the town. The bitter cold wind slashed a young man's lungs as he took a deep breath, savoring the smell in the air. Marion Armais pulled his hood over his head and started walking, passing a church with a foggy graveyard. A black cloak fluttered behind him as he picked up speed, his hazel eyes glancing dangerously in every direction. The small town of Reise had shuttered their windows, locked their doors, and stayed inside by the fire.

Very few people lingered out here in this weather, especially with the small quakes they got every now and then. Calidor was the furthest from the Barren, but the quakes were starting to worry even them. Normally, the people of Calidor explored the Unventured Lands, to the south. The towns were usually busy, and the sun would shine down on the constant commotion of the country. But now... no one was sure of anything. *Too scared to come outside, hiding from something they can't even see. Hiding from something they can't escape.*

Marion, at twenty-seven, was old enough now to realize he didn't have anything worth hiding for, and though the future was uncertain, at least there was no one on the streets to question him... at least, no one who cared. He glanced over at a homeless man slumped over, leaning against a wall, a bottle in his hand. Whiskey, maybe. Marion was tempted to take it, though the poor man looked so pathetic he found that didn't have the heart. Marion had to admit, Calidor was short of hope. Soon enough, he reached a square full of shops, with a gurgling pale fountain at the center.

Marion looked gloomily at the gray stone buildings and foreboding dark windows, watching people dressed in cloaks and boots exchange their money for food and supplies.

An older woman stood by, chatting with a market vendor. "I've been needing new forks for ages, do you have any left?" The vendor nodded. She turned to her daughter beside her. "Oh! And we need to stop at Villian's on the way home, if you don't mind. I need meat for supper tonight." The other woman nodded, handing a few coins over to the marketer as he collected her forks.

No one turned to look at the young man in the cloak as he passed, swiftly moving towards a customer-free stand. The vendor behind the counter looked up as he approached, but didn't stop what he was doing.

"Mr. Armais? I didn't expect you so early." He continued to tinker with a greasy machine part. "The usual?"

Marion nodded. "I've got business to attend to." The vendor nodded, his amused smile slightly visible over his short, scraggly beard.

"Got the devil in you today, eh?" He laughed. "Don't get into too much trouble, Mr. Armais. There are some rotten apples out there." He reached under his counter and brought up a loaf of bread and a bag of nuts, pushing over the items to Marion. "Especially with the Enforcement on your back." The man gave him a toothy grin, handing him a beer. "This one's on me."

Marion took the bottle and handed the man a few dollars for the food, which he wrapped up in a cloth and stored in his cloak. "Thank you."

He gave the man a nod and left the square, heading towards the forest. Marion Armais was considered a criminal for many reasons; though having grown up on the road, he viewed it differently. He would be hired to steal from, say, wealthier people, and bring whatever it was back to the person who wanted it. Some criminals were so dangerous they couldn't risk showing their face outside; often times they couldn't even risk being caught over trying to buy food, so they hired him. He ran simple errands, mostly.

Marion was a man of the streets, had been as long as he could remember. A Rat. *That's what they call them in Malivia, isn't it?* But at least he was a Rat with coin in his pockets.

The trail got darker and narrower as he went into the forest, as he searched for Ellison Mane; an old murderer, rapist, and a thief. He had never been fond of Ellison, no, but his money was still money, however tainted. It was Marion's last resort, when he was free of other duties, when the main markets were closed, and he felt the need to pay the bar a visit later in the day; when he felt he could bear one trip for the criminal.

Soon enough he found the carving on a stone where they were supposed to meet, and with an air of hurriedness, left the bag of food by the rock. Marion collected the dollar bills and pile of coins, looking as if stained they were with blood, from under it. This was a dangerous man, but he was fair. He gave money to Marion to buy the supplies, and gave him his pay when he returned. The criminal was afraid an Enforcer would follow Marion to his location if he stole.

As Marion walked away, he heard Mane humming to himself, creeping out of the bushes like the Rat he was. With a slight look of distaste, Marion tread deeper into the forest, wondering if one day he'd become like Mane. Dangerous. Alone. Cruel. *Insane.*

Glancing around, he pulled his hood up further, vowing never to go far enough to end up like that. If this is where it led, he didn't want any part of it. Suddenly, Marion stopped. Something was watching him. A chill went down his spine, and the hairs on his neck stood up. A tense feeling in the air... something was about to happen. He turned, but the trail was empty. Empty, but for a note set in the middle of the path. A note, with a message.

> *Prey are the fools lost in their own minds.*
> *My friend,*
> *Watch for the predators.*

Mane. What did he mean? It was surely a mockery, a tease... a trap. Before he could register the betrayal, half a dozen Enforcers came charging out of the trees, four with guns, two with daggers. They surrounded him, closing all exits before he could run, which was exactly what he was planning to do.

"Surrender into the custody of Rendar, by the order of the people and the Castle." The statement, though professional, sounded so rehearsed and bland it was almost laughable. Almost.

"What did I do? There's no need for the hostility, I assure you." Marion pulled back his hood and tried to look confused, only to find he was staring into the barrel of a gun. He hoped desperately he could talk his way out of this. If not, at least he had his dagger.

"You were associating with a well-known criminal, possibly working for him." The Enforcer scowled, pulling out a slip of paper. "And though *he* slipped past us, we're assuming you're Marion Armais, the one who's been reported stealing from the towns of Wellston, Launen, and Kennington, as well as here and numerous other places."

Marion gripped his hidden knife tight, sweating. "Look-"

The Enforcer interrupted him. "We don't have time for this." One of the other men sheathed his dagger and pulled out handcuffs, the guns clicking in the hands of the Enforcers.

The man with the cuffs approached him. "Now don't you cause any trouble." The others scoffed. They really didn't believe he was going to fight. The world around him seemed to slow, the chirping of birds and the rustle of dry leaves becoming ten times louder. Marion pulled out his shining dagger, breathing heavily. Without hesitation he lunged at the man with the handcuffs, digging his dagger deep into his gut, twisting it before pulling it back out with a sick gasp.

With a cry of pain the Enforcer dropped to his knees, holding his stomach in a hopeless attempt to keep the blood back in. The life seeped out of his eyes, so in pain, so hurt, so helpless. Crumpling into the dirt, he closed his eyes, the blood creating a darkness that slowly spread along the shirt. Marion ducked as shots rang out above him, then whirled to face the man closest to him, who had risen his gun threateningly.

"Stop! Set down your weapon!"

Marion ignored him, grabbing the gun and twisting it out of his hand. The Enforcer punched him, then reached for the fallen weapon. Marion heard a click and ducked to avoid a shot. He ran behind the one reaching for his gun, slicing his throat effortlessly before he could stand up again, and kicking back an Enforcer behind him who had slashed his back.

His hands were sticky with blood. *I won't go, I won't be one of them, the criminals, I'm different, you don't understand, you don't understand-* his knife was knocked out of his hand. More of them seemed to have come from the trees.

They had not been aiming to kill. At least, harm him, but not kill him. Marion earned a bullet slash past the arm and a cut in his back, taking down one more before he was overwhelmed. The stench of blood and sweat flooded his nostrils, his own throat sore and scratched- but he continued to scream, scream, scream as they cuffed his hands and dragged him along the path, the glazed eyes of the dead Enforcers starring, their blood seeping into the ground.

His screams echoed through their last thoughts as they lay still among thousands of crinkled leaves, among rotting trees, among living things submitting to the cold mercy of winter- among thousands in an endless battlefield of dead.

OLIVER MONTEROSE
SILVERSTONE, ALERIA

The kitchen of the Monterose Manor danced with sunlight, silent in the early morning. The only movement was the family's cat. The soft ginger fur on her back moved up and down as she slept on a pile of blankets in the corner. Birds chirped faintly outside, where they could be seen in the garden through the window. There were roses and bushes and tall, waving grass. There were other houses in sight, buried in the hills and valleys of Aleria. The cracked road wound down as far as one could see, like a river, the lines a faded yellow.

Back inside the kitchen, A dark-skinned man of about forty five was shuffling around, sipping from a mug of coffee. Sitting down, George Monterose put his head in his hands, looking not only tired, but as if he hadn't gotten any sleep at all. His stubble was hinted with specks of grey.

He was pouring over the newspaper, deep into it's content when another man came in. It was Oliver Monterose, the man's brother. Upon entering, he looked around, with brown eyes, dark skin, and a fedora atop his shaved head. Though wearing just a gray dress shirt and bland sand-colored breeches, Oliver still managed to look powerful, professional.

Yes, his brother was a politician, one of the Castle, but sometimes George lacked the stature Oliver himself could not seem to be rid of. Oliver, at thirty three, was staying with his brother for the next few days. His brother was very rich, with a wife and kids; to say in the least, he was very jealous of his sibling's success.

"Morning, George."

"Oliver! Nice to see you up so early." George adjusted his glasses and ruffled the newspaper.

"Reading anything interesting?" Oliver stretched and walked over to him, leaning over his shoulder.

His brother tried unsuccessfully to hide the article from him. "No, it's just-"

Oliver saw it, sighed, and closed his eyes. He shook his head, a shocked, pained expression on his face. *No, it can't be true.*

"George, that's not good."

"I know, I know, I was waiting to tell you." He said, exasperated. *Waiting to tell me? This isn't something you can hide.*

"You were convicted of murder? Why aren't you incarcerated?"

His brother's expression hardened. "No! Well, yes, but I swear, it wasn't me. I was just at the wrong place at the wrong time. It's all just a... huge misunderstanding. And... they're not holding me because of my position. I still have very important work to do within the Castle, confidential works, and should I be deemed guilty I'll have time to... well, wrap things up."

Oliver picked up the paper, reading aloud in a confronting tone. "The highly respected Alerian councillor George Monterose convicted of the murder of Paulen Denroe, son of Mary Denroe, nephew to Ekiliador's leader. Natalie Denroe, the boy's aunt, states it as *A tragedy that we hope we can overcome with the country of Aleria.* Paulen's funeral is at dawn tomorrow, while Monterose's trial shall be held the 49th of Fall."

Oliver looked sadder and sadder as he read the dark, bland print. There was a moment of silence. "Why were you in Ekiliador?" He asked.

George shook his head. "I wasn't, I-"

Oliver interrupted him. "Don't lie, how could you be convicted of a murder if you were in another country as the victim?"

"No, really, listen. Oliver, I was at a meeting in Newtown, which is, if I have to mention, in *Aleria,* and decided to go get a drink at the local bar. It wasn't great, it's very poor down there. I am very lucky I got a councilman's job-"

"George."

"Right. Paulen was visiting in Aleria with his grandparents, or so I've heard, and I saw him in an alley with another man. They were yelling, the man pushing the boy around, so I went up to see what the problem was. I knew I should've let him be, but I didn't want anything to happen to either of them, and... well...when he saw me approaching, the man... stabbed Paulen and ran, throwing the knife at my feet. A couple walking by saw us and reported it to the Castle. I swear that's the truth. I would never kill someone." Oliver still looked frustrated, but confused and worried, as well. *No, he wouldn't, the fool. The kind, kind fool.*

"I- fine! But you should have told me sooner, I really got-" A loud, sturdy knocking cut him off, leaving them both wondering who was at the door this early in the morning. George got up, pushed in his chair, and walked down the hall. The knocking continued.

"I'm coming!" He looked concerned.

"George? Honey? Who's that?" The quiet, sleepy voice came from upstairs.

"No one, Sara. Go back to bed."

Oliver followed his brother down the hall to the door. It shook with every knock.

"God, stop banging, I'm right here!" George grumbled, annoyed. The knob squeaked as he opened the door, revealing two Enforcers standing side by side. Sara, despite George's confirmations, rushed downstairs, coming up behind them. Two kids hid behind their mother's skirts, watching with fearful eyes.

"George Monterose?" Asked one of the Enforcers. Oliver looked at them from behind his brother's shoulder. One was rather burly and unblinking, while the other seemed to have more wits about him.

The former observed them while his partner spoke. "The councilman?"

"Yes, that's me. Why? What's this about?" George asked. However, the worried gleam in his eyes betrayed the question. He had already assumed the worst. The clever one smiled, risking a quick glance at Oliver. Him and his brother looked a lot alike, and whenever they were seen together were quickly presumed related.

"We've come for your payment." And with that, the stronger one grabbed Oliver by his arm, clicking handcuffs around his wrists before he could think. The Enforcer's partner pushed George into Sara, before he grabbed the doorknob and closed the door in their startled, terrified faces.

As they dragged Oliver to a cart lead by two horses, he wondered why they had taken *him*. It had to be because of the crime. Apparently the trial didn't matter. He was the sacrifice. What they wanted him for, Oliver didn't know. *Or could it be they know? Do they know what I did, what I wrote about the famous leader of Malivia?* Yet a nagging feeling inside him just wouldn't go away. The Castle didn't work like this. There was something more going on here.

The Enforcers threw him into the back of the cart, which was really more like a cell. Oliver had often seen carts like these, harboring criminals with dead eyes and bleeding hands. The walls were thick wood, stained with dust and dirt and what looked like blood. He couldn't even stand, as the ceiling was so low. The two small windows on either side were barred with rusted steel.

Unfortunately, the only exit was the door Oliver had been tossed through, and it was certainly locked. Smelling the air, he was suddenly grateful for the windows, which let in light and fresh wind. The lingering smell of blood, urine, and filth nauseated him, and Oliver crawled hopefully over to the bars, wishing for a breeze that would blow the smell away.

For hours he stared at the dents in the wall, imagining himself spitting into the streets, screaming at the top of his lungs until he could no longer move. Sadly, no matter how strong the longing, Oliver knew he should not waste his energy or act like a criminal. Like a Rat. No matter what happened, he would not lose his dignity.

CHAPTER 4
LANUS ELMER
VIAJAR, MALIVIA

The two officials stood in a bland looking room, staring wearily at the door that would present the captives. Four metal chairs were lined against one wall, while an open window breathed a lazy wind through the curtains. Outside, rain poured down onto the city of Malivia. The gloomy mood became gloomier when one of them spoke up.

"Shame they couldn't get one from Ekiliador, Lanus."

"They tried. Mchenry don't have many enemies there."

"Now *that's* unusual."

Lanus smiled. No one was quite fond of the leader of Malivia. "I guess so. I heard he picked the people who screwed him over some time or another. And that case in Aleria... it seems they're using this as punishment, too." He sighed, and they fell silent once more. Mchenry did like to get his revenge.

Before Lanus knew it, the door creaked open, revealing a group of Enforcers. Each held one man; save the two holding a particularly filthy one, covered in blood and dirt. Yet the one they held tightly seemed to have given up fighting... for the moment. *Questions with answers so close always kept one at bay.*

They were all male, and though he knew Mchenry had his fair share of quarrels with women, perhaps he had done so on purpose. Send them out on an impossible quest, with no women to lighten their moods and keep their company. Lanus almost felt bad for them.

The Enforcers lead the men to the chairs, throwing them down before they left, taking guard around the room. The man who

46

had the escort of two Enforcers saw this positioning, and fell back into his seat, defeated. There was no way out. Grinning, himself and Rickson approached the chairs, standing tall, appearing powerful.

"This is Joseph Rickson, one of our top Instructors. He's here to fill you in. I'm Lanus Elmer, a government officer and here to answer any of your needed questions." Lanus nodded at Rickson, who gladly started his well-rehearsed introduction. *The lies we've practiced.* He was fearful they would let something slip. *Don't be so quick to answer their questions, Rickson, the filthy one might be able to smell the lies- or perhaps you'll slip up yourself and lose both our jobs.*

"So, let's start off by introducing yourselves."

The men, though looking well emotionally, were bloody, dirty, and weak. Some were cleaner than others, but still had a look of exhaustion all the same. All were reluctant. They surely thought this to be some kind of trick or game. There was a moment of silence before the men realized nothing would get done if they didn't talk.

"I'm... Nathan." His voice was rough, scratchy, his light skin heavy with sweat. *The Rat,* Lanus thought, grinning. *Or maybe he's more of a dog... his behavior certainly supports it.*

"Real name please, Marion."

The Rat looked unsurprised, but glared with a deep hatred all the same, almost growling. "Marion Armais."

"Oh yes, we know everything about you, Mr. Armais." Lanus taunted. "Quite interesting, actually. How you love to meddle in affairs of the Castle, how your criminal record is longer than the list of nights you spend drinking away, how you enjoy both the company of women *and* men on lonely nights. It's true, you know, we do have eyes everywhere."

Marion snarled, clearly furious, struggling against the chair he was tied to.

"No biting, Rat."

Rickson moved on, his eyes now on the dark one. Lanus, shooting Armais a snarky grin, wrote them down, labeling their descriptions and names with ease.

47

"Oliver Monterose." The voice cracked, fearful, ashamed.

"Jacob Fortemer." The man said it without looking up. It was clear he was cursing himself for getting into this situation.

"Louis Willson."

Rickson gave the cripple a second glance. His crutches and lost leg made him look slightly weak and helpless, though he would be much stronger in personality than one would think, Lanus assumed. If he was strong enough to anger Rovas, well... that was more than most.

"Good. Now here comes the hard part. Why did we bring you here?" Rickson adjusted his glasses and went on. "You have been... well, chosen, to go on a journey. A favor, say, for the Castle. For Rendar. To make up for... past crimes."

The men sat there in shocked silence, their backs leaned, heads forward, eyes wide- eager to hear their fate. They didn't dare speak. Not now, so close to the truth.

"To the Barren."

There was a moment of silence, a pause with tension and emotions so high it was almost unbearable.

Rickson continued, taking notice of their shock. "You'll be paid, of course. We just couldn't seem to find anyone who would go voluntarily."

For a moment there was silence, then laughter cut through the air. They clearly thought Rickson was joking.

"*What?*" Oliver sniggered, his face a mixture of amusement and surprise. The others were chuckling, smiles on their faces; yet another moment of silence told them that the insane proposition was, in fact, very real. Jacob looked too shocked to say anything, while Louis was taking the news by looking down at his missing leg with a grimness that knew it had lots of work ahead. Marion clenched his fists, clearly angry.

Jacob whispered. "You can't be serious. Are you?"

Rickson nodded.

"Why-" Marion's voice was shaking, furious. "Why do we.... why us, why-?"

Rickson interrupted him. "There is an orb in the Barren that can temporarily stop the spreading of the dark-radiation, even reduce it- or banish it entirely. Your job, my lucky friends, is to retrieve it and bring it back to us." He continued, ignoring Marion, who was trying to speak. "We will give you horses, supplies, whatever you need. We'll also give you guidance. Don't worry, we are very aware of your lack of knowledge surrounding Maros and the war."

Rickson held out a book, a hard-leather cover with splotched pages. One of the first copies. Lanus laughed to himself. One of the the ones most difficult to read. Rovas really had it in for them. He vaguely wondered what the men had done.

"It's the only copy we have here, so use it wisely."

It was obvious that this wasn't so- the Castle wasn't willing to give away something so valuable, but the way Rickson said it made him want to believe it. It would make the poor criminals feel somewhat valuable, in the least. He enjoyed the way Joseph Rickson told his lies, admired it. Almost better than himself. To be involved with the Castle, you had to learn how.

"With our sincerest wishes, we send you with it, in hopes that it will lead you safely." He placed the book in Jacob's hands, probably because anyone else in the group would have torn it apart. They had plenty of other copies, and this happened to be one they no longer had use for- it was barely legible. A cruel joke.

"It was written by Andrew Felton, who died at age seventy six. He wrote this, <u>After Maros</u>, to record his journey through the Barren as Maros became a rotting wasteland. He made his way to Rendar with countless others, but him and very few made it here."

Rickson paused to take a breath. "For many years, years of peace and prosperity, the Barren has let us be. But now, for some reason, it's spreading rapidly."

Lanus knew that overwhelming them with information would give them a purpose to reach the Barren, but he doubted the council's decision. Giving them classified knowledge of the spreading was risky. Rickson had to inform them of it correctly, to keep them from yelling it out into the market and street crowds as they departed. It would undoubtedly cause a panic; people would run, would kill and be killed, would fill in the last of their debts and do all they'd like to do before they died. The public would figure out the truth soon enough, but the Castle needed time to secure itself before the city went to hell.

"We know the orb is towards Vandor, possibly as far back as the ocean. You're to leave tomorrow, while the city is distracted with the Enforcement's send-off to Ekiliador in order to deal with the bandits in the mountains." Rickson gave the men a nod. "Should you return..." He paused, glancing a Lanus. "Should you return alive *with* the orb, or have stopped the spreading by other means, the reward is... fifty thousand dollars."

The anger had dissipated, replaced with awe.

"Fifty *thousand dollars*? *Fifty thousand?*" Marion still looked frustrated, but the offer was clearly luring him in. None of them had worried much of the Barren, seeing as they knew little about it (except perhaps for that Jacob), so naturally they thought it worth the while. The Barren couldn't really be that bad, could it? Bad enough to refuse fifty thousand dollars?

Lanus held back a grin. *Oh, the fools. They will see soon enough the wrath of the Barren. They will wish their deaths before the end of winter, that was certain.* Louis had his head in his hands, as if he were trying to imagine the money but couldn't quite grasp the image. Another official walked into the room and motioned for the guards to come with him, leaving Lanus and Rickson to deal with the chosen. Before the Enforcers even got through the doorway, however, Marion spoke up.

"What is this orb? Why are you doing this? Why do *we* have to do this?" It seemed that a part of him still thought that this was some kind of ploy. Looking at him with exasperation, Lanus yanked him up from his seat with an iron grip.

"Let's go."

Marion looked startled, the look of one who had been cheated and left alone in the dark, pockets empty and dignity lost. "What are you doing, dammit? I want answers!" Marion fought, but at the noise more Enforcers came and dragged him and the others to the hall, effectively removing them out of the room.

"In case you all decide to not do what is asked of you, there will be someone watching your progress. Making sure you get to the Barren... alive." Lanus grinned. "They will be scouts, freelanders, people who will report to us." He refrained from mentioning the spy that was to join them; someone known as Amicus Vanner. The spy had been asked to join them here, but plans might have changed.

"Now go."

The men were taken away and Lanus was once again alone with his fellow official. "So, the beast has the prey in it's claws. A success, I'd call it." He said to the other man, giving him a small smile. "What now?"

"Now Mchenry gets his revenge."

Rickson winked and left, leaving Lanus to wonder.

CHAPTER 5
JACOB FORTEMER
VIAJAR, MALIVIA

Under the gaze of the guards, Jacob did nothing. He would make his move later. He would escape; and he had a feeling this Marion would try to as well. Behind him were the other two, Louis and Oliver; who were only dreading what they would have to do, and if they would be able to do it. There was silence, save the scuffling of feet, Marion's muttering, and the faint voices from distant rooms.

What have I gotten myself into? I mean, shit, the Barren? Jacob still struggled to believe it. The Enforcers glared ahead after they were confident their captives would behave, standing tall and strutting importantly. Just as Louis (still clutching his crutches) was getting up the nerve to ask how much longer, one of the guards stopped and turned to knock on a door. That air of authority and dignity loomed in the air around them, but they seemed worn. Bored, even. Taking a deep breath of the crisp, clean air, Jacob waited for whatever persecution was behind that door.

"Ciarra! Open up! These street-filth-" He was cut off as the door swung open. Blandly, the man introduced them. "This is Ciarra Waren, She'll supply you for the journey tomorrow."

The woman in front of them was small, young, and sturdy. Her dress was a mix of dark and light brown, like melting chocolate. She had soft features, with a confidence in her eyes. There was a distinct scent, one that Jacob instantly identified as marijuana; it overwhelmed the doorway, causing the Enforcer to wrinkle his nose in disgust.

"Oh, them! Yes, they'll definitely need some supplies." She smiled sweetly and let them in, winking at the Enforcer as he walked away. Three guards followed him, while two stayed behind to guard the door.

Once they were in the room, the smell got ten times stronger. The group gagged, putting any chance of escape behind them. Jacob almost fainted, while the rest of them were overcome with drowsiness. Mirrors, cabinets, and windows lined one long wall, opposite of racks and racks of travel clothes. A worn carpet led down the middle, to the end- where several shelves of weaponry and survival supplies made their display. Jacob did not fail to notice the jars of green leaves that were among collections of strange labeled containers and remedies only the wealthy Oliver might have heard of. Living well was something the man was used to, that much was clear. *The way he acts around us, you'd think he's leader of Rendar.*

"O-kay," Ciarra turned to them, ignoring Marion's disapproving gaze at the drugs on the wall. Jacob saw this, and resolved to ask the criminal about it later; someone like him, Jacob assumed, would surely have approved of such activities.

"Wait right here." Ciarra walked through double doors behind the clothes racks, coming out a few minutes later with a basket of clothes. "Pick and chose, the there should be about three pairs for each of you, just put 'em in these bags." As they finished packing, she lead them to another room, filled with supplies.

"What do you need all this for?" Louis asked, shifting on his crutches behind them.

Ciarra shrugged. "We supply the messengers. Oh, and the scouts for their trips to the marshes and desert to deal with the raiders and such. We also help Calidor, sending supplies, so they can help explore the Unventured Lands. It always helps to have people in the right place at the right time."

Louis didn't respond. Why was the Castle giving them so much information? Spilling it to them honestly and giving them every detail. *Aren't they worried we'll tell someone?* Rendar's government, especially here, in Malivia, was very secretive.

"Well, pick out what you need."

The rest of the group ran and grabbed whatever they thought necessary, but Marion and Jacob looked at each other, confused. This was irregular. Very. In the corner of his eye, Marion saw Ciarra looking at them, and pulled Jacob over to a rack of blankets, grabbing some. Louis, who had been busy thinking about how he would get through the Barren with one leg paused to pick his choice of weapon. Oliver gazed over everything, rushing as if someone would try to stop him. Awed at the quantity of it all, Marion paused to admire the guns and ammo available to him.

They finished quickly, clutching their packs, their only lifeline. *How long will we have to play this game?* Jacob wondered, nervous. Oliver helped Louis, and they shouldered their packs. Ciarra lead them out of the room, the two guards accompanying them. The thunder and pounding of rain only got louder as they walked through the eerily empty halls. The Castle was mainly stone and brick, with electricity and even heating, something that was rare nowadays. There were many windows, although they were rarely open. It was clean and orderly, and that was more than you could say for most parts of Viajar. There were many places like this, Jacob knew, all a part of the Castle. *And all are as corrupt and despised as this one,* he thought.

The rooms they passed were always filled, some with as many as fifty people, and others with only one or two. The few that did come through the halls gave them wary glances, as if they were animals being put in a cage. Some even looked sorry for them. Beside Jacob, Marion slowed his pace, knowing the faster they walked the faster they would be imprisoned. He wasn't stupid enough to believe anything else. Jacob had been thinking the same thing. His new companion looked for an escape route, though Jacob doubted he could find one.

"Now I trust you'll be smart enough to reconsider, Mister Armais. We wouldn't want to make a mess, now would we?" Ciarra's voice had become stern, punishing, harsh. The kindness in her gaze had all but disappeared.

The two guards had their hands on their weapons, their eyes narrowed and focused. Any fast motion, and the point of a dagger would be at thier throats. Of course, all of them had considered fighting or making a run for it, but they were against the highly-trained Enforcers of Malivia. Definitely not the best, but Enforcers nonetheless. Top Enforcers worked as military, or protection for the politically important. Ones of lower status worked as a sort of police, taking patrols and keeping crime out of the area. The lowest of all were guards, placed wherever needed or by whoever hired them. Jacob knew this well from his years on the street- they all were different in their own ways.

These were definitely of a higher rank than regular guards, but Jacob thought it wouldn't be too hard to bring them down if he had the help of that man Marion. He looked a fighter, but you could never be sure. *Are they cowards? Will they watch me bleed and do nothing, leave me and run?* There was no point, really. There were many other Enforcers in the castle, and two would soon become five, ten, twenty. And to put their lives at risk? Jacob might not have been the strongest, but he wasn't stupid. They were all so tired they could barely run, much less make it outside the castle grounds. And what of Louis? It would be more than cruel to leave him behind at the mercy of the Castle. The man was too slow on those crutches, too vulnerable. It just didn't add up. There wouldn't be a fight today.

The others seemed to realize this as well, for Marion lowered his head and submitted. Once again they were lead through the halls, closely watched by the Enforcers. Before long they came to a room with a single window and peeling wallpaper, bare of furniture and decor alike. Ciarra snapped her fingers, motioning for the guards to stay outside the door. She walked away, and Jacob heard the distinct sound of the lock clicking. A moment of silence fell on them, before they realized they were safe to rest. *What's done is done, you can't go back, just look ahead and choose your path...* The quote popped into Jacob's head, although it didn't quite fit their situation. They didn't have a choice here. He sat down in the corner, not wanting to speak to any of the people in front of him. The one named Marion was not much of his liking, and Louis already seemed defeated. Oliver had obviously come from a place of wealth, given the look on his face when the bloodied dirt-covered Armais brushed by him as they'd come into the room. They all were much too different to ever get along.

One by one they settled down, Louis falling right to sleep, his head buried in his pack. The others soon did the same, but could not go as easily as Louis. Some stayed awake, listening to the sounds of footsteps in the distance; for they did not entirely trust their new companions to let them be.

AMICUS VANNER
VIAJAR, MALIVIA

"Come here, Amicus! You can almost see them!"

The woman's voice called out to him, and Amicus answered, pushing and shoving through the crowd to get to his wife. Upon reaching her, he put an arm around her shoulders and looked out to see what was the matter.

The smell of packed bodies was whisked away in the afternoon wind, along with streamers, flowers, and fall-colored leaves. The sky was a light blue, but shifting to a sunset pink as the Enforcers moved down the cobbled street, cloaks fluttering and flags waving. They rode fine horses, mares and sprinters and war-steeds. The faces of the officials were hard and unforgiving, though some gave in and smiled at the crowd. The soldiers were off to the mountains, it seemed, and it appeared likely most of them would not return.

Oh no. Amicus looked around him. *Shit!* This was the ceremony. This wasn't some wedding or party, it was a ceremony! *The* ceremony. He had been told it wasn't until tomorrow; now everything was set off plan. He was supposed to be brought in with the others, the travelers, the ones that Rovas told him were so deserving of punishment. It had been the bar, the girls, the ale. What a time it had been, the dancing, the laughter. Amicus had left before he could get too drunk and perhaps it was for the best, now. For his wife, he hoped he could stay loyal to her.

As for the job… he had been given quite a lot of coin to do this, to make sure the poor souls reached the Barren. To make sure they didn't get killed along the way. To make sure they suffered, as Rovas had wanted. Amicus couldn't mess it up. Another beer would be the death of him.

And so he bid his wife a rushed farewell, and disappeared in the rush of bodies. He could hear her confused voice behind him, but he did not stop. Glancing around the crowd, he noticed there weren't many people from Ekiliador here. They never visited much, although when he'd come here he'd much preferred it to his own land. Most of them were rich and living well, due to the plentiful old world artifacts in that area. *They live the dream, those bastards.* But the Barren would come soon enough. They would see it fall upon them. Soon, all would perish.

***

A few minutes later Amicus was behind the crowd, now clutching a man's satchel and travel bag. It had been so easy to snatch them it was almost funny. Thankfully everyone was so focused on the Enforcement he had been able to get away easy. As Amicus walked, he passed restaurants and homes, junk shops turned from old gas stations, and the alehouse. The street girls at the bar giggled and waved at him as he passed. He visited there often, though only to tease. He paid them no mind, however, and instead rushed down the street and turned a corner.

Now, walking fast along the buildings, he came across an alleyway. A dead end. Amicus walked in and sat down, breathing fast. Think. The Enforcers didn't know he was with the Castle, he would have to sneak past them. He was meant to be a spy, a part of the group that would be able to bring back information, the status of the spreading and the land. To tell Rovas his revenge had been fulfilled. Amicus wasn't a part of the company; but those men weren't stupid. They would figure out what the Barren really was soon enough. What he had to do was make them realize there was no other way- that they would have to try.

Amicus looked down at the bags, his only last-minute supplies, picked them up, and got ready to move. Perhaps there was still enough time to catch up to the travelers. Yet before he could get any further, a group of young men blocked his exit. They smelled filthy, with ragged torn clothes and hardened expressions. Street filth... Rats. Amicus backed up, unsure of what to do. He saw the glint of a dagger. They had weapons. He had bargained his own off last night.

"What do we got here?" The oldest one grinned, his face scratched and covered in dirt. They were much younger than him, but that didn't seem to be an issue.

"Looks like good one to me." The one beside him said with a toothy grin.

"Give us all your valuables, and we won't touch you, alright?" The poor boy was desperate, that was clear enough. They approached, Amicus now with his back pressed to the wall. He could take them, but even a clumsy boy with a dagger was lethal; and Amicus had a thought that maybe the one he was facing wasn't clumsy at all. In a panic, he reached into his satchel and pulled out anything he could grab, which happened to be a few coins. He threw the money at them, though a little too high. The silver flew right over their heads, but luckily it didn't matter. The group saw the coins clatter to the ground and lunged after them, greedily fighting over them as Amicus made his escape.

How convenient, losing his dagger to a bet the other night. It had been a fine beauty too, light and recently sharpened. He would need another weapon soon, to face situations like this. To face freelanders, and whatever else was out there. He looked back at the boys. Fighting like animals they scratched and clawed, yelled and growled. There was even a girl, covered in dirt, who bit and punched the one nearest to her and fought to get her hands on the money.

The cheering in the background continued as if nothing had happened, the cool sting of wind biting his sweaty skin. The gray clouds gloomily floated overhead, giving Amicus the feeling similar to how he would feel alone on a stormy day. They blotted out the sun completely, giving him no relief from the chill. Sprinting away from the frenzied children, Amicus found himself alone in another world. He grinned. A cold world, a lonely world. A world of freedom.

OLIVER MONTEROSE
VIAJAR, MALIVIA

The horses trotted down the street, their hooves clomping on the worn, chipped stone. A cool breeze soothed him, but his travel clothes still stuck to his sweaty skin. He was nervous, scared. Cheers, whistles, and clapping flooded his ears, and he strongly wished for silence.

Faces and colors stood out like spotlights amongst all the gray, his fellow companions staring solemnly ahead. They rode away from the commotion, though they could still hear it in the distance. This went on for a while, the neighing of their mares and the rattle of their saddlebags filling his ears.

No one spoke, for they knew they were being watched. This quest might destroy him, he knew. But silver was waiting, as was the chance to save them. He thought. Save all of them. Oliver was in an unbelieving daze, as if he couldn't believe what he was doing, although when a startling tremble shook the city he quickly regained his senses.

Small cracks, barely noticeable, appeared in the ground, the crowd's once excited voices yelling out in fear. Dust rose from the openings, rocks and rubble where the fine stone road had once been. In just a few moments it stopped, but there was no more cheering. Silence gripped their throats, the faint sound of birds, the rustle of paper, and the brush of wind on trees finally heard after the commotion. Not until a minute later was there hushed muttering. The people knew somehow just how important this was, felt the tension of it in the air, the secrecy of it in the wind. Something was coming, and they would not be able to stop it.

CHAPTER 6
AMICUS VANNER
THE BRIDGE, MALIVIA

Crouched in an uncomfortable position, Amicus shifted, trying to adjust himself. The damp smell of fresh water was strong under the bridge, but he didn't mind. Dirty jobs were what he got paid for. This one was rather complicated, but for a reasonable thousand dollars he would do it. Especially if he wasn't even required to go into the Barren. *Oh, in my line of work you hear stories, yeah, stories that'll keep anyone away from that place.*

Under the bridge it was dark, with only small cracks of light weakly shining down onto the river. The bridge was the only passage from Rendar into the grasslands. The river split the country off from everything else.

The bridge itself was beautiful, the designs and construction nothing if not impressive. The wood was a rosy brown, the stone worn grey. Amicus could barely see it; the sun was on it's descent to the horizon, and it was getting darker by the minute. Mud, rocks, and grass dirtied his clothes, the water lapping up at his boots. For hours he'd sat there, waiting for the sun to set. Frustratingly, the men had passed the bridge hours ago, but Amicus would never make it across without being spotted.

Guards watched the bridge and the shore, to insure they didn't sneak back into Rendar. It was a priority to get the travelers to the Barren, alive. After that, it was on them. By then, if they were the people Mchenry thought they were, they wouldn't turn back. The leaders just had to hope they didn't make a stupid mistake.

Soon, the sun sank blissfully into the distance, and Amicus crept from his hiding spot. Two Enforcers stood by the entrance of the bridge, one leaning up against the side, dozing. Another was seen fifteen, maybe twenty feet away, standing by the tide splashing onto the shore.

With a deep breath, Amicus snuck into the water, grimacing at how cold it was. With one swift motion, he ducked under, knowing it would be easier to get it over with than to go in slowly. As silently as he could, he swam through the darkness. It seemed like just a few seconds before he had to surface again, though Amicus dreaded that an Enforcer would see his head. Bags that had once been light now weighed him down, but he could not get rid of them. They would be his only tools out in the grasslands.

Taking a deep breath, he went under again, the shock of cold water just as surprising as before. An eternity later, Amicus felt the weedy bottom under him, and he flopped onto the shore, exhausted and even colder than when he had entered. Swimming with tense muscles through a freezing river was not something he had wanted to do, but it was the safest way. *At least I made made it,* he thought as he lay down. *At least I made it.* So under the safety of the bridge, in the arms of the mud, with only the warmth of his thoughts, Amicus slept.

LOUIS WILLSON
THE GRASSLANDS

Night covered the grasslands in darkness, the sun slowly surrendering to the moon. Four horses made their way through the tall green grass, the wind making the riders pull on their cloaks and jackets. The city smell of people, food, and smoke had been forgotten, replaced by the cool scent of earth and trees. It had been a ride of silence so far, but they still rode close together- harboring a secret fear of attack, of the wild animals they had never wished to encounter, of the freelanders that may have been watching in the mysterious, waving grass. They were haunted by the the stories they'd been told as children and had never forgotten.

Suddenly, in a rough voice, Marion spoke up. "You don't suppose we should stop for the night?" He looked around at them. His companions nodded, Jacob muttering a quiet response.

"I suppose."

In twenty minutes they had the horses tethered to the ground, a pile of dry, thin wood they had brought with them in an area they had cleared of grass. Marion was working on starting the fire, flicking the lighter on, while Jacob threw on some kindling to help get it started. Sitting in silence, Louis sat on a blanket next to Oliver. After a flame lit up their camp, he decided to speak. The question had been bothering him ever since the ceremony started. *I'm sure it's bothered everyone.* He still couldn't even believe he was here.

"Why did they send us?" Louis asked. "I can't run, I'm assuming we have no experience outside of Rendar, and no idea how to survive. That is… for me, at least." He coughed nervously. "There are hundreds of people who would be better suited, if not willing to go. So why us?" His face was confused, puzzled. "There's a high chance we won't even make it to the Barren, much less retrieve this... orb and make it back."

There was quiet. Tense quiet. Louis looked at the others. A suspicion gnawed at him; a strange suspicion. He froze, thinking hard. "How many of you know Rovas Mchenry? Or knew him?" They looked up at him, recognition in their faces. He thought so.

"I did." Oliver said, almost proudly. "Though that shouldn't be a surprise, my brother-"

"Yeah, I knew the bastard." Interrupted Marion.

Jacob nodded as well. "As... as did I, for a short time."

Louis frowned. He himself knew the man from when he'd come to Aleria each week a few years back to visit family. Rovas would pass his home and ask for hospitality- for the lack of inns and such along the roads were surprising to the man. Louis refused him each time, when he'd had much more confidence, stating that his sister was unwell and that they couldn't take company. Him and Rovas would have a conversation at the road nevertheless, short but friendly. Although he refused him his home, Louis did give him an apple each visit as an apology, and they would have longer talks as the year went on. They had become acquaintances, even; Louis was glad to have company other than his brothers.

However, the last time Rovas came, they'd had a fight. A terrible one, one where Louis had threatened to do some things he wasn't capable of doing with one leg. He'd never seen the man since. It had been only a fight, only words, but Rovas could have taken it for something else. A warning. It would have been nothing, but for the fact that Rovas's sister was murdered the following day in a town nearby, as he'd learned a few weeks after. It could be the man blamed him for what had happened. Louis assumed the others knew him better than he had.

"I know just what this is." Oliver said, his face sour. "This is some plot, some trick for Rovas to get his revenge. He wouldn't dare send my brother, too much of a risk, and there was rumor Rovas was close with the Nenroes...." He seemed now to be just thinking aloud.

Jacob shook his head. "No, I'm almost positive this is real. The people he chose might have been affiliated with interior motivations, but there has to be a reason for all these strange happenings." He fidgeted with a small stick, teasing it into the fire. "There's a... a chance we can succeed, so they would have given us the truth, I would think. At least some of it. We can't tell anyone about it now, and we surely can't tell anyone about it if we're dead." He tossed the stick into the fire, deep in thought.

"That doesn't explain much." Marion glanced up at them. "We give them nothing, nothing but Mchenry's satisfaction. We'll be dead before nightfall. Some of us will be, at least."

Louis interrupted, ignoring the last comment. "His satisfaction might be a part of it, yes, but there has to be a higher purpose behind it. He wants us dead, perhaps to suffer, so maybe we're the..."

"The scouts. The ones to see what's out there to do the dirty work." Guessed Jacob.

Marion scowled. "Scouts? Really? You think he would just pop up out of nowhere after years to send us on a scouting mission? He means for us to die." He closed his eyes and put his head on his knees. "Rovas is a cruel man. I know him, and I know him well. He isn't kind, and he certainly isn't merciful. We're being taken advantage of, there's no use in denying it. For what, I don't know, but no matter how real this is there's no chance for us and he knew it. Mchenry thinks he's so clever, and he's right. No matter what we do, there's only one path to follow."

The rest were silent, contemplating.

Sighing, Louis looked at the defeated man. "*That's not true.* It will never be true. There's always a way. We can escape to the sea, the mountains, sneak back to Rendar, live among the freelanders... die how we want to die."

"You don't suppose we could go back?" Jacob said hopefully, gazing glumly in the distance, in the direction of Malivia. "Sneak into the city?"

"They won't let us get away that easy." Marion said. "I saw Enforcers at the bridge, and they will have placed them all along the border. They are not be be dealt with lightly."

"They have enough Enforcers to do that?"

"*No,*" Marion scoffed, almost laughing at the ignorance. "And leave the city undefended? There will be people from the Castle and trusted ones among them. But they'll all be armed. *And* they'll most likely stay that way for a few more days, maybe even weeks, possibly until they know we've gone. Long enough for us to be sick of these useless fields."

Jacob fell onto his back, all hope lost.

Louis too looked grim. *This is my death. I know the stories, I know the tales. The travelers who dared. I need to, as a cripple, make it there and back alive. Ha.* The odds were almost impossible. *I'm screwed.*

"So we join the freelanders." Louis proposed, scratching the stump of his leg. Nervously, the group looked at each other.

"Sure, that sounds wonderful." Oliver said tiredly, yawning. His sarcastic tone made it clear he viewed the freelanders as savages.

Marion sighed. "You all don't see it, do you? If the Barren really is spreading, then it'll just reach us if we don't stop it. No one else knows about the spreading, even if they *can* sense something is wrong. We stay, we live for a year, maybe two. If we leave, to the sea if anything else, we'll die of thirst or hunger."

"So we can't go back."

"And we can't stay."

Marion looked at the others. "*And* we can't leave. We're the only ones who can do something about this, with thousands of dollars on top of it all. A chance to save millions of lives, see your families again."

Oliver smirked. "And come back rich into the arms of women desperate for a bit of hero. Not so bad."

"So we just do it." Jacob said, sighing. "We just do the damn quest and come back heros. It sounds easy, doesn't it? Do you remember what happened to those who tried to venture into the

Barren? We'll die any way we go, I think it might be best to make it a year without suffering than certain pain and an even earlier end."

Marion scoffed. "That's a coward's way, you idiot. Our lives were doomed long before we got thrown into this mess, and we've been given a chance to change that. Doesn't that mean anything to you?"

Louis glanced at Marion, seeing right through him. He clearly didn't care for any of them, much less the people back in Rendar. Louis didn't blame him; the man was clearly a Rat. He had to admit, however, the criminal looked as smart as he was wild. *Though too shady, too many secrets.* Yet however much Louis disliked his companion's character, that did not mean he disagreed with him. *What was my life before this? I worked as a cripple on a farm for a sick sister and brothers who cared little for me with no future but the chair on the porch.* Best to make a difference in their scrap of a world. The silence was heavy, and it seemed to him most shared his own point of view.

Shrugging, Oliver lay back, pulling his blanket over himself to call it a night. "You all can do whatever the hell you want, but if the Barren is truly as it's told out to be, the only thing I'll be facing is this bullet in my head."

The others shrugged, knowing he was joking, but Louis worried. *Let's hope it doesn't come to that.* Everyone else lay down as well, before he realized they needed someone to watch the fire. He turned to Jacob, told him to take first watch and to wake him up when he needed to sleep. Nodding, Jacob took a stick and prodded at the burning logs, waiting for the night to pass. It was now so dark that the fire's sparks and flames held the most light, but Louis could still see the stars as he lay back and gave in to sleep.

CHAPTER 7
AMICUS VANNER
THE GRASSLANDS

Amicus gazed up at the sky, so full of stars it was almost white. The tall grass rubbed against his skin, along with the wind that became colder and colder with each step. He had gotten little sleep under the bridge, and had woken up to the stars shining overhead. Covered in mud, cold to the bone, and tired as he had been in quite some time, Amicus had stumbled into the grasslands, the soaking bags slung over his shoulder. *I should have listened to Rovas, he said to be there, he said to act like I was one of them but now everything's changed...*

He was sore and filthy, aching for a drink and a bed. Had he not forgotten his job, he would be riding alongside those ahead of himself right now, eating with them and sharing their fire. Now he had to work even harder to gain the travelers' trust. He could remember his conversation with Rovas, could recall their negotiation so clearly.

"So. Amicus Vanner. We meet at last." Rovas Mchenry stood in front of him, his back to his guest, facing the window over the city. They were in a conference room, a long table in the center and a carpet below. "Sit."

He sat. Amicus was here for a job, and though many had warned him against dealing with the man, he was desperate for coin. His wife didn't know anything about it, and he preferred it to stay that way. He had been told beforehand this was an out-of-city gig, and though he hadn't been anywhere past the borders of Rendar, Amicus reckoned it couldn't be too hard.

"Do you know what this means? How important this is?" Rovas asked, turning to face him. His voice was anything if not harsh. Amicus shook his head; in truth he was scared, and wanted as much information as possible.

"No. Fill me in, will you?" Inside he was relieved that he sounded confident, but he doubted the man was fooled.

"I have a plan, now, and I need an inside man. It doesn't involve the gangs, I don't control them anymore, but something of my... own personal interest." Rovas paused. "I've managed to convince the other leaders of something, you don't need to know the exact details, but they expect a deed to be done in the progress of dealing with the recent quakes. In truth I have seen the danger. I have a ship prepared, though I hope it does not come to that."

"What's this got to do with a job?" Amicus asked.

Mchenry grinned, though it was a cold grin. It made him nervous. "I've gathered up some men. Some men who... have angered me in the past. You are to guide them to the Barren, though you can desert them before they enter. They have been told to gather an artifact from Vandor- you are to make sure they are set on their path, and that they do not return here unless they have it. In fact... I don't mean for them to return."

Amicus rose his eyebrows, trying to remain interested. There was no damn way he was going that far out of Rendar. The Unventured Lands, maybe. But this? No. Instead of leaving, however, he found himself asking how much he would be paid.

"Hm. Well, a thousand should you do the job right. If you lie, take the money, and I find my old friends wandering the streets, you'll quickly find yourself dead. If you fail and admit to it, you will get nothing but your life."

Amicus nodded, thinking. A few months, that's all it would be. Not even a messy job, not even one that would put him in trouble with the Castle. A thousand dollars. A thousand. Smiling, he reached out his hand, and Rovas shook it.

The memory shook him, so Amicus focused instead on his surroundings. Looking behind him, he noticed that he could no longer see the river. He had walked for quite a while, it seemed, though there was no way to tell- he had been in a daze. The smell of fire smoke tingled his nostrils, and for the first time, he noticed a small flickering light in the distance. Exhilarated, he ran towards it, ignoring his body's tired cries.

Amicus slowed down as he approached, not wanting to startle anyone. As it turned out, there was no one to startle. Figures under blankets rose up and down as they breathed, sleeping, shadows and firelight moving over their forms. The man sitting next to the fire was fast asleep, his head tilted down as if he were praying. Horses lay on the ground or stood munching on grass as they waited for their masters to wake. Amicus stood there, unsure of what to do. In his vision of meeting them, they had been conscious. Shrugging, he decided to go into their camp and wait.

Suddenly, a couple of sparks from the flames landed on the dry grass, igniting it before he could react. The horses whinnied in fear, running as far as their tethers would allow. The travelers before him remained motionless, unaware of the danger rising around them. Frantically Amicus ran through the wall of grass and into the camp, stopping to shake the man beside the fire until he awoke. With an even faster speed he grabbed a blanket off the closest person and ran to the flames, trying to smother it before it could spread.

Those idiots! Disaster on the first night. Rovas certainly chose some interesting men for the job. He hoped he didn't have to carry the poor men to their doom. Amicus had been sent out into the wilderness before, in the forests of Calidor, and was experienced in such survival; though he highly doubted his soon-to-be companions were. Amicus was starting to think they should have sent Enforcers. Would have been smarter on Rovas's part- but it was none of his business- he was getting paid, and that was all that mattered.

Smells of smoke and heat burned his nose, the licking flames as hot as they were beautiful. The watcher of the fire ran to his aid without question, taking his own blanket and finishing the job. The man suddenly turned on him and yelled out, pointing; that was when he noticed the warm, tickling sensation crawling up his arm. Soon it was painful, and Amicus looked down to see a blazing flame devouring his shirt.

"Put it out, put it out!" The man yelled, as the others in the camp rose and saw what was going on.

Screaming in surprise, Amicus dropped to the ground and rolled around in the dirt. After he was certain the fire was gone, he rose, looking around at the damage. His shirt was in tatters, black and dirty, his skin an unpleasant red. The air was cool on his burns, and Amicus gave thanks that it wasn't summer. Ashes swirled in the air, in harmony with the wind, settling on the confused, bleary-eyed travelers. His screams must have roused them. The watcher of the fire walked over and handed another scraggly man the ruined blanket, but he tossed it aside as he saw Amicus, puzzlement mixed with anger etched on his harsh face.

"Who the hell is this?"

OLIVER MONTEROSE
THE GRASSLANDS

In the grasslands, dawn painted the sky with blotches of pink, yellow, orange, and blue. A soft breeze ruffled the tall grass, as well as the few leaves that had been blown from the land behind. Freelanders roamed in the distance, their occasional huts dotting the horizon.

Five travelers mounted their horses, the burned man mounting behind Oliver. *He smells,* Oliver thought as he lead the horse into the fields. *Smells like river, and mud.* The scent of alcohol was also strong on the man's breath, stale and dry on his neck. They left a clearing behind them, burnt and scorched from the touch of the fire. They would have to be more careful.

"How did you find us?" Marion asked, calmed after Jacob's many reassurances that the stranger had tried to put out the fire, not spread it. "How did you even know we were here? And what's a freelander doing wandering so close to Rendar?"

Marion sounded confused, as if he still couldn't see the reason in him wanting to come with them. This so called Amicus Vanner had explained it to them many times; how he was a freelander, how he knew the lands like the back of his hand, how he had been wandering for years in search of his missing wife who'd been taken in a village raid. He had offered to guide them, to see them to the Barren. The man did not look like a freelander, however. His hair was dark and pulled back into a ponytail, while his brown eyes gleamed mischievously. He was well-spoken, well-dressed, well-mannered; Amicus Vanner was *neat.* Oliver knew privilege when he saw it, and this man was definitely not a freelander.

"I wandered upon you, is all. I was going to visit the city. Maybe find a bar. A girl, maybe." Vanner shifted on his saddle. Oliver did not like the looks of him, not at all.

"You go looking for women while on the search for your missing wife?" Louis frowned.

"Alcohol mainly, I said, and… well, she's been gone much too long anyway, and a man needs some cheering up every once and a while."

This stranger certainly was good at lying. Oliver may not have been a warrior or a survivor, but he was a man bred of the Castle and knew a truth from a lie. *What does he want from us?*

Amicus sighed. "There isn't much else for me, but I could use an adventure. Off to the Barren, you say? Well, I'd like to see the place before I go, might be that it isn't so bad as they make it out to be."

Oliver wished that was so as well; they could only hope. Whoever this Vanner was, it couldn't hurt to have him. "What do they call you? Is Amicus your real name?" Oliver asked, curious.

The man smiled. "Yes, it is. It means friend in one of the old languages." He seemed to find it a little too amusing.

"Which one? Which old language?"

"French, I think it was called." Oliver bit his lip, thinking. He had heard of it, but he knew nothing of how to speak it. Jacob was frowning, his face puzzled. If anyone knew any bit of French, it would be him; yet Jacob remained silent.

Oliver assumed the man most likely was lying, perhaps in name and meaning both, although there was no way to tell. Not to mention Vanner's choice of appearance was not very convincing for what he was claiming to be. They were fine clothes, and although they were covered in filth and smelled like a swamp, it was clear they were not the usual rags of the freelanders.

"You don't look much like a freelander, *friend.* Where'd you find… " Oliver paused. "Clothes like that?"

Amicus laughed, to the surprise of the others. "You really have little trust in you, though that's not really uncommon for

Rendarians. If you really need to know, I took them from a scout heading to the mountains. He'd fallen fatally ill, and it seemed to me that he deserved the mercy of my dagger through his throat."

There was silence after that, although no one told him to leave. It seemed no one wanted to confront him, Oliver least of all. At camp that night, they took note of his supplies. The two soaking bags, now only damp, were actually quite useful. The satchel held a gun, black and dented. Old, but sure. It was felt good in his hands, and it made Oliver wonder where the man had gotten it.

"I'll tell you sometime," Amicus said, though he spoke of it no more. He spoke not of why he was soaked to the bone either, but Oliver let it be. He had held a gun on a few occasions- the most recurring being his grandfather's. It had not worked, and was only an old relic. And though it was illegal to keep guns without the knowledge of the Castle, his grandfather had kept it anyhow, saying it had been in many wars of the past. It had been his father's, and his father's before him, and apparently not even law could take that away. Looking at this gun he felt remembrance, and it tore him to give it back. Oliver might not have been a fighter, but the comfort of a gun in his hand was something no man regretted. An open box of rusted bullets came with it, along with a few more coins and a cross necklace.

The other pack gave them two extra blankets, a bag of nuts and dried fruits, a half-empty water bottle, and clothes. The food itself would last a few weeks; but Oliver had a dreading feeling that this journey would be a lot longer than that. Oliver had been told stories as a child of the Barren, and perhaps that is what made him terrified to go on and face it.

Terrified to hide from it.

Terrified to run.

Terrified.

MARION ARMAIS
THE NORTHERN MARSHES

Around sunset, Marion started to notice change in the land. The grassland was just a strip between Render and the marshes, a transition into something a little less welcoming. The air became damp and humid, the dirt beneath them becoming looser, wetter. Grass was shorter, with hints of brown, and the strong smell of lakes, earth, and freshwater reached their noses.

Before they went any further, Marion asked to stop for the night. "This will most likely be the last time we'll be able to sleep on the ground without getting wet for a while. The marshes are unforgiving lands, or so I've heard."

Amicus nodded. "You're right on that count. I've passed through many times and haven't enjoyed it."

The others took his meaning to heart and started to set up camp, thinking about what perils the marshes might bring. *It's not the marshes we should be worrying about,* Marion thought grimly. He had struggled through his life to survive, gone through too much torment, and knew from experience that they would be facing much worse in the weeks to come.

In the morning, they once again set out, but not at all prepared for the challenges of the land. Wet dirt, grass, and muck stuck to their horse's hooves, making their progress even slower. Bugs were everywhere, and only the small pieces of solid land were sanctuary. Thanks to the surface coating algae, they could not tell the deep water from the shallow, and more than once had a horse gone up to it's stomach when falling in. Despite the cooler air, the waters were warm and full of fish, snakes, and other slimy creatures. If this was just fall, summer had to be ten times worse.

Marion was suddenly grateful for the cold. He would be drenched in sweat and horribly uncomfortable if it were any hotter than this. Granted, he was still uncomfortable, but the wind made the travel much easier. Sitting on a horse all day didn't help matters either; while the bugs, smell, and humidity made Marion want to puke. Well, puke up what little he had eaten. They all were strict about rationing, and warned themselves that if they weren't careful, they would end up starving to death in the Barren. Better to be hungry here and well fed there, in the times when they would surely need their strength.

Days passed, the marshes seeming to never end. Sometimes it would be dry enough to sleep (though they were always damp), and sometimes they had to rest on their horses as they trudged through the water. Often, in the worst of times, Marion wondered what it would be like to have fifty thousand dollars. He had heard that money can't buy happiness, but silver was silver, bronze was bronze, and the thought of several glittering coins shining like the sun running through his fingers made him much more happy than it should have.

"Do you think we should stop at that freelander hut?" Jacob asked, brushing sweat from his brow. "I'm not looking forward to sleeping on the ground again. And maybe they'll give us food too."

Louis gazed blearily into the distance, noting the small brown lump that might mean a good night's sleep. There was a glow as well, a fire, though they could hear no voices yet.

"It wouldn't hurt to try," Louis said, patting his horse's neck. "But I don't want to be wandering around in the dark. We should get moving if we want to sleep there tonight."

Marion nodded, looking up at the sun. He put his hand in the air, his arm straight out, counting the finger spaces between the sun and the horizon.

"What are you doing?" Oliver asked curiously. The whole group had stopped, now looking at Marion. Amicus only smiled as if this were old news, but it was clear to Marion that their strange companion had not an inkling of his little trick.

"Figuring out how much time we have left until night."

A trick of thieves and scoundrels and wanderers of the Unventured Lands, Marion thought, though he dared not say it. They still thought of him decently, he hoped, and he intended to keep it as such. Squinting, Marion looked into the bright sun. "Each finger is fifteen minutes. We have around forty-five minutes left until the sun sets." He started towards the distant home, the others staring after him as their horses plodded forward. Marion led them, the others soon behind him, occasionally putting up their hands to the sunset.

***

Smoke rose from the chimney of the hut, rising into the crimson sky. A fire was clearly visible through the small window, which had no glass, but instead a curtain of cloth that waved with the wind. Inside, a small table leaned against a wall, a cracked porcelain bowl of rice left half-eaten by one of the chairs. A counter on the other wall had stacked dishes by a grimy sink, a faded striped towel beside that was used to dry them. A worn carpet lay on the dusty wood floor, by a bed that had clearly been slept in. The freelander who lived here was not one who liked to move around, for this living space was as permanent as any; with the privilege of running water, apparently.

Suddenly, a voice called out from behind the travelers. "What brings you fellas to a place like this?"

An old man came up to face them, his eyes foggy and calm. The freelander came closer, examining, observing. His accent was strange, though Marion couldn't quite place it. A lot of the freelanders were from different parts of the old world; Jacob would most likely know more.

They were silent, and the man raised his eyebrows. "As it's clear y'all ain't no freelanders."

"We're..." Oliver paused, hesitant. "We're scouts, heading up to the mountains."

"You're a little west for that, fellas. Get lost on the way?"

Jacob shook his head. "No, we simply have to pick up supplies from some traders up at the border. Then we head east."

The old man nodded, hobbling to the front of his hut. "Well, if you need, my home is open to ya. You look from Rendar, that's the truth, and it's not my place to refuse weary travelers like yourselves. I don't have beer, but bread and soup should be good enough for ya."

They glanced at each other. He had seemed almost too eager, though it would not help to be suspicious. None of them wanted to walk away from a free meal and rest. The old man went back to his house, leaving the travelers to dismount their horses and tether them. Louis shrugged and was first to enter the hut, not bothering to worry about the old man. From the look of it, he could barely see, and it wasn't likely he could come up behind and stab the travelers without having them notice beforehand.

The others followed after a moment, clearly not trusting how easy it had been to be invited inside. Freelanders lived out here for a reason, and, for the most part, were neither kind nor inviting. However, as soon as the travelers were seated in chairs by the hearth, all worry of trusting this old man vanished from Marion's mind. They were brought watery soup and hard bread, which they were more than grateful for. Luxuries such as butter and salt were absent, but the meal filled their stomachs nonetheless. Surprisingly, they were invited to stay as long as a few days, but Marion told him they would only be staying the night. The longer they stayed, the harder it would be to leave.

The man nodded, smiling. "I'm just glad to have some company, it's been so long since I've been in Rendar." He frowned. "Is Jordan Falimer still leader of Calidor?"

Marion shook his head, taking a sip from his flask. "Nah, he died on a hunting trip in the Unventured Lands, the forest by the border. His son Brias leads now. It's all pretty much the same with the Castle, though Rovas Mchenry does now lead Malivia."

The old man shook his head. "I'm glad I left. Those men have no right to rule the Castle. No place to rule the people. Rovas, especially. Whatever happened to his uncle, Sorase? How'd the leadership pass on so quickly?"

"Sorase didn't have any little ones, and his sister had married and run off to Aleria. When the quakes started he panicked and gave the rule to his niece Sage, but she didn't want it and handed it off to her brother... ah, Ryan, I think?"

Louis nodded. "I've got to admit he was cunning, but he made some poor decisions concerning the trade with Ekiliador and the council voted him off for his younger brother Rovas."

The politics of the Castle was, frankly, a mess. According to their law they could hand off their own responsibilities to rule to their closest family member, but the council, who was elected by the people, could easily vote their leaders on or off, and make various recommendations. There were restrictions, but they were few. The councils held most of Rendar's power, though they were easily manipulated.

The old man spoke up again. "Other than Malivia, how are things there? Last I heard, Natalie Denroe's been expanding her family." Oliver winced at the mention of her, though no one noticed. "How's her husband these days? Her sons?"

"Fine, though her nephew was killed in Aleria recently."

The old man didn't look shocked. "Oh, he was mixed in with all sorts a trouble, he was bound to get himself killed eventually. And you mentioned the quakes?"

Marion's eyes widened. "Yes, but there's more. There's been some strange weather... and yeah, the quakes." Marion leaned back, trying to make it a casual topic.

"Why, I didn't think it would reach Rendar." The old man said, scratching at his grey beard, his eyes truly puzzled. "I've been getting some recently as well. Some freelanders have told me, though I can't vouch for it to be true, that the closer you get to the Barren, the worse the quakes are." His voice lowered to a whisper. "And I'd be careful going up into the mountains, fellas, I've heard they're breaking apart. The paths have been cut off by fallen rocks, rocks broken off by the quakes."

The old man sighed, glancing nervously around. "I'd go back to your homes, fellas. I might be leavin' too. Too close to the Barren for me. Get a boat, maybe escape into the Unventured Lands. Somethin's stirrin up, and I'd best be off and away before it comes. I suggest you all do the same." And with that the man got up and left to his bed. "Y'all can sleep on the floor, got nothin else better for ya."

Well, the quakes certainly made him nervous. Marion feared what the disruptions would bring as well, and the idea of turning back and running to the never-ending forests of the Unventured Lands was very tempting. Marion shook the thought out of his head. *No, it's not that bad, it can't be, the truth's just been twisted and exaggerated. We'll get the damn orb and come home to fifty thousand dollars.* This reassured him, and all thoughts of the Barren left his mind. In the warm hut, with dry ground and full stomachs, there was little they had to worry about.

The group sat in silence for a while, sipping their drinks and eventually going out to get blankets from the bags on their horses, who were tethered safely by the hut. They slept well for the first time in weeks, and at dawn they headed out, the man giving them a bag of food and yet another warning. They considered it for a moment, but all agreed the old man might be exaggerating.

The money had not yet been forgotten.

CHAPTER 8

LOUIS WILLSON
THE NORTHERN MARSHES

According to Jacob, it was now the 57th of Fall. They had slept on the ground the previous night, and it had not been an enjoyable experience. He yearned for the safety and comfort of the old man's hut. Louis could remember bits of conversation, including yelling at Marion to be quiet and to stop tossing stones out into the water while he was trying to sleep. Now, however, he would rather be sleeping wet on the ground than knowing they would have to pass through the abandoned village. It had been on the horizon since yesterday, and already they could tell it had been burned and left for nature to decay.

Currently it was early morning, and the light dew glistened on the marsh grass as they traveled. Louis savored the fresh air of morning before they would have to breath in the rotting smell of the village. A weak sun was just peeking out over the horizon, but clouds covered much of it. The sky was gray, and rain seemed to be in the future.

"Marion? How much longer to the village?" Amicus asked, his voice thick with exhaustion. He had been growing weary, and had mumbled for alcohol more than once in his sleep.

"I don't know."

"Use the sun."

"Amicus, look around you. Do you see a sun for me to use?" Marion wiped the sweat from his brow and pushed back his hair, clearly tired. "Besides, it doesn't work like that. It only tells when the sun will set."

Amicus didn't seem to be listening; none of them were. They were tired, sore, and battered. Louis knew they would grow used to the conditions, of thier blisters, saddle sores, and exhaustion. He himself had gone through such a time, at the loss of his leg. His other was now stronger than ever, but for the longest time he had been as weak as a hatchling from a nest. Soon they would grow used to the hard cold ground at night and the endless landscape ahead.

All of the travelers were hungry; the need to preserve food was strong, yet the need to eat was stronger. Louis wished he were traveling with people who had smaller appetites. Most of them were unfamiliar with the sting of starvation, the endless gnawing of hunger, most of all Oliver. In truth, he was too. He feared it, feared the time when he would try to fight the pain inside him, but could not reach it. Louis Willson feared when the simple thought of bread became his utmost desire over anything else.

Soon the village loomed just ahead of them, the old buildings, houses, and markets crumbling with age. Ivy crawled up the loose stones and metal, deteriorating it, making it one with the earth. Remains of bones, belongings, and furniture were covered in dust or dirt, so worn they were not recognizable.

The hidden smell of rot and decay was better than Louis had feared, but it was still there- lingering beneath the wind. There was silence, save the crows overhead and the faint crumble of stones. Their mares wandered through the town, shaking their heads and snorting, as if trying to shake off some unseen dirt. The place was filthy, and even though he hadn't touched the ground he felt an itching nonetheless. The town had a strange feeling, a feeling of... desertion. The horses trotted unwillingly along through the ruins, leading their tired masters away from the open land. Oliver had been dozing, his head on his chest, but Louis now felt the need to awaken him. He shook his friend awake.

"Where are we?" Oliver glanced around fearfully at his new surroundings.

"The village I saw." Marion said, looking warily at the dark open doors of the deserted buildings.

A shiver went down Louis's spine.

"This?" Oliver asked.

"What else?"

A prickling feeling crawled up his neck, and he turned around. Nothing. He'd had too many experiences with criminals. Maybe that was why he was worried. Stealing from their orchard, always trying to stay unseen in the shadows of the trees and the fields. Was he the only one feeling this? Louis glanced over at Oliver, who was observing the village with disgust.

"Whatever was here, it's long gone."

"Why do you say that?" Marion sounded concerned. With dreading realization, Louis hoped that his feelings were wrong. Hoped they were nothing but anxiety or exhaustion.

"Because there are footprints."

The whole group stopped, looking over at Oliver.

"Where?" Amicus asked, scanning the ground around him.

"*What?*" Louis whispered. "Why the hell didn't we see-"

"Shut up!"

Jacob was glancing at the windows, looking so frantically his eyes were almost a blur. His body was shaking from fear, drawing his mare close to the center of the group. They went silent, knowing in their gut what Jacob had seen. *Why weren't we more careful?*

"Run." Marion whispered, his voice shaking. Seeing the glints of eyes in the windows, the creak and clicks of the bows and guns being put in position.

"*RUN!*" He yelled, and the others reacted as if they had been ready their whole lives. They hit their legs against their horse's flanks, their frenzied energy putting the poor animals into a state of panic and adrenaline. Cries came from the buildings, indistinguishable shouts mixed with the thunder of footsteps and the hustle of movement.

Dust and stones were flung up into the air behind them, as they urged their horses to go faster, faster, faster. Gunshots rang out in the air, and cry of pain and a thump as one of them fell to the ground. Louis did not look back to see which one, who was it? *No, just run just run just run-* However the rest of the group slowed and looked behind them, seeing Marion laying on the ground, clutching his bleeding side, gritting his teeth, grunting and trying not to scream. Blood pooled around him, letting out a scream that ripped at their hearts, though they had barely known him.

Louis grudgingly turned back, and felt guilty for wanting to leave Marion behind. *You're better than this, you have more honor-* He argued with himself in his head- *No! You idiot, you fucking idiot, you should have run, you would've escaped, now you're done for! You can't run, you can't walk-* It was too late now. *Go to him.*

He rushed over, trying to calm Marion's frightened horse. Oliver dismounted and attempted to help him onto his own horse's saddle, but by that time they were already surrounded. Louis managed to get the mare under control, and so he crutched over to his companion. Knowing he couldn't get him onto the horse, he set his crutches aside and kneeled down next to him.

Louis had ripped a part of his shirt off and pressed it onto the wound. It was the least he could do, all he could do. A moment of silence passed before they heard a click. Not from the circle, but from their own group. Amicus had taken out the gun from his bag, taking a second before turning off the safety. It was rusted and small, but Louis had no doubt it would work just as well as the other guns around them.

"Get away!" Amicus yelled, his hands shaking. "Leave us alone!" The gun kept shifting positions, shifting targets as he tried to figure out who was important enough to shoot. There was a moment of silence. Then, instead of backing away as he had expected, they laughed, making way for a person approaching the middle of the circle. He was middle-aged, stocky, covered in tattoos and wearing a gold chain against a worn shirt. It was ripped, stained, and dirty, much like his cargo pants. No shoes were on his feet, but he did have a lot of hair; it was black and greasy down to the nape of his neck, framing a smirking pale face.

Amicus had a second to wonder why he was leader- there were plenty of stronger, more dominating men in the crowd. Ones with scars enough to make a woman faint, ones with muscles and emotionless, murderous stares. Before he could come to a reasonable conclusion, however, the man stepped up and put his hand out for the gun. In the midst of people, he could see bows and guns at the ready. The leader's brown eyes were dark and cocky, and the lack of hesitation in them was somewhat chilling. *Very* chilling. Cold.

Amicus reluctantly handed it over, knowing that if he did not, he would be shot from his horse and killed. These were not people to joke with- they were raiders, attacking scouts and traders and even others of their own kind. Placing the gun in his satchel, the man walked over to Marion, who glared with undenying hatred.

"Well, well, well. Looks like we got ourselves some travelers." He circled around them, smiling with a cold smile that would make any grown man tremble. "Weak, pathetic... I wonder if we should just leave them to die."

Oliver backed away towards his companions, shuffling along on the cold stones and dirt. With one arm he dragged Marion, who groaned in protest.

"What're you filth doing out here in a place like this?" His taunting voice made Louis want to punch that smile off his face, but he knew it would do no good. "Seems a little too dangerous to me..." The leader turned and kicked Marion in the side, causing him to scream out in agony.

"Stay away from him!" Louis rose, grabbing his crutches and hobbling up to the man.

"Now, now, don't cry yet. It's going to get a lot worse. Take their other weapons."

Louis spat in his face, though the man only wiped it away with a frown. The raiders disarmed them of their other firearms, much to the travelers' dismay. The leader walked away, the men clearing a path for him, staying a respectful distance apart.

His voice was clear, the taunting tone vanished.

"Tie them up."

85

JACOB FORTEMER
THE ABANDONED VILLAGE

Jacob awoke tied to a post, his companions still out cold and tied up beside him. His wrists were red where the rope had cut into his skin. He looked over. Marion's wound had been left unattended, but thankfully had clotted; his breathing was heavy and rasping. Dried blood stained Jacob's shirt and the floor around him; a drop of it ran down from his mouth and to his chin, where it lingered. It smelled like pennies, metallic and warm.

The others were bruised but otherwise unhurt, himself included. Looking around, Jacob noticed how inexperienced these raiders were with holding prisoners; probably because the few who wandered around here were smart enough to stay away.

They were in a stablehouse with an open door, which let in the chilly afternoon breeze. There were no guards that Jacob could see, though he still stayed quiet. Tools, hay, rags, and more were scattered around the floor, while the travelers' horses snorted angrily, trying to escape their confining stables. Jacob was scared to see the lash marks against their hides, their strangely wild look without riders. It was almost as if they had never been tamed. Jacob continued to look around, struggling a bit against his bonds. The rotten, old smell was stronger inside the buildings, but the cold and the breeze lessened it.

Another gust of wind blew through the door, swinging it on it's weak, rusted hinges. He shivered, longingly gazing at the pile of rags and blankets in the far corner. After a few moments of silence, Jacob tried to get to the wood axe lying in a pile of hay just feet from him. It's edge was rusted and blunted. *Yes, but it can still cut my bonds.* His foot almost touched it, he was so close, just a little further…

"You won't get out."

Jacob jumped, looking around.

"What I mean is, you won't get out without help." The woman stepped out from the shadows, walking up. Her accent sounded familiar, maybe Russian, but it was hard for Jacob to tell. Russia was an old country from the old world, and he had rarely seen any of it's native people. He only knew this from his books, his history books he had loved to read so much. And the recordings, of course, down at the library.

This woman looked older, around her late forties, with shoulder-length tangles of black-gray hair and strange, pure white eyes. *Blind?* Was Jacob's first thought, but the woman seemed to know exactly where she was going. She wore an old leather jacket, brown boots, and jeans. The woman walked over and sat down, cross-legged, and looked at him with a mixture of worry and contemplation; like Jacob was a bug she wasn't quite sure how to get rid of. She tilted her head.

"Who are you?" Jacob backed up against his post, not sure whether he should trust this woman or not. He probably couldn't, but he held on to his hope.

"I'm no one. Someone. A friend. Or not. Whatever you make me." The strange woman smiled, and leaned in close. The smell of filth and smoke made Jacob wrinkle his nose, but he stared back, determined. Stared into the white eyes, the swirling white of a hurricane.

The woman's voice lowered to barely a whisper. "There are two guards outside the door. Another exit is behind those boxes. Use it to get the horses out. Go to the lake. There's a boat." The woman grabbed a knife from her pocket, admiring it's gleam, before cutting his bonds. She moved on to Marion as Jacob started lifting boxes from the stack, slowly uncovering the door.

"Why are you doing this?" Jacob asked as he pushed the last box into the corner. The woman didn't respond, just started pulling away the rags on the pile Jacob had seen earlier.

87

The raider lifted their bags out and started putting them on the horses, a pained expression on her face. She started to work faster, shaking her head, warning off any more questions.

"Why are you doing this?" Jacob asked again, confused at the reaction. Suddenly, the woman let out a long sigh, then shivered. She turned to look right at him, the white in her eyes fading away to reveal angry brown ones. The panicked, fearful face was slowly being replaced with a confused, irritated one.

"Why *am* I doing this?" As the woman realized where she was, she became furious. She looked around for a second, blinking, confused. "You, you're the prisoner!" She yelled, recognition in her voice. She ran at Jacob, who picked up the axe in defence, raising it. *What the hell?* It was as if the raider had been possessed.

The woman pulled out her knife, forcing Jacob into a corner. "Oh, Weston will be so pleased when I tell him I caught the escaping prisoners." She lunged, Jacob leaping out of the way. "Maybe he'll let me have my way with you... before he burns you." The raider's voice was mocking and full of lust, almost a whisper, threatening and eager. "He likes to burn."

Panting hard, Jacob raised the axe, but it was so heavy, he didn't know if he could swing it...

"Wouldn't he be mad you were the one helping them escape in the first place?" Out of nowhere Amicus grabbed the knife from the woman's sweaty hands and put it against her throat.

The raider tensed, her voice shaky. "Now, now... I didn't mean anything by it. Honest."

Amicus pressed harder into her throat, and she sucked in a breath. "Who's Weston?" He asked harshly.

The woman laughed. "Oh, I think you've made an acquaintance."

Amicus's confused expression soon turned into one of spite. "He had the tattoos. The one who kicked Marion. So, he's what? Your leader?"

"That's the one." The woman snorted. Amicus motioned his head at Jacob, who grabbed the cut rope from one of the posts, tying the woman's hands behind her back.

"Who are you?" Jacob asked. He gazed into the raider's wild eyes, searching for the trace of white that was gone from existence. The woman glanced toward the door, but Amicus saw and lead her to a post, where he tied her there.

"*Answer him!*" Amicus whispered menacingly, the knife gleaming as it pressed against her sweating skin. "And if you're too loud, I think you can guess what happens."

There was a new light in his eyes as he said this, though Jacob still wasn't sure whether Vanner would actually kill her. He didn't know Amicus, not really. Jacob didn't know him well enough to know his pride, to know his courage; to know whether he would really draw blood.

"Fuck you." The woman spat in his face, and Amicus, with a swift motion, rose the knife and sliced open her cheek. Dark red blood dripped down the raider's face, staining her shirt.

Amicus was strangely calm, his voice dangerously low. Almost as if he had done this before. "*Who are you?*" Shoving her into the pole, he lowered the knife to his victim's neck once again, and the woman's eyes showed a glint of fear.

"Sasha Rintos." Her accent became more pronounced a he spoke, and Jacob hoped that it was from fear and not amusement.

"Why did you take us prisoner?" Amicus relaxed a bit, taking a moment to wipe the spit off his face.

"You have to ask? We're raiders. You're the usual scum that comes through. We use you Rendarians for whatever we need. Supplies, of course. Wes likes to burn 'em, but he lets us have our fun. Most of the men were hoping you'd have some ladies with you, but I guess we'll just have to make do with what we have."

Looking much to happy about that fact, she tilted her head and smiled, revealing yellow teeth and a sour breath. The woman's eyes glittered menacingly. In a matter of seconds Amicus had lost control, dropping the knife to the ground and punching the raider as hard as he could. Truthfully, they were impressive punches, and the woman was helpless as Amicus released his anger. With her hands tied behind her back, it was hard to defend herself. Around them, the air started to smell of blood and sweat, and the horses neighing nervously.

Jacob moved to pull him away. "Amicus! Be quiet! There are guards outside!"

Amicus stopped, panting. He was much stronger than he looked. Sasha was out cold, her face bloody and bruised. Her jaw was out of place, a mess of maroon seeping from a swollen mouth. Their companions were waking up. Oliver was starting to stir, Louis staring at them, forgetting about his crutches hanging out of the bags on the horses. Standing in the eerily silent room, Jacob forgot how to move. Amicus was dangerous, and he was no freelander, that much was for certain. Those were practiced punches, aimed hits, solid blows. Trained. If they were going to get through this they needed to support each other, help maintain each other's sanity. They needed to be trusted. The travelers had only been out here for a few weeks, maybe less, and they were already falling apart.

"Okay. Okay." Jacob said, frantically trying to think of what to do next. After a few seconds, he spoke again. "Oliver, get the horses over here. We need to get Marion on the saddle and Louis on his feet... er, foot."

Oliver nodded, casting a worried glance at Amicus. Jacob looked at their supposed freelander companion, examining his hard features and relentless eyes. His face was hard and emotionless, but within moments Amicus had regained his normal feel, if not with a little more confidence. Jacob's shocked gaze did not go unnoticed, however, and Amicus quickly turned away.

Marion groaned as he lay on the floor, coughing from the dust, ash, and dirt. A horse was beside him. Jacob did not respond to the several questions bombarding him, and instead picked up Marion and helped him onto horse. Oliver and Amicus aided best they could. Marion slumped forward; he was weak, but despite his wound he was able to hold himself up on his mount. *The poor man,* Jacob thought as he mounted in front of Marion. He would've had him in the front, though they would need to ride fast; Marion was both taller and broader than himself, which would block Jacob's view. Marion had been the strongest among them, in skill and strength alike.

Now however... Marion gripped Jacob's shirt and held tight, as if any moment he would fall off. He probably felt as if he would. Before long they were ready to go, and Amicus took a peek outside the open door. Guards did not stand just outside as expected, but a little further away, talking with occasional glances at their building. The rest of them mounted their horses.

"Let's go. Before they decide to come check in on us."

In single file they exited their prison, nervous and exhilarated. They moved slowly, taking advantage of their chance to sneak out. Jacob did not want to have to outrun the raiders, especially with Marion in such a condition. Quietly, silently, they snuck through crumbling buildings, the shaded afternoon sun sending weak glimmers onto the ruins.

They had slept through most of the day, Jacob realized, as they made their way out of the village. Soon it would be dark. He squinted past some buildings into the distance, spotting a wide, eerie lake just beyond. Marion, growing mildly uncomfortable, shifted on his mount, holding back a cry of pain. He could feel the horse's muscles beneath him, rippling and strong with each motion. The sun finally admitted defeat and sunk behind the gray, unwelcoming clouds, the last shimmers of light fading away.

"Wait!" Marion's voice came out in a helpless wheeze, cracked and dry. "Stop!" this one was louder, and the group halted per his request.

"What? What's wrong?" Oliver dismounted his horse and came to his side. "Do you need something?"

He looked through the window of a building they were passing, a shine of metal glinting in the light. Marion couldn't seem to find the strength to speak, so he just pointed to what he had seen. Oliver looked at it for a second, confused, worry etched on his face.

91

Jacob too was confused. *Is Marion having hallucinations?* But then he saw it, and his face melted into an expression of awe.

"Get over here, all of you!"

Amicus and Louis turned their horses and trotted back, a look of anxiety on each of their faces.

"*What*? And keep your voice down!" Louis whispered.

Basically leaping with excitement, Oliver pointed through the window.

"Damn, we're lucky." Louis abandoned his horse and walked over to gaze at the rusted gun hanging from the wall.

"Do you think it works?"

"Yes. Probably. What kind is it?"

Jacob, who knew it was his cause to know these things, answered promptly. He had been particularly interested in history, and there happened to be a lot of guns in wars back then. What could he say? It was interesting.

"It looks like a sort of rifle. But I'd have to hold it to tell you more." Jacob's nose pressed against the cracked, stained window as he tried to get a good look of the room.

The overall stability of the building seemed intact, and it looked unnaturally clean. Piles of rubble were cleared to the side, put under the few cots. It was a bedroom, Jacob realized, as he saw the ragged blankets and belongings by each one. A small fireplace, secured with extra stones, was on the wall opposite the cots, and Jacob could still smell the smoke from the dead black logs and ash. A hole, big enough to fit an arm through, was behind the fading fire, probably to let smoke out. The chimney had either collapsed, or they had just build the fireplace themselves. The gun was placed on two metal nails jutting out from the wall, it's wood polished, the metal a bit rusty.

"See any way in?" Amicus asked, looking at Jacob intently. He had been taking up the window space.

"Well…" Another glance showed him door on the other side. Closer inspection showed that it was barred. "There's a door, but it's blocked off. We'd have to go on the road, but there might be raiders."

"Have they noticed we're gone yet?"

Jacob strained to hear shouts of panic, anger, and chaos. "No. I don't think so." It was silent, the cheers and shouts a good distance away. "There must be some event going on."

Louis shrugged, speaking up. "Well, we don't have guns anymore, so we don't really have much of a choice. Just a few knives isn't going to get us fresh meat, which, by the way, we should get while we can. This rifle is the best chance we have of saving our preserves and hunting before we get to the Barren, where I doubt there's any game. Or people. Or anything." He shifted nervously on his crutches.

Jacob observed the cracks on the glass, an idea forming. "We could just break the window. Jump in, grab it before anyone notices." There was a moment of silence.

"Yeah, okay." Oliver turned to the bags on the horses and started searching for something to break the window with.

Marion swayed a little on his mount, but gripped the reins tightly. He was clearly more aware now, more awake, and more aware of the itch that seemed to be spreading over his body. Warmth from the horse and possibly what could be called a fever made him sweat heavily, and he most likely cherished the cool breezes that occasionally reached him. Jacob knew what it was like to be sick, really sick, and sympathized with him. He hoped his friend's wound wasn't infected.

There was a crash to the left, an echoing sound that seemed too loud in the dead village. The good-hearted cheers in the distance suddenly turned confused, hostile, as the sound echoed. Marion turned his head to see Jacob pulling the gun off it's rack. He had underestimated the weight of the weapon, and he almost dropped it before regaining his hold. Not too heavy, but sturdy. Comforting. *Don't drop it, don't drop it, don't drop it.*

It gave Jacob a feeling of power, of strength and respect. The feeling that he was the leader, the reassuring one, the one who knew

93

what to do with unhesitating confidence. An even deeper feeling rose inside him, like he could do anything, could change the will of fate with one shot. It felt *safe*. Greed rose up, gathering in his gut like a vicious snake, and Jacob had a sudden urge to keep the gun close, keep it for himself. Yet one look at his weary, sullen, painfully hopeful group forced him to hand over the tool of smooth wood, of sturdy metal, of luring and longing.

He saw the same look in the other's eyes, a look that now disgusted him. To anyone else, it looked like they would go too far to own that gun. Kill for it, even. Kill *with* it. It was a dangerous look, and Oliver seemed to realize it too, as Amicus tried weakly to take it, to feel it's power, feel the weight, the bullets, the unseen workings of magic. Shoving it in the bag, it disappeared from view, and everyone seemed to get ahold of themselves.

MARION ARMAIS
THE NORTHERN MARSHES

"Get over here! They're coming!" Marion yelled hoarsely, hating himself for not being able and well. Now, he was a burden that might get them all killed. *For once I know what Louis feels like,* he thought, grimacing.

Marion gripped the side bag for comfort, but instead found the haunting weight of the rifle. His midsection stung, and Marion felt a loathing for the gun. *No one deserves this much pain. Oh, God, no one.* The stinging continued, and Marion could almost feel the bullet inside him, feel the metal and dirt spreading an infection. With a helpless thought, Marion knew they needed to get that bullet out. He wanted it out, and didn't care what they would have to do to make it so. It wasn't far in, not at all. Regret seized him. If he had been well, Marion would have stolen that gun himself, without hesitation. They would be sailing across that lake right now, taunting those angry, foul-mouthed freelanders. *Goddamnit, I'm supposed to be the strong one.*

"We have to leave, come on!"

Marion was frustrated, his face pale and looking like he might pass out at any moment. Yet he still took the role of leader, still was anxious and impatient. Oliver had just mounted his horse when they saw a smaller group of raiders behind them, also on horseback. The savages yelled out in anger, their leader at the very front. The travelers were fairly new to situations like this, and as a result they made mistakes; it was unavoidable. However, mistakes usually determined if they would escape or be recaptured, and Marion didn't like the thought of that at all. If they were ever going to survive in the Barren, they all needed to have a talk. Hell, most of them had snuck extra food from their supplies, as some of them weren't used to rationed food. Marion could exclude himself from that group; he was used to hunger. So far, at least.

They would need to talk, talk not only to set rules but to get to know each other. Get to know each other so they could protect one another, so they could work as a team, a team with no secrets, lies, or deceptions. A team that knows when another is hurting, a team that knows how to lift each other up. For their path through the Barren would not be easy, and their only savior from insanity or depression would be each other. From the start of the journey, they had been distant, unsure, wary of their new comrades. But if they were going to survive, that needed to change. Marion could see that now. A part of him worried that wouldn't be possible. Maybe they were too different. Already he could see Oliver was having a hard time coping with his new life, and that Amicus was starting to realize what he had gotten himself into. Jacob was stronger, young but reasonable, Louis seemed smart but weak.

And himself? Marion was willful, good at hunting, skilled in fighting and so much more; though he had faults as well, and he sure as hell knew it. He lacked empathy. He didn't know his limits. He had a tendency to get angry quickly, to lash out unexpectedly. There had been consequences for that, a long while ago. His mind flashed back, back to when his life had been… rather complicated.

"Marion?" He was shaken awake, the face of his friend above him. "Marion, we have to go. Now."

He was in a shack in the woods just outside of Wellston, Calidor, covered in dirt and wearing torn clothes. Marion lay on his side, his head resting on his bag.

"Marion!" Seth. That voice was Seth Blair. "Get up, goddamnit, get up!"

Marion scampered to his feet, looking around. His friend, his companion through all of his struggles was there, short black beard, green eyes, and worn leather jacket over a flannel. There were footsteps outside, louder than they had been before.

"What's going on?" Marion asked.

"*They found us, idiot, get moving!*" Seth whispered. He rushed to pack his things.

"*Enforcers?*"

"*No, no, the Vipers!*"

"*The gang?*"

"*The dealers.*" His friend was looking out the stained window, into the mist outside. "*They have guns.*" He whispered. "*Dear God, they really have guns.*"

Fear filled Marion. They had angered Rovas Mchenry, the well-connected man not yet ruler of Malivia, but the notorious head of several gangs and the source of the dealers. Dealers, the men who dealt, grew, and collected various old world drugs, tobacco products, alcohol, or even simply outdated medicinal reliefs. These were not illegal- no, that wasn't the issue. That was never the issue. The problem was ownership; who stole what from who, who got their hands on something they shouldn't have. Who, in the end, got the money.

The infamous Marion Armais and Seth Blair had not only stolen Rovas's money, but foiled various schemes of his and undone years of work. They had been hired by his opposer in the dealing business, and been paid good money for it too. Though now, it seemed, they were being punished for it.

"*Run, Marion. Go.*"

Marion turned to look at him.

"*The cash is hidden at my place, up in Ekiliador. Go. Take it. Get out this mess. Get out of this life. Promise me.*"

Marion stood there in shock, in anger. He felt trapped, conflicted, hesitant. He didn't want to leave Seth. Hell, the man was his cousin, his friend. His only friend.

"*But-*"

"*Promise me!*"

The voices outside were threatening, and they thudded in his ears. Weakly Marion nodded, backing away as his friend drew his dagger and ran out into the open. Blair, the heroic son of a bitch, was causing a distraction. With a moment of hesitation Marion *opened the back window, jumping out and racing into the fogged, gloomy woods beyond. A gunshot rang out behind him, and another. A yell, and silence. He did not turn around, did not go to help or to fight. He didn't even look back.*

The memory pained Marion, not only because he did not turn from that life as he had promised, but he had wasted Seth's money; on bars, on drugs, and even a few that were willing to give him company in the night. It was now that he realized that he had changed quickly in the last few weeks. *Or has it been a month? Two?* Marion couldn't seem to remember. Loud yells, sounding like orders, alerted him to his surroundings.

The travelers urged their horses onward, attempting to gallop faster. The village was now behind them, and they were in an open field. The lake was just ahead, glimmering in the light of dusk. Wind rushed past them, adrenaline pumping through their veins. Everything was a blur, so Marion looked behind, yearning to see how far they were from failure, and how close they were to success.

He squinted in the distance, blinking a few times because of the rising darkness. The sun had set, but only just, for there was still light in the sky. The leader was almost upon them, followed by at least a dozen others. Though the bandits had mounts a well, the steeds could never hope to best their own. The freelander's horses were weak, sick, and obviously not well taken care of. The travelers' own mares, pure-bred in Malivia, were strong, fast, and healthy. That made all the difference, and Marion knew it was the only reason they hadn't been caught so far. Those raiders had lived in these ruins, knew these roads, breathed in the rotting air around them. In retrospect Marion realized that by all odds they should have been caught. When he looked back at the riders, he saw flashes of white in their eyes. Just as one was about to raise their gun or bow, the flash of white appeared and they would lower it. The white would fade away only to reappear in another's eyes, to shout wrong orders, lead the horse astray, or slow down.

However, as this white ghost was busy with such actions, it seemed to have forgotten about the leader, Weston. The man urged his horse faster, faster, faster, until he was galloping just feet away from Marion. The leader pulled out his gun, the wind pulling his hair back to reveal a snarling face.

"I'll finish my job this time." He yelled, his voice was strangely clear despite their distance. Marion never heard him click off the safety; maybe the sound was lost in the wind. Perhaps he had never even turned it on. Marion felt a horror growing deep inside him, a fear that he would die like this, be gone, just like that. He couldn't go anywhere, could barely function being so weak from his wound. He gripped the sides of the horse, feeling for anything in the bags that he could use as a shield, or to throw at his attacker. His hand came across the barrel of a gun. A rifle. *The* rifle. A second passed, though it felt like eternity. What was he waiting for?

Marion pulled the gun out, praying it was loaded, and aimed it at Weston's shoulder. Clicked off the safety. Shocked, the leader had no time to react as Marion pulled the trigger. It wasn't that hard physically to pull, but he felt the tension, the enormity of it pulling him back. There was a loud bang that left his ears ringing, startling him, causing him to jump. A splotch of red started to make it's way along Weston's thin shirt.

"Son of a-" The leader shouted, falling off the back of his horse from the impact. His horse, no longer with a rider, stood there, breathing hard, taking a rest. The raider undoubtedly yelled more, but they were too far away to hear.

Catching up, the group of freelanders came to his side, and Marion could swear he saw Weston glaring back at him. He let out a sigh of relief, sliding the gun back into the bag. His shirt was soaked with sweat, yet a chill went through him, dotting his arms with goosebumps. He had shot someone. With a gun. It was a strange feeling, like releasing all his hatred and anger into one bullet. It wasn't so bad; and though he'd experienced firearms well enough in Calidor, something about this was different. This time, Marion Armais wasn't on the wrong side of things.

The horse swayed back and forth as they approached the lake, though that might just have been him. Marion's vision had begun to blur. The rest of the group was nervously silent; each one had yearned to turn and look back at the fallen leader, but at the same time were worried about what they would see. They were in a state of denial, denial that they were really out of trouble. The only way to fix that, in their minds, was to outrun it. The darkness settled down on them like a dreary fog, and they breathed it in and out, in and out. Saddle bags thumped and clattered while the horses galloped on, never slowing in fear of a hand reaching out of the darkness to pull one of them back.

And as the new black landscape came, the wind became cold and harsh. The crickets chirped, the birds fell silent. An inky sky punctured with holes let starlight down into the world below. The lake had become a glitter of the moonlight, growing larger with each passing second. Soon it was before them, intimidating, troublesome, gleaming hungrily as if it would like to swallow them into it's depths.

"Where's the boat? Jacob, didn't you say there would be a boat?" Louis asked, a panicky edge in his voice as he scanned the shore. Looking for a dock, a boat, anything. "They won't take long to follow us, they saw the direction we were heading." His voice shook, the horrified look in his eyes proving he was already thinking about what would happen to them if they were caught.

"Don't worry, we'll find it, it's only a little dark." Jacob said, his tone reassuring. Oliver looked down at his horse, stroking it's mane nervously. The night air was chilling to the bone, making them shiver. One of them took the lead along the shore. Marion gripped Jacob's hips and clung to his jacket, holding himself steady; black spots were appearing, and his mouth felt dry. A throbbing had settled itself into his head, like a heartbeat.

"It has to be here somewhere..." Jacob said. "That woman, the one who told me, her eyes were strange at first. They-"

Marion jerked upright, trying to stay awake. "They were white?" He turned his head to face Jacob, wondering. Well, he wasn't quite sure if it was Jacob. He was feeling quite lightheaded, and his breathing became labored and heavy.

"Yes, they were. How did you-"

"I'll... tell you later. What were you saying?" Marion felt the multiple pairs of eyes burning into his back whenever they got the opportunity to glance.

Jacob continued. "Well, yes, they were white. Foggy. A storm, like a hurricane... she didn't have pupils, like she was blind, but she knew where she was going. If that makes sense. It felt unnatural. "

Amicus looked confused. "You got all that from just looking at her?"

"Yeah- well, no. I could *feel* it. And the woman, she sounded Russian, had the accent from the old world. Maybe it was something else, German maybe, but it was harsh and foreign."

"I didn't know people still spoke with old world accents." Louis said, vaguely interested. His gaze was settled on the horizon, deep in thought as they trotted, searching for an escape that was hidden from their sights.

"Well, apparently some of the freelanders still do. When I kept asking her why she was helping me escape, she looked like she was fighting with herself. When I asked her again, the white in her eyes was gone, but not only that. She became a whole new person. Walked differently, acted differently, talked like a raider would. Possession, maybe? Is that even possible?"

There was silence for a moment, before Marion spoke. "I saw it too. The white. It kept the raiders from shooting at us when we were being chased. It-" He coughed. "It flickered in and out of their eyes before they could realize what was happening to them. They-" He was cut off by the crash of old wood. *A dock?* He couldn't think. Everything was slow, and he felt empty. *Hunger?*

"What was that?" Amicus asked, trying to look up to the front of their group. Jacob looked down, unbelieving, at the hole his horse's hoof had made in the small, old boat.

"Well, I think I found the boat." He said, as realization dawned on their faces.

"No," Oliver said, getting off his horse. "Oh...no, no no, this is bad. Oh, this is very, very bad."

The boat lay upside down, the hole seeming to laugh at them as he stared at it in disbelief. The rest of them dismounted, staring at the damage in the worn, gray wood.

CHAPTER 9
OLIVER MONTEROSE
A STRANGE LAKE

"Are there any other boats?" Louis asked, looking over his shoulder. More shouts had begun, louder now. Jacob was holding Marion up, his arm around him, trying to somehow support the barely conscious man.

Oliver knelt by the boat, surveying the damage. "We don't have the time to find any other boats. We have to-" He tripped over the root of a tree and lay sprawled on the ground.

"Oliver? Did you fall?" It was already getting too dark.

"I'm alright." His hands brushed what he had fallen on and he froze, an idea forming in his head. Jacob saw what he was looking at and grinned. The tree they had come upon was known as the ceiba pentandra; they were rare and their seeds valuable, though that wasn't exactly what Oliver was excited about. The pentandra's pods held a cotton that was water resistant, buoyant, and durable, though very flammable. It was a very desired tree in Rendar, due to it's rarity. Oliver had once written an article about someone who had sold them.

"Oliver?"

He was jolted out of his memories. Amicus stood before him, with a handful of the fibre. "Is this what I think it is?" He asked, holding it up so he could feel it.

"Yes, yes, get as much as you can." A spark of joy lit up inside him. Not only could it fix their boat, but it could start their fires. It's uses and value were beyond measure.

And right now it would save their lives.

103

AMICUS VANNER
A STRANGE LAKE

Amicus fingered the soft cotton-like fibre in his hands. When they got back they could sell it for a fortune. *No, not they. Not us. Me, I'll be returning with it, sneak it out in the night and make for Rendar, the moment we reach the edge of the Barren.* He had forgotten himself for a moment, although the thought did not appeal to him as much as it had before.

He felt almost obliged to help them- he would be leaving the travelers to their death. The others did not see his confliction in the dark, and so smiled in relief. They were lucky. They had been captured by raiders and had escaped with a gun and their lives- not only that, but they now had insight on the phantom, the ghost of white. The demon, the friend, the blinder, the possessor. Whatever it was to be called, Amicus knew they were being watched. Followed. Helped, perhaps. The thought scared him. This wasn't supposed to last longer than a few months, a short term work with good pay. But now they had lost their horses, and there was a new mystery to be solved. Simply put, it was getting too complicated for Amicus Vanner's liking.

"Hurry, we have to leave, they'll be on us any minute now." Jacob noted, as he looked at the dark forms of his companions pull the boat out into the water and seal the hole. The lights of torches, orange and yellow and red, flickered in the distance. Their light and warmth was far, however, and the travelers sat in the chill shivering and waiting.

"What about the horses?" Louis asked, stroking his mare sadly. "Will we leave them to the raiders?"

Oliver frowned. "We'll have to let them run." However, he made no move to make this happen. Not just yet.

Jacob was mumbling to Marion, trying to keep him conscious. His wound had started to bleed again, and Amicus wished they could keep him still and let him rest. Marion's face was one of pain and discomfort; the others felt pity, gratefulness that *they* had not been shot. Amicus was grateful as well, but that didn't make him pity Marion any less. He pitied them all, in fact, though there was something there that hadn't been there before. A trust, maybe. He suddenly felt a little guilty.

Himself and Oliver flipped over the boat, Louis coming over on his crutches. Amicus approached Marion, helping Jacob get him into the boat. "You'll live, don't worry about that." He said, reading Marion's worried face.

Marion grinned, and despite his wound he had not lost the ability to use sarcasm. "Thanks for the concern, but nobody knows who's gonna to live or die. That's up to the dying man, I'm afraid. And all men are dying."

"And will you die today, Mr. Armais?" Amicus asked, his tone curious and slightly amused.

Marion smirked. "Not today, friend. Not today."

"Quit talking, they see us!" Jacob yelled.

The others scrambled into the boat, rushing as they heard the distant yells get louder and louder.

"Okay, okay. Get Marion in here."

The boat was big enough for at least seven people, but it would be a tight squeeze with all of their supplies.

"Wait, wait, the horses!" It was Jacob who said this, glancing worriedly at the tired beasts. There was no way they could take them across the lake, but across the lake was their only option, unless they wanted to try and go around it. But even then their pursuers would likely catch them, and would keep going until they got revenge. Until the leader got his revenge.

Someone spoke up in the dark. "They can go back to the grasslands, but we can't take them with us."

A sadness passed through the group, mainly through Louis, knowing they would most likely have to walk the rest of their journey. An angry yell awoke their sense of urgency, the voices much closer than they had anticipated. Jacob swiftly leaped out of the boat and hit the horse's flanks, causing them to neigh and run to disappear in the darkness. They were left alone.

"Come on!"

Louis sat at the end, surrounded by bags and supplies. Jacob, with many fearful glances behind him, hurriedly pushed the boat back into the water and jumped in. Dirty, wooden oars had just come to Amicus's notice, and without hesitation he picked them up and started to row. Shouts and yells became louder as he desperately tried to move the boat, to move it away from the dangerous freelanders at the shore. The raiders yelled and swore, throwing rocks and shooting arrows. *The damn bastards.*

Looking over the side of the boat, Amicus noticed that something was wrong, something wrong with the lake. A dead fish, all bone with little pieces of tissue, floated up onto the surface, a ghostly figure in the dark. Strange, poisoning smells breached his senses, and he covered his nose with his shirt. Freelanders had come closer to the shore, but they weren't yelling or pointing their guns and bows anymore. They were laughing.

"You should've stayed with us," One of them shouted out across the water.

Weston shoved his way to the front, a surprised smile on his face. His shoulder was bleeding, but it had been hastily bandaged. "Things much worse than death are in that lake, little travelers. Take care."

The leader turned away, him and his followers fading into the night. The shore disappeared and suddenly there was silence, no sounds but the whispering and splashing of dark water against the hull. The men had momentarily forgotten about the hole in the boat, and with a sickening slyness the water had forced its way through. Louis pressed more fibre into the leak, holding it down. The material quickly clotted and stuck to the wood, strong, like the webbing of a spider. It would suffice, but it would not last forever. With the warning from the raiders now thudding in his head, Amicus now seemed to notice what they had really gotten themselves into.

Ghastly fumes rising from the lake made Amicus gag, blurring his vision. The oily water now started to inch it's way up along the interior of the boat, but none of them took any notice. Marion had passed out, Louis looking frantically around as if he seen something in the fog. Amicus lifted his boots to find them dripping. His feet were wet. The boards were old and thin- no wonder it was falling apart. Everyone then, instead of panicking, seemed to calm down, even relax. A strange serenity seemed to be falling over them. The group knew they had to be calm and accurate to get past the lake, but this was something else. A feeling of rest had settled upon them, a feeling that was lost and sleepy.

"This has to be the Barren. It's sorcery, dark-radiation, it's-I-I've never seen something like this before. It's spreading faster than we thought. Much faster." Jacob said, blinking. "We have to hurry. It might poison us. Well, I'm not sure sure what it'll do. If the Barren has already spread it's influence here, or even a shadow of it, then we can't stay."

It's not as if we have a choice. We'll be drowned by morning. The fumes were making him tired, exhausted, but fear and adrenaline kept that sense of urgency inside him.

"Wake up!" Amicus yelled to the other men, saying it harsher than he had meant. They had glazed eyes and blank faces. Slowly, one by one, they drifted off to sleep, slumping down to the wood. His mind felt groggy, tired.

"Wake up, wake up!" Amicus blinked, blinked again, shook his head. Something wasn't right.

Something wasn't right.

Something wasn't right.

107

JACOB FORTEMER
A STRANGE LAKE

Jacob Fortemer was on the boat, the others asleep around him; all but Amicus, who stared with an unblinking gaze. Darkness swirled around them, figures in the lake, floating, staring up with eyeless faces and rotting white skin. He recognized each and every one. They covered the lake as far as he could see, breathless. Jacob looked down to see he was skeletal, weak, starving. A dark stain spread along his shirt. When he glanced at Amicus again the man was covered in blood, his face torn and mauled, so much so that it was unrecognizable. Dead, but breathing. Arrows were through him, bullets as well. Slashed by swords, scratched by claws. He looked in the water to see his own reflection, and saw that he had eyes as white as snow.

(Jacob,) his companion whispered, through a broken jaw. The voices echoed in his head. *(Jacob. Jacob. Jacob. Jacob. Jacob. Jacob. Jacob. Jacob Jacob Jacob Jacob Jacob Jacob JacobJacob-)*

He opened his eyes.

All around him was calm, though his heart was beating too loud in his chest. Dreaming. He'd been dreaming, that was all.

"Where are we?" Jacob asked, looking around. His voice was dry and weak. It was a lake. A lake, on and on in each direction, the sky grey and the birds silent. Only the winds and the small splashes told him this wasn't a dream. They were drifting, they were asleep, on a lake as despairing as tears and under a sky as grey as storms. It was morning, and the water now seemed more like the sky, a grey and dark blue, less like oil and more like rain.

The fog hadn't quite cleared, and though it was visible around them he could see nothing but a gloomy horizon. *This* was not a dream, and his senses were telling him so. Jacob Fortemer was aware, awake. He started to shake Oliver beside him, but a glimmer in his peripheral vision forced him to turn away.

A skeleton, small and stained with dirt, floated past him, and it somehow looked familiar. Somehow. But that didn't make sense. *How would...* a golden bracelet hung on the dead wrist, shining with rust and blood. It was his daughter's. Emilia's. The one she'd wear all the time, the one she'd seen hanging from the merchant's display, the one she was so fascinated with that Jacob couldn't help but buy it for her. It was worth at least ten dollars, rather expensive for someone like him, but a gift was in order for his little Emilia. She had deserved it.

"No, no, oh God, please no." Jacob blinked and it was gone. He was seeing things. Hallucinating. He put his hands over his face, breathing in, out, in, out. Then he heard the voice.

(Jacob, Jacob, Jacob, Jacob-)

"Jacob?" Louis sat up, confused and yawning. "Jacob?" He rubbed his eyes, wiping the dirt from his face.

The others started to wake as well, though none of them spoke. They'd all had dreams, that much was clear, though Jacob wasn't sure if they were different dreams or the same one. After a few minutes they managed to clear their heads. Oliver took the oars and pushed them on, leaving the rest of them to think. His own thoughts were confusing, strange, and wandering. It was like they weren't even his own. Jacob felt his eyes, his curiosity, dragging him to look at the still, rippling water. What was it this time? He didn't want to know. He didn't want to know what else was out there, in the lake. Some things were better left unknown, for there was always a price for knowledge. Marion had drifted off to sleep again, though it was most likely no cause of the lake. He wound was worsening, as was his fever.

"No! He's dead. Dead. I made sure of that-" Marion's face went slack, and Jacob assumed the man was still dreaming. The rest of them looked away, uncomfortable.

"Wait, don't shoot, don't take me," He groaned, sweated, tossed and turned. "I'm sorry, I had, to, it was... you bastard!"

109

Marion fell once again into a deep sleep, and Jacob hated himself for wanting to ask the criminal what had happened. It wasn't his business. *Or is it?* Shouldn't he know what type of person Marion was, so he didn't murder them all? Jacob chided himself- it was no time to think about that. There was never a time to think that way of someone who'd been shot. Someone that needed them. With that wound, Marion wouldn't be murdering anybody, especially if they couldn't get that bullet out. If it was in too deep, it would most likely be best to just let it heal as it was, in risk of harming Marion even further. Being just six years above twenty, Jacob didn't know much about murder or injuries, but he still had his history, his education, his experience as a lawyer. And to be honest, those subjects had a lot of such things.

He was positive Oliver had an education, probably a good one, but Jacob knew he would be the one in charge of taking out the bullet. Oliver, he thought, didn't have the guts. Jacob didn't know if *he* did, either. Yes, it probably had been a long time since his older companion had been taught such things, but Oliver was bound to remember a bit. He could help. Amicus was a freelander, or so he said, so he might know some remedies, though past that he wouldn't be of much help. With Louis, he wasn't so sure. Paerdan was mostly farms and markets, and many people were much too far away from anything to learn much other than farming. He'd have to ask them.

Looking around at his group, his weary, hopeless group, he figured they were in no shape to perform anything medical. Jacob doubted they could even lift a knife without shaking or dropping it during the process- and that included him. He found himself wondering where they'd be now if they had never been captured; but Jacob knew they never would have been safe from the Barren. Soon enough these lands would be filled with dark-radiation, making them see and hear things that weren't there, making them sick and weak. They all would be dead within a matter of months, maybe weeks. Insanity, isolation, and terror would likely drive them to a sooner death by their own hand. They *had* to do this. Jacob saw this more and more as they got closer to the Barren- there was no other choice for them. Not now. Not anymore.

Submitting to the pull of his curiosity, Jacob looked ahead, hoping to see a shore line, or perhaps even shallow water. There was nothing. *Does this lake go on forever?* Just mist, fog, and endless dark water. If they were stuck out here much longer, he thought, he would fall into sleep again. The image of them drifting around until they starved was a propelling, motivating picture, causing Jacob to take the rows from Oliver and push on, harder and faster until he couldn't move his arms. It seemed like hours, though it was hard to tell, especially here.

"I can row, if you want." Amicus said, leaning back. "You don't have to do everything."

Nodding with relief Jacob sank to the floor of the boat, closing his eyes. Just a little rest.

Just a little...

CHAPTER 10
LOUIS WILLSON
A STRANGE LAKE

Louis awoke to the crash of wood against rock. For some strange reason he thought about horses, before wondering where they were. *A boat. Right. Why? Horses... horses, we left those behind. A lake. What did we hit?* A smooth, hard surface was below him... *wood, maybe?* It smelled of rot and wet plants. He raised his head, got dizzy, and lay down again, taking a few deep breaths. Focus. Think. *You need to be awake.*

Louis tried again, this time forcing himself into a sitting position. Feeling around for his crutches, he grasped them and held them close to his chest. He didn't want to open his eyes, in fear of what he might see, but he knew he had to. Seeing, after all, was better than being blind. After a few blinks from the sudden light, the blurry shapes started to clear.

"Louis!" A loud voice called. It echoed in his ears. "Louis! Wake up! We got through!"

"Almost through."

"Damnit! We're not, Oliver, are you blind?"

"We're close enough."

Louis blinked again, sighing with relief as his vision cleared. Looking around, it didn't take him long to find the source of their latest problem; a large, jutting black rock stuck through the front of the boat.

"What happened?" Louis asked, trying to form a scenario in his head. His mind, however, felt scattered, like cards fallen out of their deck or pages out of order; useless.

"What does it look like happened?" Amicus huffed, frustrated. "We were rowing, facing backwards so we couldn't see the rock. The fog was thick. You were out cold. No one was paying any attention."

Oliver was looking over the water, eyes focused on something down below. "Louis, give me your crutch. Just one." He asked, holding his hand out. His eyes didn't leave the water.

"What? Why?" Louis clutched his precious possessions to his chest, worried of what Oliver might do with them.

"Oh, for God's sake, just give it."

Unwillingly Louis passed over a crutch, waiting for Oliver to fumble and drop it into the water. With his hand on the top, he lowered it into the black, poison lake.

"No, come on!" Louis begged. "Whatever you're doing, I don't care, just let me have it."

As Oliver lowered it, some part of his mind waited for a dead white had to grab it and pull his companion down, to a dark, horrible death; but it was just his imagination. The crutch hit the stony bottom, and Oliver grinned. Before, as Louis had looked down, he'd sworn he had seen stones, and perhaps ghosts that had only been the bodies of dead weeds. He was right.

"We're getting out."

"What?" Louis said, reaching for his crutch. "Are you insane? We're not going to swim through a dark-radiation infested lake. That's- it's....."

"Our only option." Jacob sat up, a grim look on his face.

Louis looked at them in disbelief.

Amicus was glancing down at the water, a disgusted look on his face. "Well... I don't particularly *want* to, but-"

"-but the shore is close. And look, it's only a few feet deep." Jacob said, pointing.

Louis looked ahead through the fading fog, and saw his companion was right. The shore was near. He glanced at the unconscious Marion, raising his eyebrows. Oliver bit his lip but said nothing, not willing to offer. Jacob, sighing, gathered Marion into his arms and stepped out into the water. It went up to his knees, the small waves lapping at his thighs. When no one else moved, Jacob looked back expectantly. The rest of them grudgingly gathered supplies and followed him, dreading to leave but loathing to stay. *Who knows what'll happen to us if we step foot in that water? And yet who knows what'll happen to us if we stay, and drink it?* There wasn't much choice in the matter, once Louis thought about it, but this weary group of travelers weren't very good at thinking at the moment.

One day that'll get us killed.

OLIVER MONTEROSE
THE NORTHERN MARSHES

Oliver, touching Marion's shoulder slightly, tried to wake him up. He did, if not only a little.

"Oliver?" Marion muttered, blinking. He laughed softly, but suddenly cried out in pain when Oliver accidentally pressed on his wound to set him on his feet, and out of Jacob's arms.

"Oliver?" Marion asked, half asleep. "Where... where...."

Oliver sighed, looking sadly down at his companion. The dark-radiation and his wound must not have been the best combination, he thought. For the first time, it hit him. *Marion might die.* Before, it was just a gunshot wound. They could fix that, they'd deal with it later. Yet now, as Oliver pondered it, another thought rose inside him. If Marion didn't get medical treatment, he would die. Gone, just like that. One of their strongest members reduced to nothing. Well, there was little they could do about it now. All they could do was focus on trying to get Marion Armais out alive.

And so they climbed up the foreboding rocks that stuck up out of the water, hands slipping and sliding on the loose, wet stone. A cold gust of wind stung their faces, on a lake that had previously been absent of any wind at all. The air became colder, the breeze stronger. When Oliver stepped back into the water, it was so cold it felt as if he was burning. Despite the shallowness of the lake, they had an awfully hard time moving through it. Each step was ten times harder than the last.

How did I end up in this shithole? How did I come into the company of a cripple, a freelander, a criminal and a commoner, wading towards my death? He was George Monterose's brother, one of the wealthiest people in Aleria. Respected. *How the hell did I get here?* This was not his fate, this was a mistake. He was higher than this. *As soon as they sleep I'll leave them. Not that I'm much use anyhow. Just an extra mouth, swallowing up their food and hopes alike.* Their boat was soon flooded behind them, and a powerful thought hit Oliver, one that scared him to his bones.

"It doesn't want us to leave."

His panic increased tenfold, realizing this wasn't just radiation they were facing. This was mixed with some sort of black magic, a strange dark chemical never meant to be seen by the light of day; something the core had released into the world as it slowly dissipated, as it had cracked, as it had broken. Something he had heard about only in drunken stories, until it all came back to him in a rush or fear. *I have to escape before it's too late.* This was much more than they'd thought it was. This was twisted, wrong, formed out of pain, suffering, and misery.

This was only a taste of the Barren.

This was only the beginning.

***

Dry winds blew across the land, a land that was no longer quite the marshes, but now a borderline to the Ashen Desert. A mix of dying brown grass, trees, dirt, and dunes of cool sand had replaced the wet marsh. The change brought a sense of achievement to the group, one they hadn't had before. The travelers were covering ground, they were achieving their goals, if not slowly. Yet as they hiked up the dunes on the cool autumn day, Oliver's confidence seemed to have left him. The loss of the horses had been rough, and now Jacob and Amicus carried most of the supplies. Louis hobbled along on his two crutches, excruciatingly slowing them down, though no one had the heart to say it. His face was beaded with sweat despite the cool weather, his leg clearly aching. A single bag was slung over his shoulder, but the group didn't give him more to carry. If there was a pain the others didn't know, it was having to hike all day as a cripple.

Oliver now carried Marion in his arms, panting with exhaustion. Marion had passed out, his chest rising slowly up and down, red-stained shirt still fresh with blood. Oliver felt it hard to hate the man in his arms… though he so wanted to. The criminal was heavy despite losing weight, and made Oliver's arms ache in pain. Any moment it felt as if he would drop the man, and every moment he thought of the relief it would bring. It was like carrying a rock, heavy and unmoving. *No, a bag full of rocks,* Oliver thought, gritting his teeth.

It had been one full day since the lake, but something was pushing them onward. The pull of this mysterious orb, or just the fear of the dark-radiation following them in the forms of their worst fears. However, someone could only walk so far.

"That's it." Louis fell to his knees, rubbing the end of his severed leg. He couldn't even feel his other one anymore. "Stop. Marion needs help, we need rest, and one more step is only gonna make it hurt more." He groaned. "And I don't care what you all think, tonight I'm sitting right - the - fuck - here."

They all froze for a moment. No one argued, just shrugged and sank to the ground. The travelers were sheltered under a weeping willow, old and dry, battered with sand. Soon the sun gave way to the moon and the clouds to the stars.

Before long they huddled up and fell asleep, dreaming of lands and rivers too far from their reach.

117

CHAPTER 11

MARION ARMAIS
THE ASHEN DESERT

Hours later, Marion awoke. It was midday, the sun shining weakly down. His thoughts were muddled, but the pain in his midsection jolted him to reality. They needed to get that bullet out. Now. Now. *Now.*

"Wake up!" He yelled, his voice hoarse and tired. He choked back tears. "*WAKE UP!*"

The group, their faces slack against the sand, groggily sat up, brushing themselves off.

"Marion? What is it, how're you feeling?" Louis blinked sleepily at him.

Anger mingled with his pain. "Oh, Louis, I'm great, I just have *a fucking bullet in my stomach!*"

That woke them up.

"Marion! Oh, the bullet, I forgot, Oh…"

Oliver helped to lay him on his back and slowly peeled the cloth from the wound. The blood had dried, clotting the thin material to his skin.

"You *forgot*? What the hell do you think this is?" He yelled angrily, but Oliver worked without comment. Marion yelped like a dog, gritting his teeth, feeling nauseous. It started to bleed again, and yet Oliver only stood there, hesitating, at a loss for what to do.

"Who knows anything, about… ah….?" Marion asked, turning his head towards them. Jacob nodded. The others looked uncomfortable. "You do? Know how to remove a bullet?"

Jacob nodded, his face pale. "I- I've read about it."

"Good enough. Get your ass over here." Marion looked up at him, annoyed, when he did not move. "Well, come on then, we don't have all day!"

Jacob looked taken aback for a second, looking almost queasy. Then, after stern glares from his companions, he adorned a determined look and moved forward to help.

"We've got to remove the bullet first," Jacob said, examining it. "It's not far in. But it's going to be messy... and painful. Then we need to disinfect it and wrap it. That's about all we can do; well, all I know to do. After that we just need to make sure you rest."

"Are you positive you know how to do this?" Marion asked, suddenly wishing there was a doctor here to do the procedure instead of an inexperienced stranger. It surprised him, really. By now he would have thought they knew each other well, but their trip had been mostly silent, each one of them contemplating. Thinking. Jacob's answer interrupted his thoughts.

"Yes. I used to get hurt all the time stealing. Eventually my little girl begged and we ended up taking lessons from a retired doctor that lived by us. It helped."

Oliver looked uncomfortable. Perhaps it was the notion of stealing gone unpunished, or the unfamiliarity with people such as him; the less fortunate.

Jacob pushed aside his black hair, looking nervously over Marion. "You might pass out, so, just..." Jacob unbuckled his belt, folded it, and gave it to him. "Just bite on this, I guess."

Searching through the bags, he pulled out a knife and rolled up his sleeves, breathing before looking down at the wound. Marion shuddered. *Calm down. Stop shaking, oh God, what if he messes up-*

"Okay. Okay. Here we go. Amicus, get some water ready. Marion... I... I'll get it out. Promise." Jacob tried for a grin, but it was less than reassuring.

Blood stained Jacob's fingers as he tried to access the opening, to feel where the bullet was. This wasn't so bad, Marion thought, as Jacob felt around the wound. He winced, biting down on the stick a bit. Surprising. He had really expected it to be wor-

Then it hit. A pain so great filled him like fire, the cutting of the knife stung like ice, *it hurts so bad, it burns, it stings, oh God, when will it end-* that was when Marion blacked out, and all faded into darkness.

***

Marion awoke to the night, to the chilly air and gritty sand. Stars dotted the sky, a sky so clear he felt as if he were dreaming. He was leaning against a tree, the bark rough and cold behind his back. The others slept, peaceful and silent. It relaxed him, and he closed his eyes to try and drift back to rest.

"Feeling better?" A voice asked, and he opened his eyes to see Jacob sit down beside him.

"I guess."

His wound was wrapped and it felt, to be truthful, much better, but Marion knew his limits. He would need Louis's crutches to walk, and even then he wouldn't be able to last a whole day. Marion glanced around, not letting his eyes linger on the bloody bullet tossed aside in the sand.

Jacob sighed. "I- I'm sorry. I tried my best, but your days of recovery are limited. The Barren is... well, you were passed out for most of the time across the lake, I remember, but I think the Barren is spreading faster than we thought. You'll be affected. We all will."

For a moment, there was silence.

"There was a story I heard once, as a kid. It's stuck with me. Do you wanna hear it?" Jacob wondered, tilting his head. It was clear that the man only wanted to help, so he nodded.

"Go ahead. Might help me sleep." Marion said, leaning back and sighing.

Jacob grinned. "Alright, then." He cleared his throat. "Once, a long time ago, in the old world, there were these islands, far out into the ocean. So far out that sailors that most didn't know they were there. On these islands, there were several volcanoes."

"A... what? Volcanoes?" Marion asked, confused.

"Yeah. Those, uh, fiery mountains." Jacob looked back out into the horizon. "Anyway, one day a sailor came upon the islands to find them deserted. How this was possible, he didn't know. It seemed like a heaven. The volcanoes rose high, but they were dark, black, and cold. Dormant. The sailor saw no danger in them. So he brought others to these islands, many and many who came to live away from all the conflict of the rest of the world. Still, the volcanoes were cold.

They settled in, and built and established and populated until they had metal ships and smoke flowing from concrete towers. Still, the mountains remained cold. It wasn't until many years later, when the people started disturbing them, did the great black hills awake. A heat rose inside them, sudden and furious. Out from the holes at the very peaks touching the stars came a raging fire, in bursts of cloud and smoke. The sky rained ashes on the islands, the light disappearing with the shrouded sun. Molten rock-"

Marion interrupted. "Melted rocks? Is that even possible?"

Jacob smiled. "Yeah. Yeah, it is. Anyway, all of that flowed down to the towns and melted and burned, leaving nothing but ruin and charred bones. When the islands had been cleansed, the volcanoes slept again, turning cold and silent as yet another sailor came and fell into thier trap." Jacob looked over at Marion, who was smiling.

"I liked it. Haven't heard a story in a long time." He paused, a softness in his eyes. "You're good at it."

Jacob rose his eyebrows. Maybe the man beside him wasn't as wild as he'd thought. "Anytime."

Without warning, Marion suddenly sat up, wide-eyed and very much awake.

"What is it?" Jacob asked, looking his friend over, somewhat confused at the reaction.

"I just realized something." Marion sat up straighter, ignoring the sharp pain in his side.

121

"What?"

"The Barren is like these... whatever you called 'em. Volcanoes. What if something woke it up, started the spreading? What if something is creating these, like, spots of dark-radiation? Does that make any sense?" Marion wondered thoughtfully. His mind felt much clearer. It was the air, or maybe the fresh breeze.

"Yeah, maybe. The Barren could be too overwhelmed with radiation, it might need to spread out. Something might've just unlocked it's cage." Jacob's expression became cold. "You've gotta understand, Marion, this radiation doesn't stop. It grows and grows, like a volcano'll get hotter and hotter. There's definitely something wrong with the Barren. Something isn't right, I can feel it. We're missing a big piece of this puzzle."

Jacob paused, taking a breath and turning to look into Marion's eyes. "Dark-radiation's got a mind of it's own, and it's choking on it's own medicine. Being subject to poison like that for so long, the Barren might just fall apart into the ocean. The land's weak. The radiation probably just needs a new land to suck the life out of. You follow?" Jacob asked, his worried face illuminated by the starlight.

"Yeah. Yeah, I think so."

How did he end up here, sitting in the sand bleeding in a land far far away? It had all started with Rovas. *It's always him, isn't it?* Marion sighed, and tried to push those troubling thoughts from his mind. The travelers sat in a comfortable silence and looked over the water, over the dunes and the fire of their camp. Together they looked past the stars and the mountains, wondering of what lay in the vast and distant ocean beyond.

LOUIS WILLSON
THE ASHEN DESERT

The flames burned and blazed as the sun rose, as the morning light draped itself over the arid land.

"So." Louis commented, as the travelers sat in a circle in the sand. The bright fire flickered in the center, drawing the eyes of those around it. There was an uncomfortable silence. He coughed, winced, then continued. "So. What do you suppose we do now?"

Marion looked up at him, brow furrowed. "Nothing's changed. We keep moving."

Louis remained unsatisfied. "Don't you suppose we ought to… you know, talk?" He asked. *How are we to survive this if we know nothing more about each other than our names? If we know nothing of what we are about to face?*

"And what exactly do you propose we talk about?" Oliver fumed, a slightly irritated tone to his voice. "The money we'll most certainly never get? The lands and homes we'll never see again? The people we'll never get to speak to before we die?"

Louis sighed. "Why not? But I'd rather talk about what's coming. This orb, this Glass Shadow. The white eyes. The Barren. I'm sure there's no doubt left that the Glass Shadow exists."

The others nodded at this, leaving them sullen. Louis had no doubt they all were having dreams. He was, at least; his last one had shown a dead forest with a crow in a tree.

"What about it, though?" Amicus said. He opened his mouth, closed it, licked his lips, then spoke in a soft tone. "I'm worried it might hear us, if we talk too much."

"What'll hear us?" Oliver smirked. "The trees?"

Amicus did not laugh. In fact, he seemed almost frightened. His voice lowered to a whisper. "The closer we get to the Barren, the more dreams I've been having. I've seen the orb, I've seen us, I've seen the white in my own eyes. In the dreams. Don't you see? The orb *is* this white ghost. I don't know what's been sending us visions, but it feels like a different power. A warning. But if this orb can speak with another's mouth as Jacob claims, it can hear with another's ears, see with another's eyes. *It'll always be watching.*"

Marion looked confused. "You're talking like it has a soul. It's an *orb,* a source of power to be harnessed. A horse can't run unless it's let out of it's stable, like this orb can't use it's own power unless is has a master. It's gotta have someone do that for them. This orb is probably just a pawn."

"But of who?" Jacob wondered aloud. "Who would ever want to live in such a place, much less be responsible for the spreading of it?"

Louis tossed a log into the fire. "It doesn't concern us if the Glass Shadow is acting of it's own accord or if it has a master. What concerns us is whether it- or they- is on our side."

But how could it be on our side if it's the one spreading the disease of the Barren? Louis thought. *It's not on our side, to think so is false hope, but then how come it helped us at the village?* It was too much, too confusing. Why would it help them if they were out to stop it?

Then, suddenly something else was there, in his head, alongside his own thoughts. He shivered. *(because it isn't)* the voice told him. *(it isn't it isn't spreading it, the King the Kingis is Louis Louis Louis can't you see can'tyou see it the orb has a will of it's own)* He ignored the voice.

Louis couldn't deal with that right now. There was too much going on, he didn't have time to deal with the crazy voices and visions in his head. They were all puzzled, as it seemed, so they returned to the silence of the crackling of the fire.

"How did you lose it?" Oliver asked, and Louis looked up at him in surprise.

"Pardon?"

"The leg. How'd you lose it?" His expression proved he was genuinely curious. The others did not look him in the eye, but waited for him to speak.

Louis shifted; he was clearly uncomfortable. "Uh, well, when I was ten I wandered into the woods alone. I got too close to a bear and her cubs. When I tried to run it chased me and got ahold of my leg. My brother heard me yelling, saved my life, really. The bear had..." He couldn't finish. Truthfully, Louis couldn't quite remember it. All he could recall was the pain, and darkness, and the looming face of a growling beast. It was no doubt a saddening story, though many of them had dreaded something worse.

"What about you, then?" Jacob asked Oliver. "You're well-born, It's not hard to see. How did you come to be hated by Rovas Mchenry?"

"I, well... my brother's a councillor, he-"

Amicus started to laugh. "*You!* You're George Monterose's brother, the one on trial!"

"On trial? For what?" Marion asked, intrigued.

"What country did he council?"

Oliver sighed. "Aleria. He was accused of killing Paulen Denroe, the nephew of Ekiliador's leader, you know the one. That's why they took me away. His only sibling. George himself, of course, is too important. He didn't do it, though. The murder. At least, that's what he told me."

Only Amicus didn't look surprised. He was the only one who had seen it in the papers. "I saw that. In the news. Front page. Did no one else see it?"

Jacob, who never really bothered to read the paper, looked down at his feet, while Louis shrugged. "We never got the paper. We were too far from town."

Marion, if he could have guessed, looked somewhat ashamed. "I was a little busy at the time."

Louis thought he had an inkling of what 'busy' really meant, but he said nothing.

Amicus grinned. "So, how were you all captured?"

125

There was silence. They had told him of their unfortunate encounters, though had not specified. Marion turned away, pale, Jacob staring into the flames. Oliver opened his mouth but thought better of it, and Louis himself had a sure feeling that those were not memories they wanted to recall.

Amicus seemed to regret his question the moment he'd said it. "I... apologize. That was uncalled for."

No one responded, so he merely lowered his head. No one wished to talk of their past, and less of their future. The fire crackled, sending sparks up into the air to dance with the wind. A drizzle of rain came down on their camp, but Louis hardly seemed to notice. It was a good night of rest, for the tree above seemed to shelter them well, and the fire was warm. The conversation was soon forgotten and forgiven. And as they sat huddled by the fire, wrapped in blankets on the cold sand, the dangers they were soon to face vanished from their minds.

For now, they were at peace.

AMICUS VANNER
THE ASHEN DESERT

The five travelers left footprints in the sand as they walked, observing the change of landscape around them. As they had left the marshes, and the ground had become solid, grittier, less grassy. More trees had popped up in this transition, giving them shade from the warming sun.

Before long they'd trekked into dunes, part sand, part grass, little dirt. The abundance of trees had dwindled, taking the shade along with it. Now, as the travelers hiked, they were truly in the Ashen Desert, with the sand, the heat, and endless horizon. Winter was coming on, but the closer they got to the Barren, the less that mattered. Days were slightly hot, nights a chilly cold. Most of the time it was like this, but further in that started to change. Sometimes it was opposite, the nights sweaty and the days yielding storm or rain. Weather was unpredictable, though it was always miserable. Amicus found himself yearning for the simplicity of the grasslands, with it's simple blue sky and pleasant fields.

In the light of day this company hiked on, packs swinging at their sides, on their backs, or dragging along in the sand behind them. Marion had taken up a stick to help him walk, wincing as he pushed on. Louis held tight to his crutches, now scratched, crusted with sand; but still strong. Amicus could see that Louis's worst fear wasn't the Barren ahead, but the chance that his crutches would break or be lost- and he would be left helpless. *I pray for him, I really do,* he thought. Amicus could only imagine what Louis would have to endure. He felt a guilty relief that he wouldn't be there when they died.

Sand dug into their feet, felt through the thin soles of boots that had worn down to almost nothing. The sky was a light, faint blue, the sun weak in it's shining. The land looked as if it had been drained of color, dribbling out into the air as time went on. Despite these strange changes in the desert, the travelers took little notice. They had never ventured outside of Rendar, had only heard stories, seen faded pictures of other lands. Nothing, in their heads, seemed out of place, besides the strange weather. Yet even that could be explained, made sense of, whereas the lack of color was paid no notice. It was the small things, as one might say, that made all the difference.

"How much longer until sunset?" Louis panted, hobbling along with great effort. Jacob moved forward to support him.

"It's noon, Louis." Marion said, not even glancing up. The heat of the sun was bearing down on them, burning in spite of its weak glare.

"Noon, noon... can we just rest for a second? Sorry, but any further and I'm either going to pass out or throw up."

Louis stopped for a second, breathing hard. His leg obviously hurt like hell, his arms raw and sore; Amicus didn't even need Louis to tell him that.

"How're we going to make it across this desert? I knew it was going to be bad, but not *this* bad." Amicus said, looking worriedly at Marion, who had knelt over in pain, clutching his wound. *How will I ever get them to the Barren alive?*

Blisters, sunburn, and weariness were all you could see on their faces, the lack of hope almost as strong as the heat around them. This early morning, before the sun had risen, it had been almost cold, drizzling. Now, though... it was heat as they had never experienced before. Much more of this and they were done for. Louis, in a state of delirium, suddenly paused and looked off into the distance. His mouth hung open, his eyes glistening, wet.

"I see it..." Louis said, squinting with all of his might. "I see it!" His voice was raw and scratchy, but the excitement came through well enough.

"What?" Marion asked, still clutching his wound. He was trying to decide if it was a hallucination or the real thing; they all were. Amicus was starting to worry about the cripple's sanity.

"Maros!" Louis said, his voice cracking.

Jacob squinted alongside him. "That's impossible."

But belief was in Louis's eyes, firm and hard and true. "Yes, it's there, look at it! It's alive! We have to go there, we've gotta hurry, we have to..." His eyes glazed over, an awed expression softening his features.

"No..." Louis stuttered, in complete confusion. "No, nonononono-" The once hopeful expression on his face turned cold, terrified. "What the hell is that thing? What the hell-" His voice cracked, tears in his eyes- tears of utter fear.

The others stared at him, unable to turn away. *What the hell is happening?* Amicus thought. This was wrong, this wasn't right, it-was it a vision? While he was awake?

"NO!" Louis yelled, frenzied and panicked. "No, we have to LEAVE! It's coming, they're coming, it wants us *all, all of us, every single one-"* He stopped, panting. His glazed expression became emotionless, and after a few seconds he shut his eyes and fell back onto the searing sand.

"What's wrong with him?" Jacob asked, voice shaking.

Oliver rushed to his side to check for a heartbeat. He nodded, sighing with relief. "He's alive."

"And?" Amicus asked, looking over at the motionless body. He opened his mouth, seeming not able to find the right words. "Why?" It was the only thing he could think to say.

Louis's skin was pale, shining with sweat. His faint freckles and longer auburn hair usually accompanied an encouraging face, but now it was almost painful to look at. *This is all too much. This is not what was asked of me, not at all, this is not worth all the coin in Rendar.* In that moment Amicus could not have been more eager to leave, to abandon his companions at the border of the Barren. A strange feeling filled Amicus with dread, and with lonely hearts they gathered around Louis. With a knowing realization the travelers stood there for a moment. He did not fully agree with his thought of leaving. Somehow he felt as if he owed these broken men, however little he knew them. He was a man set in his ways, after all; one to fulfill his debts as best he could. So Amicus picked Louis up in his arms and lead the doomed group into the deadly lands beyond.

***

There was, in fact, something in the distance, a building that got clearer as they moved towards it. It wasn't a city like Maros full of life, as Louis had described in his delirium, but quite the opposite. As they approached the old structure, runes and markings in the stone became apparent, while the absence of life set a sore feeling in their hearts. No one was here. Why would there be, with the Barren so close, and everything else so far?

The temple, as Amicus assumed it was, rose over them, creating a long, daunting shadow. Trees with long twisting branches and wide canopies of leaves surrounded the structure, while a small muddy stream ran alongside it. The sand was a pale yellow-brown, as if it had forgotten it had to carry a color and was now letting it drain away. Rough, scorched, and sandy, the stone looked terribly old, crumbling as if the faintest push would cause it to topple. The entrance, a passage leading into darkness, hid halfway under rubble, but was still accessible.

Amicus blinked sand out of his eyes, hauling their bags over to the shade of the temple. With the stream and the trees, Amicus found it strange no one was here. *How would they know of the disease the Barren is spreading?* But the answer he knew already. He could feel it, they all could. The freelanders would know that something was out of place.

"Water!" Jacob exclaimed, rushing over to the drying stream. His lips were chapped, his throat parched, his skin dry and flaky. The man's once bright blue eyes were faint and dull, weak with thirst and hunger. Without their horses, and in their state of health, they had to ration their little food into very small amounts.

Hopefully animals would be near the small river, and one of them might be able to put use to that gun.

"Do you think we should take shelter in there?" Amicus asked, turning to Marion, eyes cautiously moving over the temple. There was something strange about it... something that drew him forward but warned him away at the same time. It was clearly abandoned, but was it safe?

Marion scanned the building as well, taking it in. "No, no. It looks unstable. I think we'd better-"

He was interrupted by Oliver's gasp. "Look, look at it, by the entrance!"

They focused their gaze on the doorway, and the runes above it. Rendar's symbol stood on each side of an image that caused them many moments of shocked silence. It was a carving of circle on a pedestal, an orb on it's stand. An orb. *The* orb. The Glass Shadow.

"Change of plans." Marion said. "This looks important."

"You think?" Amicus mumbled sarcastically.

Marion ignored him. "Amicus and I can scout it out. You all go under the shade and rest." Amicus walked over to the stream, where Jacob sat in the middle of the water, washing the sand out of his hair and skin. "And take care of Louis, will you?"

Setting his unconscious companion down in the shade, Amicus dug through their bags, pulling out a knife. His dagger was already at his side. "If we aren't back by sunset, presume us dead. If you hear us yell, send in Jacob. Yes?"

The travelers sent grim looks over to the temple. Marion looked at Jacob for confirmation, and the man nodded. Oliver shoved a blanket under Louis's head, while Jacob retrieved the pot and filled it up by the stream.

"See you soon. I hope. Don't do anything risky without us." Marion made a gagging sound as he examined the water from the stream. "And we'll have to boil this water. It's disgusting."

Amicus Vanner and Marion Armais departed from the group with one last wave.

131

CHAPTER 12
MARION ARMAIS
THE TEMPLE

Stones rolled down the pile as the two travelers climbed over and into the temple. They appeared in a long, winding hall, broken with age and life. Dim, faded sunlight poured through the holes where the foundation had grown weak, where parts of the temple had collapsed. It was cool inside, though the shade was a relief. The lingering scent of a dead animal had tingled their noses, but they took no notice. They were too focused on their objective to care. Amicus took the lead, Marion following closely behind. As they walked, Marion noticed holes in the wall to their right. Perfectly carved, scattered in a pattern that was meant to look natural; yet really was organized and well-thought out.

"Wait!" Marion yelled, grabbing Amicus's arm, freezing in position. "Don't move."

Amicus started to protest, but the fearful tone and grip on his arm caused him instead to look around for the danger.

"Is that what I think it is?" He asked, warily watching the holes. *This isn't a temple,* he thought grimly. *This isn't a place of worship.* Maybe not in the way he thought. In truth he had no idea what it was.

"Let's find out."

Amicus stepped back and picked up a decent sized stone, rolling it onto the ground ahead. Arrows shot out with a click, clanging against the opposite wall. The shafts were weak, the tips blunt. Some shattered on impact. Still, another injury would have really hurt, even if it was a small one. Marion was doing surprisingly well, considering he'd been shot, and had overcome his fever. *Nice*

132

work, Jacob, he thought to himself, silent thanking the man. Marion was convinced he could manage a scouting trip... though this might have been more than he'd expected.

Their reaction to this trap was grim. He had anticipated some sort of challenge within the temple, but now a new dilemma loomed ahead. How many more traps were there? And would they make feeble attempts such as this, or would they be fatal? There were a thousand thoughts running through his mind, but Marion focused on just one- that there was something more here than just a temple. It was a protector. It was a guardian. He dared not even hope the orb was so close.

"What do we do now?" Amicus pondered, looking down the hall. God only knew he was imagining the multiple mechanisms that might try and kill them.

Troubled, Marion looked around. They had to get to the center of the temple. Whatever the temple was guarding, they would find it there. *But how to reach it?* The path ahead was much too perilous, but going back would only leave them wondering what they had missed. It was too risky. *Yet what if...* he paused, glancing around. *What if...* with hesitation Marion pulled out his dagger, taking a moment to admire it's power and deadliness.

Amicus looked at him with a serious face, a look that said, *so, what is it we're going to do?* He raised his eyebrows. Without looking back at his companion, Marion grasped the hilt and bashed it against the wall, causing a cloud of dust to settle around them. Careful not to hit Amicus with the shining blade, he did it again, cracking the stone. A few more kicks with the end of his boot, and Marion had forced an opening big enough to crawl through.

With a grunt of satisfaction, he knelt down and peered into the next hall, scanning for any danger. It smelled significantly more than the last one, like blood, and the air was cooler. Strange. Marion started to suspect something was off. There might have been more guarding the temple than just traps. However, as they crawled through and started to walk, he saw no sign of any animal, not until they were deeper into the halls. Blood, a dark red, stained the floor, often matted with fur. It was fresh. That was what worried him the most. Fresh blood, human, animal, which one? There was no telling for sure. Marion shuddered at the thought, focusing his gaze not on the blood or fur, but into nothingness, fazing it all out until it was gone. *Focus. Walk. Think.*

The temple was so old, and blood dried fast. The only way it could have gotten here was if... oh no. Someone was here, *something* was here, and they most likely had not yet left. Something was waiting for them. Amicus seemed to have realized this too, so Marion didn't bother to clarify it. They stayed silent; their voices would echo through the halls, alerting anything here not only that they were present but to where they were as well. It also gave him a feeling that something was watching them, taunting them. No, they would not speak here. Marion looked down to see his hands shaking in the gloom. Their footsteps thundered in his ears, a lone sound in the strange temple.

After what seemed like hours, the light grew brighter, more holes letting in streams of light to illuminate the dusty air. They walked down the empty hall, side by side, and Amicus gripped Marion's arm. His companion tried to pull him back, for perhaps he was afraid. With a shake of his head Marion continued onward, pulling his arm from the other man's hold.

He too wanted to turn and run, but it would get them nowhere. Marion was glad he was not alone. An entryway was ahead, covered by an old wooden door swinging slowly on it's hinges. Even though he only got a small glimpse of the room, Marion discovered it's feeling right away.

All rooms had feelings. They could be depressed, with sagging furniture and chipping paint and the patter of the rain on the window. They could be mischievous, with hidden secrets and the masked smell of perfume. Even joyful, with baking bread, familiar smells, and plenty of light. But whether angry, happy, cozy, or clean, it exemplified the owner's personality. This room was powerful. A deadly power, one used for evil, evil things. It was a place where shadows glared in corners, hiding behind assumptions, hate, and greed. A place where when Marion would walk in, he could only guess at it's feeling, for something much bigger than himself was at hand.

"No. Let's turn back. No, no, no, please Marion, no. Oh, God, please. Don't go in." Amicus had held in his panic as long as he could in the silence, but it seemed to have taken him over.

Coward, Marion thought, *though I can't blame him.* He wanted nothing more than to run away as well, but the sense in his mind rooted his feet to the ground. He was full of fearful adrenaline, his curiosity being the only thing keeping him from bolting away as fast a him legs would allow.

"*No...*" Amicus groaned, his voice lower than a whisper, pulling him back. "Marion, we have to go, I feel it, something's not right, it's *not fucking right-*"

Marion shook his head, putting a finger to his lips. With a forced calmness Marion looked at his fellow traveler strictly, turning to face Amicus and holding his shoulders firmly. And with that look he knew they could not turn back. Not now. Whatever awaited them in that room was too important, much bigger than them, than their friends, or anyone in Rendar. It was too powerful to be ignored.

As they walked towards the door, Amicus held the hilt of his dagger in an iron grip. Marion had many thoughts about what might be behind that door. Oh yes, many thoughts indeed, but none of them seemed to click, none of them seemed right. Yet as Marion gripped the rusty handle, as he listened to the creak of the hinges that sounded oh so much like screams, he knew he could never guess what was behind that door, not in a million years.

***

The room was much like any other in the temple, if Marion looked only at the stone and crumbling bricks. A hole had opened up from the ceiling, dropping rubble onto the ground below. Light shone on the dust that floated through the room, though it was an eerie light. Clouds had covered the sun, and the world grew darker.

Snow started to come down, flakes of white slowly falling from the grey. There was no wind; for a moment it seemed almost peaceful. Yet that was before he saw the pit in the middle of the room, the message, with words engraved in the wall, faded and old.

The will of the orb,
The will of the King,
They die for what the quakes will bring.

That was before Marion saw the splatters of blood on the walls, before he took a deep breath and smelled the scent of rot, gore, and ruin.

It was before he noticed that the fur and blood in the halls had come from a strange wolf, barely alive; hanging halfway in at the edge of the pit, thin and sickly.

It was before he saw the sticky blackness clinging to the sides of the depths, leading down into darkness.

Before he realized the wolf had opened it's eyes to reveal a swirling, cloudy white.

***

"Holy *shit-*" Marion stumbled back, eyes wide, mouth open in a silent scream.

(MarionMarionMarion free us FREE US) The voices screamed in his head, and for a moment he felt as if he were going insane. *(coldcold it's so white so cold)* The voices were the same one he'd heard before, but louder, so much louder, almost screaming, like the pit was a direct phone line to whatever was deep down below.

Amicus seemed to have lost his voice but ran, pulling Marion along with him. The image of the pit, the skeletal desert-wolf at his feet and the message was torn from his vision as he ran, as he ran through the bursting pain in his side that was not only a cramp but his wound as well. In minutes they had leapt through the hole and crawled back outside, too panicked and scared to do anything but run over to their startled companions. Amicus was breathing hard, stumbling around, as if he were dizzy and did not know what to do about it. Marion fell to his knees and put his face in his hands, rocking back and forth, trying so hard to erase the memory from his mind. Somewhere he could hear Oliver, Jacob, and Louis asking if he was hurt, if it was alright, what had happened. Marion tuned them out, trying not to think, to to hear, not to see. They would not get an answer to their questions. The two were petrified, horrified, too traumatized to speak. *This is all wrong, so wrong, what is happening? What's going on?*

And the snow fell in the desert, fell onto the sand, silent and peaceful; it shrouded the path ahead in white, the white of sea foam, of a dove's feathers, of the relentless eyes that would forever haunt his dreams.

CHAPTER 13
OLIVER MONTEROSE
THE TEMPLE

Oliver sat on the bank of the river, occasionally glancing at Marion and Amicus. Much too often he would look back at the temple, worried after he got the feeling something was watching him. *Something's always watching,* a voice told him in his head. How much Oliver wished he were home; and yet somewhere deep in his gut he knew he wouldn't be home for a very long time. The leaves rustled lazily above him, the brisk wind getting stronger with each passing hour. The snow still fell, sending a shiver down his spine. Rushing and gurgling, the stream in front of him bubbled happily, muddy and freezing but plentiful.

Closing his eyes, Oliver pretended he was back in Aleria, home with his brother and nieces and nephews and sister-in-law, Sara. The crackle of the fire behind him was only from the hearth in the living room, the fatigue, hunger, and thirst only from working all day in town, the rock he was sitting on only the hard wooden chair at their table. Memories of home pained him, thinking about his brother and wondering where he was.

Does George feel guilt, or pity? Perhaps he's glad to be rid of me. Better me than him, I suppose. Does he know his only sibling is headed for the Barren to die? That he isn't in jail but somewhere much, much worse? Oliver could not bear to think of it. His brother was the only family he had. No one liked him much, he'd found. He was not someone people remembered, not someone people were willing to trust.

A lump had formed in his throat, and Oliver choked back the despairing feeling. This was no time to sulk. Marion and Amicus still would not talk about what they had seen in the temple, and were more than eager to leave their current camp. However, this was their only source of water, a good chance for sustenance, and shelter if they needed it from storms or wind. It was a haven, and the rest of them intended to lay low for a couple of days. Especially since they were in no immediate danger, and had no idea what was inside the temple. The two had made it clear that nothing alive was inside… or so they thought. But no matter how many times Oliver reassured them, it did not change the fact that they thrashed in their sleep, talked only when necessary, and portrayed a grim, defeated mood.

We are done for, if even the bravest of us shy away from crumbling stone.

JACOB FORTEMER
THE TEMPLE

Jacob knew what they had seen. He had seen it too, in his dreams. In a vision. He had been there in the shadows, when his companions saw it. The wolf, with swirling white eyes and the strange pit teeming with dark-radiation. The message.

The will of the orb, the will of the King, they die for what the quakes will bring. Someone was trying to tell them something, that much was clear. It was an old message, one from long ago, most likely written by freelanders or Marosi escaping to Rendar. A warning. Jacob was trying to forget but also trying to remember. It was in his nightmares, in his head, and a few times he thought he saw movement or the glimmer of an eye within the temple. *Something is watching us,* he thought. It was the orb, this he knew. Jacob also knew they needed to confront the others. There had been little to no conversation about such things as of yet, at least none that any of them could remember.

They needed to talk, to rationalize, to put the pieces together. No one, however, seemed to think it necessary. Only Louis and Oliver did not know, and it grieved him to see them keeping secrets from each other. Louis, the poor man, had woken in good health and mind, though seemed confused by what had happened. *It was like I was having a dream, but I wasn't sleeping. I can't really remember,* he'd said. A vision, he'd told them, of warning. Not to keep them away but to help them see what they were to face. The travelers had listened intently to Louis's story and puzzled over it long after, but none of them had yet come to a conclusion. The past few days had been hard, and all of them drifted apart. They slept, they ate, they thought. They had no answers. Without Marion's usual leadership, the travelers seemed quite dead. Marion had held them together, and seeing him so defeated made them all less confident they could handle what was to come. Jacob had become worried for what would become of them, so he took it upon himself to hunt for food. Nothing like a small bird or rabbit to lift up their mood. With this attitude, they would never make it to the Barren. Never make it past this temple, most likely. Something *good* needed to happen.

And so, with hopeful determination, Jacob hid among the dead underbrush by the river, waiting patiently for an animal, any animal, to come in for a drink. As he lay on his stomach and listened to the sounds of the desert, he contemplated what would happen to them. The smell of smoke, sand, and muddy river water flooded his nose, and he took time to cherish it. There would be little of this in the Barren. *How will we survive?* Jacob chuckled. *Off pure willpower, most likely.* Sighing, he gazed out onto the river, wondering hopefully if there were any fish.

Suddenly, a bird flew down on the opposite side of the bank, not bothering to look around before sticking its shiny black beak into the water. Jacob was still for a moment, admiring the bird's dark blue and black feathers, before he realized he was supposed to be hunting, not bird-watching. With a swift motion he readied his gun, the faint click of the safety grabbing the bird's attention. It popped it's head out of the stream and looked around, it's body rigid.

Now. He had to shoot now. Without a second thought Jacob aimed and pulled the trigger, gasping at the power he received from the shot. The sound echoed through the air, leaving his arms trembling. The bullet hit the ground several feet from his target, sending a cloud of sand into the air. The bird squawked in fear and flew up into the sky.

He'd never used a gun before, much less a rifle. He guiltily looked down at the bullet hole in the shore. *Can you reuse bullets? Should you keep them, or just leave them?* Best to make sure with Marion before he started throwing bullets away. Jacob had a gut feeling that you couldn't, though. *Marion should be doing this.* When he walked over to gather the bullet, Jacob had found it deformed, dented, misshapen. Good luck getting *that* into a gun.

The rest of the day was much the same. A bird, rabbit, snake, or even a coyote would come to the river, but they were either too far downstream or too fast and wary to waste a bullet on. Sometimes Jacob shot, sometimes he didn't, but it didn't change the fact that he still had an empty stomach. Even later that day, he noticed that most of the few animals he'd seen had looked... strange. Sickly. For some, this aura was almost unnoticeable, a faint shadow; such as the bird he'd wasted his first shot on- but for others it looked as if the animal had been dead for quite some time and just didn't stop living.

The coyote had been without half it's face, it's wound seeping pus and dark clotted blood. None of them would have been willing to eat it anyway, if he had managed to kill it. With a long, dreary heart, Jacob returned to the temple, the gun feeling far too heavy in his hands.

***

They would be leaving today, Jacob realized, as he looked over at the figure of a sleeping Marion. His friend's chest rose up and down, up and down, his eyes motionless and face calm. He was at peace, a dreamless sleep, for once. Jacob smiled softly at the sight, before turning back to the black, ashy remains of their fire. Both Amicus and Marion had agreed to tell the rest of them about what they had seen that afternoon, then resolve on what to do from there.

The travelers could leave and march onward to whatever fate thought they deserved- but it was today that the others would know the truth. *I know what they saw, I know it yet I have no hint of what it means.* Was it a warning? That was likely to be agreed upon, though a warning of what? The Glass Shadow was twisted, that much was clear. Jacob wasn't sure if it was on their side. It was only watching, helping, though for what purpose he did not know. What did the Orb even want them to do? *What is the right thing to do?*

They had discovered something much bigger than themselves, something Jacob was afraid they could not conquer. Yet they had to speak of it, however much they hated to do so. *We have come to save the last bits of our world, not to see strange pits in temples and ghosts haunt our dreams.* But that was a price they had to pay, it seemed. This was no longer a simple matter, and perhaps it never had been in the first place; but they could not turn back now, not after all they had seen. For him, at least. Jacob still felt he did not know the others as much as he would have liked to. Marion, yes, and maybe Louis, but Oliver and Amicus still remained a mystery.

Today, Louis and Oliver would hear what had happened in the temple. Today, some of them might leave. Jacob wouldn't blame them. Today, those true among them would continue their journey with no secrets bearing them down.

A soft rain had started to batter the trees, a light drizzle that they hadn't had in weeks. The snow was gone, and the air had chilled, if only slightly. The water was welcomed, although they were slightly upset to see winter approaching so quickly. Jacob didn't bother to try and take shelter, though. The dead tangling leaves and branches of these trees were thick, dense; he barely felt a drop. Thankfully, it didn't rain hard or long enough to wet the ground, so the travelers were content as they slept through the early morning.

The moon was fading, the stars disappearing and reappearing as the clouds above made their way across the lands. Louis threw more wood onto the sand, digging the lighter out of his pocket before lighting it. Their rekindled fire sent sparks into the cool air, but the wind was still as pestering and bitter as it had ever been. Jacob wrapped his blankets around himself, telling himself he preferred the cold to what would come. The afternoon ahead would most likely bring heat and sweat, and would continue through the day as they walked. He hoped the rain would last, and Jacob wondered vaguely if there had ever been a time he had wished something like that.

Abruptly, a rustle in the brush by the stream caught his attention, causing him to leap up, listening as if his life depended on it. Jacob listened for a moment, hearing all. It could be nothing, it could just have been the wind- but if it was something…

Trying to make as little noise as possible, he dug through Marion's bag and pulled out the rifle, walking carefully into the darkness by the stream. Mud and sand mixed with melting snow sank under his feet, branches brushing his his arms and legs. The rustling continued, and Jacob could see a large shape kneeling down to drink, intent and oblivious to it's surroundings. After a moment it rose its head and froze, sniffing the air as Jacob inched closer and closer. This was his shot. His one chance. It was too big to miss, to close. His finger gripped the trigger, the moments after feeling like eternity. Jacob exhaled his breath, his hands trembling; though his dark blue eyes were determined and focused. A blasting, echoing shot hit the animal in the side, causing it to fall over, writhing in pain. In a panic he shot it again and again, dark blood spraying his face and his clothes. His ears rang and he felt almost weak. Before long the beast lay motionless, dead as the Barren, dead as winter, dead as the still night air.

MARION ARMAIS
THE TEMPLE

Marion awoke to the sound of gunfire. Three shots rang out, echoing in his head. His mind was groggy, disoriented, as he looked around at his confused companions. Another shot rang in his ears, but it was enough to get him awake.

"What the hell was that?"

Marion flinched, sitting up. He looked around anxiously, expecting bloodshed, violence, panic. Instead he found the others much like himself, looking around in confusion. He counted, and came up short.

"Where's Jacob?" Oliver asked.

In fear for their friend they looked worriedly at each other, the worst scenarios forming in his mind. Was it the freelanders from the village? Had they come at last? Or had Jacob shot something? *Did he shoot himself?* The thought drove Marion to get to his feet. They heard laughter, soft at first but soon it grew louder. They hadn't heard a laugh in so long it took Marion a moment to recognize what it was, what it meant. He dared not hope too much. Jacob came back to them splattered with dark blood, his face bearing a grin and his hands holding the gun high to the storm above them. His laughter was proud, overjoyed.

"Jacob?" Oliver yelled, eyebrows furrowed. "That you?" They received a response very unlike Jacob, but he was in a mood of domination- that much was clear.

"Damn right it is!" Jacob walked closer into the clearing, smiling more than anyone had for the entire journey. The rifle hung loosely in his hand, but they saw no prey. No meat. *So what the hell did he shoot?* Jacob saw the puzzled looks on their faces as their sleepy minds tried to work out what had happened. He gave them an answer, pointing out over to the riverbed, his eyebrows raised in expectation.

"Well, I can't very well carry it up by myself."

Shock followed. A dawn of realization formed on Oliver's face, his mouth dropping in shock. "It's too *big* to carry over here? What the hell did you shoot, Jacob?"

His smile faded a bit, and he bit his lip. "I'm not exactly... sure about that." He looked confused with himself, and with that left them to see his kill. With eager though questionable faces they walked over to the river, treading carefully in the dimness of the early morning. Marion dared not become too hopeful, in fear that this perfect moment would somehow be twisted, that something would be wrong. But never fear, for as they came upon the beast, it was more than they could have hoped for, though not quite what they had expected.

"What *is* that?" Louis asked, hobbling over. Marion looked at it, blinking as if what he was seeing wasn't quite right. At first he assumed it was a stag, though a second look told him otherwise. The beast was large, larger than a lion, but took the resemblance of a deer. It's skin was a pale gray, it's dark black fur hanging in patches along it's body. It looked sick, certainly *felt* sick, and deep in his heart Marion knew this was not a creature put here naturally. It had probably been close to death even before Jacob shot it.

The next thing he took notice of was it's figure. It had two heads, one the head of a doe, the other the head of a stag bearing antlers. One head had multiple shiny black eyes, around eight of them, as Marion could have guessed. The other had two, though one was scarred and seemed to be taken by infection. Nevertheless, all the eyes gazed glassily up into nothingness, black, empty, and lifeless. Antlers grew out of it's back like the mane on a horse or the scales on a dragon, twisting, while it's tail was long and split off into three at the tip. The bullet wounds were obvious, as they had caused a lot of damage at close range. Black blood seeped out of the holes, staining the gritty, rocky sand below it. One of the wounds was larger than the other, more apparent and... graphic. It's entrails and

146

blood spilled out onto the sand. Jacob had apparently shot it in the side first, before backing away, panicking, and shooting it in the neck, then again but perhaps missed. The whole beast stank of death, blood, and gore, but Marion knew it would be much worse once it started to rot.

"Is it good meat? Can we eat it?" Amicus wavered slightly, looking down at the animal with a hopeless look of disgust.

To give him an answer, Marion pulled out his knife and knelt down by the creature, who had clearly been suffering long before Jacob gave it its grisly end. He examined the shining blade for a moment before plunging it into the bullet wound, cutting along its flank from there. The dagger was sharp, deadly, and quick. What normally would have been a hard job was done in minutes, for the flesh was thin and easily pulled across the skeletal body. Before long Marion peeled back the section he had cut to look in. The animal was clearly deep into the stages of radiation poisoning. *Dark* radiation poisoning. The meat closest to the skin had turned a deep, purple black, like blotches of ink on fresh paper.

Marion cut off a section of it and sniffed. Rancid. However, when he looked deeper, he saw that not all of the meat had been infected. Those parts of red venison would be fine... Or so he hoped. *Would that I could, this beast would go right into the river, to feed the fish and the flies. Would that I could.* But he couldn't. They needed this, and any worry he showed would only make the others less certain.

"Come on." He said, batting some hopeful flies away before grabbing a leg. "We can still eat most of it."

The others exchanged worried glances, but Marion knew they would trust him. He was a hunter, an explorer, a thief and a murderer. They would trust him, or starve. Jacob, Oliver, and Amicus grabbed the other hooves; yet that did not diminish the fact that it was so *heavy.* The smooth, enlarged hooves were a useless hold, and even gripping the ankle didn't help much. They ended up dragging the beast, and slowly, at that. It was almost impossible for them to move. The meat in that deer, no matter how infected, looked better and better with each passing step. Louis had gone ahead to start a fire.

By the time they reached the camp, the sun was bright in the sky, the rain having faded away, and the travelers were drooling for the fresh meat. Jacob, who had been given the honor of killing it, and Marion, who knew how to cut up an animal this size, got to work. There would be occasional groans and winces as Jacob would have to plunge his hand inside the animal, along with the usual stomach-churning sounds of dissection. Marion seemed to have no problem, though Jacob did not seem quite as fond of the animal as he had been before.

It was noon when they finished. Marion and Jacob walked to the river to wash off the blood, the flecks of innards, and the warm, horrendous smell of rancid flesh. They were covered in blood and ended up having to wash their clothes as well, after they'd bathed.

When they returned, the others had stuck the good meat over the fire. The guts and inedible flesh lay in a pile by the carcass, now only bloody bones swarmed by flies. Jacob had suggested they save the horns and fur coat, which, if done right, could make decent wear, something they would likely need for the upcoming winter in the Barren.

For a while the thoughts of the temple slipped Marion's mind. *And I am glad of it.* These men may have not been the best at shooting or fighting, but after all they had been through so far they certainly were good at surviving. They had forgotten about the need to talk of the dangers ahead, though no one minded. And, when the sun finally set on the hard day, they devoured most of the well-earned meat; salting and drying out the rest. That night, the travelers slept with full stomachs and good dreams.

LOUIS WILLSON
THE TEMPLE

The travelers sat in a circle around a dying fire, some munching on the last of the meat. It had been several days since they'd arrived here, though it felt like much longer. But this was it. Right here. They were finally going to talk about it. *What can possibly be so bad? What did they see?* It had bothered himself and Oliver ever since, although Jacob seemed to have no problem with the waiting.

They were silent for a moment before Marion spoke, his voice soft. He told the story slowly; all the rest of them could do was sit in a shocked silence. The travelers had seen much and heard more, though even this worried them. The orb was present here-things like that couldn't help but make a wolf and a pit a little more interesting. But now, they knew. Finally they would talk about the white eyes, the strange messages and what *really* lay in the Barren. Together they would figure out what was happening, what they should do next; how to save the scrap of world that was left to them. It would give Louis a sense of security, knowing what he was going to do and that it was right. Having no secrets, telling no lies. It somehow made the situation bearable.

With friends at my side and a cause I would die for... that is as good as a life I could wish, Louis thought. *And if we survive, I can live an even better one.*

CHAPTER 14
AMICUS VANNER
THE TEMPLE

"TALK!" The man bellowed, spitting into the air. "Talk, goddammit!"

Amicus was crying, sobbing softly, quieted by the angry shouts of his father. Blood splattered his clothes, the nice clothes that fit well on his eight-year old body, a body that was crumpled on the floor. He remembered it now... the gathering, his friend, someone had (stabbed?shot?mauled?) killed him, but who? Was that blood on his clothes, it wasn't his, no, it was Peter's, but where was he? he was gone. Dead? What had they been doing? It was blurry, so blurry...

"TALK!" His father yelled again, causing Amicus to jump. "Why won't you just fucking talk?"

The Enforcer came and put a hand on his father's shoulder, making him flinch. "Sir, please, calm down. You're scaring him."

"Get your hands off me." His father stormed away, leaving the surprised, offended officer alone with Amicus.

"Do you know what happened to Peter? Peter Fereath?" The Enforcer asked him, kneeling down to meet his eyes. "Do you know who hurt him?"

With a fearful glance at the doorway his father had gone into, he stuttered. "The man..."

The Enforcer nodded, eager for him to go on.

"He, he..." Amicus Vanner looked up at him with trust in his teary eyes.

He talked.

150

"Amicus!" Someone shouted, and he tumbled out of him daze, blinking in confusion. He must have drifted off. What had he been dreaming about? It had been a sad dream, but one that had happened to him nonetheless. *The reason I ended up selling my service to do the dirty deeds other people don't have the guts to do themselves.* His father had driven him away, and he had been left with no one. It was the incident with Peter. His friend, murdered. The Enforcer. But why was Amicus thinking of this now? Was he being reminded of all the terrible things in his life? Was he starting to feel guilty about spying on his new companions? To be a traitor, ears and eyes to sell information? He looked into the depths of the fire, wondering.

"Are you alright?" It was Jacob, he saw, who had noticed his lack of attention, and he hoped they hadn't discussed the matter at hand without him.

"Yes, yes, I'm fine."

But Amicus wasn't, not really. He was tired, weary. Not from lack of sleep, but of lies and deception and always being on guard, from the guilt gnawing at him from the inside. There was an uncomfortable silence, as each of them wondered how to continue.

"The village." Blurted Oliver, who was shifting nervously in his position. "Marion saw some white eyes in the raiders that were chasing us out, but-"

"No, no. It was earlier than that. The woman, remember?" Jacob said, looking at his feet rather than the eyes bearing down upon him.

"Yeah, her. Right. Wasn't she helping you though?" Marion asked, confused.

Jacob frowned. "Yes. But that's the strange part about all this. If someone is using the orb's power to spread the influence of the Barren, why would it be helping us? We're the ones trying to steal it."

Amicus remembered the woman Jacob was talking about. He remembered the village, clearly. Confident in their abilities, Amicus had known they would escape the moment they were captured; the raiders had been pitifully unorganized. And if anything, that was the reason they were here now.

Amicus shifted uncomfortably. The Glass Shadow, this King that had been mentioned in the message in the temple, all that was to come- none of it mattered. Not to him. *But it does,* a voice in his head told him. *It does and you know it.* Amicus knew he would not have to face the Barren, not have to face anything they were discussing now. He wasn't a part of this. That instilled some comfort in him, though there was still that pang of guilt.

"But when you asked her who she was, she must've registered she was being... possessed? She fought it away."

"So apparently unsuspecting victims are the easiest targets," Marion mused, leaning forward. "When they were chasing us, I saw it, it flickered in and out of their eyes. I think it kept them from shooting at us."

Louis nodded in agreement. "If it weren't for this orb, we'd probably be dead."

Amicus looked at him grimly. "Then how come the message, the blood and ruin? The fucking hole in the ground? Why? It makes me question it's intentions. If it's got it's own intentions at all."

"It left that as a warning, a sign," Jacob said, thinking. "To tell us something."

"To tell us what?"

"That it has power, and that we can't turn away. It might be afraid. It might need us."

Amicus snorted. "It needs our help, so it tells us by leaving a vague message and some pit to nowhere? Yeah, sure, that makes sense."

"That, or it's something else. Something other than the orb." Contemplated Louis.

"Wolf, white eyes, remember?"

"Yeah, yeah, you're right. It has to be the orb."

Marion looked into the horizon, sighing. "So now what? What's our goal? Before, it was just to retrieve the orb and, if we can't stop the spreading by ourselves, bring it back to Malivia. Now, though? What does this thing want us to do? Is it messing with our heads?"

Oliver shook his head. "This is much bigger than us. That won't change, and we won't get any stronger. If anything, we should turn to the ocean." The message on the stone rang in his head. *The will of the orb, the will of the King, they die for what the quakes will bring.*

"And? What then? We'd be leaving everyone in Rendar to their death, and sailing off to our own. I say we go on." Jacob looked up, his eyes determined. "I *will* finish what we started." The rest of them looked at him with surprise, but also with respect. Not many would make that decision. "I say we get the orb and bring it home, whether it wants us to or not."

"Alright." Marion responded, as if approving the plan. "Alright. I'll come."

"Count me in." Louis said, almost grinning.

Amicus wondered if it felt good to know that their friends would stay loyal, and stick by their sides. He knew it must have felt better than this, and he suddenly found himself hating what he was doing to them.

"Well, if we really are going to figure out what's going on, what we're facing, well... There might be something in that book they gave us, something historical to help us."

"History? More like fantasy." Amicus laughed, mocking.

Jacob frowned. "It was written by someone who was really there! Well, at least for some of it."

"Yes, but the others are just old stories." Amicus said, tossing a rock back and forth between his hands.

Jacob, purposely ignoring the comment, pulled out the book they had been given, ragged and worn, and opened it to look for the anything that could be of use. As Jacob started to read, the others realized it wasn't only to revisit the history and legend, but for comfort and solace in a hard time; for reassurance that they had a chance, for hope. The travelers leaned in close to the dying fire, listening to the story as the sun said goodnight and gave way to the full, bright moon. And Amicus, however dedicated he was to money, found himself somewhat attached to these travelers. Yet the words of Rovas Mchenry echoed in his head, haunting.

"Men like us, Mr. Vanner, are above the game of loyalty. We are the faces that blend in the crowd, the ones who are not specifically one thing but all things at once, not an ally to rely on but not an enemy to defeat. We are above it because we play the greater game- don't we, Mr. Vanner?"

The Three Kings

"Once, in a flourishing land known as Maros, three kings expanded and grew their domains. The first leader, Harrison, lived in the city to the west, by the sea. The second, Ilius, lived in the center city, to the north. The third, Amor, lived in the city to the east. All was well, and continued to be so even as Rendar formed its civilization and grew to be a powerful opponent.

Soon, however, the councils of Maros began to worry. Rendar would want their supplies and riches for themselves; Maros had plentiful lands, oil, valuable old-world artifacts. The last thing Rendar needed was war. Instead, they sent several envoys to Maros to negotiate a trading treaty, so they could maintain peace, to negotiate for the land between their countries. The two countries disagreed on many things- Maros ruled with kings, while Rendar attempted to rule with diplomatic leaders. There was difference in their economy, their government, their culture and even language and accents. Rendar was very diverse, while Maros was not. The Rendarians had come on ships, sails raised high. It was a land of the people, of the adventurers; Maros had been there all along, since the old world.

While the envoys of Rendar were passing though Qalle, a small town on the outskirts of Illius's city, a fight broke out between two rebel guilds. The larger guild that lived in Ilius's kingdom very much agreed with the treaty, while the other did not. They believed all of the world rightfully belonged to Maros, through Rendar and into the Unventured Lands beyond. The guilds held many supporters and the country was on the brink of civil war. They fought, slaughtering many Rendarians as well as Marosi. Rendar was enraged that Maros caused such a thing, and many of the Rendarians visiting Maros whispered rumors and told lies, rousing people up. The guilds grew stronger and more feared each day, and *it had come to notice that it no longer was about the treaty- they were fighting out of anger, and revenge. Rendar had no choice but to become involved, for their own people were at risk.*

Before long both sides had declared war. It was known from then on as The Lost War, as no side had gained what they wanted. Harrison was assassinated when the war started, a rioting group shooting him down as he ate his breakfast on his balcony, which overlooked much of the city. Amor was betrayed by his own guards, killed while giving orders. Ilius supposedly died from a sickness unknown to anyone before; the illness was deadly, long and painful. With fever as hot as the fire in the sky, and bleeding from the mouth and ears and eyes. Rendar, being very immigrated and skilled in the medicinal field, knew hundreds of remedies- but none were offered to the King. He may have survived, he may have died, no one knew.

When the war was passed, there were so many dead in Maros that one could not walk into a building or down the streets without seeing a dozen or more bodies. There were more dead than living, and most of the survivors were too wounded to walk, much less rid the cities and towns of the corpses. As a result, Maros fell into devastation. Just a year later, when they started to recover and peace started to reign, a strange, twisted form of radiation took over the land, killing many more. When Rendar heard the stories they refused to believe it, until they saw a man taken by the dark-radiation sickness. Most of the survivors fled to the opposing land, where they were grimly accepted. The dark-radiation took over, and turned the once glorious land of Maros into an unlivable wasteland."

The Orb

"Once, at the shore of a land called Maros, a box floated in from the sea. It was made of rusted steel and clasped tightly shut, but the metal was starting to weaken from what had to have been endless days on the ocean. A lone fisherman had been sitting on a rock, looking out, cherishing the cool, salty breeze and and evening sun. He had seen the box and opened it, amazed at what he had found.

It was an orb, very beautiful, very fragile. It was lying on a bed of fine black silk, wrapped in pure white cloth. It's glass was shiny and flawless, so clear that it made the white clouds inside of it stand out. The heavens seemed to swirl in it's very depths, casting a faint light onto the sand. But just as he had a moment to enjoy it, a cloud of black smoke shrouded the inside of the orb, turning it dark and mysterious. The clouds overhead grew sullen and wet, drizzling down on what had previously been a beautiful evening. The blue sky turned gray, the sun disappearing, covering the land in cold and shadow.

The moment the poor fisherman pulled himself away and shut the box, the clouds and rain subsided, the pleasant beach returning to its usual state. He carried the box up to his shack-like house on a wispy hill nearby, his dirty plain clothes billowing in the wind. Inside, he ignored the whistling the wind was making through the boards, the smell of stale bread and sea breeze, the dry taste on his tongue.

The fisherman grabbed a belt from his cot and wrapped it tightly around the box, as if he were afraid it would jump out and escape. He then made his way to Harrison's city, the one closest to his home. He gave the orb to the King, who gave the fisherman a bag of coins, told him to keep it quiet, and sent him on his way.

If it makes you feel any better, I could go on to tell you he bought a cottage far from there, fishing to his heart's content and living a full life. However, as fate would have it, Harrison's life wasn't so simple. He took the box to Vandor, to Ilius, where they invited Amor and exploited the orb's powers- No doubt they were curious. They then hid it at the topmost tower of the castle, where the trapdoor to the top was guarded and had a strong lock of which each of the Kings had one key.

Unconsciously they agreed that the orb wouldn't like being trapped up in a cellar deep underground, so they put it in the only place where it's power seemed rested and serene. And there it lingers to this day, in the ruins of the city. As far as I am concerned, it is depressed and desolate, among rot, death, and radiation. Wasting away in a land with no life, a sky with no stars. Perhaps it was destroyed in the war, perhaps it had been stolen, or perhaps it might not have existed at all."

A MAN IN THE CITY
VIAJAR, MALIVIA

The city of Viajar sunk drearily under the gloomy, cloudy sky. Banners, dirty and torn from the strange weather, fluttered in the wind like dead leaves. It seemed lifeless, drained, without hope. The feeling of tension before a battle filled the air, the deep breath before the jump; it swarmed around people like flies, causing hurried talk and wary glances.

The people here dressed in cloaks and boots, coats and knitted hats, rushing along the streets, keeping their heads low, staying out of sight. One man was among them, looking rather ominous in his black trench coat. His blond hair was slicked back, luggage in hand. The father was packing, loading his goods into a car. A small boy gripped tight to his arm, scared and wide-eyed. Taking a moment, the man looked down at his son and smiled with kind eyes, though it was obvious that deep down he was worried. Bags were packed, out on the street and into cars and carriages before dawn, heading south. Word had gotten out; and once the word was out, it was panic like nothing he had ever seen before. The Barren was spreading. It was spreading, *and oh God, Malivia will be first*. The man ruffled his son's hair.

"Better get a move on, buddy. How 'bout Calidor? The Unventured Lands?" He turned away, and whispered to himself. "Far as we can get, son, 'fore the radiation takes us all."

159

CHAPTER 15

OLIVER MONTEROSE
THE ASHEN DESERT

The desert, to say in the least, was bland, dull, and continuous. The weak wind battered at their dirty, forlorn faces, gritty with sand. Wearily the travelers pushed through it, their torn shoes crunching on the ground. The only sound besides heavy breathing was the occasional clunk of objects inside a bag.

These sounds echoed in Oliver's ears, making it seem like a dream he would never come out of. The sand was now dulled, becoming grayer as they walked. He kept his eyes on the ground, and noticed the change as they got closer to the Barren. The gritty gray sand soon stopped crunching beneath them, and when he reached down to touch it, it was soft and fell apart in his hands. Ash was lifted up by the wind and fluttered away into the distance, leaving Oliver breathless. They were walking on ashes. Gray, powdery ashes, in a range from black to almost white. Now, the ash puffed up around their feet as they walked, soon settling back onto the ground behind them.

The Ashen Desert. Oliver scoffed. What a fitting name. *I can't wait to get out of this hellhole,* he thought, looking back in the direction of Rendar. *If we get to the Barren and it's anything worse than this...* he shuddered, shaking his head. There was nothing worse than this, he was sure. He longed for his home, his brother, his family, his luxury.

"What is it? George, you can tell me. A politician like you can't keep all the secrets in the world. I can help." Oliver told his brother, concerned. *They sat outside on a bench, observing the rolling hills, fields, and woods of Aleria.*

160

"I'm not sure you can. I'm just stressed, is all. John Keller has been having some trouble with Mchenry-"

"Rovas?"

"Yes. He came back from that council meeting shaken up. He won't talk much to anyone, the Castle's at a standstill. And not only that, but I've overheard things... strange things." George fell silent.

The breeze was chilling, and Oliver pulled his jacket closer around himself. "What? What have you heard?"

His brother took a breath, and sighed. "Rovas. He's romantically involved with Natalie Denroe's sister, Mary, who, if you didn't know, is married. Natalie's nephew, Paulen, that's Rovas's son. They don't know, no one knows, but there have been rumors, and more. I have proof." He looked around, wary. "I shouldn't be telling you this."

Oliver's eyes lit up. "I could write about it, for the paper- I can expose him!"

"The paper? You mean the Silverstone Tribune? You haven't written for them in years."

"They'll accept this one. I'm respected there. The news will spread, and quickly. I can do this."

George nodded, uncertain. A week later Oliver submitted the article to the paper, though it was never printed. The Silverstone Tribune was shut down before that could happen. Soon after that his brother was accused of the murder of a Denroe boy known as Paulen, and Oliver was dragged to Viajar, Malivia- dragged here, into this mess.

He had left out that part to his companions, to say in the least. He assumed that was the main reason he was here, though the murder surely must have made Rovas angry. And who would be more missed, a councillor of the Castle in Aleria or his unnoticed brother? Sighing, Oliver's attention was turned back to the hike, but his thoughts wandered elsewhere.

Their packs got lighter everyday, lighter and lighter as they diminished their food supply. The deer-like animal Jacob had shot was gone, but it had saved them days and days of rations. They scavenged what they could. Nevertheless, Marion continued to lead them onward at a fast, steady pace, as if the food supply was almost gone. Yet they all knew the real reason, the reason that kept them from asking him to slow. The travelers wanted to get through this ghastly desert as fast as possible; they hated the heat, hated the sweat, hated the dryness in their throats and the sores and scabs and the sunburn. But after this… it would be the Barren. A place Oliver dreaded arriving at but couldn't wait to be done with.

"It seems we're getting closer to our destination," Oliver noted, kicking up some ash before pointing into the distance. "Do you think those are ruins?" He pointed out the structure on the horizon. It was a stone archway, large and dominating.

"Could we be there already? At the border? At the Barren?" Marion took a few more steps, squinting as hard as he could. The others gaped at it in awe. They had calculated another week, a few at most. Not this soon. Marion took off at a run, but Jacob grabbed his shirt and pulled him back.

"Wait! Don't rush into this, Marion. Something's wrong. We weren't supposed to arrive this early, I'm sure of it."

"So? What else could it be?"

"A graveyard. It's a graveyard, Marion."

Jacob started walking, looking grimly into the distance. "When the Marosi started to flee the Barren, many of them buried their dead at the graveyard near the border, where the corpses would be out of the radiation. Well, so they thought. It was a better option than just leaving them there, or carrying them all the way to Rendar. But so close to the Barren… so close to dark-radiation…" Jacob didn't finish. The twisted magic in the radiation would have affected the land somehow.

Somehow in a way that likely wouldn't leave them be.

AMICUS VANNER
THE GRAVEYARD

The travelers approached the archway, dread settling in their hearts as surely as the ash settled onto the ground. It was crumbling, the runes engraved upon it too worn and battered by the weather to make out. The graveyard stretched for miles, so vast that none of them could see the end of it. Gravestones, some wood and some rock and some no more than a pebble to mark it, lined a white stone path; leading, as they assumed, through the graveyard.

With just a moment's hesitation Amicus stepped onto the trail, looking around as if he were a thief who had just set off an alarm. Nothing happened, and with a few more cautious steps, they had to admit that they couldn't wait forever. Hastily they set off, careful not to step off the path. The air smelled of staleness, of old things in an attic collecting dust. It smelled of age, of ruin, and a faint, barely sensed smell of decay.

Somehow, despite all they saw and heard, it smelled *alive*. Not empty, like a graveyard should be, but alive and burning with a unyielding hunger. It looked abandoned, but bad things always hid in the shadows. Once or twice Amicus thought he saw movement, heard a shuffling, or even saw a pair of eyes. There was always the feeling that they were being watched. It was silent, making Amicus feel disruptive and vulnerable.

Within just minutes of walking, the air around them became cold, causing him to shiver. The heat of the day was gone, though they were not relieved; it only made Amicus nervous. Miles of graves and ash passed them by, though it seemed like much longer. Progress was slow, yet they were always watchful. Careful. Precise. The travelers wanted to get through this graveyard, that much was true, but they also wanted to get out alive. Unscathed, preferably.

They no longer doubted the power of the Barren, not after their experience with the lake.

They walked and walked, until their legs were sore and breath ragged. Unwillingly Amicus was about to call for a rest, when, suddenly, they approached a clearing in the path, a wide circle of stones. Three other pathways lead off into the mix of graves, north, west, and east. Amicus was right to assume it was the center of the graveyard; this was where the tension was greatest, where the fear was strongest. However, the group barely noticed. Together they had fallen into the unavoidable trap of exhaustion, and with that came the inability to process information or catch small details. Therefore they continued on their long trek with no second thoughts about the circle, with no hesitations or caution. It was what many other travelers had done before them, and the graveyard had expected no less.

"*RUN!*" A voice yelled, frantic. A young girl came bursting out from behind a grave. "They know you're here, *RUN,* they're coming, they're coming, *RUN!*"

She dashed past them, a freelander in torn unfitting clothes with a stone in one hand and a small blade in the other. Her face was panicked, bloodied, but she clearly wasn't worried about that. What this girl *was* worried about was much, much worse than a couple of cuts.

"*RUN!*" She shouted again in a hoarse, drawn-out voice. "Run, you idiots!"

That was the last Amicus heard of her, but he only knew they should have run by her side. What was scarier, though, was that she hadn't yelled loud. *No, her voice had been lowered, as if she were afraid she might awaken something.*

"Look!" Louis said, his knuckles white on the handles of his crutches. "What... what *is* that?"

This new sight awoke Amicus momentarily, causing him to stare fearfully at what Louis had seen. Another girl approached them, a very young girl, coming out from behind another grave. She was clutching a tattered, dirt stained blanket, wearing a very filthy green dress. The clothes were almost reduced to rags, very much so that Amicus was surprised he had been able to identify the color at all. Skin, pale and, though he hated to think it, almost gray, drifted off the girl almost like ash. Her eyes were gray as well, gray like a stormy sky or the weathered stone of an abandoned building.

"Hello?" Amicus asked, reaching out his hand. "Are you okay? What's your name?"

Back away, run, back away, run! All his instincts told him so, yet he ignored them. The girl stumbled forward, looking at each of them with a blank, desperate stupidity. She reached for them, opening her mouth and screaming, a scream so pure and real it drew him in, wanting to help this poor girl who... Amicus paused. *Who... who...* the girl's skin. It was... strange. He had thought she was just sickly or weak, but it was something else. He felt his hand grasping out to touch the girl, but before he could she burst into clouds of ash, her scream echoing in their ears.

Seconds later a new ash figure appeared, a man with gashes and scars on his face. The wind fluttered his clothes as he called out to them in helpless screams. They turned around, and there were more, men women, children, even animals. The abominations all had injuries, all screaming and screaming and suddenly Amicus couldn't think he couldn't hear he couldn't see it was all over it was over he was done *oh God please* make it *stop-*

The figures exploded it a storm of ash, and the travelers stood there in shocked silence as the flakes flurried down and drifted away. The sun rose, the wind blew, the stone graves crumbled in their ancientness. Silence. Was it over? Amicus dared not move, dared not make a sound. Oh, and that was their downfall. Thinking that where they were at the moment was safer than the paths ahead. Yes, it was indeed.

With a disturbing silence the ground opened up before them, revealing nothing but darkness, and the travelers were swallowed into the jaws of the earth. Barely a moment passed before the hole started to disappear.

Their sudden and horrified screams were cut off as the opening closed once again, the stones clicking back into place, the dirt, dust, and ash settling back down into what looked like a solid circle that hadn't moved for hundreds of years. Oh, and the sun rose, the wind blew, and the stone graves crumbled in the bare, undisturbed silence.

MARION ARMAIS
THE GRAVEYARD

Marion awoke in a dark prison cell, a cell that smelled of urine and rot. It was small, but it held the five of them well enough. The others had not yet strayed from the path of sleep, so he didn't bother them. Straw was clumped into pitiful beds on the hard rocky floor, a grimy bucket in the corner.

It made him feel like an animal, trapped, and Marion didn't like it one bit. The cell doors were strong and secure, the slot, he presumed, for food. Though he was tired, his curiosity won over and he crawled over to the bars, gripping them tight and looking beyond. They were in a huge cavern, the inside of which looked like the interior of an old building. Torches, glowing with orange fire, let off a strong light, illuminating the underground they were confined in. Just outside his cell was a rusted metal staircase that spiraled upward along the wall, leading to other cells filled with howling animals, sobbing humans, and pitiful things that had deteriorated to almost nothing. The other prisoners dared not scream; instead they choked back muffled sobs, and Marion knew why. Something was watching.

The stairs did not lead all the way up to the ceiling; instead they stopped a good distance from it, forming a sort of balcony or watchspot with a faded yellow railing. This was a place from the old world. What it had been he did not know, but signs of it were everywhere. The metal, the rust, the strange objects scattered about and the signs on the walls. But it was not silent, and as Marion looked past the stairwell to the ground below, he almost fainted.

There were *ghosts*. Not ashen ones such as they had seen on the surface, but transparent. They would have looked almost normal if not for their sharp, jagged teeth and eyeless sockets. The ghosts were dressed in simple clothes, yet ragged and bloody, no doubt from when they had died. They were talking amongst each other, cheering, and circling around wooden stakes in the center of it all. Their echoes were faint in his ears, due to the massive size of the chamber. An opening in the ceiling revealed the sky, to either let in more light or for a... ceremonial purpose?

(getoutgetout) Voices came to him, stronger now. Louder. *(Marion getout get out danger cold white blindMARION)*

Suddenly, before he could retreat to the corner of his cell, a ghost appeared in front of him, grinning with it's eerie white teeth. Skeletal, frightening. It's sockets were empty and rotting like the others, but it's gaze made Marion want to shrivel up into a ball. Rope was circled around it's arm, a key held in hand. It wore a flannel and jeans, both of which were stained and worn. A loud click and the cell was unlocked, open to the horrifying world around him. The ghost grabbed Marion with a hand that felt like cold, bitter air, and tied his hands behind his back with the rope. Two more of them came and tied his friends, who were shaken awake and were looking around with faces that could truly resemble pure terror. They were in shock, as he was, and could not muster the strength to react. There was nothing for Marion to do but wait for what came next.

Shuffling, they filed down the staircase, often tripping or stumbling forward. Louis had left his crutches in the cell, but that didn't stop the ghosts from pushing him down at the same speed as the rest of them. At times the cripple clung to the railing, struggling for support. He pretty much had to be carried, and Marion knew if those cold arms were around him he wouldn't be able to breathe. The rocks peeking through the walls were sharp and lethal, the stairway narrow. By the time they reached the bottom they were covered in bleeding, stinging cuts. The eager breath of the ghosts around him made Marion wince, made him shrink back from their overwhelming presence.

The travelers were tied to the stakes loosely, rushed, in an eagerness to begin. Despite the sagging ropes and free legs, Marion found he could barely move. Didn't *want* to move. Moving would mean facing those ghosts, having them grab his arms, yell into his ears, look into his soul with their eyeless, empty sockets. No, he would not move. He couldn't. A shout made Marion forget about the torments to come, drawing his gaze to the ledge at the top of the staircase, now seeming so far above. A dizziness came upon him, but he shook his head and bid it away. Not now. Now, he needed to listen. To be focused. And maybe, just maybe, find a way out.

"The time has come!" A ghost yelled from the balcony, his arms spread wide. He wore several articles of leather and metal, looking like some sort of raider. His face was set in a victorious expression, covered with what looked like a... was that catcher's mask? Jacob had told him about those, from- *what was it called again?* Baseball. Marion had thought the sport was fascinating.

The ghost looked down at them. "The time has come when we shall feast on the souls of the living, when we shall become stronger than the race of men, when we shall prosper off the surface of this world!"

The yells and cheers that came after were loud and dominating, strong and unmerciful. It made Marion want to cover his ears. Thousands of ghosts surrounded them, thousands of dead gathered in the world below. Thousands to feed off their souls. The thought made him shiver.

"This is the day! The King has promised us much to gain if we caught these meddlesome men, and who are we to deny him? Who are we to deny the one who harnesses the power of the Glass Shadow? Who ruled over the land of Maros at it's finest?" He shook his head, his brow furrowing in anger above his dark, empty sockets. His pointed down at them.

"*THESE MEN SHALL FALL BY OUR HAND! WE'LL RAISE AN ARMY, JOIN THE REIGNING KING, THE KING OF MAROS, THE KING OF THE GLASS SHADOW!*" He bellowed, his voice echoing loud and dominant throughout the cavern.

His fist shook with triumph, and with this motion the ghosts raised their swords and yelled back, lifted their rusted guns, knives, axes and bows in the cold chamber below the earth.

169

CHAPTER 16
LOUIS WILLSON
THE GRAVEYARD

As the ghosts finished cheering, they approached the travelers, a hunger in their glares. Louis stood there, petrified, the rope seeming to weigh a thousand pounds on his chest. His leg ached, his mind even more so. *This is how I will die, surrounded by things I thought for my entire life did not exist.*

The room grew cold, or maybe it was just him, for the ghosts seemed to rise with heat. In their motions, Louis could tell the spirits wanted to rush at the travelers, devour their souls as fast as possible before anyone else had the chance. Despite this, the abominations moved slowly, licking their lips and and pushing each other aside to get to the front.

Louis felt himself back into the stake, and he gripped the hard, splintery wood with pale hands. Their stench was of rot, their clothes rags. He wrinkled his nose in disgust, his heart racing. Some looked more solid than others, their feet leaving footprints on the wet ground. Some were almost transparent, stumbling through their counterparts as they tried to find their way. Sniffing, cherishing the smell of fresh life, the ghosts surrounded them, coming much too close for comfort.

One ghost, a daring one at that, came close and brushed it's hand through Louis's arm teasingly. It passed right through him, as if the ghosts were only a hallucination, shapes of dust in the air. The spirit circled around the stake before it stopped, it's hand settling on his shoulder.

Flinching, Louis tried to shrug it off, but the cold grip remained firm. Unlike before, the grip was now solid. Louis felt himself weakening, his life, his energy being sucked right out. Before long, the hand on his shoulder was warm, and he turned to see a battered woman, with brown eyes, braids, and dark skin. Solid, real, and very much alive.

More came to see, to steal his soul, to become whole. Within minutes he was surrounded, and they could hold in their greed no more. They yearned to touch him, to place if not just one finger on the man with blood flowing through his veins, with life pulsing in his heart. Louis passed out, the cold hands on his skin fading away into memory.

The ghosts were coming alive.

***

Louis blinked, groggily opening his eyes to find himself and his friends back in their cell. His limbs felt like weights, his heart beating slowly and faint. Whispers from the others penetrated his hearing, as well as the talk and chatter of the ghosts below. The light of the torches swirled and blotted in his vision, and he faded back into unconsciousness.

***

Louis awoke once again to a loud thump, and a cursing voice. Amicus sat at the bars of the cell, reaching out with one dirty, struggling hand to the outside wall next to their cage. His face was torn with frustration. Whatever Amicus was trying to grasp was out of his reach.

Louis picked himself up with a grunt and sat beside him. His companion was reaching for a ring of keys, which dangled on a rusted hook. After a few moments Amicus turned to him, irritated. Loose strands of his dark hair had escaped his ponytail and now hung down over his sweaty face.

"Well? Do you want to try?" Amicus looked out along the winding stairwell, scanning for any watchful ghosts.

"If you'd like." Louis said, and moved himself over. *So I'm not dead. Not yet, anyway.* He reached for the keys but came up short, and gave up much too quickly. Louis noticed, for the first time, that their bags had been piled up in the corner. He looked at Jacob, who was closest.

"Jacob. *Jacob.*"

His friend awoke with a flich, looking around groggily. "What? Where-"

Louis cut him off. "Jacob, our bags. A dagger."

Jacob saw what they were attempting and nodded. He rushed over, stepping across his sleeping fellow travelers, and grabbed the dagger. They had been disarmed of their other weapons, but Louis had kept a spare.

Why the ghosts didn't take out their things, he never knew. *It's here and that's what matters.* The dead had underestimated them, he thought, as Louis stuck the knife through the bars and hooked the keys. Anyone could reach far enough if they had to. He was careful not to drop the keys on the floor, for it would make a clatter that was bound to attract attention.

Amicus gaped at him. "Thanks. That-" He scoffed. "That should've been obvious. My mind's a bit scrambled after... well, you know."

Louis nodded, understanding. Had he not seen the bags, he would have never made the connection. Not as fast as he did, anyway. As for the ghosts... Louis knew the spirits would feed off of them again, and it was only a matter of time before the travelers didn't make it. Having to go through that again... it was one of his nightmares, now. His fears. Louis felt drained, older, weaker. It was as if the ghosts had pulled years of his life away from him, and he had somehow, unwillingly, let it slip through his fingers. It was like trying to keep water in a broken glass.

"Are you alright, Louis?" Amicus asked, concerned. "You look sick."

"Don't we all? I'm fine. Wake up the others and we'll get out of here."

With that Amicus stood, keys jangling in hand, and went over to nudge his friends out of unconsciousness. After a few tries of shoving the key through the cell bars and into the keyhole, they heard a click, and the cell door swung open. Silently, carefully, the group shouldered their bags and rushed out of the cell, eager to get out. Why the ghosts had left the keys so close to the cell, or placed them highest near the balcony did not matter. Louis only knew that they had escaped. *We're free.*

"Don't get too excited," Marion said, looking behind them worriedly. He must have seen the excitement on Louis's face. "We're not out yet."

Louis knew these words to be true, and looking down at the ghosts below, he realized they were far from escaping. He himself had only his crutches to use as he ascended the stairs, and if they were chased, he certainly would not make it. The hole above them was open once again to reveal a setting sun, though Louis did not waste time to sit and enjoy it.

They needed a way up there, before they were spotted and forced into another cell. He vaguely remembered a rope on that ghost's arm, which he had used to tie them up. *Where had he put it?* Louis scanned up and down the spiraling stairwell, and to his relief finally saw a crate full of it just ahead.

"We need that rope, then we can tie the end into a loop and hang it from that." Louis whispered, pointing to a jagged rod of metal sticking out just below the open hole. It looked like it had been used as a hook to lower things up and down, a pulley of sorts, but had since then been forgotten. Sticking out alongside it from the ground of stone and dirt were pipes, steel, broken and disfigured.

Jacob agreed. "We'll have to be quick, those things won't be far behind us. We can all climb, right?"

Amicus looked nervously, not at the rope, but at the ground of the chamber. He swayed a little before nodding his head like the others. Louis sighed. Yes, he could climb, though not very well. *It's not as if you have another choice,* he thought. Marion also looked down at the ghosts below, but not because he was nervous about heights. He was scanning their weapons.

"They might shoot at us while we're on, but we can't let go, you understand? We've got one chance to get this right."

A strange, almost confident feeling spread throughout the group as they looked into each other's eyes. They would be okay. They would get out. It would all be-

"Hey! *Hey!* They're escaping, damn you! *Someone get them!*" A ghost patrolling the walkway glared up at them, drawing his handgun.

"GET THEM!"

Several more came running up the steps, grinning sickly as they exercised their whole, lively bodies. In their eyes Louis could see they wanted blood, wanted death for the living, breathing souls in front of them. These creatures wanted to *do* something that would affect the world around them, to have purpose for as long as they could. For no matter what they did, they would always fade back into a rotting hallucination, and if not fed would soon fade out of existence. These abominations would do as much as they could as long as they had physical form, and would not let a chance for glory slip away that easily. The travelers were frozen for a moment, gaping at their already foiled plan.

"Run, come on, run!" Oliver yelled, and they sprinted for the balcony. Louis had been ahead of the others and hobbled up as fast as he was able. Jacob tied the rope as he ran, his hands shaking, his feet tripping on the stones.

Louis was out of breath, holding his crutches in a death grip while Amicus helped him up the stairs. The travelers moved slower than they would have without him, and they could see the clear guilt in Louis's face. He feared that the day would come when he would slow them down and bring them all to end. Thankfully, it was not this day. He would make sure of that.

They reached the top in a panic, the ghosts only minutes behind them. In their eagerness, the undead pushed and shoved, yelled and slashed to be the first capture the travelers; they wanted to be rewarded. With a nauseous feeling inside him, Louis handed the rope to Marion, who swung it around before letting it fly. It fit loosely around the hook, but was secure and would not slip off. There was a moment of satisfaction before a loud shout jolted them back to the present.

"Grab the rope!" Marion yelled as he tied his end of it around the railing. It would be easier to climb that way. They all obeyed, but Amicus only stood there, staring at the ghosts just moments away.

"We'll never make it," He whispered. His face settled into a firm expression, a look that said the man had made a decision and wasn't going to change his mind. A look that filled Louis's heart with a depressed, aching feeling. The ghosts would cut the rope if they were not held back. Louis knew deep down what their freelander friend was going to do, however much he hated it.

"Amicus, don't…" Louis begged, but Amicus payed him no attention. The man was set in his resolve; the luring reward of silver had left his mind, the fear of the Barren growing more prominent. It was all in their heads, Louis knew, but for Amicus he sensed something different. Something had been different about him from the beginning.

The oncoming ghosts charged up the steps, their eyes glinting with murder. A few toppled over the side and fell, while others kept a sure footing. Amicus drew his dagger and stood ready, his torn and dirty traveling clothes seeming to Louis like knight's armor. He was truly brave, or perhaps just too scared to go on, but it would do them no good to waste his sacrifice. In a choked voice, Amicus whispered, so, so quietly that it could barely be heard by any of them.

"I'm sorry."

And with that he charged into the swarming mass of the dead; his dagger glinted in the dim light, and was soon covered in hot, thick blood.

"We have to go." Louis told the others, but his voice was so quiet he doubted they heard him. He didn't want to watch; none of them did. So, they started to climb the rope, Louis sliding his crutches into his duffel. He looked back to see Amicus fighting to his best ability, slashing the dagger, ducking, kicking unwary ghosts off the ledge. Blood spilled over him, splattering, shocking the ghosts into submission. *The only thing keeping him alive*, Louis thought, *is that these spirits are still getting used to their new forms.* Manifestations such as themselves weren't used to weapons actually cutting instead of passing right through.

Amicus roared in anger, in triumph, in surprise he had lasted this long. Sweat poured down his face, and he narrowly avoided a lunge from small, rabid child. They stood paralyzed on the rope, watching as Amicus grew weaker and weaker. He was the reason they weren't being shot out of the air right now. He was a hero. Oh, but even heroes have an end; for after endless, tiring minutes of fighting he was overwhelmed. Yet Amicus had absolutely no intention of going back to that cell; he had no intention of feeding these monsters. Yet there was no way he would make it up that rope alive, and if he did, carrying the guilt that he was a spy. A traitor.

With one last, warning look, Amicus lunged off the balcony, salty tears streaming down a pale, scared face; he fell fast, shattering bones, crashing to meet the cold, dead rocks below.

JACOB FORTEMER
THE GRAVEYARD

No. No. No, this was a dream. Alive, not dead. Couldn't be dead. Not Amicus. He had gone on with them despite being only a lost freelander, despite the danger and challenges they faced. Always he was there for them, and his last moment had been for them as well. No, not Amicus.

Suddenly, an arrow whizzed past Jacob's face, so close that another inch would have killed him. *No, this is real. Amicus is dead. The ghosts are alive.* And they needed to escape.

"Climb!" Marion shouted hoarsely, heart beating fast. Several ghosts were shooting at them, merciless. A bullet skimmed the rope, and the loose strands started to come apart. Louis was panting, gasping, frustrated. He fell behind, and yelled out in pain when a black arrow skimmed his arm. Marion was already at the top, helping Oliver off the rope and onto the last stones.

The cry had escaped their ears. Jacob looked back and saw Louis slip, but his sweaty hands found a hold before long. He needed help. And so Jacob, the good man that he was, allowed himself to slide back down the rope in order to help his friend. He wasn't sure what he was going to do, but the cripple wouldn't make it up by himself.

"Louis!" Jacob said, turning to face him. "Take-"

He was cut off by a loud, painful cry, one that just happened to be his own. An arrow had pierced Jacob's back, and could feel the blood running down from his shoulder blade. He couldn't move. Jacob felt his hands give way, felt them slip off the rough, hard rope.

Louis grabbed his arm, and held him up with strength he didn't know he had. Both their hands were cut and bloody, slippery and weak. Soon, he knew, Louis would let go of him. Jacob needed to grab the rope, though he was light-headed and in pain. He needed to grab the rope. *The rope.* Louis's arms strained, hurt like they were on fire.

"Jacob!" He yelled as another arrow flew by. *"JACOB, GRAB THE ROPE!"*

Jacob looked into Louis's dirty face, his terrified green eyes, and gathered all the strength he had to pull himself up. Even when he did, his shoulder burned with an agony he didn't know existed. Jacob was so tired, so weak, he knew he couldn't make it. Maybe it was best to let go. Before he could think more about plunging to his death, he felt a strong tug on the rope. Marion tugged it again, and Jacob grew confused.

Why would- there was a loud snap, and suddenly they were dangling horizontally from the rope, hanging on for their life; it had snapped. Marion had counted on that, had noticed the bullet that had set the strings astray. They were out of reach from the ghosts, but not from their range of fire. In fact, they were closer to the ground than they had been before. *What now?* The answer came when Jacob realized they were rising. Oliver and Marion were pulling them up towards the light, they would be free, they would be safe…

And that's when the hole started to close.

CHAPTER 17
JACOB FORTEMER
THE GRAVEYARD

Stones clicked back into place, dirt rising up to fill the cracks. The sun grew fainter, reduced to a single ray of light shining down upon them as if they were souls rising up to the heavens. Jacob was holding on to the rope with all he had left, the pain clear on his bloody, scraped face. They rose faster, and he knew Marion and Oliver had seen the hole start to close. If their only escape did shut, him and Louis would be stuck, and eventually they would let go of the rope; unless the ghosts got ahold of them first.

All the scenarios that rushed through Jacob's head were hopeless if the hole shut; this was their only hope. Jacob looked up at the sky, up at the blurred faces of Marion and Oliver who sweated with the effort to pull their friends to safety. He thought of how they had arrived here, so oblivious to the horrors below them, almost unscathed. They had been given just a taste what it was like to suffer, though Marion had had a glimpse when he was shot. Oh, but they all would soon learn what it was like to suffer. *Yeah, the Barren'll make sure of that.*

And so it was fate, Jacob dared to think, that wanted them dead. Or perhaps it was just the way of the world, for he got one last look at their friends' terrified eyes before the hole closed above them, the last stones clicking back into place with an echo that seemed to send the world into a shocked, horrified silence.

OLIVER MONTEROSE
THE GRAVEYARD

Marion and Oliver stood with the rope in their hands, now stuck below the earth. This wasn't supposed to happen. Not any of it. *What'll we do? We're running out of time.* If they sat and waited, the ghosts could easily take them back down, and there would be no chance of Rendar's survival. Oliver knew there was something going on that was much bigger than them, but now they were separated. Their group had gone from five to two in a matter of minutes.

If Jacob and Louis were still alive, they would be dead soon enough. The ghosts were starving, anxious, filled with a desire that made Oliver shiver. Oh yes, their friends would be gone before long. All they could do was hope the two could find a way out, catch up to them later on. *Because we can't wait.* Oliver looked over at Marion, who had tears streaming down his face. Oliver coldly turned away, shouldered his bag, and dropped the rope.

"We can't stay here." He said, and Marion weakly nodded.

The others would have to survive on their own.

LOUIS WILLSON
THE GRAVEYARD

Louis's hands were red and raw, his face a mixture of defeat and disbelief. Jacob hung just above him, the blood from his wound dripping down onto Louis's face; he could taste it in his mouth, metallic and warm. An earthy, underground smell filled their noses, the fresh air now a distant memory. Dirt and dust fell upon them as the ground shut with one final groan. The hole was closed. They had no way out.

The balcony was full of angry spirits, and he could say the same for the ground below. Louis looked around the chamber; there was nowhere to go. Unless... No, that would be impossible. He spotted something opposite of the balcony, an opening in the rock. It was small, and blended in to the cracked, faulted walls well. Louis never would have noticed it had he not been hanging almost eye-level with it.

"Jacob!" He whispered urgently, his eyes gleaming with hope. "Look!"

Jacob turned his dirt-streaked face to the wall, showing he understood with a slight nod of the head. "Do you think we can make it?" He asked, his voice scratchy.

"I think we don't have a choice." Louis responded as he looked down nervously at the screaming, howling ghosts below. They scratched and clawed at each other as they climbed spider-like up the walls and stairs, spilling each other's blood- blood that had begun to run through their veins once again. They were monstrosities, stuck between the land of the living and that of the dead. Neither Jacob nor Louis were too eager to end up in their clutches.

"We have to swing," Jacob concluded, taking deep breaths, wincing in pain every time he moved. The arrow still protruded from his back, soaking his shirt.

"I know."

"Are you scared?"

"Yes." Louis looked up at him, fear in his eyes.

"Good."

And with that they swung, swung, swung.

And they jumped.

MARION ARMAIS
THE ASHEN DESERT

The ash swirled up under the dark, cloudy sky, shrouding the light. Two travelers walked on the surface, wrapped in nothing but cloaks. Cold, bitter air froze their faces, but it was not unusual. Winter was near. Winter, and the cold along with it.

"Oliver?" Marion asked grimly, his face streaked with tears. His eyes were frozen, dead, no longer the bright hazel they had once been; full of grief and suffering. "Should we have left them? Should we have gone?"

Oliver didn't answer. Instead he looked up into the distance, into the dark gray fog beyond. Under the wind, under the scent of ash and dust, there was a strange smell. The two took no notice of it, for their noses were clogged and their minds troubled. But it was there, nonetheless, that strange smell. It was there, a smell that was not of death but of something *alive.*

Alive and pulsing with blood, a strange blood, a strange smell.

Strange with darkness, sickness and uncontrollable hunger.

Strange.

CHAPTER 18
JACOB FORTEMER
THE GRAVEYARD

To put it simply, the wall was hard. Hard, and sharp. Jagged edges scraped their fingers as the travelers scrambled to find a handhold. It was an almost perfectly vertical wall, and, being so, a rather difficult one to climb. Louis had managed to grasp the ledge, and so he pulled himself up. Jacob's hand, however, had slipped off the side of the opening, leaving him frantic and fumbling. Though this was not quite a problem, for a moment later he was also at the entrance of the tunnel, having grasped one of the wider cracks below to use as a hold.

"Jacob?" Louis asked over the startled shouts of the ghosts below. The undead below had certainly not expected such a suicidal attempt at escape. "Are you alright?"

"I think- I think not." Jacob winced. He nervously glanced behind him, down at the undead scurrying up the walls like spiders trying to catch a fly.

"We need to leave."

Louis squinted down into the small, dark tunnel. The opening would be tough to squeeze through, even for them, but it lead into a passageway tall enough to stand and wide enough to walk side by side. Louis threw their packs in first, landing with a thump. With a deep breath, he went in headfirst, trying to go as quickly as possible. He couldn't help but imagine a ghost grabbing his leg and pulling him back out. It was dark, and there was barely enough light to see by. Sniffing, Louis thought he could detect the smell of a different air, smelling of oil and metal and rust. Jacob came in just after him, crying out as the arrow in his back snapped against the rock.

"Jacob, they're right behind us, we need rocks, we need to block it, *hurry!*"

He shook himself out of his daze and joined his friend in feeling along the floor for large rocks. *So lucky, too lucky, we should be dead,* Jacob thought, breathing heavily. They settled on a boulder, one large enough to block the entryway, but heavy enough as so not to be moved. Gasping, sweating, and grunting, they only just finished the task before hands reached in the cracks, grasping for something that wasn't there. Louder thumps and yells suggested the dead were pounding on the rock, pushing it. Their own work paid off, for it did not budge. They wasted no time, though, and hastily picked up their supplies and rushed blindly down the passageway.

Picking up his crutches, Louis went along as fast as he could, not worrying about the darkness or what dwelled inside it. Whatever it was, they would just have to face it. After a few minutes they stopped, breathing heavily in the pitch black. There were no echoing footsteps, no angry yells or clatters of arrows against the walls. The barrier held. As they felt their way along the tunnel, they heard gunshots.

Probably trying to blast the damn rock to bits. Jacob smiled at the thought, smiled because they had escaped. They had won. They had succeeded. And even though they knew not where the tunnel lead, they had a certainty nothing would be there. Not this close to the chamber of the ghosts. Jacob only prayed it wasn't something like a cliff or a dead end, for that would be even more disastrous. They needed rest, sanctuary; they needed to heal. But most of all, they needed to reunite with their friends. Jacob hoped the others had gone on without them. If they had stayed, there would be many more problems to deal with. Problems they wouldn't have time for. These thoughts were interrupted by the stop of footsteps, and he grabbed Louis's arm.

"We need to rest." Jacob was wheezing, the pain in his back almost overwhelming.

"Here?"

"Where else?"

Louis nodded respectfully, setting down his pack and grunting as he sank to the floor. His crutches clattered on the hard rock. Jacob sat down beside him, the enormity and power of the darkness now settling upon him.

"We'll have to catch up to them." Jacob whispered, his voice shaking with fear. He unwillingly imagined the ghosts grabbing him out of the darkness.

"Tomorrow." Louis responded, already drifting off to sleep. He didn't know when they would get to rest again.

Their voices echoed through the tunnel, and Jacob cringed with each word. His eyes flitted frantically into the darkness, unseeing. A monster would come, a beast succumbed to the forces of dark-radiation. A ghost, perhaps, or a hidden, murderous freelander. Something would come, would grab him, and he would be slain in the night- in the night that had no moon and gave way to no sun.

OLIVER MONTEROSE
THE CROSSING

The pillars of black marble stood high, establishing an invisible wall along the border. The two travelers stood in front of the archway, staring at it's crumbling frame and intricate designs as if it were from another world. It was large, more monumental than purposeful, but set a tone of power and intimidation nonetheless. Here, the ashy sand started to diminish, revealing black rock such as that in the graveyard's chamber. Cold winds blew across the land, blowing dust into the air. Silent. It was a desolate wasteland, but the horizon was endless and the feeling of peace was almost comforting. It was the Crossing, where everything seemed to freeze, when the dangers waited for later and the travelers need not have worried.

Marion lingered behind him, wary, his head down and feet shuffling; the bruised shadows underneath his eyes proved he was lacking sleep. He did not take much interest in the archway, in the pictures and words that had now faded to almost nothing. Oliver walked up to the marble, tracing his fingers along the cold lifeless carvings and runes.

HERE AT THE CROSSINGS, TREAD LIGHTLY, WE SAY
COME ONE NIGHT, BEGONE THE NEXT DAY
SAFETY HERE, WE ASSURE YOU, BUT BE WARY, YOU SEE
THE DANGERS WILL GET YOU, IF AFTER DAY THREE

Oliver set down his pack upon reading these words, looking around. "We could do with a few day's rest."

His voice was meant to be comforting, but it was hoarse and full of despair. Marion only nodded in response. The other man had been silent ever since he'd asked Oliver if they should have left.

Weak, tired, and quiet, Marion was no longer the person he had once been; he had given up. Though, to a certain extent, so had Oliver. He'd never really thought he would make it to this point, had just assumed he would turn back before they got here. Yet now here he was.

They had barely any supplies left, now that the other two had disappeared under the ground with their packs. Oliver had watched his companion die, abandoned Jacob and Louis to the mercy of the ghosts. All for the sake of the quest, which they weren't even meant to survive. *What's the point anymore?* He and Marion sat down on the hard rock, looking through the archway and into the hazy Barren beyond.

"I'm waiting." Marion said, a sternness in his eyes. It was more of a statement than a request. "I'm waiting for them. And if they don't show up after three days, then I'll go on. But if there's even a chance they're still alive, I'm not going without them."

A soft grin covered Oliver's face, and he sat down beside Marion, looking into his beaten, determined face with a kind sympathy. "Well, I'll wait with you then."

Nothing more needed to be said. A new courage found him, and Oliver thought that maybe he should try to honor himself and this world, finish the quest they had started. Maybe he should take this responsibility seriously. They fell silent, leaning on each other with the comfort of friendship that can only come with the understanding of hard times. And so the travelers sat on the rock at the crossing, the cold wind blowing the last of the ash past the archway and into the lands beyond.

LOUIS WILLSON
THE TUNNEL

The men awoke to the sound of thunder. Echoing, furious thunder that faded away only to come back unexpectedly just minutes later. Sounds of wind rushing through the tunnel and of rain battering rock filled Louis's ears. However, the two travelers were still dry, and for a moment Louis forgot where he was. There was only darkness, but the sounds gave him a visual he didn't like. How could he hear such things when so far below the surface? There had to be an opening somewhere close; somewhere ahead.

He felt around for Jacob, who was curled up on the ground, shivering from fear and cold. How long had he lain there, clouded with fears, searching the unwavering darkness? Searching in the emptiness for something that wasn't there? Of course there had been rats. Louis had heard some in the night, but there were rats alone. This scurrying, though, might just have kept Jacob on the lookout. Regretfully, Louis shook Jacob out of his slumber, causing the other man to flinch at his touch.

"Are you ready? I think there might be an opening ahead."

Jacob nodded, blinking his red-rimmed eyes. "Do we have any food?" The voice was weak and desperate.

"Oh!" Louis crawled over to their bags, which lay forgotten against the wall. "Of course."

Jacob merely grunted in reply, but Louis knew he was glad. They hadn't eaten since... well, he couldn't remember. And Louis was thirsty. Parched. Drained. He pulled out a water bottle and a package of salted meat with crackers; it wasn't even close to enough, but it was something. They sat in silence and ate, the salt burning their chapped lips and making Louis want to drink more and more of the frigid water. They devoured their meal, finishing it to the last

189

drop of water in the tin canister, licking their fingers. Louis set the empty bottle firmly on the ground, making a metallic clink against the stone. It echoed through the tunnel, sending chills up his spine. In silence they packed up, stowing their things in their bags and listening grimly to the storm as they did so.

Why are you here? You should be dead. You slowed them down. You killed Amicus. It's your fault he's dead. Why are you here? The voice asked him. *You killed him. You killed him. You killed him.* Louis tossed the thoughts aside and helped gather their things. It was moments later, (such packing did not take long) that they set off, not even looking back at the place where they had spent their sleepless night.

As they walked, Louis yearned to distract himself from his sore, aching body. Blisters and small sores had appeared under his arms, where the crutches rubbed against day after day. He seeked to distract himself from his thoughts, which constantly drifted back to Oliver and Marion. Wondering if they were still alive. Wondering if they had gone on without them. Wondering, wondering, wondering. And Amicus Vanner; the good man, the poor man. It pained him to think of it. Louis's mind almost split open with a searing headache. Distraction. He needed to focus on something less stressful.

Gratefully his eyes settled on Jacob just in front of him. Settled on the severed arrow lodged in his back, the splintered wood and dark clotted blood. Jacob was tired, yes, but also weary with depression. It was one thing to be weak, but being weak with defeat was on a whole other level; it meant giving up. It meant losing. This air of feeling was around Jacob now, and it only made Louis hopeless. With everyone so low, so drowned in despair, how would they ever make it? Amicus's passing had been unfortunate, but that didn't mean they should waste his sacrifice. They needed to get their act together, himself included, or they would all be dead soon enough. Louis cleared his throat.

"What can be broken but never touched?"

"Excuse me?" Jacob asked without turning around.

"It's a riddle."

"It's old, that's what it is." There was a slight tone of annoyance in Jacob's voice. "You're insane. You're fucking insane." He slowed his pace. "This isn't the time, Louis. Just leave me alone."

"Do you know it?"

"A promise." He responded grudgingly. Then, after a few seconds, "What about that book?"

Louis frowned. "What book?"

"That book they gave us in Viajar. In Malivia."

Yes, he remembered now. Still wondering what Jacob wanted with the old storybook, he dug it out of his pack and handed it over.

"We already read everything important." Louis added, looking over his friend's shoulder as he flipped through the pages.

"I know."

They walked in silence for a long while, or at least it seemed so, until Jacob handed him the book once again, his thumb holding open a page.

"This one. Read it."

Louis sighed, rolling his eyes. "Jacob-"

"Please?"

Grudgingly, he tried to make out the smudged, inky words on the page. There was now enough dim light for them to see by. It was a poem.

Of places I have wandered, of mountains I can see
Of joy and love and fear and hate oh now I come to thee
I see that you are anguished, I see your hurt and pain
I see this and weep bitter tears wetter than the rain
And so with that I look into the sky so darkly grayed
And unto you I grimly bade
A fairly fond farewell.

Of battles I have fought in, through torments now are we
In darkness, death, and sorrow, oh now I come to thee
I see you are forsaken, I see your loss and grief

I see this but come upon you, hoping to be brief
And so I sheath my bloody blade
And unto you I grimly bade
A fairly fond farewell.

Of journeys we have been on, of laughter we have shared
Of times when for a moment we forgot to be so scared
I see your face and cherish the last sight of it to see
So now I come upon you, and you over to me
I smile in the midst of blood and war around us soon to fade
And so, for the last time I embrace you and so bade
A fairly fond farewell.

Louis smiled, just a small grin. It felt strange on his face, but it was comforting. It was good. A good poem. A good story.

"This isn't farewell. Not yet, anyway."

Jacob tensed, taking a few moments to answer. "I know."

They continued to walk, and so Louis slipped the book back into his duffel. He would read more, another time. His friend was acting rather strange, and Louis didn't like it. He would not lose Jacob, he would make sure of that; he only wished he had the courage to tell him so.

For a second Louis forgot about the Barren. In fact, he forgot about everyone, everything. It was bliss, neglecting his troubles; but good times, as they say, cannot last. Soon they were in empty silence again, and Louis focused now upon his surroundings. Cooler, fresher wind blew past them, cold and damp. The sound of rain and thunder was now so loud that it could no longer be ignored.

"That's a storm, do you think?" Jacob asked quietly, tracing his hand along the wet, black rock of the tunnel. This question was not unusual, for such had to be considered this close to the Barren, and Louis did not judge him for it.

"Yeah, sounds like it. Be careful, when we get there."

Louis realized he had used the word *when*, but did not correct himself. The *if* he did not want to think about. There was no doubt that there was an opening, all the signs were clear. There were no separate paths to follow, no other choices to make.

Suddenly, there was a loud screech, but not one of any living thing. It was the scream of rock grinding on rock, the boom of the earth cracking. Like lightning, it was, a sound that he'd never known until he'd heard it. They both put their hands to their ears, Louis almost losing his balance because of it. Dust came down from the ceiling, the sound of rocks crumbling and falling still at work. Hurriedly they continued down the passageway, Jacob shoving Louis's crutches into his bag and putting his arm around him.

"We'll go faster, and stay together," Jacob reassured him, but Louis wasn't so sure. His worst fear, he could feel it now, was having his friends hurt or injured at his expense. Because he couldn't go fast enough. *Because I'm not strong enough.* These thoughts hurt, and so Louis shoved them away. This was no time to be self-critical. He nodded to Jacob, and so they rushed as fast as they could to where ever fate lead them. Jacob winced as they moved, though Louis paid little mind to it. *The wound will heal,* he thought, but he wasn't too sure. He would have to remove the shaft of the arrow, somehow.

Many minutes later, as far as they were concerned, they arrived at the opening. Though, unfortunately, it wasn't quite as they had expected. Jacob and Louis stood, petrified, at the gaping hole in their path. They looked down from the ledge into an unmeasurable precipice, as they could not see the bottom nor the end in either direction.

Their tunnel had ended, leading out to only air. Jacob stuck his head out into the storm, and Louis grabbed his shirt so he didn't fall. It made him swoon, and they backed away. Rain was pouring down from the dark sky, and lightning struck stones, making them fall into the bottomless ravine below. Wind raged, and all was chaos and destruction. *We're done for.* Louis sank to the ground, his clothes soaked from the intruding rain. He looked at himself using a puddle beside him, but all he could see was a corpse. Covered in dirt and grime, weak and sick. Disgusted, he looked away, only to see that

Jacob wasn't much better. His face shone in the little light they had, shone with shock and fear.

Looking across the cliff he could see the other side, see the opening in which their tunnel would have continued. Now, there was no hope. No way out. Climbing would be suicide in this storm, and they were much too weak to walk, much less do so vertically. They would rest, Louis decided, and see what the morning would bring them.

Before he could even close his eyes, a disturbance came to face them. A loud roaring echoed through the valley, echoed in their ears and settled dreadfully in his heart. The rumbling got louder and louder until suddenly they could hear it no longer, and there was only a silent darkness. The entryway had been blocked up, and Jacob fell backwards in surprise. Oh, but it was not covered up by rocks. No, it was that of something foreign to them, and as Louis reached out to touch it he felt it moving.

Only for a moment he got to feel the thing, for his hands were cut and bleeding from the- *rocks, dirt? falling?* His hand came away covered in a dark black liquid, like blood. Perhaps it was their world collapsing, infected with dark-radiation. No matter what it was, it rushed past the opening, creating a sliding sound that wasn't unlike the sound of an earthquake. The masses of dirt and rocks were huge, seeming to go on forever. Another thought struck him. *Those aren't rocks. Those are scales.*

But no, no. That was insane.

In the darkness all was indistinguishable, and he only made these assumptions from what he had felt and heard. Before long light rushed once again into the passage and the two sat there, shocked. Louis's hand was bleeding, shedding blood onto the ground below. Jacob crawled closer, and Louis remembered the arrow, and the clearness of it was in his mind. It was still in Jacob's back, and made his poor friend wince as he made his way over.

To his surprise Jacob leaned beside him, looking out into the storm. He choked out a sob, silently, the tears coming suddenly like rain. His eyes, which had been glazed and horrified, were now closed as he buried his face into his hands.

Louis remembered now his friend was older than himself by six years, and from what he knew, Jacob had a daughter and sister he might never see again. With a hope to comfort him, Louis sat closer, his bloody hand staining Jacob's already torn shirt as he put his arm around him. After all this, he'd cracked. His friend couldn't take any more. Jacob was worried, hopeless, petrified, and Louis felt he might never be able to recover.

So in the rage of the storm and wind, he put an arm around Jacob as he wept, as he wept out his sorrow and grief and loss. Louis sat staring into the distance, feeling empty. They sat together as they suffered in their pain and agony that they knew would not end anytime soon.

The rumbling under the earth soon faded away.

CHAPTER 19
MARION ARMAIS
THE CROSSING

It was dusk of the first day, now, that they had awaited the arrival of their two friends. The air was still, the sunset bright. They had set up camp, more permanent than usual, in the hope they would be able to grant their companions a somewhat comforting return.

Marion hoped their friends were not angry at himself and Oliver for leaving, and could only imagine the arguments that could arise; arguments none of them had the energy for. Yet even if they did fight, Marion hoped for their return more than anything. He didn't think he could deal with another death, much less one that had happened because of some injury that had been inflicted while in the chamber; then it would truly be his fault. The blood of Jacob and Louis would be on his hands. He was the one who had wanted to go, not because it was best for their mission but because he didn't want to be captured again. Marion had done it for himself, and he regretted it more than anything.

He felt he was a coward. He ran while his friends suffered, ran to leave his friends to die. *Because I wasn't brave enough.* Marion wasn't, as he now realized, like Amicus, who he had thought so little of when they first met. Regret swarmed over him, and he looked over at Oliver, who was sleeping by the fire. He would make it up to all of them. There was no doubt about that. He would never run from his friends again.

They were all he had left, after all.

JACOB FORTEMER
THE TUNNEL

Beams of light penetrated Jacob's eyes, making him blink in confusion. He had fallen asleep, it seemed, in his delirium. It was bright out again, the air clearer and somehow less suffocating. Maybe it was just because he had gotten a full night's rest, but he also felt healed. Jacob had been sick, but now he felt... better, somehow. Being so close to that *thing* had made him feel weak. Light-headed. Strange. It might have all been in his head, he couldn't know for sure.

Jacob shook those thoughts away, not wanting to remember the storm. Instead he focused on that which was around him, and it was brighter than he recalled. The stone seemed to glimmer in the sun, the puddles of leftover water shining like they were pure, molten gold. It was the most beautiful thing Jacob had seen in weeks. But where was Louis? Where was he in this strange, unfamiliar tunnel?

Jacob spotted his friend sitting on the brink of the chasm, looking out. His form was only a shadow against the sun. As he got up to ask him how they would get out, Jacob realized not all of him had been healed. A pain shot through his back, and every move felt as if he were lugging bags of stone instead of limbs. With a groan he sank back to the ground, dreading another move would finally kill him. Dreading the pain that would come with it.

Louis heard the commotion, turning around. The man told him something about rest, but Louis didn't know that Jacob didn't want to sleep. He wanted to leave. He wanted to find Oliver and Marion, lay by the comforting fire of their camp, out of this mess. Together. Have this damn arrow pulled out before it killed him.

197

But his body protested, and right now he could not overpower it. Jacob drifted back into a deep sleep, welcoming it like one would embrace a long lost friend.

***

Again he awoke, and again he felt fresh and sane. But he dared not move, for fear he would make the same mistake. His mind might have been unharmed, but his body was far from it. Instead, he closed his eyes and focused on something else, anything else. Jacob's memory flashed back to his time in Malivia, with only Emilia and himself. A hard time, but a better time.

"I'm selling, Choker, don't waste your time." *Jacob stood in an old garage, large and filled with junk. License plates hung on the walls, machine parts and tanks of oil scattered around on the cracked concrete floor. It was otherwise empty, but for a hispanic boy in his early twenties, wearing jeans, a torn greased shirt, and a seashell necklace with a strange black rune on it; he sat in a stained chair, observing them casually as he scratched into the concrete wall with a wrench.*

Jacob stood, waiting, behind an overweight man tinkering with an overturned car. He was old, with grey hair and yellowing teeth. Sebastian Choker, though no one dared called him by his first name. The man turned, wiping his hands on a towel and taking a swig from the silver flask at his side.

"Bit early to be drinking, isn't it?" Jacob said, an all too serious look on his face. He was in no mood to joke around today.

"Aw, Fortemer, lighten up. Whadda you got for me?"

Jacob handed him the bag, and the man grunted his approval as he held the parts up the light.

"Good haul."

"How much?"

"Hm. I'll give you five for this and twelve for the others."

"Give me seven for that and you've got a deal."

"Fine."

Choker dug in his pocket and handed him the money. He motioned to the boy in the back of the garage. "This new lad is Gabriel. You can deal with him too if I'm gone."

Gabriel gave a wave, and he nodded in response.

"You leaving somewhere, Choker?" Jacob asked. The man was not one to leave his business to others. Something suspicious was going on, that much was obvious.

Choker fidgeted, nervous. "You have a good day now, Jacob. Tell that little girl of yours hello for me."

Jacob was jolted out of memory lane when Louis came into his sight, a duffel bag on his back, crutches inside. He sat in front of him, and started talking. Louis's words didn't seem to reach his ears, for his lips moved but there was no sound.

Jacob blinked, blinked again, and heard the voice, faintly, as if his friend were far in the distance. He couldn't make it out, though, so Jacob decided he needed to move. How long had he slept? If it was longer than he thought, he might be okay. A spot in his back was numb, and his limbs no longer felt heavy. In fact, he felt almost drugged, or what he thought being drugged felt like. Lack of experience in that particular area left him almost clueless, but Jacob had still learned of their effects from books and such. Just in case. His mind was a bit disordered, and Louis's voice was only now becoming louder.

"Do you think you're ready to climb?" Louis asked, looking him over with clear concern.

Jacob nodded, and started to push himself up. "Well, I can't really feel anything, so it's probably best."

From the look on his friend's face, he knew Louis wasn't sure, and inside Jacob kept wondering if they should take the arrow out. Wondering if it was tipped with deadly poison, or barbed like a fishhook. Wondering exactly how much time he had left before infection found him, before he died.

But there was no time, and this was definitely not the place. What they needed was to get out. If they removed it here, who knew what condition Jacob would be in? They needed to leave. To find their friends, whether close by or far into the Barren. They could deal with his injury later.

Louis started digging through their packs for anything that might help them scale that dangerous, rocky wall. They were close to the top, but it was still high. And in their weakened states, they didn't know what would happen. It took the cripple only moments, for they didn't have very large packs, to make a pile of items they needed and to pack up the rest.

The excursion ahead of them was certainly formidable, the rock wall looming above composed of jagged edges and loose stones. *Before the end, rubble, ruin, and skeletons are left forgotten under the blooming flowers of new life.* He thought, rubbing black dirt between his fingers. Jacob wasn't frightened for his endurance, but for a mistake that would send them both tumbling down into darkness. It would be hard, he knew. Harder even for Louis than it would be for himself. *God, much harder.*

There was some food they would eat before they left, the last bit of water and an extra layer of clothes for both of them. It was getting cold, winter cold, and it got worse when climbing. Jacob was open to the elements, welcoming them to freeze him, bite him, soak him, make him want to let go and give up. These contemplations were not comforting at all, so Jacob pushed them away and focused on the wonderful thought that they would *not* be climbing in a storm. A storm with thunder, wind, rain, crashing rocks and strange things from the shadows. No, it would be under a clear sky, the sky that made him look into the great blue emptiness and ponder. The sky that made him almost miss the shelter of the clouds, wisped away from memory.

It was a good a day as any.

"Jacob?" Louis asked, tapping him lightly on the shoulder. "You ready?"

He shook his head. "I'll never be ready, Louis." With that statement, he shouldered his pack and tied his end of the rope to his waist. "But I'll go when you are."

200

Nodding, Louis grinned sadly, and turned away. Jacob's hands shook with nervousness, faltering and slipping as he tried to tighten the straps on his bag. This was going to be impossible. Hard even with all limbs, for that matter. He would never make it, and he would pull Louis down with him. Pull both of them down into the dark, endless depths. Jacob could see it now, oh so clearly, and realized he was starting to lose his nerve.

Louis was looking at him again, perhaps sharing the same thought. "Okay?"

Jacob nodded, and forced his feet towards the ledge, closely after Louis. His stomach plummeted, tightened, and he started to panic. *Oh God I can't do this I'll die I'll die I'll die I'll slip I'll fall God please-*

Louis disappeared around the edge, and he felt a tug on the strings of his heart. He could let Louis go on, find another way out, or even not at all. Stay behind. The thought was tempting, very tempting, but Jacob knew in the back of his mind there was no other way. It was this, or starving to death in a tunnel and leaving Louis alone to make his way to the others. That fate sounded worse than any he could imagine, and so he left it at that. He didn't have a choice. And besides, his friend's arm strength was exceptional, from working so hard on that farm with just one leg. Louis would be fine- and if a cripple could do it, so could he.

Whispering hasty prayers under his breath, Jacob grasped a rock, pulling himself quickly out of the cave, before he could be tempted any longer. He dared not look down, dared not sway to the rhythm of the swirling fogs below. Instead Jacob looked up, looked up at Louis and the sky and the rocky wall that wasn't really that tall from here, no, it was okay. *It's okay.* The rock was dry, surprisingly, dry and cold like ice on his skin. There were some frozen puddles as he made his way higher and higher, sometimes causing him to slip and cry out in fear as he dangled with one hand above the chasm. Seldom it happened on their journey up, though those few times always left him shaking afterwards. He was relived that the holds were good, and their footing stable.

201

"*Jacob*!" Louis yelled, his voice carried away in the wind. "*Jacob*!" The other man looked down, his hair and clothes billowing in the wind. "*IT'S COMING!*"

Then Jacob felt it. The rumbling. The loud cracking of the earth so much like gunshots filled the air, along with the banging of stone on stone, crumbling down. It was here. Again. A quake was upon them. Jacob felt himself climbing faster, though a voice in the back of his mind told him it was nothing to fear. That thing he had seen just days ago, it was just rock falling down over the tunnel opening. The rumblings, the roars, were just the earth in a slow transition. But the rest of his mind refused to listen, and he climbed ever faster up the rock.

Soon enough he was side by side with Louis on the wall, both of them climbing with haste. Fear filled his mind, fear and nothing else. Though just as suddenly as it had appeared, the quake was gone, the silence and emptiness now filling his ears. Jacob dared not look anywhere but up, up into the endless sky where it seemed that no dark things lurked.

After what seemed like years, Jacob's grimy, numb, cut fingers grasped the ledge that lead to the surface. With a grunting, sweating effort he pulled himself up and collapsed onto the ground, woozy and disoriented. The pain in his shoulder was excruciating, almost unbearable. Grimacing, he tried to look over at Louis, who was beside him, but his knees buckled and sent him sprawling into the dust.

With that he fell into a deep, exhausted sleep, just as the clouds swept over them in a grey shadow and the rain started to drizzle down.

OLIVER MONTEROSE
THE CROSSING

Oliver and Marion sat upon the rocks of the crossing, waiting. Waiting for what was to come, for it would be either friend or foe, no one could tell. Though they had rested for as long as two days now, Oliver felt weary within his heart and pained within his soul. Hunger escaped them, water being only a necessity to survive. Circles sat drearily under their eyes, hopeless eyes that were empty and teary with sorrow.

Dirty, filthy, and weak they waited. Waited upon that rock, staring into the distance, searching for the hint of movement, the secret wisp of a shadow against the bright, blurry horizon.

CHAPTER 20

JACOB FORTEMER
THE ASHEN DESERT

The light of dawn was upon them, shining in splotches of colors through his eyelids. It awoke him to a stormless, clear morning, a morning of which Jacob took as a blessing. The gloomy clouds loomed above, his clothes damp. As he woke, he blinked droplets of water from his eyes. That morning the rock seemed not as hard, the air not as cold, their wounds not as painful. A day of travel was ahead of them.

"Louis?" Jacob's voice asked hurriedly, worried the man had not made it up alongside him. After a moment he remembered his friend had been ahead of him on the cliff. "Louis?"

He was answered by a groan, and a rustle of movement. Looking around, he saw his friend much too close to the edge of the chasm. Jacob pushed himself up and rushed over to Louis, putting his arm around him for support.

"I'm fine, I'm fine."

However, despite Louis's reassuring tone, Jacob knew otherwise. Neither of them were okay. Far from it, actually. He himself was sore from yesterday's exertions, but he could not even begin to imagine what his companion was feeling. Louis shivered, trembled, and in his face Jacob could tell all he wanted to was rest. Rest, and possibly never wake up.

Louis saw the concern and shook his head. "Whether I'm fine or not, it doesn't change anything. We have to leave today if we ever want to catch up to them. They might already be in the Barren, for all we know." He paused, sighing. "Come 'ere. Help me up. We have a long way to go."

Jacob nodded in understanding as he grasped Louis's hand and helped him to his feet. Together they gathered their packs and took off, going slower than usual but at a consistent pace. Using all of his effort, Louis continued on, his crutches now comparable to sticks found alongside the road. The crutches were scratched and dirty, much like himself, for that matter. Jacob knew the day would come when they would break, were forgotten, or were lost. It was a miracle Louis had even been able to get them through the graveyard at all, much less all the other hell they had been through. *Yes*, Jacob thought, *the day is coming*. They would be stripped of all their dignity and honor, and left with nothing but each other.

The Barren would give them no mercy; for there was no mercy in the land of the dead.

MARION ARMAIS
THE CROSSING

Sleeping, unaware, vulnerable. They were no longer wary, no, they were desperate. Marion had the feeling, the dark feeling, that they were waiting in vain. Waiting for ghosts. Waiting for their own shadows. By each hour Marion grew grimmer, with a gleam in his eye not so different from a madman's. He grew sick with pain and grief, sick with the fear that his friends had died alone. How he regretted it now. He barely slept, only sat upon the rock and waited. It hadn't been in his nature to leave those in need of his help. It never had been.

"I would have stayed, you know." Marion said spitefully, his eyes furious, his face a scary calm. "I would've stayed."

There was a moment of tense silence. Oliver turned on him, obviously frustrated. Marion was out of patience, and needed to take it out on someone. Anyone. It wasn't his fault the closest someone happened to be Oliver.

"Are you joking? You would've died! You- you would've died trying to save those who don't need to be saved! Don't you trust them?"

Marion scowled. "It would've been *loyalty.* It was the least we could've done. I would've died for them, yeah, but better to die there than without them here."

"Who the hell said you were going to die here? We still have a damn job to do, if you haven't noticed, that has everyone's lives on the line! Is loyalty abandoning them all to save a- a cripple and a commoner? They're nobodies, Marion!"

Marion looked at Oliver as if he had never met him before. It had only started as a small argument, but something about the way Oliver had said that made him furious.

"They were your *friends*. Like *brothers* to you. They've kept us alive, in case you haven't noticed. They're the reason we're here at all!"

Oliver looked at him, his anger taking a firm hold. "Really? A man with one leg and someone who's trust would have gotten him killed if he hadn't died in that chamber? *They only slowed us down.*" Oliver turned away. "They're dead, Marion! Dead! We've waited and waited. They won't come."

"Then go. Do your damn mission. Don't come back." A pause came between them, but it did not last. "Just *go,* Oliver."

Angrily, in his storming fury, the man grabbed his bags and left. Left with eyes blazing fire and heart plotting revenge. And with no words of forgiveness and no regret, Oliver Monterose faded into the great unknown, delving into the great dark nightmares of men.

LOUIS WILLSON
THE ASHEN DESERT

The horizon was never-ending, the sky a desolate gray. Drearily the rain fell upon them, dotting their clothes and soaking their hair. The two beaten, weak figures of men pushed themselves onwards, hoping beyond hope they would meet their friends at last.

But days passed, and the only signs of Marion and Oliver were their deserted camps, the fires dead and the charred wood dripping wet. All footprints had been washed away, and the only thing that kept them on track were the remains of their camps. The sun rarely showed it's face anymore, rarely peeked out to let the travelers know it was still there.

"Louis?" Jacob asked, turning to look at him as they walked. "Do you think they're in the Barren yet?"

Louis shrugged casually, as if to say he couldn't tell, but it had been on his mind since they had set off. *It's all I can think about... What else?* Their two friends almost surely thought them dead, but wouldn't they at least wait a few days? Didn't they trust they could make it themselves? *No,* a voice told him. *You're a fucking cripple. They last saw you hanging onto a rope above a chasm of ghosts. Of course they think you're dead.*

Instead Louis said, "If they aren't waiting, they're very far ahead of us."

Because of me, I can't run, I'm too goddamn slow. Louis heard his companion sigh. Jacob had rarely spoken, if only to ask to rest or to eat. He might have even been weaker than Louis, and that thought alone worried him. They continued their trek, hoping and thinking. It was at a slow pace, a very slow pace. His friend kept falling behind. Just minutes later, Jacob let out a shout of pain and crumpled to his knees.

"Jacob? Are you alright?"

Louis turned back and helped him up, thinking he was just sore from his wound. That was until he saw the splintered wood. The wound had coagulated, and, to his dismay, a part of the snapped arrow was still in Jacob's back. Wood, splintered, bound to scabbing skin and sealed into flesh. The arrowhead, and a part of the shaft. *How could I have been so blind?* Louis remembered it snapping in half when they pushed themselves through the tunnel, but after that it was hardly noticeable; Jacob must have thought the arrow had been torn out in the process.

"Jacob, I'm going to need you to not panic, alright?"

His friend tensed, waiting. "What is it? Is it not healing?"

Louis almost laughed, but the severity of the situation held him back. "No, Jacob, the... some of the arrow's still in there."

Silence. Neither one moved or spoke for what seemed like eternity. His head spun, trying to figure out how they had missed such a thing.

"We... we never took the rest of it out? Louis, *you never took it out?* It never got..."

Shaking his head, Louis helped the shocked Jacob sit down, before pacing beside him in worry. "When it snapped, I'd just assumed... I thought..." He broke off.

How, how did we forget? How did we miss it? Jacob clearly had no idea, had probably just thought the numbness meant it was healing, that the soreness and ache were all just a part of it. That Louis had taken it out while he was unconscious, maybe. Jacob most likely didn't remember much. Louis had been so disoriented and tired and worried, he hadn't put any thought into managing the wound properly. Louis felt disgusted with himself. What kind of friend let his companion walk around with an arrow in his back? Sure, he hadn't noticed it, but he *should* have. Hell, he thought more about the scars on his hands than he did about Jacob's injury. *Selfish, selfish, selfish.* Jacob looked up at him pacing, worry on his face. Louis obviously wasn't one to pace, but he attempted. It was now, as he hobbled back and forth, that Jacob started to realize Louis was blaming himself for this mess.

"Look, Louis, let's just leave it in and move on. We can take it out once we reach Marion 'n Oliver. It'll- it'll be better that way." Louis moved to interrupt, but Jacob hushed him. "No- no. If we wait any longer they'll be too far ahead of us. They most likely already think we're dead."

Jacob started to get up, but Louis pushed him down again, shaking his head. "Jacob, I get it. I understand, trust me, I do. But we don't need them-" Jacob started to get up again, but Louis stopped him. "No, wait, just hear me out. Listen. We don't need them at the moment, do we? Jacob, if we go on, you'll die. And if you die, I-" Louis broke off, thinking, trying to find a way to explain. "I'm a cripple, Jacob. You're my support right now, I *need* you. Hell, you and the others are what get me up everyday. So we're getting that damn arrow out of you and we're not risking your life just to catch up to them. We will eventually, that's all we can hope for now."

Jacob opened his mouth, but paused and decided against arguing. Grimly he nodded, leaning forward with his hands to his face almost like in prayer. But this was not the case. He was preparing mentally for the pain, for the pain that would be merciless in its endeavor to kill him, for the pain that would save his life.

"When you do this, you have to make sure the arrow doesn't separate from the shaft, okay? That's most important. And- and there's more, let me remember, to make sure it's not stuck in bone..." Jacob sighed, rubbing his temples, mumbling instructions under his breath.

Louis listened as intently as he was able, nodding, observing the wound with worry. The medical procedure was complicated, especially with the limited tools available, and Jacob admitted that the would would likely never heal fully. It was unfortunate, but Louis was determined to do this right- to do one thing right. And so the cripple knelt beside his friend, gently peeling aside the blood-soaked cloth. Bruises, yellow and purple, swelled around the hollow of clotted brown blood and scabbing; infection would be inevitable.

There was the unfamiliar slicing of the knife, frozen water washing away dark red, prying of fingers sending shockwaves of lightning through the wreaked body below him that only whiskey could numb; torn and broken coughs, sobbing and screaming.

The sounds broke his heart.

MARION ARMAIS
THE CROSSING

Marion sat and waited, the silence ringing in his ears. He wanted someone to talk to, even if it *was* Oliver. He regretted what he said and now was starting to think that his entitled, rich companion might have been right.

The dangers would be coming soon, whatever they were, and Marion's mind told him to get up and find Oliver. Otherwise, he would be alone. Yet no matter how much he urged himself to, Marion just couldn't get up off that rock. He couldn't admit defeat. He couldn't leave Louis and Jacob, if they were even still alive.

Sighing, Marion Armais looked out into the horizon, the suspicion growing in him that he was waiting for something that would never come.

CHAPTER 21
JACOB FORTEMER
THE ASHEN DESERT

Screaming, filling his ears. Filling the air, which came into his nose, his mouth, spread over him like a suffocating wave of heat. It was an agonizing sound, animalistic, gut-wrenching. Jacob couldn't help it, he screamed, screamed, screamed until Louis couldn't stand it anymore and backed away for a few moments, putting his hands to his ears. Soon, though, as Jacob's screams turned into gasping sobs, Louis got back to work. His face was sweaty despite the coolness of the wind.

The procedure was supposed to be quick, fast, effortless; yet pulling an arrow out of someone's back seemed to be trickier than they'd thought. Jacob had tried to tell him, to guide him through it, to aid in preventing further harm; yet he was teeming with fever, his mouth dry, his skin pale.

The arrow was almost out, it was almost done, but how was Jacob meant to know? For him, the pain could go on for eternity, his screams continuing until his throat was so torn that he could only sob. Shudders raked his body, uncontrollable, seizure-like, tears blurring the world into a mess of flashing black and white. Jacob clenched the stones and rocks beneath him, cutting into his palms, unfeeling compared to the agony pulsing through his wound.

And so as Louis pulled for one last time, as Jacob imagined his hell, not so far away Marion sat up a little higher, his ears detecting a distant sound; the only sound he'd heard besides for his own breathing in what seemed like forever.

And so Marion listened, listened to the scream echoing from the motionless horizon.

MARION ARMAIS
THE CROSSING

Marion was so shocked that for a moment he couldn't move. The screams had stopped, but that didn't matter.

Someone is out there. Close. Oliver was wrong, they made it, they would- no. Oh, no. Shit. They'd been screaming. They'd been screaming. Screaming.

Marion rushed and packed his things, the one goal now set in his head. He had a plan. No more waiting, no more wondering. They could go on. Together. Quickly he rushed around the camp, not even bothering to put out the fire. Then Marion ran, ran back the way he had came, ran looking for his friends and praying he hadn't gone insane.

LOUIS WILLSON
THE ASHEN DESERT

Louis held the bloody, snapped arrow in his hand, staring at it. So much pain, over such a small thing. In disgust he threw it away, hearing the pieces clatter on the stone before falling silent. Jacob had passed out, with his wound still bleeding. Exhaustively, Louis crawled over to his bag, pulling out the last of the bandages.

Marion had used a lot, and the rest of the medicinal supplies were with the others. Careful not to wake him, Louis disinfected and wrapped the wound as best he could, though he was no professional. Worried, Louis felt his friend's forehead, and found that Jacob's fever was still running high. Out here, with little medication, he would most likely die.

After all that, all they had done was for nothing. He would have been better dying sooner than later, and Louis discovered that he had only caused Jacob more pain. He had done this for himself, so that he wouldn't be alone. Yes, he loved Jacob like a brother, and he wanted him to stay. But was it really for the best? Would he save Jacob more torment by letting him go in peace? By ending it quickly, a slash to the throat, to spare him the pain to come?

But the fate of his friend wasn't his to decide. *No, it's not.* Relived, Louis sighed, holding his friend close, guarding him from the chill and wilderness alike as he slept, as he healed, as he recovered.

MARION ARMAIS
THE ASHEN DESERT

Rocks scattered and ash flew up in the air behind him as the criminal ran, ran jumping over the cracks and boulders and hills. The terrain was mostly stone, black as night and mixed with the ash from the desert. It was hard to navigate, but Marion managed. It was his excitement that drove him on, his eagerness to find someone, *anyone* to talk to about this whole mess.

He dashed forward blindly, following nothing but a guess that it was the same road that had led him before. It was only when Marion did not come upon them that he started to wonder. Should he go farther, or head back and give in? There were no signs of people, friends or not. Had it just been his imagination? *Am I going insane?* The thought itself drove him mad, and so he pushed on, telling himself that it had *not* been his mind playing tricks. It was good that he did so, too, for just minutes later he saw a dark form on the horizon. Marion ran as best he could, now making care to not trip or fall. He was so close.

And before he knew it he saw Louis grin, saw him shake Jacob awake, saw him reach out with open arms. Then there Marion was, helping his friend up and embracing him. He breathed in the scent of Louis, inhaled the smell of sweat and blood and *him* that was just so human. Marion laughed and cried in the relief that he was not alone, that he was not insane; to just touch another person, to feel their presence and to know that they were not a figment of imagination was an amazing feeling. Marion held onto the warmth a moment longer before turning to Jacob, who was just coming out of sleep.

"Marion?" Jacob asked, trying to sit up. His voice was too quiet, too broken, too rasping. Louis rushed to help, but warned Marion before he moved to hug his wounded friend.

"Look, he was shot, we only just got the arrow out. Just... be gentle, okay?"

Marion nodded in understanding, but the grin didn't fade from his face as he carefully embraced Jacob.

"Are you alright? Is the wound deep?"

Jacob shrugged, and took his seat on a boulder. "It hurt like hell, I can tell you that."

Marion looked on with sympathy. "Trust me, I know."

There was a moment of satisfied, peaceful silence, until a thought wandered in and the air turned tense.

Louis looked around. "Where's Oliver?"

Marion grew angry, his serene expression soon replaced by a scowl- a look Louis had grown used to. "I'd ask him myself, but I guess some people are just too impatient."

The memory felt so much like poison to his stomach he turned away and started to walk back towards the Barren, not wanting to face his friends. His grin had vanished.

"Marion, what does that mean? What does it mean?" Louis took his crutch and hobbled as fast as he could, calling out after him, concerned. "Marion!"

"It means he left us!" He turned back around, yelling. "It means he left us and moved on!" Marion scoffed. "As if he could do it alone."

Jacob looked surprised. "He... he deserted us? *Why?*"

Marion raised his eyebrows. "Why? He thought you both were dead and that it was a waste of time waiting for you. He said there was something bigger than us, more important than us."

Louis sighed and walked back to Jacob, settling back down beside him. "The fucking idiot."

Marion had been harboring the same thoughts; Oliver would get himself killed. The rage had almost dissipated, now as he realized what Louis meant. Oliver would be alone. In the Barren. By himself. *Hell, the poor man has no chance.*

"So what do we do now?" Jacob looked up at them.

"We keep going, I guess." Louis said.

They nodded, but after a moment Marion froze. "Oh no. no, no, no...." He searched frantically through his pack, then rummaged through the others. A few moments later he sat back, defeated, hand over his mouth.

"What is it? What's wrong?" Louis worriedly searched his face for an answer.

"He took it." Marion looked around at them, too shocked to think. "He took the gun."

LOUIS WILLSON
THE ASHEN DESERT

The group of three once again trekked together, Marion ahead, leading them to the Crossing. Jacob was now running a high fever, and was incapable of walking for more than a few minutes at a time. Therefore he lay passed out in Marion's arms, looking worse than ever. Dirt covered him from head to toe, along with crusted blood and other various injuries. His breathing was soft and ragged, like wind through autumn leaves, his body as thin as a bone. His raven hair was tousled, unmanaged, his eyelids fluttering over a faded blue as he clung to consciousness. They all were exhausted, but Jacob seemed the worst of them all. He hadn't eaten the last few meals and his wound, though nonbleeding, looked as if it would leave a significant scar.

Louis felt extremely guilty for not being able to carry Jacob, for he could see the toll it was taking on Marion; it was hard enough having to carry himself through the journey. And, though his friend understood that having one leg was already enough of a worry, Louis still did everything he could to help. Marion was left with what? A bundle of breathing rags and a crippled dog he had to drag behind him? *We're better off dead.*

The men traveled in silence, thinking about what would become of them, what would become of Rendar. They'd fallen apart; what once had been five was now three, and what they all thought was soon to be two. Oliver had taken the gun, along with a good deal of supplies. They hadn't even stepped foot in the Barren yet, but it had still torn them down to nothing. From far away, it had filled them with it's poison. It had still driven them insane with nightmares, fears, and worries. Without hesitation, it had seen them come to bring it down and showed them that something as powerful as it could not be destroyed by the likes of them; yet there was still a mystery here.

The orb, the Glass Shadow, was watching them. The white ghost, hiding in the bodies of others. It was helping them, though through what motivation Louis did not know. They also had no idea what it was, or where it came from. Their handy book of legends and poems had come to no use, for it was barely mentioned in the text, as far as they knew. Only the one story. *This we"l have to solve for ourselves,* Louis thought.

He hoped they could do it, but he doubted they really would. He knew, they all knew, that they would perish.

It was just a matter of when.

CHAPTER 22
A BLIND BIRD
THE CROSSINGS

The Crossings loomed before the travelers, dangerous and foreboding like a cobra before the strike. It was here where the tired, weak group rested for three days, a three days of which weren't very eventful. However, it would be the last moment of real hope and happiness they would have together for a long while. There was no fire that night, for there was no wood. What Monterose and Armais had been using before was from a ruin not far off, and even that had been dry; more turned to dust than actually burned.

The bird knew. It saw. The bird gave its eyes to another, it's wings to one who could not fly, its ears to one who could not hear. The travelers lay in the darkness, dreading for the light of morning to come, for it would mean looking once again out into the lands that somehow felt darker during day than during night.

The bird watched.

The next day they did little but eat, though they had no appetites, and sleep. The bird saw this, as did another, though the bird was blinded white and the other could see. It knew of their troubles. Their water was scarce, but there was enough for several more days, at least. If they were careful, if they didn't walk. Armais was the only one who knew the Crossing's warning, but took no heed and decided to rest one more day, for Fortemer's sake, it seemed. Perhaps for Willson as well, or maybe he needed some rest himself. The bird saw this, too, and deemed it unwise. Later this day, though, the travelers noticed movement farther out, behind them, around them, everywhere besides the road ahead. It was a warning, they knew. Even the bird could see it. If the things in the distance came closer, the bird would fly and the travelers would depart.

Midway though the fourth day Armais seemed to realize he was delaying. The others were happy to stay there for as long as they so wished, for they thought this was a place of rest and talk and calm. The bird saw this as well, in their faces. They were easy to read. If anything, they wanted to stay, but this didn't help Armais. Didn't they didn't know a place like that so close to the Barren wouldn't come without a price?

Armais told them to move, and they had no energy even now to protest. So in a slightly better condition from when they'd come, the travelers left the Crossings, all of them now wary of the slight movement in the distance. It could have been their misleading eyes or the shadows of the clouds but the bird saw it too, saw it with eyes whiter than snow.

The bird flapped it's wings and flew swiftly behind them.

A BLIND HARE
THE BARREN

The Barren was, for the most part, composed of rock; black, sharp, and uneven. Sometimes the ground rose to create hills, sometimes it sank to create valleys or even ravines. The earth below seemed at peace, but if someone so happened to have their ear on the surface they'd hear a faint rumbling, feel it in their bones. The hare saw this, as did another. The orb was watching. To the travelers, the Barren seemed deserted. All was quiet besides the wind and themselves.

As they walked, they came upon trees trying to survive in the inhospitable terrain, their trunks twisting and branches bare. There were plants that might have been something green once, but now were indistinguishable in their origin. Some were strange and some were not, some were harmless and dead and others had thorns. They never came across a plant that was untarnished, in all their time in the Barren. This hare, the orb knew, had not either. The sky was blue but whenever the travelers looked up at it, it seemed to have no color, no emotion, just... nothing.

Surprisingly, within their first couple days of their venture into the Barren, the travelers spotted animals. Once, a rabbit, with albino white eyes and no fur- only patches of burnt red and black skin. It watched them curiously before hopping off again; though not too far, the orb made sure of that. Fortemer, who had been the one to see it first, harbored the suspicion it was the Glass Shadow, but dismissed the thought. The animals were strange in the Barren. The hare knew this well.

Second seen was the bird. A nest, hidden in a dead tree was inhabited by what looked like an eagle. Ferociously it warned them off it's territory, snapping its black beak and ruffling it's marron-brown feathers. Armais was particularly intrigued by its four wings, two on each side atop one another. Spiky ridges trailed down it's back, almost as if it were reptile instead of bird. Three murky yellow eyes glared at them, and they decided it was a good idea to stay away from those claws. The hare agreed.

The travelers came next upon the cave of a bear, but steered clear when they smelled the inside. It was a good thing, too, for the bear was not as fascinating nor as forgiving as the eagle. This the hare knew. It hopped and hopped, careful to stay out of sight.

All of these forsaken creatures not only made the travelers worry about the power they were up against, but made them fear what fate lay in store for themselves. They knew almost nothing of dark-radiation, knew not even how to know where it was strongest or how to avoid it. They were weak.

This, the hare knew.

CHAPTER 23
MARION ARMAIS
THE BARREN

One evening under a lightless sun, the travelers referred to their last hope; their worn, tattered book of legends.

"Can you read any of it?" Marion asked curiously as Louis flipped through the pages.

"Yes. But nothing important, yet."

There were a few moments of silence before their companion's grin led them to believe he had found something.

"Alright, there's something here, a few pages. Most of it's unreadable." This didn't affect the others at all. They just wanted to know something, *anything,* about what they were facing. Louis cleared his throat and started to read.

***

Dark-Radiation: A Warning

Dark-radiation is one of the few forms of radiation that can mix with another destructive force. The name "dark-radiation" originates from the fact that it is, in fact, a chemical composition of new age black magic and pure radiation. When the old world sank into the sea, the weapons that had been radiation-active were affected by the drastic changes of the core. They mixed with released core chemicals and, as a result, started to spread. Black magic, a new combination of core chemicals that were being introduced, today can be harnessed- however, it's extremely dangerous to do so. This new form of radiation acts almost as if it's alive. It thrives by using, wasting

the land it infests then moving on for more. It's a disease, with no cure we yet know of. It dreads me to think of what will happen to one of the last lands in the world, but I fear there is no power great enough to stop it. Not with the limited technology and resources we have now. It's the greed of radiation, bringing sickness and deformity to any living thing that breeds, lives, or journeys in it. It's the cruelty of black magic, causing illusions and suffering. It, well, it drives you insane. My fellows who I've traveled with have lost hair, gotten sores, and started, if anything, to look like the living dead. They vomit, bleed, and are constantly hungry; myself included. Most have dry peeling skin turning grayer and grayer with each passing day. It's the dark-radiation, no doubt, and though I have no way to see myself now I know I must look the same. Please, I beg of anyone who reads this, be careful. I warn you to stay far, far away.
Nothing is worth this.
Nothing.

***

That was where it ended- or, perhaps, where the rest was illegible. They all regretted reading it, even if it did warn them of what was to come. It set a grim feeling in Marion's heart, telling him they'd not only be dying but dying in pain, dying after all they had worked for. It was hard, believe it, for them to turn back to the road and keep going. *Harder than I'd ever could have imagined,* Marion thought.

The thought of just ending it seemed like a reasonable proposal, almost an attractive one. It would be simple, a cut to the throat, a quick death. *The only problem is, no one else is going to do this. No one but a few have ever gotten this far, and there's a reason for that.* Only ignorant men, men who knew nothing of the terrors ahead, would do it for a price. And that's what they had done. The amount of money they had been offered had slipped away, a vague memory. He only knew it wasn't enough. Right as of now Marion would give all the gold in the world to taste something like a strawberry. To lay in a real bed, listen to a song, or sit by a warm fire. The money was almost nothing to him now.

But what waste was it to be thinking about such things, when most likely they would never set foot in Rendar again, much less get the money they were promised. Oh, what a world it was, where fish still took the bait and the fishermen still cast it.

***

It was many days into their journey of the Barren when Marion began to spot sources of water. Often they were just puddles, but occasionally it would be a stream, possibly a pond or maybe, just maybe a small waterfall. They had come upon a few waterfalls like these, when a stream flowed down over the uneven rocks. Despite the sickness devouring the land, there was still fresh water to be found, if they looked in the right places.

Even more often they would come across fresh camps, just days old. Oliver traveled further and further every day, and Marion began to wonder if the man was right. *Are Jacob and Louis just slowing me down?* These thoughts were useless and selfish, Marion knew this, and remembered that it wasn't their fault. For God's sake, he himself had been shot and done his fair share of halting progress. Louis had one leg, Jacob was on the brink of death and Amicus was already past saving. Oliver seemed to be frustrated with this. *The bastard.* It wasn't their fault they kept on living, though the thought of death was even more so appealing to them- Marion knew his two friends felt guilty every day for slowing the group down, and the thought almost made him laugh. *We're all too worried about ourselves, and what the others must think of us. We all worry about disappointing each other or being a burden, yet none of us are proud to have made it this far. None of us realize what this really means.*

Louis was useful, was valued, much more than he realized. They were venturing lands unknown, not knowing what was around the corner, however harsh a journey it might be. Oliver was unable to look past himself and sympathize, and Marion could not blame him.

He was who he was. Marion was determined to not desert his companions as Oliver had, though he doubted he could make a day without them. Marion doubted *they* could make a day without him. In truth, Oliver wasn't the enemy. He was just a different person with different views, using a different tactic to complete the same goal. Marion had to remember he wasn't the enemy. *He isn't the enemy. He isn't the enemy. He isn't the enemy.*

The real enemy was far ahead, somewhere by the sea in a tower of crumbling stone.

LOUIS WILLSON
THE BARREN

Louis was in pain. It was as simple as that. He had no time to think, there was only pain. Pain in his one good leg, pain in his arms bruised, sore and rough from carrying himself, pain in his hands, and foot and heart and mind.

Each step, the thought repeated. Pain in his leg his arms his hands, and foot and heart and mind. No time to think. No time to complain. His body ached, but soon it numbed.

The few rests he got were short, dreamless. Louis hadn't spoken in days, maybe weeks. The sounds around him were distorted, like the pieces of a puzzle he just couldn't solve. This was eternity, the ground below him and there was nothing else. Nothing else but pain. Pain in his leg his arms his hands, and foot and heart and mind...

JACOB FORTEMER
THE BARREN

Then, there was Jacob. His fever had risen, and couldn't walk to save his life. He felt as if he were hanging onto life by a thread, with a few reasons to hold on and a thousand reasons to cut it. The arms of Marion soon became his home, where he lay journey after journey passed out and praying, praying for the pain to go away. Praying to just make it stop.

To be brutally honest, he wasn't that heavy now, just skin and bones. The world was so cold, and Jacob shivered constantly. He tried to speak but his voice was weak and dry, and just led to him coughing. More than once he refused to eat, for fear he would be the cause for their starvation. Sometimes he didn't even drink. It was the least Jacob could do, but his health was slowly waning. He didn't know if he could last another week. His name echoed in his head, urging him to wake up, to keep going. (*Jacob Jacob JacobJacobJacob*)

At one point Jacob cried silent tears in the dark as they lay there, bodies rising under blankets as the cold wind blew; the night was empty and asleep. *Let them be okay.* He thought, praying to whatever was listening. *Let Emilia be okay. Let Marion be okay. Let Louis be okay. Let them all be okay.* In his delirium he waited, waited for the time when he would walk again or when he'd be left behind in a cold, hard grave.

MARION ARMAIS
THE BARREN

For the travelers, it was coming to the point when they no longer discerned day from night, when they ate restraining themselves from devouring more than their share (despite the food tasting like ashes in their mouth), when they started to act, look, and smell like something other than human. It was a point when Marion needed something to happen, something to talk about.

Everything was endless. Everything was the same. Once it had snowed, probably many times, though he could not remember. They had taken shelter under an outcrop of rock and huddled together in the fireless camp. Cold and hunger were often topics complained about, but that too soon stopped. They all knew of each other's struggles and it did not help to hear them aloud.

The snow had been a strange sight, for the crystal white perfectness of it didn't seem to mix with the Barren. Marion would have commented on this if he hadn't noticed the runoff from the melted snow was foul-smelling and tinted; meaning it had most likely come from infected water of the Barren. Had they been out in the snow, they most certainly would have felt some effect from it. However even then they did not talk much, only simple phrases such as *pass the water*, or single words and sounds.

The travelers eventually just made motions and gestures, finding even speech a hard task to manage. They did not despise each other, nor were nervous to speak to one another. It was merely the fact that talking made them think, think about their situation and what they would do- and to them it was much easier to not think, to go along in silence, the mind blank and at peace with the strange world around them.

In the unrelenting silence, Marion found himself constantly reminded of his past, of his life before all this chaos. His mind would wander to memories he didn't even know he had.

"Marion, buddy, there's no way. How much is that?" Seth Blair asked him, pushing forward. The basement was damp, dark, and harbored the smell of old parchment and books. The safehouse had been guarded well, but skilled fighters such as themselves were able to make it inside relativly unschathed. It seemed Rovas had underestimated them. Again.

"It's more than enough."

Without a second glance, Marion zipped the duffel and slug it over his shoulder. They walked back upstairs, Seth starting to whistle. They stepped past the pools of blood, the bodies they had mutilated, the scattered weapons and bullets on the stained wooden floor. They stepped past the room filled with dust and dirt, leaving red footprints in their wake.

Together the pair stepped out into the dim sunlight, stepped away from the bloody mess they had made with nothing but smiles on their faces.

That was only one raid. One time, one moment, one memory so faint he barely could recall the details. Marion didn't know why they had been there, or why they had wanted the money. It didn't matter anymore. And Seth. Poor, poor Seth Blair. An honest man, really. Honest in the sense that he had a good wife, though Marion couldn't remember her name. Honest in the sense Seth never once cheated, never got too drunk, never *actually* used the drugs they stole. Marion was only his pathetic little cousin, the boy that had always come running back into his arms when things went bad. And they always did.

"Hey!" The man yelled as Marion ran off into the distance. "You little Rat! Get the hell out of here! Enforcers'll be on your ass soon enough, boy!"

Marion dashed through the streets, ducking through alleys, the stale bread clutched tightly in his hands. He panted, adrenaline filling his body. This boy was young, too young, to be stealing

232

anything. A child. When he arrived at the field, he slowed his pace, looking around. No one. He was alone. Slowly he approached the grave, the headstone crumbling.

"Hey there, little brother." He whispered, breaking off half the bread and setting it beside the dried flowers he had brought last week. Marion then sat, facing the stone, tracing his fingers along the words carved into the stone as he ate his half of the bread. The sun shone bright, the breeze soothing on his skin as it created waves in the tall green grass. The air smelled like a river, like spring, like soil. He was there for what seemed like hours when he heard the crunch of footsteps behind him.

"Hello, Seth."

"Don't waste the bread. You're hungry enough as it is." Something in his cousin's voice was weary, as if he had already told the younger boy this. As if he already knew it was useless.

"Come on. Let's go home."

"I am home."

Something, perhaps it was impatience, seemed to rise within Seth. "No, you're not. You don't have a home, Marion. You don't have a family. You know what you do have? Me. So stop wasting your life on people who aren't around to notice."

Marion sat there, unfazed by the ridicule.

"I know," He said quietly.

He didn't move.

That memory was so old, Marion had to really search back to find it. God, how he had wasted his life; his little brother would have been disappointed. Anyone who would remember him fondly was dead. Anyone who knew his name would wonder vaguely what had happened to that pathetic excuse for a man before forgetting all about him. He doubted anyone he'd ever slept with would even care to recall his face.

Despite the silence in the air that let him drift off into his past, Marion had the strange feeling they would soon have something to talk about; and they did. He was jolted back to the present by the sudden noise.

"Do you see that? Marion, do you see it?" Louis stopped walking, squinting into the distance. His voice was scratchy, raspy, from lack of use.

Frowning, Marion looked as well, though in the back of his mind he considered the possibility of hallucinations. It had happened before, it could happen again. However, it took him less than a second to identify what Louis was talking about.

"Do you think-"

"Maybe."

Marion grinned to himself, and he couldn't say they didn't rush as they made their way over. Soon a huge lake loomed in front of them, gleaming despite the lack of sun. Truthfully it wasn't quite much of a lake as it was a pond, for they could see the end of it, but it was the largest mass of water he'd seen in a long time; and to him it seemed alright to call it so. Small waves lapped up against the shore, which was now black, rocky sand. The water itself was no good for *them* to drink, this he knew from the moment they came near enough to smell it. However, they didn't lose all hope.

Wherever there was water, there would be life, and Marion knew for sure that those foul creatures would be more than fit for water such as this. It lowered their chances of such dinner without the gun, but that barely mattered now- there was nothing to do about it. So, right then, he just enjoyed the fact that they had come across something new. The thoughts of the return journey were too daunting to enter Marion's mind.

The only thing we can do is go one step at a time, forwards, don't look back Marion or you might stop forever. It's a dangerous place out there, you're in a dangerous world, you can't deny it; and once you get caught up in it you're never coming back.

CHAPTER 24
A DEAD CITY
VIAJAR, MALIVIA

Viajar was silent, abandoned. The wind carried newspapers though the air, blew dust across the marketplaces, whipped past flags no one could see. No people, no horses, no carts. Nothing. Rusted bikes lined the sides of the roads, and somewhere windchimes clinked softly in the breeze.

It was so… quiet. So sad. So strange.

Dark windows glared, glass lay shattered, and the city seemed utterly, totally, empty. Abandoned. There was soon yet another quake, one that sent stones falling to ground and birds into the air, but there was no one to notice. It shook the city, cracked the buildings, split the roads.

The people had fled, and they would not return.

LOUIS WILLSON
THE BARREN

Louis was tired. Shadows lurked under empty eyes, exhaustion looming, intricate fears clinging like a web. His mind was plagued with nightmares, visions of searching white eyes and growling beasts in the dark; of fields filled with dead flowers and snow-peaked mountains crumbling into bottomless ravines. Fragments of a broken past pieced themselves back together with stitches and string, flaring with reminders of venom in memories pushed down deep. Yes, Louis Willson was tired.

He was tired of each step having the same pain, having to walk miles of those steps over the same rocks, same dead grass, past the same grey trees. He was tired of thinking, he was tired of pain, he was tired of life. The lake had been something different- it had taken his mind off all of that, had put aside the thought of just ending it. Though the lake didn't do much for them, it was a sign. A sign that their journey wasn't pointless, a sign that they were accomplishing something, that there wasn't just endless dreaded landscape ahead. It made Louis almost happy, but that didn't mean much to him either; he didn't quite remember what happiness felt like. But that wasn't really his fault, was it? No, that was the fault of his brothers.

"Here," May said, pulling a small box from under her bed, blowing off the dust. They had shared a room, for him to care for her sickness and her for his disability; the two were able to help each other. This was not long after he had been injured, and the stump of his leg was still wrapped and bandaged. The space was small and cramped, though May kept it neat- the patchwork quilts pulled neatly over the beds, the wooden floors swept clean, the scattered belongings organized and their clothes folded into dresser drawers.

The window was open, letting in a breeze, and the yellow curtains blew up to reveal their brothers in the fields.

"I've been meaning to give this to you." She pulled out a little figurine, carved from wood, of a dog. "Her name is Lucy. Dad carved her for me when I was little. I thought you might like her. Faylon wouldn't let me get you a real one."

Louis smiled. "She's beautiful." He looked over at her lovingly. "Thank you."

Suddenly he heard the door slam, and heavy footsteps thudding towards them. Louis flinched. His brother's head appeared in the doorway, sweat lining his forehead. Caios.

"Well, what are you two doing sitting inside on a nice day like this?" His eyes locked on the figure. He laughed, a slight anger in his eyes. "Playing with toys? Louis, I thought I told you to feed the horses."

He sauntered into the room and grabbed Louis by the arm holding the dog. "You never listen, do you?" Caios said, pulling him out of the room. "You might be a cripple but you can still as hell do some goddamned work around here."

"Stop it! May yelled, though her voice was weak. "He didn't do anything wrong!"

His brother didn't seem to hear her. Louis winced at the firm grip, though not dared said a word, even when his hand was thrust over the blazing fire in the hearth.

"Drop it." His brother said, his voice harsh.

"Please…" He managed to stutter, tears brimming his eyes. Louis let out a shout, and Caios lowered his hand to the coals.

"Drop it!"

The burning was so strong he let go, though not of his own will. Pulling his hand to his chest, Louis crawled away from the flames, his brother kicking him in the side, hard, knocking him to the floor. "Do your damn work, and if I see you in here again before dark, don't expect to have dinner tonight."

The door slammed, leaving them alone. His ears rang, his hand stinging. May rushed over to him, embracing him. Together they watched the wooden dog burn into ash and coal, the light of the fire reflecting in their eyes.

Louis remembered that day so well, and vaguely he hoped that his sister was doing well at home. His siblings could never bring themselves to hurt her; she was so sweet, caring, so much like the mother they never had.

And oh, now there was Jacob. Louis felt terrible. It was his fault the poor man was sick. How in hell he had forgotten about the arrow was a mystery to him, and even being a bit delusional did not excuse that. And yes, his vision had been blurry and the broken arrow had been deep inside the wound, but *still.* A raspy, weak voice called to his attention, and out of curiosity he abandoned his train of thought and turned to face Marion.

"What did you say?" He asked, but Marion wasn't there. After a short glance Louis saw he'd run down to the shore, having left Jacob to lay in the sand. "Marion?" Louis tried to raise his voice into a yell, but he couldn't; all that came out was a rasping sound. While he looked to the distance, Jacob lifted his head beside him, squinting.

"Where-" Jacob stopped when he saw Marion running back to them, running despite his sore, tired legs. Louis wondered what his friend had discovered. Anticipation rose inside of him like a wave, unbreaking. His heart skipped a beat. *Something good, maybe it's something good at last-* and Marion walked up to them, smiling. He was laughing, laughing out of relief and joy, and only then did they notice the bag he held in his hands. It was theirs, but they hadn't had possession of it for awhile.

"Do you know what this means?" Marion was smiling. He searched through the bag for a moment, pulling out the rifle. It was the same gun, and to their excitement there were plenty of bullets to spare. Rations, enough for weeks accompanied it, along with their missing supplies. There was more, undoubtedly, but that was all he had to see. Marion pulled them into an embrace, and they couldn't help but smile in their relief. They were saved.

Then the thought struck him, struck him hard. It took Louis a second to think- the pack was Oliver's, there was no doubt about that, but why would he leave his supplies behind? Curiosity filling his mind, he stared down to the shore, where Marion had found the bag. The remains of an old campfire and a boat for the lake were all that was left... an old boat of rusted steel that must have been there before Oliver came upon it. There was a dock that had somewhat sunk into the water, and remnants of past inhabitation. The only streetlamp had been cracked, and was half-consumed by the lake. Then there were the tracks. The footprints of what could be no other than Oliver's boots led away, and to him it was clear he had been running. Other tracks followed his, tracks of four feet instead of two.

Large tracks, paws. He was chased.

Suddenly as Louis looked around him, at the eerily calm water and silent horizon, he didn't feel safe. He felt anxious, like he was being watched. His companions had noticed Oliver's absence and came beside him, now noticing the tracks that led out of their sight. The bag wasn't a gift, it was a sign. Something would chase, and they couldn't run.

***

It seemed that the beast that had been chasing Oliver was still hunting, for they saw no sign of the creature all of that afternoon and throughout the night. The travelers had meant to leave the following morning, but Jacob, to their surprise, was somehow recovering. Louis did not know how, and in some sense he didn't want to know. Louis had given him pills from Oliver's pack, given him herbs and remedies Marion had not once heard of, and it had seemed to help. He hadn't expected what he did to actually work.

Jacob could stand and walk a few feet with relative ease, and his fever was going down by the hour. Out of fear of cutting off the recovery, they decided to stay for as long as they needed, and leave only as soon as they were confident Jacob was well enough. Louis was, to tell the truth, greatly excited, for he would have blamed the death on himself if Jacob had not been able to recover. It was a time of aspiration, a time when the future seemed almost bright and worries were vanquished. It was this day when Louis went out with the gun in hope of hunting, though Marion had disagreed and insisted he go instead.

"I'm a hunter, Louis, I know what I'm doing with a gun. You can help Jacob more if you stay here."

Louis sighed. "I *need* to. I need to do something." He motioned over at the sleeping huddle that was their friend. "He's fine. Resting. I won't be gone long." Louis paused. "You've been carrying Jacob, let me carry back a hare or two."

Marion nodded reluctantly, and said no more. It would be hard, Louis knew, but that didn't stop him from sitting himself down in the sanctuary of some rocks and waiting, gazing out onto the still lake. It was afternoon when Louis gave up and started to head back. There had been nothing, nothing living that he could see. His hope dwindled, but he promised himself he would try until he caught something, that he'd try until his efforts paid off and luck came to their side. Then he saw it.

At first it filled him with exhilaration and joy, but soon, after another moment of looking, the joy faded into fear- a cold, panicked fear. It was a squirrel, fresh and scraggly, with patches of gray fur and muddy yellow eyes. It was already dead, but had not been for long, that much was clear.

What scared Louis was not the fact that it was dead, but the claw marks and scratches, still bleeding from whatever attack it had endured. Whatever had attacked this poor mutation was obviously big enough and confident enough to kill and leave the meat to spoil. *Killing for fun.* With a rush of adrenaline Louis tossed the squirrel into his pack and made his way back to his companions as fast as his crutches would allow.

The beast, he assumed, was back.

CHAPTER 25
JACOB FORTEMER
THE BARREN

Jacob could finally think clearly. He let his mind wander, enjoying the entertaining company of his thoughts. Before, in his delirium, he was confused, and felt as if he couldn't breathe- it was the state of unknowingness and exhaustion that he so dreaded to endure again. But while he was recovering, he decided to enjoy his time of peace. They had food now, much more of it, as well as supplies. Nothing could make Jacob more content at that moment, because, for now, they were well. Just a few day's rest and he was almost certain he would be able to walk alongside his fellow travelers and once again embark on their long, foreboding path.

As it was said, Jacob could think, but apparently not quickly enough to figure out what to do when Louis came back to warn them. His face was one of relief as he saw his friend approach unscathed, but melted into a look of concern and worry as Louis started rambling, letting them know of the danger as fast as his mouth would allow.

"The beast, the one we thought was gone, it's back, Marion. It's probably watching us now." Louis looked around, shaking, wary. He stared at them. "Do you hear me?"

Jacob blinked, utterly confused. Marion seemed to be just as puzzled.

Louis rolled his eyes. "It *means* that our enemy isn't just a ravaging beast but something smarter, with a… a thirst for violence I *really* don't want to mess with."

Louis's eyes were filled with fear, a prey-like panic. "We have to leave, it's close, it's not safe here-"

Marion put his hands on his friend's shoulders and looked him in the eyes, so seriously that tension rose in the air around them. Louis's anxious looks and rushing adrenaline faded away, his stuttering now a whispered mumble.

"What did you see?"

It was a simple question, but meant not only that they had no time for rabble, but that they needed an explanation before they set off blindly.

"I-It was, well, I was on my w-way back, and it, well-" Louis cursed himself for stuttering and resolved to just take the bleeding, mutilated squirrel out of his pack and show them. The claw marks were clear on the animal's hide, the dripping blood glistening like rubies.

"Where'd you find this? How far did you go out?" Marion's voice was harsh, worried; the feeling that they needed to leave, get out at that very moment was intensifying, and he shook with the fear of it.

Jacob looked almost like a child, panic filling his wide eyes as he scrambled back to hide out of sight by a gathering of rocks. His breathing was heavy, his body tense, as if expecting an attack. To the others he looked almost wild, and the sight filled their hearts with sadness. Jacob tried to collect himself, though one thought just wouldn't go away. *What is more pitiful, the beaten hound to bow to man, or the beaten man to bow to hound?*

It was a line from a book Jacob had read not long before he had left, and it stuck out in his mind now more than anything. Here they were the men, and the hound was the Barren, wild and ruthless in it's beatings. Jacob cowered before it, and neither Louis nor Marion could withstand for long.

Soon enough all would bow to the Barren.

All would fall at the feet of the hound.

THE BEAST
THE BARREN

I prowl in the night, I am the beast, the beast is me. My prey is plentiful, but rancid; there are no feasts of times forgotten. Where, I ask, is the life of the land? The lightning strikes green and the clouds gather, stones crack at the rumble of the earth. All perish. The meat I have is rough and foul, and does not fill my hunger. Oh, where the sky is gray and misery endless, I wander; I chase but do not catch, run with no soul or grace, wallow in self-pity and misery. I'm a foul beast, ruined by unseen magic and pain. Oh, what a miserable- wait... wait... wait...

That smell of blood, of weakness, it's here!

I've smelled it before, when I chased, when I prowled.

The night is fulfilling, they're exhausted, weak....

Why, fate is on my side.

MARION ARMAIS
THE BARREN

Never before had Marion seen such a hideous creature before him, and he resisted the urge to turn away at the sight of it. Upon the rock not too far away was the beast, sitting close to the ground, hoping to see, not to be seen. It could have once been a panther, a lion, perhaps, some sort of large cat. It had grown to be much larger than either animal, though, and once he thought about it, the only thing the beast had in common with either of the animals was it's figure.

All in all, it was ghastly, so much so that Marion just knew God would never put anything that hideous on the face of the earth. It bore a grey head, with two pure maroon eyes that, though the travelers didn't know it, shed blood instead of tears. It's mouth was filled with black teeth, long and sharp as the tip of a sword. Two wings, which would in no way help it to fly, folded out on either side, thin and peckered with holes. The rest of it's body was skeletal, lethal. Grey and white fur covered the flaking skin, stained with blood and dirt. A tail swiped back and forth behind, while sharp ears perked up on each side of it's head.

Had Marion been any closer he would have smelled the thing, and he would have wrinkled his nose in disgust. Eerie, menacing and foreboding as it was, the creature smelled of death. Not death in the way that it inflicted such upon others, but in the sense that it *itself* was dying. The scent was sickening and pitiful, rotten. Any closer than that, and Marion would have been just a pile of bones, wasting away as the beast got its fill.

So, not daring to look any longer, Marion turned his head and pretended nothing was amiss. It took more than he knew to tear his eyes away. Casually he walked back to his fellow travelers, sweat lining his brow. His heart thudded, each step seeming longer than the one before. An instinct in him wanted to run, to run as fast as he could, while he still had the chance. However his mind knew he'd be killed before he ever reached any shelter, and that his body would fail him if he tried. Weak and tired as he was, Marion knew the beast was waiting for the cover of night, and any sign of them trying to leave before then would trigger the thing to make an attack. His only coherent thought was to tell his companions of the approaching danger.

"Jacob? Louis?" His voice was barely above a whisper, and he gestured for them to sit across from him. Shaking, his eyes resisting the temptation to look behind him, he asked his friends first to look nowhere but at him or the ground.

"Don't, don't look, even when I tell you!" It was meant to be a shout, but Marion restrained and kept his voice low. "Don't seem shocked or anything, just… just pretend this is all… normal."

In his head he pictured the beast behind him, *knowing he had seen, ready to pounce, ready to kill-*

"Marion?" Louis said, looking into his eyes. Calming him. "Just tell us. What is it? Oliver?"

Marion shook his head, almost wincing. *If it was, you would've seen him already.* "No… well, no… it's ah," He paused, not sure how to say it. "The beast. It's here, up on the rock just over there."

Jacob spoke, his heart fluttering with panic and anticipation. "The one that chased Oliver, you think?"

He nodded.

"What's it look like? Is it…" Louis paused, unable to find the right word. "Scary?"

Marion looked at him in shock. "You're damn right it's scary, Jesus, it's a fucking terror." His voice shook, and he put his head in his hands. "And you'll see soon enough, I bet. Look, we can't run, we can't hide-"

He paused. The sound of the lake, of water, filled his ears for just a moment. He inhaled the cool air, an idea forming in his head.

"The lake, that's it-" Marion looked up, at the boat that sat on the shore, it's owner long gone.

"You think we could go? Now?" Questioned Jacob, now also looking at the boat.

Louis bit his lip, scratching at the stubble on his chin. "I can go down first, 'cause of my leg, pretend I'm taking a piss or something, then you both grab what you can and run down. I don't know if that thing can swim, or- or how smart it is, but, well, if it sees us trying to escape…"

There was silence once again between them, for they knew not what to say. After a few uncomfortable moments, they felt the urgency to get it over with. With a slight nod, Louis got up and brushed himself off before heading down to the lake. Marion and Jacob watched with anticipation looming over them, nervous. It was only when Louis reached the water when they realized they needed to move.

In just seconds, for there was little for them to pack, they grabbed their bags and rushed down to the shore. Noticing their haste and smelling their fear, the beast arose, angered that it would have to put up yet another chase. The travelers rushed, stumbling and tripping, though even at their fastest they couldn't get off the shore in time.

JACOB FORTEMER
THE BOAT

The world, in the moments that seemed so long, was a blur of sky, water, and sand. The lake reached into darkness, and reeked of salt and filth and disease. This became more evident as they splashed their way hastily into the chilling water, pushing the boat out and intending to board. Before that could happen, the beast was upon them, growling, pawing at the wet sand that led out into the small lake.

It was apparent that it's wings were useless, and Jacob was very much grateful for that. Yet that moment's hesitation was a mistake, for the travelers took advantage of it and started to board the slippery boat. Sweating, wet, cold, and afraid, they awaited to see what the creature would do.

Marion, the last to get on, was just pulling himself up when the beast lunged out into the water and slashed him, from his shoulder down to his lower back. Blood instantly colored his shirt, and with a shout he loosened his grip on the boat.

"Marion!"

Louis threw his crutches at Jacob and turned to help his friend, who was barely hanging on. The pull of the water grasped him, urged him to let go, to sink into the cold icy depths below. Louis grabbed his arm and hauled him onto the raft, pulling Marion away from the lethal claws of the beast. The weight of them all on the unstable boat caused it to wobble and sink a little, more than it should have, striking a slight panic in their hearts.

The beast had given up for the moment and was now prowling along the shore, glaring, unresting. There was no longer the threat of the beast, but they would not last long soaking wet above a cold lake, on a slowly sinking boat. Their only chance, it seemed, was to cross, though they still were unwilling.

Jacob looked around, petrified. "You don't think the beast will follow us to the other side?"

Louis shrugged. "I suppose we're the best thing it's seen in a while." His voice was reassuring, but the words held a different meaning; there was no telling if they would be followed.

Inside Jacob knew this was not the last they would see of the beast. The thing had chased Oliver for God knows how long, and most likely got him- it was certainly a possibility. Yet, in his gut, he felt that he hadn't seen the last of their former companion.

CHAPTER 26
LOUIS WILLSON
THE BOAT

Their journey on this lake was much different from their one in the marshes; here it was almost worse. The calm before the storm, the clear before the cloud. Soon the sight of the tormenting beast got smaller and smaller in the distance, and before long faded out of sight. Louis was glad. His eyes had kept wandering to it, seeing the creature prowl up and down the shore in quick short paces, It's anger felt clearly even after they had escaped its clutches.

The wind battered him, freezing his clothes and skin, biting at his eyes and ears. Exhaustion filled Louis, despair and worry. *What will happen to us? After all this, all our suffering, is this how we'll die?* In that moment, as the air cooled and the sky grayed, as the smell of death filled their noses and the blood froze in their veins, they knew. As the feeling of fear rose within him, as Louis wondered why he was still so afraid, as a pale white fin breached the surface of the water, he knew. When the fading form of the white creature disappeared again into the darkness below, he submitted. This was the end.

There was no one to save them now.

***

The small chilling waves lapped up against the sides of the boat, pleasing to the ears yet dreading when they heard no other sounds. Their boat was still buoyant despite the hours on water and the age of the metal, though it couldn't have just been luck. Louis had the feeling, just a small feeling, that something wanted them

249

alive. Wanted them to come so far and then fail, to suffer while knowing they were under the hand of a destined fate. That no matter what they did they were subject to the pain and misery by the will of the more powerful. That it held them up just enough so they could float, that it pushed them just enough so they could walk, that it fed them just enough so they could live.

And the worst part of it was that they would keep going. They would give in to the torture and go until they could no longer, or, more rather until it was seen fit for them to die. These thoughts swarmed in his head relentlessly as he lay on the boat, his back to Jacob, his feet to Marion. It was cramped, and Louis yearned to stretch out over the sides, but after the appearance of the strange things in the lake, he dared not.

It felt as if it had gotten much colder, but that wasn't all. Their clothes had deteriorated, so much so that they could be considered beggars, wearing rags on the streets. At this time it was night, long and never-ending. There were no stars to guide them nor any light beside for the moon, which glimmered somehow dangerously on the water. The creatures of the lake were still here, that much was clear. Their ghostly white forms drifted below them. Marion still bled from his wound, and though Louis didn't want to place blame, he couldn't help but see that as the reason they were being followed by these creatures under the water- and there was most likely more than one. Blood attracted all beasts. It was the summoning that always came through in the end, even if they did not wish it to.

Sometime during the night, by the time Jacob had fallen into a light sleep, the creatures resurfaced. Marion had passed out from exhaustion, breathing heavily, while Louis sat up, glancing around. He had heard them, their rumble, a change in the sound of the water. Louis expected to be frightened, to be paralyzed with fear, to not dare to move a muscle. It was the creatures, he knew it. There was something off, though. The air felt clearer, the moon brighter. He felt strange, sick, light headed, nauseous.

250

Louis had the feeling something much bigger was going on here. Something dangerous. By now he was pretty sure it wasn't just luck that had gotten them this far.

Just as his friends started to come to their senses, the world around them froze, from every droplet of water to the forms of the massive creatures down below. The air stilled, and there was a silence so shocking that none of them spoke. A sound, the only sound, drew them towards a spot near their boat. A mist rose from the lake, forming a human-like figure in front of them. The man glowed with an unnatural light, making the water around him look almost purple.

There was a rasping sound as the man breathed, harsh and bitter with cruelty. He wore a thin mask, silver in the light, with engraved carvings that even Louis had to admit we're a work of art. The mask covered his entire face, leaving neither holes or a place to see through. It was curious to imagine how he survived, though Louis put no thought to it now. Black hair covered the back of his head, untamed and slicked down to the nape of his neck.

He wore faded old-world clothing, a black cloak, boots and a silver ring that shimmered in the dim light. Unlike the rest of his apparel, he'd donned torn purple jeans and, strangely, some sort of shirt with illegible letters on it. The overall image was all very intimidating, despite the unusual clothes. The voice that came after was clearly a grown man's, and yet sounded a little high-pitched; almost psychotically so. He paced around them, marveling at their confused faces.

"I pity you, you know." He said, with a slight english accent. Just the voice told them he had relation to Maros, as their people had spoken in such tones. *So, he's Marosi.* The thought was frightening, and so Louis pushed it from his mind. *What's happening?* This was not possible, could never *be* possible, even now that such a thing as dark-radiation existed. In this world, though it had changed, the halting of time itself was still an unimaginable feat. This was a dream, or an illusion. It had to be. The man spoke again, pacing across the still water.

251

"You must be so confused, so..." He snorted. "*Worried*. I admit I've forgotten what that feels like." He turned towards them, seeming to look at their unbelieving faces. The man tilted his head.

"You don't believe this is happening, do you? Well, that's a shame. I've been rather lonely for a while, but now, whose fault is that?" He laughed. "Don't- don't worry. Really. I'll explain."

"Excuse me," Marion said, in an almost sarcastic voice. "But I don't recall having met you before."

They all sat up, trying to look stronger than they felt.

"Of course you haven't. *I'm in your head*."

They looked at each other, frightened, panicky. The courage leaked out of Marion's eyes instantly, fear filling them.

The man suddenly laughed. "No, you idiot, I'm not in your head. You really don't see it, do you? I must say it's been amusing watching you all on your little adventure, but the fun ends here. There's a power greater than you, than everyone in your wretched land, and, well, it's a-coming."

He sighed, like he was annoyed. "It's just that watching you stumble along in your misery gave me an a little idea. My orb- you boys know it as the Glass Shadow- gives me my power. Okay, that's all fine, but I have a problem. It's resisting me. It remembers it's past." His voice reached a high level of mocking at the end, and if the man had been showing his face, Louis would have sworn he'd rolled his eyes.

"Bla, bla, bla. All you need to know is that it's grown to hate me. I think it's got a plan of it's own. But *you,* you kids who call yourselves men, you give it hope. It's been aiding you through your struggles, protecting you throughout your journey, watching over you. Seriously, believe me, it does not care about you. It wants to use you for it's own purpose."

The man rubbed his fingers together as he paced, trying to find the right phrase. "Lemme tell you something, yes, well, I guess it wants *freedom*. Any white eyes you saw, that was probably my orb. Clever, you might say, of it to encourage you to come further. You might think you're strong, but I'm really sorry to tell you that

252

that's *so not true*. I mean, come on! You're a cripple, a bookworm, and an outlaw. In *no scenario* do you come out of this alive. It's the orb that's protecting you, and all that's kept you alive is the fact that it's not seen it fit for you to die yet."

The man paused, in both voice and stride. "The orb is wise, strong but... unknowing in it's power. It thinks it rules me, but who is the one trapped in a cage?" He shook his head, chuckling.

He's fucking monologuing, Louis thought, utterly confused. *Who the hell is this?* The strange man continued talking, and Louis thought it would be wise to pay attention. He was *literally* telling them everything they needed to know. Was this the man they were supposed to kill? Was he even an enemy? It seemed that he knew where the orb was, even had an influence over it.

"You're all adapting to the Barren. You might've seen this demonstrated already. The dark-radiation is poisoning you, and though your body will try to live, it'll fail. You're only human. It'll be an illness as you have never known, painful and everlasting until you lay dead upon the ground."

Louis sighed. *As if we don't already know.* Yet the next thing the man said made him look up in surprise.

"I know how to help you. To just get to the point, you're at my mercy." He giggled through the mask. "So...now that you know what you're really walking into..." He paused, tilting his head once again. His movements and gestures were fast, almost like a salesman appealing to a client. "Here, uh, lemme make you an offer. It's simple, really. I want full control of Rendar. I have the means to make this happen. The Glass Shadow doesn't want this, and even though I imprisoned it, it's power is far beyond mine. I'm using it for... certain purposes, you don't need to know, but it still has hope that someone'll set it free. It's secluded but it's influence still goes as far as the marshes, probably even the grasslands."

The man laughed again. "But look at me, going on and on. I suppose I *have* been lonely. No one to hear my struggles but my wretched orb and the- oh, well, you'll meet them soon enough."

Louis shook himself of his shock. "Why're you doing this? What do want with Rendar? What do you want with *us*?"

The man grinned, like he knew everything there was to know. "Well isn't it obvious? I want you to destroy the orb."

JACOB FORTEMER
THE BOAT

There was silence. Jacob sighed, putting his head in his hands. They had come to retrieve the orb and instead would destroy it. Ironic, almost. This had turned into something much bigger than he wanted. They weren't heros, weren't brave or true or loyal. They were commoners. People who just wanted to make a bit of coin and get on with their lives.

"Not anymore." The man said, looking into his eyes. He seemed to know what Jacob had been thinking. The mask melted away, dissolving into thin air. The face Jacob saw was not what he had expected. The man's eyes were a deep blue, but there was a dangerous gleam there that made him nervous. His thin smile was unnerving.

"This journey has made you into much more than just commoners." He spoke to all of them but looked mainly at Jacob, who gaped at him.

"How did you-"

"The power of the Glass Shadow gives me many advantages. But, hey, you're easy to read. The problem is I'm like a slave to it, and it to me. We're, ah, connected, and because of this I can't touch the orb, and it can't touch me. I can only kind of borrow it's power. The reason Rendar isn't mine already is because I can only use my power as far as the orb can reach. We're at a stalemate- but I've found a flaw. Only in this state, in the moments between time, can it not see us. *They*- they've granted me this one victory. But that's a story for another time. In all other places and times the orb is watching, listening. But now I've got the upper hand- when you submit the orb, destroy it, the power will be mine, all under my command. I can harness it."

He came closer, his face twitching slightly. "Now, now listen. This is very, *very* important. You'll crack it's glass, not shatter it, *only a crack. Only a crack, do you understand?* Then it'll have no mind, no will of it's own. Only a pawn. Destroyed, in a spiritual sense. *Just make sure it stays intact.* And you, you will receive the cure for your sickness and be on your way, the last and only ship to ever sail from this land again. The rest'll be mine... and if you refuse, well, I'll kill you." He smiled, the mask reforming over his face. "Farewell! Though I can trust I'll see you again soon."

"Wait!" Jacob yelled. "What are we supposed to call you?" There was a moment of silence before he said, "I was a king once. Still a king, though over different subjects... the title still stands, I suppose."

And with that he snapped his fingers and disappeared, the waves resuming their splashing, the strange creatures swimming unexpectedly down into the depths and the wind whispering eerily in their ears.

***

The shore's black sand stuck to their shoes as the travelers abandoned the boat and stumbled to dryer land. The air was quiet, the wind soft and smelling of the ocean. Not too far in the distance the land became drier, scattered with rocks, waving brown grass, and the occasional tree.

It was a dead place, but it was clear it had once lived. The colors were faded and the feeling quiet, but for the moment the travelers knew they were safe. For a second they just stood there, looking, their feet sinking into the sand. Jacob turned in a slow circle, stumbling a bit as he did so.

"Well, what do we do now?" Jacob asked, his voice weak and defeated.

Marion was silent, at a loss for words. Louis did not say a word either, though after another moment he handed out their bags and crutched up to a nearby tree, leaning up against the trunk and

256

sinking to the ground. His companions followed, and before they knew it they also were asleep, listening to the whispering of the wind and the heavy breathing of the only living things for miles.

CHAPTER 27
MARION ARMAIS
THE BARREN

Morning came slow and in a daze. Marion yawned and, for a moment, forgot of his troubles. He thought himself to be back in the woods in Calidor, where he would spend the nights under the stars and surrounded by trees, the only sounds being the rustling of trees and the call of the owls. He would breath in the fresh forest air, the air he had come to know and love. But as Marion opened his eyes it all flooded back- the comforting memory gone to be replaced by the sight of the wasteland before him. Pain in his back shot through him, the claws of the beast still fresh in his memory.

The wound would heal, as did all things in time. It could wait. However, other matters were not as patient. The travelers were going forward thinking they had no choice, that it would all be worth it in the end. At the beginning, so long ago, they had gone on for the coin. Before long, when they realized they had gotten themselves into something bigger than a simple job, they had thought they must go on for the sake of their world. Now, as they sat obedient like puppets of this King, Marion knew they had missed their chance to go back. If they did they would surely be punished for trying to escape their fate.

"What now?" The voice came from Louis, who squinted as he propped himself up against the tree. He shook Jacob, waking thier friend up. "What choices do we have?"

We don't have any choices, Louis. Well, at least none where we live." Marion snorted, somehow amused.

Jacob stuttered in response. "But-"

258

"Look. If we go back, we die. We'll never make it. We help the orb, we'll probably die. We help the King, we live, but regretting every decision we've ever made, never seeing our families or friends again. And, well, that's basically just a big *fuck you* to Rendar. We've got almost no chance of survival. This King, whoever the hell he is, has clearly waited a damn long time for an opening like this, from what he told us. This is his moment."

Louis frowned. "So what are you suggesting? That we just let him take our land?" He looked around at them. "We've come so far just to give up?"

"We're not giving-"

Louis interrupted him, frustrated. "No, no, we are. You think he'll just take over peacefully? How could he? It doesn't work like that, Marion. He'll kill whoever he needs to get what he wants. The man's a phycopath. I don't know exactly what he's going to do, but do know that *our people* will die because of him."

Marion opened his mouth, but closed it again. "Fine, we-we'll help the orb."

They would destroy the King, destroy that sickening bastard before he killed them all. It felt right... no, it didn't. Not really. It felt like their best option. Not right. Nothing felt right anymore. He looked into Louis's eyes, scanned his face then did the same to Jacob. They were covered in dirt and blood, their expressions looking as if they had lived a thousand years. He imaged he looked the same.

Marion perceived the land around them, a land that struggled to grow again, struggled to live. He thought of his past friends, their families, and the countless other lives that all depended on him. *On us.* He thought of what he had left, what he had to lose. All that came to his mind were the people in front of him, and that was enough.

To the others' surprise, Marion laughed in disbelief, and suddenly embraced his companions. He knew what he had to do, he knew his purpose, he knew what mattered in the world. His friends looked confused at first, but grinned, surprised, and embraced him back. The smell of each other, to feel each other there, to have their support, was all he needed. To have someone to talk to, to understand him. To be sane.

If I were here alone, Marion thought, *I would've blasted a bullet through this useless head long ago.* As true as it was, he didn't dwell too long on that thought, and instead closed his eyes to take in the last happy moment he would ever have for a very long while.

LOUIS WILLSON
THE BARREN

The waves of grass seemed alive, breathing to the song of the wind, dancing, mixing their colors of beige and faded green. The travelers could see into the distance, to where the fields ended and the rocky forests began. The air smelled fresh and new, and for the first time in a while, he felt safe. The sky was clear, and for a moment Louis didn't recognize the Barren. However, there was one thing missing; the chirping of birds, the signs of life. It made the scene silent, eerie.

Just as the King had warned them, Louis started to feel weaker; they all did. It was as if he had a slight fever or sickness and had no way to be rid of it. *No way but the cure offered by the King, though I doubt he'd let us live.* Louis suspected they were being played, by every possible player on the board.

Starting to grow tense at the silence, Louis stopped for a moment and searched through his bag, pulling out the long forgotten book of Maros, now tattered and torn from their journey. His companions looked back at him, waiting, curious. Louis opened the book to a random page and paused, looking ahead. Jacob nodded, raising his eyebrows expectantly. And so they started walking again, his own voice a pleasing sound in the near silence. They had done this a few times before, when the trails they followed were empty and silent.

Listen, we say, to the call of the wind
To the drips of the rain, to the cries of the sinned
Listen, we say, to the rustle of trees
To the crumble of rocks, to the hum of the bees
Listen, we say, to the creak of the board

To the silent breath, to the will of the lord
So listen, we say, for what sneaks up behind
Whether here, far away, or deep in your mind.

There was silence once again as they contemplated the poem, thinking on the echo of the words. Jacob was smiling, falling back to walk side by side with Louis.

"What do you think it meant?" Louis asked casually as he maneuvered his way around a rock hiding in the grass.

Jacob shrugged, still thinking, mumbling some of the words under his breath. "I'm not really sure. I liked it, though. Could you read another one?"

Louis was about to start again when Marion cut him off.

"Shhhh!" Marion held out his hand in warning, looking around. "Do you hear that?"

Louis sighed, annoyed. "Marion-"

The look he received was dead serious, making him close his mouth and listen.

"No, no no...." Marion's eyes grew wide, and he turned his head to the sky. Louis looked with him, a realization crossing his tired features. There was a reason this part of the Barren was flourishing, in it's own twisted way. Nothing came without a cost, especially here. *Goddamnit.*

"What? What is it?" Jacob asked, turning in circles, scanning for the danger. Louis looked panicked. The air grew colder, smelling damp and of earth. The clouds above them grew darker, the wind blowing restlessly.

"Rain, it's going to rain."

Marion turned to Louis, his expression looking frantic. He was clearly thinking fast. Without a second of hesitation, Marion took Louis's arm, tugging him forward.

"Shut up. We need to go, now."

"Why? What's so wrong with rain? *Marion!*" Jacob's voice cut through the wind.

Louis was still trying to escape his friend's grasp. "Dammit, let me go, Marion!" The other man ignored him.

"Just go, come on! We gotta find shelter!" Marion took off running, a feat that seemed like a miracle. Jacob still was recovering from being ill and marveled at how Marion could muster the strength. However, something was obviously wrong. Wondering if his friend had gone crazy, he ran into the grass. Louis mustered ahead as best he could. *What the hell is wrong with rain?* He thought, utterly confused. He had an idea he didn't quite want to confront, and it lurked like a shadow in the back of his mind.

"Dammit, Marion!" Louis shouted. "Wait up! What the hell do you think you're doing?"

"Saving your life!" Marion yelled back, frantically searching for something in the distance.

They pushed through grass, the smell of rain, dirt and earth filling his nose. A moment later they were in the open, the grass turning to rock and soil. A cave loomed in front of them, a wide opening in a hill of stone. Louis could hear Jacob yelling out behind them, but Marion did not stop. Just as he had dreaded, the splattering of rain filled his ears, the cold drops piercing his skin like icicles. At first Louis wondered what Marion was so worried about, then it hit him. *Rain is... evaporated water, yeah, okay, and water comes from.... Oh.*

The lakes, the rivers, most of the water sources in the Barren were contaminated with dark-radiation. And it wasn't only that- the sky above them was already poisoned, and whether the water had been fresh or not it certainly wasn't now. They would be affected faster if they stayed out in the open. Louis could feel it already, the sickness, washing over him. The radiation, twisting his insides, changing him, killing him. The thought made him sick, but he held back his nausea.

It seemed that Marion felt it too, for he slowed his pace. Stumbling he reached the cave, coughing. Jacob arrived a few moments later, his face pale and thin and terrified. He nodded to Marion, looking back outside. Louis came behind them, immediately throwing up before rolling onto his back, groaning. It was pouring now, soaking the once cherished field with poison.

Squinting his eyes, Jacob walked deeper into the cave, stopping where the light did. It was dark, so dark that Louis thought it would be hard even for a flashlight to penetrate. Jacob seemed to know, though, as he gazed into the darkness. Seemed to see things that weren't there. A cold wind breathed up from the depths, the throat to a monster who wanted nothing more than to have them in it's stomach. Jacob took a fearful step back, then another. He turned to look into the rain again, as if deciding which one was worse.

"Jacob." Marion called, but Jacob did not falter from his daze. "Hey, Jacob."

"What?" Jacob sounded impatient, anxious.

"We'll wait it out. It should let up soon."

His friend nodded, but seemed unconvinced. He was right to be so, for the rain did not let up. For two days the travelers waited, two days of doing nothing but trying to avoid the streams of water that ran down as far as they could see into the cave.

During this time, they were once again attacked by their sickness. Jacob started coughing blood, while Marion was retching an empty stomach and all of them were covered in sores and rashes and blisters. It was morning of the third day, when the rain showed no sign of stopping, that Marion proposed they go into the cave.

"We know we can't go out there. We don't have a choice."

Jacob glanced worriedly into the darkness, frowning. "Most likely we'll just die wandering around in there. We don't even know where this leads, much less if it goes anywhere at all."

There was silence to this, a dawning fear. Marion started to kick the rocks with his boots, in anger and frustration.

"Still, what-" He stopped mid-sentence, with his mouth still open with the hope of an argument. Marion had spotted something buried in the rocks. How he had not seen it sooner was a mystery to him, but now it stood out as clear as the sun. It was a gleam of silver, or some other metal, and just a few moments of frantic digging revealed it to be a helmet, rusted and dented. There were bones as well, though he threw those aside.

Jacob rushed forwards, eager. Grabbing the helmet, he brushed the dust off and held it up to the dim light.

"This is the passage." He whispered, in awe. This helmet proved it- just by looking at the symbol engraved in the metal, the head of a bull, proved that the soldiers of Maros had been here. That they had stood where he stood, guns ablaze, protecting the King of the city Valca to the east, Amor as he rushed to warn Vandor of the oncoming attacks from Rendar. This was a site of the Lost War- the conflict where, ironically, both sides lost everything.

"Excuse me?" Marion asked, leaning in, trying to get a look. Recognition shone in his eyes when he saw it, understanding. Louis, too, had an inkling of what it meant.

This cave lead directly to Vandor, to the center kingdom, to their destination. It was a blessing, and should have had them on their knees thanking whatever was watching over them, yet it was also a curse. Who knew what had happened to the tunnel over the years? It could have collapsed, could have been taken by dark-radiation, and there was a good chance something was living in there. Hell, he was almost certain something was living in there. Louis didn't know much about this cave, but he knew their luck, and based on their previous encounters he guessed that at least one of those predictions were true.

"Is there really a choice anymore?" Marion asked, looking out into the rain. It might be the last time he he could see such weather, or even see the sky.

"No. I think it's this-" Jacob gestured to the cave, "-or that." He tilted his head to the storm. "And I think we know which one has a higher chance of killing us."

The others nodded, understanding. And so the travelers made a decision; one they would surely regret.

"We'll need light, then, Jacob. Or do you expect us to go in blind?" Marion's confidence had faded into frustration, and though he would not admit it, fear. The dark had always been an enemy of man, and only those willing to accept it would ever truly be safe from it. Louis knitted his brows together in confusion at the sudden hostility in Marion's voice.

Louis's own proposition was muffled by the sound of the rain, interrupting the newfound tension. "I, uh, I still have some oil left, and the lighter. If we use it now we'll have to find other means for fire afterward. Winter is close, so I was saving. We'll have to be careful."

Jacob nodded. "If it comes between being cold and having sight, I think I can stand a little chill."

Marion did not protest directly but frowned, concerned. He turned Jacob around by his shoulder. "We can't use it all. Have you ever been cold? I mean, really, actually cold? What happens when we freeze half to death? When we have no fuel left to burn, and lose each other in the dark? Please, we have to consider something else." Marion paused. "This isn't a good idea, I can feel it. There's something off."

Jacob looked shocked. "Oh, so just because you have a feeling, it means we should stay and wait? Until what? Our food is gone and we starve? The rain won't end anytime soon, this *is* our only choice."

"Hold on, hold on!" Louis looked up at them, annoyed. "Shut up, both of you! Do you see what's happening? Just... just stop fighting." They looked at each other in silence.

Marion sighed, shaking his head. "We can go. But when we're stuck in the dark as blind as dead men, all hope gone at the mercy of whatever the hell's in there, think on this moment. *Think on it.*" The last part he said bitterly, his eyes as hard as stone.

Louis rolled his eyes, shaking his head. *Jesus.* The tension in the air between them could have been cut with a knife. "Let's just get this over with." Louis dug through his bag, taking out their smallest blanket and ripping it up.

"What are you doing?" Marion asked as he tore the rags.

"Making a torch, what else?" He responded, frustrated. *To hell with the both of them. To hell with the Glass Shadow.* Louis agreed that going in was their best chance, but at what cost? He was already a cripple- and here they were expecting him to follow them wherever they went. He couldn't make it out here by himself, he knew that much, but was it too hard to take his disadvantage into account when making decisions like this? If there was something in there, Louis couldn't run, he couldn't fend for himself. There wasn't a guarantee that they wouldn't leave him and save themselves. *Men show their true selves when faced with fear. Fear strips you down to instinct and controls you like a puppet.* He pushed through these thoughts of spite as he took out the last of their oil and started to soak the cloth.

At the same time, though, he felt the frustration of his fellow travelers. It wasn't easy to travel with a cripple, and at the beginning they must've hoped for Louis to die early to spare them the inconvenience of caring for him. He had been a burden, he knew this, and he *accepted* it. There was nothing he could do to change that. So, Louis discouraged himself from thinking such selfish thoughts. They had sacrificed everything for him, as he had for them. That was that.

He kept the peace between Marion and Jacob, who both felt strongly about their reasons, but he didn't really have many opinions of his own. In truth he cared little what they did- if anything, he cared more about when it would end. Louis knew he would die. He could feel himself weakening not only mentally but physically; he just hoped he could help get his friends to their goal before that happened. Blinking, he concentrated on his work.

His thoughts were so jumbled now, so conflicting, so confusing. Furrowing his brow, he grabbed one of bones Jacob had tossed away and started to wrap it in the cloth. *Why am I here? Why am I still going? Why is this so hard? Since when have I needed to make the decision between a dark cave and a poisoned surface?* He strained to remember.

Money. That was it. He had done it for money. Louis paused and laughed at himself, recalling the memory. But no money was worth this much pain. Not even all the coin in Rendar could convince him to do it again. Not a million women, not unlimited power, not even the promise of another leg would sway him. With a start he realized exactly how much Rovas Mchenry had cheated them. If Louis lived through this, he swore to himself, he would strangle the politician with no regret and lead him to an early grave. The contemplation gave him immense satisfaction, more than it should have. Louis handed the makeshift torch to Marion, along with the lighter. His friends did not notice his change of character, however, and instead asked him if they should make more than one.

"I can't carry one, and our supplies'll go down twice as fast. Here, carry these. We'll take it one at a time." He responded.

Louis tossed the other three usable bones to Jacob, who observed them, unimpressed. "How long will these even last? They're dry."

Marion sighed. "It's all we have, Jacob, unless we can put some use to that stick up your ass."

Louis laughed, well-humored, though Jacob did not. "Looks like someone can't take not getting their way. I'm surprised, though I guess you can't expect much from a Rat."

Marion turned on him, fuming. "Yeah? And what's that supposed to mean?"

"I thought a thief like you might be smart enough to figure that out for himself, but if I have to spell it out for you-"

"And what the hell do you know about me?" Marion yelled, furious, fists clenched.

"I know that being some fucking criminal doesn't involve a lot of-"

"*STOP!*" Louis stood up, shifting his crutches. "What the hell has gotten into you two?" He felt like a scolding mother. The other men were silent, glaring. Louis sighed. "You expect more from each other, but you don't understand. After we've come so far, well, anyone who attempted this would have died a long fucking time ago. This doesn't help anyone, so *put aside your shit and deal with it later.*"

Louis's voice was deep, angry, and short of temper, causing the other two men to freeze. God, he was sick of this. It was hard enough without their bickering. His companions seemed a little shocked, but got over it quickly.

"Sorry." Jacob whispered, and Marion responded with the same. There was silence, but for the patter of rain on the rocks outside. The cold air pierced Louis's lungs, seeped into his flesh, but seeing his friends fight over a matter so small hurt more. *The cold that's outside and within us are both menaces to be wary of.*

MARION ARMAIS
THE CAVE

It was like walking in a dream, a nightmare, lost in the darkness of his own mind. Everything was an inky black but the faint light ahead, the small yellow flame that seemed helpless against the impenetrable mass of black around it. It barely illuminated the stone walls, which Marion could tell by touch alone were as wet and cold as ice.

Their feet splashed in the puddles below them, and dreadfully he thought that soon enough he would fall into one, sinking deep and never coming back up. Drops of water, their silent breathing, and the echoing of their footsteps were the only sounds. The rest was left to imagination, such as the scuttering of a nonexistent creature or the dripping of blood in place of water.

There was something about the cave that made it all the more real, unlocking barriers of the mind and releasing whatever was inside with no restraint. The travelers dared not speak, for they feared- well, of that they weren't entirely sure. Marion could feel the walls around him, sense them there; yet at the same time it seemed as if he were surrounded by his worst fears in an endless void. They were victims to it, as all men when afraid, but nevertheless they did not stop. Had they been alone they most certainly would have been gripped by panic and dashed for the light above. But they weren't. They had each other, for now.

The sound of pouring rain had long ago faded away, letting them know they were truly down beneath the surface. Marion couldn't even imagine what it would be like when they no longer had the fire to guide them. Their supplies couldn't last forever, and in truth he doubted they would last another few days. Their oil burned for a long time, but nothing could last forever. Not even the orb, the King, this land- not even the ghosts under the earth, starving for life.

***

Not even a day had passed, though to Marion it seemed like much longer. They had walked until their first torch had been reduced to ash, then had lain down where they stood and rested.

They were walking again now, the sameness and unchanging qualities of their journey making him restless. Marion was always tense, constantly looking over his shoulder, though he knew he would see nothing. It was torture, and any more of it would drive him insane, he was sure of it. This was his fault, he could have stopped them, convinced the others it wasn't a good idea. Hell, he had been the one who proposed it. Marion couldn't quite remember why he had done so.

His outburst with Jacob he regretted; something inside him had just seemed to snap. But had they waited a bit longer, the rain might have stopped, and they could have gone on. Their food was desperately low, and now there wasn't even any game down here to hunt. Marion found himself praying that the tunnel had collapsed, that they would be able to see the sky again.

Just the thought that he was wishing to be on the surface of the Barren made his stomach churn- he had never guessed there would be time when he would want to go back up there. Hopefully Marion breathed in the air, hoping for something fresh, something like the cool breeze of an autumn day- but all he got was the bitter, chilling air of senescence. They were on their last reserves, desperate for an opening to the world above. Being here, sure that the others would've thought of it, reminded him of the cave under the graveyard.

It was only when Marion was about to suggest the dreaded option of turning back, did he feel a slight change in the air. It was subtle, but noticeable, for he had become much too familiar with the scents and temperature of the cave. They looked at each other in the dimness of the torch, the light gleaming in their eyes, which were a little too auspicious for his liking. Marion hoped, but knew to be wary; they had been tricked before.

Cautiously the group moved forward. Desperately he prayed there was an opening ahead. The ceiling above them crumbled away only to be replaced with empty air, echoing and mysterious. The ground below spread out, to the point where they could just barely see the curving walls. The travelers found themselves in a large cavern, strange and dominant in it's power. A wind, icy and unforgiving, swept through the cave, creating the distinct sound of breathing. The torchlight bounced off the cave walls, glimmering on the ceiling like sunlight through glass.

At first it seemed empty, as all he could hear were their own much too loud footsteps. It was strange that this should be here, Marion thought, for never had he heard or read of any such thing; but he was the last person who would know this. It was Jacob who did the reading, Jacob who knew everything. Yet when he turned to look, even the bookworm looked confused. Stranger than that was the hint of blood in the air, fresh and tingling in his nose. Something was wrong. Something was here.

Marion took a few steps ahead, looking around in wonder. His boots crunched on what looked like glass, causing him to freeze. He looked down and saw that it was indeed what he had thought, but the question was scarier than the answer- where had it come from? None of the travelers dared move a muscle for minutes afterward. They were listening for a sound, a whisper... a trap. They weren't disappointed. There was a faint dripping sound, consistent, now unforgettable that they had heard it. Something warm dripped on Marion's face, and when he wiped some off and held it by the torchlight, he saw the dark red gleam of blood.

The others saw this too, and at the sight of it Jacob let out a little whimper, like he was about to say something but decided to hold it back. For a grown man it seemed almost cowardly, but neither Louis or Marion judged him. Had they tried to speak, it most likely would have sounded the same. Before they knew it, there was another sound, a rustling or clattering, wind chimes in a summer breeze. However, it wasn't as pleasant, as they soon came to see. In a moment Marion saw them- hundreds, what could have been thousands of crystal bats swarming down from the ceiling, their screams shrill like cracking glass. Their wings were as sharp as blades, clear as still water. They had eyes like the ice on a frozen lake, seeming intimidating despite their unusually small size.

The travelers covered their ears in response to the bats' shrieks, falling to the ground. The torch fell from Marion's hands, the flame vanishing; and the glowing embers were the only light, the only heat in the dark cave below.

CHAPTER 28
LOUIS WILLSON
THE CAVE

Pain as he had never known came upon him, but not the pain that anyone might think. It was as if Louis had a scratch on his back, in the one place he could never reach. And yet the scratch was not a scratch but a cut, slashed into him over and over and he could do nothing, *nothing* about it. The travelers scrambled in the darkness for cover, swatting away the relentless glass bats as they did so. Louis somehow managed to escape the swarm for a moment, crawling away into the darkness.

The bats, for some reason, had not bothered to attack him much. It was enough to keep him down on the ground, that was for sure. Perhaps it was because they knew he could not run. But it was no use dwelling on that thought now. Louis managed to reach the oil in his pack, and scrambled with the lid, breathing heavily in his panic. The metallic smell of his own blood was repugnant in his nose, the fear so strong in his heart he could barely think. After what seemed like an eternity Louis got the lid off, and with all he had left he threw the can at the torch, hoping beyond hope. Just as he'd expected, the shiny black oil spread slowly around it, bursting into flame the moment it touched the glowing embers.

He smiled proudly as blood dripped down his face and into his mouth. The bats screeched in fury, most of them retreating into the darkness. Their eyes shone in the firelight, menacing. Louis dared not look too long. Instead he rose, grabbing his fallen crutches and nudging his friends to get up and move. The fire still burned bright, and would for another few minutes, but that did not mean safety. They were never safe. They never would be.

"*Please, get up, get up!*" Louis begged as they got to their feet. To his despair he saw his friends were delusional, stumbling and bleeding. Their clothes were tattered and soaked dark red; in fact, they were almost as slow as he was.

Keeping his wary eyes on the creatures, he led them to the opposite tunnel, leaving their charred torch behind. Painful wheezes filled his ears to take place of the shrieks, and not too long into their escape Louis realized he almost preferred the latter. His friends choked back sobs as they brushed their fingers over their own slashed, mutilated bodies.

Marion's left eye had been slashed, the scar running high from his forehead to the top of his cheek. Blood and white tissue dripped from the socket like tears.

They were making decent speed, better than Louis had expected. It was the fear of the creatures behind that drove them onward, nothing else. The fear of pain pushed them on, not the will to live. Their goal was the same, but their motivations had changed. It wasn't something he liked.

(LouisLouisLouis freeus free us we're close now, nowfree us) He shook the voices away. *Not now, not now,* he thought. These visions, these voices, disturbed him. He hated it. They were louder the further they traveled, louder and more frantic. *(Louis pleaseplease we're blind LouisWE'RE BLIND)*

"Louis?" Jacob said, wiping blood from his mouth. The man looked at him, with sadness in his eyes. "Thank you."

There was a silence, not uncomfortable but... full of relief. Thankfulness. Bitter joy. It was an aching in their hearts, because they knew there would be no happy ending to their story. This thought filled Louis with a slight sadness, but not as much as it used to. Now he was accepting in their fate, and was very glad that he wasn't alone.

JACOB FORTEMER
THE CAVE

Jacob's eyes were filled with blood, and all he could see was red. He could still see some, however, unlike Marion. *His* eye, Jacob was sure, would be of no use to him as long as he lived.

Everything hurt so much, he wanted to fall, wanted to cry, but every time he tried something inside him pushed him onward. It seemed strange to Jacob that the creatures behind them would not follow. He could hear their screeches well enough, echoing through the tunnel. How were they not upon them? It was a mystery to him, but at the moment, there were more pressing matters at hand. Maybe the bats couldn't leave the cave. Jacob didn't bother to question it.

With a determined concentration he focused on the path ahead. There was no longer any light to guide them, and before long the blackness swallowed them up completely. Sound was their light, touch their color. Being blind was terrifying. Jacob felt as if he was searching for something he would never find; in a place so crowded that he couldn't find his way; trapped in a cage with the door unlocked, yet unable to find the handle.

And with all they had seen, Jacob couldn't help but envision the ghouls from under the graveyard around him, staring with an emptiness that chilled him to the bone. He saw them so clearly, and once he thought he even could smell them, their rotten stench, of life and death. He could hear them, scratching, shuffling. It haunted him, and he hated it. Jacob knew that the others had the same problems, perhaps even with different nightmares. They wandered for so long that eventually there was no sound at all but their own footsteps, making Jacob feel more alone than ever.

To their good fortune, the air around them seemed to brighten. A breeze filled his nose with fresh air, and although it was the air of the Barren, it filled him with joy. In his realization Jacob tried to smile, but his mouth was filled with blood, so he settled instead with a thankfulness in his heart. None of them ran towards the opening, but that was okay. They didn't have the energy, and he wanted to cherish their good fortune for as long as they were able. To his joy they came upon the exit, the place where the tunnel had collapsed and the rubble led up to the surface like stairs leading up to heaven. The sunlight blinded him, making the world above look blurry and white.

Jacob wiped the blood from his eyes. Louis had fallen to his knee, like a pawn before a king. The cripple knelt his head and took the rubble of the stone in his hands, staring. Jacob was certain his friend was delusional, but another part of his mind saw the beauty in the scene.

Despite being in the cave for no longer than a few days, it had seemed like an eternity. Jacob glanced at Marion, who was feeling along the wall, tracing the cracks- as if analyzing something he'd never seen before. After a moment the poor man reached up to lightly touch his face, his torn eye. When Marion felt it he winced and pulled back, his hand covered in a dark red.

In the corner of his vision Jacob notice something out of place, though he wasn't sure if his suspicions were correct. In wonder, his eyes never leaving the spot, he crawled over to the edge of the rubble. Half the ceiling lay across it, not to mention countless rocks and a fallen grey tree. But under all of this, under their path to the surface, was a hole that plunged into the depths of the earth.

As Jacob got closer he could feel the radiation, could feel it seeping and crawling like a starving insect. The pit reeked of it, reeked of rot and blood. He pushed away a rock, letting dust and stones fall down into darkness.

He never heard them land.

MARION ARMAIS
THE BARREN

The hole underneath the rubble was indeed a mystery, and Marion would have assumed it was a natural erosion or fracture if not for the black liquid running down the sides. He sniffed it, coming to the realization that it had the metallic scent of blood. Though his companions had not seen it before, Marion was grimly reminded of the temple, and the pit eerily similar to this. Louis and Jacob glanced at each other, and he knew they were suspecting that it wasn't unlike what they had found when they'd escaped from under the graveyard.

Eager to depart from the maw of the cave, the travelers climbed the pile of rocks to the surface and stood, staring at their surroundings. Louis was up last of all, but did not ask for help. They all were covered in blood, injured, torn. Marion was still coping with the fact that his eye had been mauled beyond repair; it felt strange. A part of him refused to believe it. He did not move, just gazed into the horizon. A breeze blew in from the west, cold and whistling through the rocks. They were once again in a barren landscape, to his disappointment.

Marion especially had hoped for something better, if only to prove his point that the surface would have been better than the cave. However, no one needed convincing on this matter, not even Jacob. He wasn't willing to say the words *I told you so,* as he knew how much himself and Jacob had upset Louis.

Now, in place of forests of withered trees and empty fields, there were hills and hills of black rock. Natural stone pillars jutted from the ground, creating shadows that grew longer and longer as the sun set. The shapes that emerged from the ground were unfamiliar, strange; as if a sea full of sinking ships had suddenly turned to stone. Perhaps it was result of the shifting of the earth,

278

similar to how mountains were made, or rifts. Marion reached again to touch his eye, and felt a pang in his heart as he felt the damage. He would never see again with two eyes. Never again.

They stood there, silent, as if not knowing which direction to go. Nothing was clear anymore. Marion had a grim feeling they would all die, whether they reached Vandor or not. *There might not even be a cure for this sickness.* Who were they to hope?

"That north, Marion?" Louis asked.

"I think... yeah. Yeah, that's north." Marion looked at them, seeming to follow what was running around in their heads. Then, a disturbing thought came to him, and he felt strongly he had to voice it. "Why would we even consider helping him?"

"Who?"

"The King." Marion responded, turning to them. "Have we come so far just to- to give in to the will of a... a...." He paused, angered. "He'll kill us when he's done. I know the eyes of a killer, and he had them. I don't know, not really, but I can't let him take our home. I can't let this spread. I just... after those things in the cave... I can't... I don't know."

"Well, I do. Whoever the hell he is, we can't trust him-" Jacob was saying, before he paused.

His face was turning from one of determination to one of absolute, terrifying fear. Jacob Fortemer's gaze was locked on a deformed bird perched on a nearby rock, staring at them intently.

It's eyes were a strange, pure white.

CHAPTER 29
A KING IN A TOWER
VANDOR, THE BARREN

On a tall stone tower under the dark sky stood a man. His hands were locked behind him, his posture confident. Acting like a royal, though there was no one to impress. Additionally, a silver spiked crown lay atop his head. It looked rather silly, as he was still wearing his torn purple jeans and old shirt, but the King didn't seem to care how strange it was.

For a long time he looked up at the night sky, pacing back and forth, back and forth. He never once looked down at the surrounding castle and abandoned kingdom so far below. The King was singing to himself, half humming the words. He walked forward, smirking. In the center of this tower was an orb, sitting atop an ornate stone pedestal. There was a cage around it, with no obvious way in or out. All was silent, as the King had stopped his singing. He sighed and shook his head, as if remembering a past thought. The King started toward the door that hung open, intending to leave.

Before he could do so, however, there was a white glow behind him that caught his eye. It was different than the usual illumination, brighter, swirling across the stone like sunlight through water. The King turned to find the orb's color changing to a midnight black, like the thundering clouds during a storm.

"You met with them. How?"

The voice was flourishing with anger and confusion. The sound was neither male nor female, perhaps both- for there would be intervals where it sounded as if multiple people were speaking, not just one. It was a harsh tone, one that was never taken lightly with the King.

"That's none of your concern. I thought they deserved to know what exactly they'd come to face." The King spoke in a way that was unwavering, showing no weakness and giving nothing away. Intimidating to some, but the orb took no notice.

"It is all of my concern. It seems you've just turned them against you." There was a smugness there that he hadn't noticed before. The King had expected some retaliation, perhaps frustration, but there was something about how the orb said it that made him think this wasn't the case. A sort of fear struck him.

"Meaning?"

"What did you expect? Did you threaten them? Tell them your unfortunate situation?"

The King stood there, opening his mouth to speak but biting his lip instead.

"Of all the stories and tales, of all the dictators and miscreants and wrongdoers, all of them have flaws. You have the most common one- you underestimate your enemy. That is a mistake, Illius. You're a fool."

"I know what I'm doing. I didn't tell them the entire truth." The man sounded more nervous as he talked, his previous attitude whisked away with the wind.

"You could have killed them. It would have been easy. So, so easy. But no. Apparently you had to monologue, give away your secrets, and waste a perfect opportunity. They're on my side of things now."

"We're on the same side! We can work together. We can *use* them."

"No, I'm afraid not. Yes, me and you want revenge, but the similarities end there. I want freedom. You want control. We can't have both." There was a pause. Thinking. *"What do you want with them?"* The voice was truly curious.

The King crossed his arms over his chest. "And you? What do you intend to do with them?"

281

"What I intend?" I intend to be freed, have you killed, and then dispose of them myself. I intend to wipe out every living soul and restore this land to what it once was. I'm not sure yet. But you guessed that already, didn't you?"

"They're at my mercy, under my command. They'll die without me."

"From what I've heard, they don't care."

And with that the King stormed through the door and down the steps, leaving the orb, as always, alone under the starless night.

CHAPTER 30
Louis Willson
The Barren

Marion had killed it, the bird. It hadn't been hard. The thing didn't even move, didn't even twitch when he had smashed it with the rock. The white in it's eyes soon faded away to reveal a beady black.

"It looks edible." Louis mentioned as he sat on the rock, picking it up and dangling it by it's leg. For a moment they had forgotten about their significant lack of oil, but the mention of cooking something brought back the grim thought.

"Could we eat it raw?" Inquired Marion.

"Could we *what*?" Jacob asked, disgusted. "You can't be serious. I want nothing to do with it." His face paled. "I can still see the white in it's eyes."

There was an uncomfortable stillness, interrupted only when Louis frowned and argued his point. "A few days from now and we could be wishing that we'd ate it."

"A few days from now and we could be dead." Jacob noted, taking the bird and dropping it on the ground. "Let's go."

Louis looked grimly back at the creature, trying to ignore the nagging in the back of his mind that told him to go back and take the risk. The thin, mutated bird looked so appetizing to him that he began to worry about his sanity. They were already sick; they didn't need anything else to worry about. Besides, the thing did look infected, perhaps on the verge of death.

His mind cleared for a moment, and so Louis turned away and focused instead on the hazy distance. They *were* sick. At first he'd pushed it to the back of his mind, like it was nothing, just a threat. It was like having nausea- he knew he was going to throw up, he just didn't know when. It would come unexpectedly. Louis could feel it, even now. *But we have time. Enough time.* His thoughts were interrupted by a voice beside him. Marion.

"Louis?" He asked, as if requesting permission to speak. It was clear both of the other men felt regret at what had conspired before entering the cave. Louis looked back, seeing that Jacob had fallen behind to walk at his own pace.

Louis was too tired to be bitter, or harbor any grudges. A part of him just wanted it to be over. "Yeah?"

"Look, I know this- this whole thing is one huge nightmare for you, and I'm sorry." Marion sighed. "I'm sorry for all the crap you have to go through. I'm sorry for arguing. But that doesn't mean you have to always be sorry for yourself."

Louis tensed. This wasn't what he was expecting. "What does that mean?"

"*Please.* I know you, Louis. I know you think you're a fucking disaster. And maybe you are. That's up to you. But me and him?" Marion gestured to Jacob behind them. "We don't think that. Not one bit. After all this- hell, you're impressive."

Louis didn't respond. He was confused. Was Marion complimenting him, or insulting him? At this point he couldn't tell. The look on his face must have given something away, because Marion's words continued in a harsher tone.

"Look, you need to face the truth, whatever that is to you. But you need to stop treating yourself like a piece of shit, because you're not. You understand me?"

Louis nodded, the tug of a smile on his lips; so, harsh love. *I can deal with that.* "Uh, yeah. Okay. I- I'll think about it. Thanks."

"Don't mention it." Marion responded. He turned back to Jacob, leaving Louis to contemplate what had just been said. It gave him a new confidence, that much was clear. It was a good feeling; unfamiliar, yet comforting. Louis's small grin did not fade from his face, even after the sun had set.

***

Deep in his heart, Louis felt the dread that they wouldn't make it. They slowed each day, their progress coming to almost a grinding halt. The travelers all were suffering the effects of dark-radiation much faster than Louis had expected- he had no doubt they would die, at some point in the near future. But there was hope. There was always hope.

He looked his friends over, at their gaunt faces, ruined clothes, and dirty skin. They were unshaven, wild. Thin, hungry, and weak. In spite of having no way to cut their hair, Louis didn't worry about it. They were losing it faster that it could grow, and when he thought of it, it wasn't really growing at all.

Blisters and sores covered them, now scratches and blood. Dirt was in every crack, under every broken nail, in every wound. Lice crawled in the little hair they had left, thought even it too died soon enough. Louis's underarms, where he leaned on his crutches, were rubbed raw. He had no idea how he was even going on, much less moving. It was undeniable that he was strong, had grown strong over the years, but this was too much. Even his companions, who had the advantage of two legs, were a sight for sore eyes.

Back in Rendar they would have been mistaken for the homeless, Rats, perhaps wanderers or criminals. Maybe even the walking dead, for there was no denying that was what they looked like. To be considered heros? Saviors? That fact was laughable. Heros were strong, powerful, special and *always* did the right thing. They were clean in sin and health, responsible... perfect in looks and personality alike. *But are they?* Louis had never heard of a real hero like that, not once in his goddamned life, only in stories. He had grown up hearing about these heros in the books May would read him, had grown up with high expectations of who a hero should be.

Louis thought fondly of his friends. No, these travelers didn't have anything powerful about them, nor were they perfect. It was the little things that were special, he found; the things that really mattered. Jacob enjoyed reading, knew too much about the world in which they lived, had a daughter back home who kept him going. Marion, if he pushed enough, would tell him fondly about his garden; hidden away in the fields of the Unventured Lands, far from his life of crime. Getting to know his friends past their guises had been something Louis never wanted to forget. If anyone should be considered heros, it would be them.

All of them.

***

They did not know what they would do to put an end to the mysterious King, and therefore it was the only thing on their minds. They walked and walked, barely speaking, wondering what was to become of them. Each one left a trail of blood, dripping from cuts no one yet bothered to tend to. They were trapped in a sea of stone, with no ship to keep them afloat.

Nausea overtook Louis. However, when it struck, all he could get out was air and spit. Often they would have to stop and fall to their knees, heaving, then coughing. Constantly they were fatigued with thirst and hunger, though none of them wanted to eat. The time came when they stopped to take a rest and Louis couldn't get up again. The travelers were plagued with despair, losing hope that they would ever make it to face the King and confront the Glass Shadow.

***

It was just a week after their escape from the cave when the travelers found the river. It had seemed an eternity to them, however, and they were relived to finally find a decent source of water. The small stream was clear, sparkling like crystals in the sun. It flowed calmly and peacefully, the gurgling and bubbling sounds filling their ears like music. Joy filled Louis's spirits, hope and relief. Unfortunately it all vanished when Marion spoke, his voice dry with hopelessness.

"It might be a trap." He said, looking into the river's rocky bottom. "There's a trick, I know it." The others payed him no notice, Louis least of all. Marion was too suspicious.

"It's a blessing, for God's sake, just drink it!" Uttered Louis, kneeling and taking the water in his hands as if to see if it was really real. Jacob too was exhilarated, his eyes wide and unbelieving. Hastily he drank, only stopping to breathe. The water was cool and refreshing, the only good thing they had come by in quite a while. Marion did not trust it, but was too tired and weak to refuse it to himself. The travelers bathed and refilled their water containers, most of which had been filled with nothing but an inch of metallic tasting water.

When Louis was finished and could think of nothing else to do, he just sat there, not taking his eyes off the the running water. This was because of the daring thought in the back of his mind, the thought that told him he was hallucinating and that there was no river at all. That it was all a dream and if he looked away it would be gone, leaving him with once again the view of the unbearable, dead wasteland. This fear, though it might sound unreasonable to others, was very real in Louis's mind.

They sat together for quite a while, drinking what they wished was moonshine or liquor or whiskey or anything strong enough to dull their thoughts, to dull their pain. Sitting and drinking until they were sure that the river was real, and until the fact that the need for a conversation came up once again.

"How long do we stay?" Louis peeled his eyes from the stream and looked at Marion. He clearly did not want to make the decision. In turn Jacob too looked over at his companion, raising his eyebrows.

Marion sighed, pushing his hair back with his hand. "As long as we like, I guess. Get ourselves back together."

Louis smiled and shook his head, looking back into the swirls of the water in front of them. "I wish. Remember that we're dying. I assume the more we waste away the days the quicker we'll go and the less time we'll have to do whatever the hell we want to do about this mess."

"So just for tonight, then?" There was a grim tone in Jacob's voice. The others nodded, and returned to just sitting and drinking like they were somewhere very far away in a bar with no worries to trouble their minds or quarrels to trouble their hearts.

MARION ARMAIS
THE BARREN

The river had indeed been a blessing, one that wasn't so quickly forgotten. They never came upon such a river again, although their luck did get better from there. Perhaps it was just their mood, or something in the water of the stream. Either way, the travelers felt better than they had in a long time.

The water had attracted many animals, and they had shot down a hare. One would have thought the meat of the Barren was pungent and foul, something not to be touched. However, it was still meat, and the hare had little to no look of disease upon it. It to Marion it was delicious, if not with a slight metallic taste.

Something so good in a land of such despair was like a ray of sunlight in the eyes of someone who'd been trapped underground all their life, the first taste of food in the mouth of a starving man, a vagrant crowned king. Yet good things such as these were not in the plenty, and Marion did not expect another miracle.

It may have simply been to keep them alive and suffering, but such a hopeless thought was redundant. After all they had been through, how far they had come- to think such things would have killed them on the inside before they could even be buried in their shallow graves. Without the river, perhaps they would have been defeated already. They could not have gone on for much longer, as every man has his limits. Marion knew this, but was reluctant to believe it.

Now they trekked through the wildest parts of the Barren, the parts where the stone turned to forest. All trees were bare, gray leaves fallen on the ground like dead soldiers after battle; a cold winter wind blew them into the air, sending them flying. It reminded him of the ashes in the graveyard, lifeless and old. There was the strange feeling again, like they were bothering something that ought not to be bothered with. There was no other life they could see, for all of it, as Marion noticed, stayed far away from the grey forest. The sky was a broken glass window, cracked where the dark branches rose and twisted above them. It was eerily silent, as was most of the Barren. It was saddening, almost, to see such things. There was a difference between just looking upon something despised, and seeing what it had once been as well. Frozen, the travelers stood for a moment within the forest, looking over their shoulders to get one last look at the place from which they had come. After that moment they looked then at each other, though there was no need to speak.

There rarely was, anymore.

***

"Marion?" Jacob came up behind him, walking slowly behind Louis, who was several feet ahead. Marion glanced over at him, waiting. Their outbursts in the cave had changed something between them now. The air was tense, thick with unspoken regret.

"I've been thinking... and... and I'm sorry. I was the one who wanted to go into the cave, not you, and it's- it's my fault for what happened. The attack. Your eye. And... I hope you can forgive me for what I said. Before we went in."

Marion didn't respond. They walked for a moment in silence, before Jacob tried once again to regain the trust of his friend.

"I lived on the streets too, once. For years. I stole, and did lots of terrible things, but when I found Emilia, when I adopted her, she- she made me realize what I was doing. I grew to despise my life, how it was, the decisions I made. It's just that all of that, all of what you were... I hated it. It just reminded me of what happened to me and my daughter. I shouldn't have treated you like that. I'm sorry, Marion. I really am."

To his surprise, Marion's annoyed face grew into a soft smile, and he patted Jacob on the back. "S'alright. I was out of line too, I wasn't thinking straight. But it's over now. We're good. Don't worry about it."

And with one last reassuring grin, he caught up to Louis, who was waiting for them ahead.

***

A forest is supposed to feel different. More confining, more… full. Here there's something wrong. The trees were spread out, alone, isolated. It lacked life, a soul. He felt out in the open, weak and vulnerable. Marion, of course, was no expert on these things, but in his heart knew what a forest should be. What the world should look like.

There should be the green of fresh grass and trees, the blue of the water and a pure, clean sky. There should be life and love and change as the seasons come each with their own new bewilderments. Most of all there should be hope, and there is none here, and there will never be. It sickened him. Marion missed these parts of his old life; the days when he would run from his past, wander to places never mapped and see what no one had seen. Discover what no one had discovered, and have it be beautiful.

He yearned for the feeling of grass or sand on his feet, the taste of a salty ocean breeze or the sight of a flower blooming on a petal. Dew on the leaves, a fall wind through a field. Fruit in an orchard, snow on a mountain, the real stars and sun and moon in the sky. It called for Marion in his heart, but he knew he would never return to such things. And money? Money was nothing. It was the falling jewels of fresh rain, the silver of the moon, and the golden sweet of honey that were worth something more to him now.

"Do you remember it?" Marion inquired one morning, as they walked through the grey woods.

"Remember what?" Louis asked, splitting their last stale crackers into three piles.

"Home."

There was a pondering silence in response to this, as if they hadn't thought about such lovely things, as if they had forgotten. A faint light came to Jacob's eyes. He almost smiled. It was in remembrance of times before.

"Yeah. Yeah, I do."

He grinned sadly, looking into the distance, pretending he was somewhere else. It touched his heart, and for a wonderful moment Marion forgot about where they were, and what they had to do. All he thought of were the rolling hills and forests and streams of a land he would most likely never see again.

CHAPTER 31
A BLIND RAVEN
A GREY FOREST

The travelers walked through the woods with the wisps of past memories clouding their sights. They walked north in vain, or so it was thought by the King. None of them noticed the raven, the only living thing in the treetops above. It ruffled its black feathers and watched, watched with it's stormy unblinking white eyes. Within the tower under the sky, the King saw them through the glass as the orb saw them, as the raven saw them.

But the travelers knew nothing of this.

They could not kill all the birds in the sky, for fists and stones could only reach so far. For a long while they journeyed through the forest, though they were not sure precisely how long. In the woods there was no change, just the light of the sun and the darkness at night. It was similar to their earlier experiences in the Barren, though even then they had different rocks and dips and rises in the land. Here all the trees looked the same, the flat earth as well, while the point they were at now and the spot they had been ten miles back could not be told apart.

The travelers had been silent for so long now that it hurt their throats to speak, so there were seldom any conversations. It was no loss, though. They had nothing important to discuss, nothing that they felt needed to be vocalized to the others. This was clear to the raven. It flew close behind them, it's black wings spread wide. This sameness was constant, and the travelers quickly grew accustomed to it. Therefore when the day came when things started to change, they were at a loss of how to react. Fortemer heard them first, the loud hoofs, the sound that was not unlike charging into battle. He stopped walking, trying to listen.

"*Something's coming...*" He whispered, as if afraid whatever it was could hear them.

"Horses?" Willson asked, squinting into the distance. In Rendar it would have been obvious of such, but they had learned not to assume anything anymore. The sound filled their ears, louder with each passing second. In panic they realized they had nowhere to go, nowhere to hide. Terror gripped their hearts as they frantically looked around, searching their thoughts for any escape.

This was amusing to the raven, or rather to the orb. It was hiding from their worst fear, knowing it was just on the other side of the door and there was nothing they could do about it.

Armais stumbled around, running his hand through his hair like someone who'd been assigned a rather difficult task with only a certain amount of time to do it. Then he spotted it- the answer, the quick escape, the classic way to stay out of sight. It was so simple, so obvious, done in so many stories and tales and even in his own life.

"*Hey!*" Armais whispered, gesturing to the tree beside him with his head. "*Climb!*"

Fortemer did what was bid of him, looking back to his one-legged friend and offering his hand to help. Willson now was the one worrying, but wasted no time. As Armais climbed into his tree, Fortemer took his friend's crutches and did the same, reaching out his hand to pull the cripple up. The bark was dry and withered, no trace of sap or even insects. It left his hand covered in filth, from the years of wind and dust and dirt.

The sky became darker though it was only midday, and the frigid cold winds picked up, biting their skin and whipping at their clothes. The raven knew what was coming and ruffled it's feathers nervously, flying off into the gray, rainy sky.

JACOB FORTEMER
A GREY FOREST

Another misfortune was upon them, and they braced themselves for what was to come. In fear Jacob gripped the branches like a child unwilling to leave it's mother. It seemed in that moment time could go no slower, dread filling his heart. Soon enough, though, the sound of hoofs approached, and it was indeed the horses that were the cause of it.

They were black as night, mares that were bred large and strong. They seemed too wild to be tamed, too reckless to be trusted. Mounted atop each horse was a man, though they were like no men the travelers had ever seen before. There were even women among them, told apart only by their breasts and shape of their armor. All had skin the color of sand, and looked as if the same could be said for texture. Gritty, strange, rough. Blue eyes, ice blue eyes scanned the expanse of forest as the horses slowed and the riders sniffed the air. Their irises, Jacob noticed, were controlled, or manipulated like a muscle; the cold colors swirled and blotched and mixed around a center pupil. All of them were bald, black marks trailing over them in various patterns and symbols. Many had scars, though carried simple weapons such as bows and daggers, even guns.

The creatures were mainly dressed in black cloaks and boots to match their mounts. There could have been no more than thirty. Their leader rode ahead of the others, no difference to him but the way in which he carried himself, confident and ruling in demeanor. Jacob tensed, not daring to move or even to breathe. The leader smiled, rose his hand in the motion that no other should move forward, and spoke in the silent air.

"Clever, I must admit, but a classic." He laughed. His voice was like rough sandpaper, the accent of someone who was meant to speak a different way. The other creature behind him looked up, and at the sight of them whispered in the ear of his master, in a foreign and strange tongue. Jacob could barely understand it, but heard the follower address him as *Taire...* or something like it. The leader nodded, responding in the same language. He did not raise his head to look at them, though it was clear who he was talking to.

Shaking his head, he pronounced, "Come. Come down."

When no one moved, two of his followers arched their bows, aiming their arrows into the trees. Their arms did not shake, nor did their eyes blink. At command, no doubt, they wouldn't hesitate before shooting the travelers down. Jacob saw this, as did the others, so cautiously they lowered themselves to the ground.

Close up, the men and horses smelled of blood and sweat, of ocean salt and wilderness. There was a strange presence about them, savage but not dark. A gun was in one of their bags, Jacob thought, but... it was too late. They could never get it in time, never fight off so many at once.

There was a demeaning silence, foreboding in which that it filled their hearts with fear. They were men grown and still their opponent towered over them, making them seem like children being scolded. Skinny, weak, and poorly armed, they felt pathetic, like street filth, like Rats in front of kings. The feeling was demoralizing, knowing they were somehow lower than even these. They were looked down upon by the lowest of the low, and with that Jacob knew they were defeated. They had become no more than rodents scurrying lost in the darkness.

The leader was silent, as if waiting for something. With this thought Marion fell to his knees; he had no honor left to hold his chin up to the skies. Jacob followed him, as did Louis. There was a part of him that hoped they would be killed and have done with it.

"You poor men. You poor, poor men."

There was silence but the wisp of the wind through the trees. The horses shuffled nervously, feeling the tension in the air. Many of the creatures craned their necks to get a glimpse of the travelers before them- it seemed to Jacob that people like themselves were rare in the Barren. He was still unsure of how that would impact their fate.

"It has been spoken that you are the pawns of the orb and the King alike, yes?" The Taire asked.

Marion slowly nodded, unsure of any other way to respond.

The man clicked his tongue amusingly. "And which, ah... are you loyal to?"

The three men on their knees glanced at each other, for they themselves were not sure exactly. Marion made the decision for them, however, before their prosecutors could come to the same conclusion.

"The King."

He was so certain in his speech that it made Jacob look over the horde in front of them, searching for any sign that may have swayed Marion's opinion. *What is he trying to do? Get us killed?* They served the orb. Or did they? Jacob didn't trust anything anymore. It was complicated, that much was certain... *So why is he lying?* It didn't matter who they truly served, what mattered was getting out of here alive- even it it did please the savages' ears that they were supposedly on the same side. Panic seized him. Jacob prayed his friend hadn't just guessed. The leader smiled, and for a moment it seemed all was well. That was until he raised his hand and motioned for the archers behind him to shoot. The seconds seemed like hours, and in his heart Jacob knew they would be dead before they could even stand up to run. He closed his eyes, held his breath and waited. And waited. And waited.

Then the moment was over, and when Jacob opened his eyes he saw that the archers had lowered their bows with a confused look shrouding their faces. He turned his head to Marion, only to see that his friend's eyes had turned a shiny, cloudy white. Louis looked just as surprised as himself. The friend beside him then spoke in a voice Jacob did not recognize.

"*They are mine, in their hearts. I have them on the end of a leash. Let them live.*" The voice was drawling, amused. Not like

Marion at all. The Tiare frowned, glanced at the men in front of him, and decided to speak in the way that would escape their ears.

"Luceir, spare me the sound of your tongue, it has no place in my company. I assure you they are mine, so treat them as such. Make certain they live to cross the bridge. I gave your people a chance, one that can be reversed just as easily. Should you fail me..." The orb did not need to finish.

"Yes, Qasyies. It will be done."

The white faded from Marion's eyes and he slumped to the ground, motionless.

"No, No!" Jacob looked down at his friend, shaking him as if he were only asleep, clutching to Marion's shirt. Louis made no motion to assist; his eyes were locked on Luceir, who glared down at them with a faint distaste, as if he were being forced to do a chore. Jacob payed no notice.

"What did it do to him?" Jacob asked, his voice weak. Luceir ignored him, motioning to a woman behind, who approached and dragged them to their feet.

"Who are you? What are you doing?" Jacob interjected as they threw Marion across a horse. The woman did not answer him, but instead pulled a black hood over his head and tied his hands behind him. She instructed him to walk. He obeyed, stumbling in the darkness.

Jacob heard the sound of hooves and rain pattering down onto the earth. The strange tongue filled his ears in whispers and harsh tones, while the scent of lakes, fish, and strong soil filled his nose. He walked and walked under the gray sky and the rain, the cold wind whipping at his clothes and chilling him to the bone.

LOUIS WILLSON
A GREY FOREST

His crutches were wet and slipped in his hands and he hobbled along, his feet crunching the dead grey leaves below. Louis did not think, but listened. The leader's name was Luceir, though his followers addressed him as Taire. *Perhaps Taire is an honorary name, for a ruler or leader,* Louis thought. This was the only conclusion he came to, though he heard the word *Qasyies* mentioned often. He figured he would find out soon enough.

Louis was blind, thanks to the hood over his head. It was strange to not know where he was headed, but he knew he was safe for now. Thanks to the Glass Shadow. Had there been no interruption, he would surely be lying dead with an arrow in his chest, blood staining the grey canvas around him; and for that much he was grateful.

Jacob marched beside him, though no one else walked. They were all on their mounts. Marion was not yet awake, it seemed, and in his mind he feared for his friend. *What did the orb do to him?* It made no matter. Marion was not dead, that much he was sure of. Whether he would awaken or not... that was up to a higher power now, or maybe the orb, the King. Louis didn't know what he believed in anymore.

"Stop," The woman commanded, her voice harsh. She pulled the hood off of him, and Louis blinked in the light. "You follow Makkei."

His dagger was pulled from its sheath, as was Jacob's and Marion's, though, being unconscious, he could not use it. She pushed him forward.

"Who?" Louis asked, and she pointed to a boy in front of him, scrawny and most likely not over the age of twelve. She handed

299

the boy their weapons, which Louis personally thought was not the smartest of ideas.

The forest was all around them, and now they stood in a village by a lake. It was large, larger than anything he would have expected, with homes made from the rubble of old buildings and worn paths formed by horses and boots. Smoke rose into the air as men and women and children alike huddled by campfires. The air was a bitter cold, though there was no mistaking the distinct scent of smoke and woods. Louis could see strange plants growing out of metal cans and a few men building a raft by the shore. The riders who had captured them had moved on, tethering their horses and greeting their friends. *People live in the Barren?* Louis thought, confused. *But these aren't people, they're...* he could not think of a word for them, for he had never known them to exist.

Jacob beside him looked just as confused, but they were left no time to think about it. The boy spoke to them, in the strange language, though when they did not respond his eyes grew wide. He turned to the woman, who nodded, gave him a rather lengthy order, and then galloped off. Marion was with her, and Louis craned his neck to see where she would take him.

Makkei smiled, an honest smile. He didn't seem to look down on them like the others had. "Come. I show you village."

He wore a simple shirt with torn sleeves and jeans, though went barefoot. When Jacob did not move, Louis took the lead, stepping over horse manure and what could be nothing else but the contents of a chamberpot. The road itself may have been filthy, but the village itself was otherwise. The people were relatively clean, as was the water, it seemed, and the buildings. There was even a working water pump.

Louis saw a smith working weapons and his assistant working guns, while another man tinkered with a rusted watch. Some were cooking, others skinning animals. A few were training, kicking up dirt and spraying black blood as they fought. As he noticed, not all of them wore the same thing- some had jeans, jackets, cloaks, a variety of new and old-world clothing. One man even walked by clutching a strange broken device, which Jacob told him were once headphones; Louis resolved to ask him what that meant later.

"Where *are* we?" Jacob asked the boy, who was waving to a friend fishing on the lake.

"We are in Maros." The boy stated simply. Louis shook his head. That much was obvious.

"Who are you, then? Who are all of you?"

Makkei spread his arms, gesturing to the village. "Children of Qasyies, of orb, of glass... glass..."

"Shadow." Jacob finished.

The boy continued. "Yes. Qasyies gave us life, we can survive here. For that we owe it. It hoped we would set it free, but King found us and told us if we *ever* left forest we would die. Qasyies took pity and left us alone, but whenever a favor is needed we listen always."

"How do you know our language? Why... why do you even speak a different one?" Louis asked as they walked. They received many stares from the onlookers.

"Your tongue is hard to us. I learned for all my life and still do not speak it good. The Taire know it best, he tell us how, in case we meet your kind again. Marosi comes much easier. This is where you rest." Makkei gestured to a building to his left, and led them in. The door was a large rag, tattered, and the boy pushed it aside. Inside it was almost cozy, with blankets on a shelf and a fire in the hearth. It was bare otherwise, save a few bags and scattered belongings. Someone had drawn some sort of graffiti on the brick, but it was very old. A chamberpot was in the corner and a pot was on the fire, filling the room with the smell of meat and smoke. Two of the Marosi were asleep in the corners, and Makkei gestured to the travelers to join them. Marion was nowhere to be found, but the boy assured them he would be safe.

"He will be taken care of. Qasyies wanted him alive."

Louis knew it was reasonable to think so, but he did not trust them. He was right be cautious, but in his heart he doubted he would

301

ever trust anyone but Marion and Jacob for as long as he lived. It was even hard to trust the young boy, who had a dagger on his side and most likely the skill to use it.

"What'll happen to us?" Jacob asked, glancing warily at the sleeping men. "What... do you intend to do?"

Makkei shrugged. "I... do not know. I think you will not stay long." He said, handing him a can from the pot on the fire. It was filled with a grey black broth and cooked meat, the scent strange to his nose. Louis rose the bowl to his lips, but the boy quickly took it back before he could eat.

"I am sorry. I forgot you are not Marosi." He poured the gray liquid into the fire, leaving only the meat. "The gray is dark. Poison to you. We boil it out of meat, but your kind cannot eat it, or you will sicken."

"You're not affected by dark-radiation?" Louis asked, surprised.

"The sickness? No." Makkei affirmed. "We can eat and drink it, though the taste is... rather..." He did not need to finish. *Rancid,* was Louis's first thought.

"The meat is good, do not worry. Eat."

So Louis ate, the meat tender, though a little rare for his taste. It was cooked, so he did not complain. He ate until he was full, as did Jacob. It was a welcome feeling, and Louis felt almost himself again.

"Rest, while you can. But can you tell me... why you come to Maros?"

Louis smiled politely, thinking for a moment. "It's complicated." Another glance at the wide-eyed boy showed he needed a more specific answer.

Jacob continued. "To free the Glass Shadow from the King, so we can use it to cease the spreading of the dark-radiation into Rendar."

The boy looked confused. "I wish you luck, it would mean our freedom. Qasyies could help you, yes, but King is dangerous.

There is something going on, Tiare and his Ehsas have been talking of it, day and night. Whispers, too. It will not be easy."

"Ehsas?"

"I am not sure of the word in your tongue. They advisors, warriors, protectors, sisters and brothers by oath. I want to be one, but father says I must be hunter. There is less food each day."

Louis swallowed the last of his meat, pulled a blanket from his bag and retreated to a spot by the fire. Jacob did the same.

Makkei rose and made for the door. "You will need furs if you are to live through this. Sleep, I will find what I can. And here-" He tossed them their daggers. "You might need them."

The boy left, leaving the room eerily quiet. Firelight flickered about the room, casting light through the holes in the walls. Outside Louis could see the darkness taking hold on the grey forest; the men and women had abandoned their practice with weapons, the few walking along the paths disappeared into buildings, and guards were starting their posts as the sun fell behind the dying trees. *What else lives in this forest but you? The birds?* Louis thought as he saw them. *What do they have to fear?* These Marosi had to have been the most dangerous living creatures in the forest.

Soon Louis drifted off to sleep, though it was restless. The reason the town was guarded became clear before long. He slept by the fading red coals hearing the growling and shuffling of beasts in the trees, with the smell of blood filling his nose.

MARION ARMAIS
A GREY FOREST

Marion awoke to the sound of shouts, and the strong smell of manure. *Horribly* strong. With a groan, he turned on his side and heaved empty air into the straw and dirt. His head ached, and though he should have been hungry, the smell had stolen his appetite. There was another splat beside him as more manure fell to the ground, and he looked up to see the rear end of a horse glaring down at him.

"What in the hell-"

"You are Marion, yes?" A young boy stood over him, a dagger at his side and a bag in his hand. "I am Makkei. You follow me now, please."

Makkei tossed Marion the bag and reached out his hand. Marion took it, though it felt like gripping sandpaper. His shoulder throbbed, through when he reached back to touch the old wound he found it had been bandaged. He had gotten it so long ago, he'd assumed it had healed... His damaged eye, he found, was also covered.

"Why..."

"Why are you in stables? Jaone told me smell would wake you up." The boy saw Marion gently touch his wound. "Do not worry about that. It was infected, but we tended to you."

"Jaone?" Marion asked as he scanned their surroundings. He had indeed been in the stables, and took a moment to gaze at the town. People were up and about, though they weren't like anything he'd seen before. The last thing he remembered was their arrows aimed at his face. Makkei started to walk down the path, talking as he went. Marion had little choice but to follow.

"Jaone is an Ehsa, very respected, but my brother thinks that should not be. He wanted the spot when Feithor died." Marion did not bother to ask what an Ehsa was, but he was inquired to ask about Feithor.

"Who?"

"He turned to King for help and tried to escape forest. He failed, and he re- uh, re-deemed himself and became Ehsa."

"How did he die?"

About this Marion was curious. *What can kill men like this?* He thought as he passed a girl shooting bullets into dirty glass bottles, shattering them. She never missed, not once.

"One of the beasts took him in the night." The boy fell silent after that, and Marion did not push him.

"What happened to me?"

In truth he'd thought he died, and had been all the more confused when he'd woken in the stables.

"The orb took your sight, Jaone told me. To speak to us. She said Qasyies told us not to harm you."

Well, that's reassuring. They walked in silence after that, Marion trying to put the pieces together in his head. As he followed the boy, he found himself observing the town. Quite frankly he could smell nothing but horse shit, but the sights were enough. Out on the lake small boats fished and children swam, while not too far from the shore he saw women skinning and dismembering a strange white-furred beast. One man was trying to break up a group of children fighting over a rusted dagger, while others dug a grave by the woods. Banners flew in the wind, their faded colors a contrast against the grey he had seen for so many days. A few Marosi looked up at the sky warily and noted the gathering swarms of gray clouds, though it was of little concern to them beside the fact that they would perhaps get wet. Marion saw no fear in their eyes, and assumed it would not affect these people as it had themselves on the day they'd found the cave. This thought led him to wonder where his companions were.

Marion opened his mouth to ask, but stopped abruptly in his tracks when the boy turned to a structure on their left and motioned for him to go inside. It was large, largest of all he had passed, with a makeshift scrap roof and wooden walls- though the size wasn't what frightened him. Above the door, facing the lake, was a mauled head with the point of a sword through its gaping mouth. And, as he imagined, the steel went through the wood and into the room inside. Its eyes had been pecked out by crows long ago, and there was barely any hair left to speak of. Streaks of blood ran down its face, as well as the door below it. It had long since dried, clotting around the neck most of all.

Had it been male or female Marion did not know, but the sight of it opened his eyes to the world around him. He felt more alert, more aware... more afraid. He looked back at the boy, who saw his panic and smirked before walking away. Marion was left alone for a moment, alone as the drizzles of rain pattered down on him and the village around shuffled about it's business.

Without really thinking he walked up and pushed open the door, careful not to touch the blood. Inside, as he had suspected, the steel hilt of the longsword protruded for the wall, stained a dark red. It was the first thing Marion saw because it was the first thing he looked for, and afterwards he turned to face the voices.

It was a smaller room than he'd expected, though it was filled with the warm light of the hearth. There were doors, all closed. The windows had no glass, with only rags of curtains that were pinned over as to keep out the wind and rain. There was a table, and upon it a great white beast not unlike the one he'd seen some of the Marosi flaying by the shore. It was wolf-like, but strangely large, with night black fangs and a gaping blood-soaked maw. It's eyes stared at him, it's curious black eyes that looked much too alive. As if it were considering him as a future meal, though that was insane. *It's dead, idiot, it's not going to eat you.*

Marion told himself this, but after all the things he'd seen it wasn't too hard to believe such things. At its midsection, the shaggy white fur stopped and thinned, changing the back half of the animal to what resembled a bull. There were even horns on it's head, and the two back feet were hooves in place of paws. Marion was reminded of the beast they had encountered by the lake, with it's eyes dripping blood and it's skeletal grey wings. This was much less gruesome, but it had a fearful power all the same.

The hilt of a knife bulged out of its throat. There was quite a lot of blood, and the room reeked of it. The people gathered around the beast didn't seem to mind, however. Most of them were like the boy Makkei, with their sandpaper skin and strange icy blue eyes. There were two like himself, human, per say, one with a slight auburn beard and the other sporting dark hair slicked back in an almost professional fashion. It took him a moment to realize that they were, in fact, his own Louis Willson and Jacob Fortemer.

In their new furs and cloaks he had barely recognized them. It scared him a bit, to tell the truth. He didn't remember if Louis had had a beard or not. He didn't remember what color Jacob's eyes were, and he would bet his life that he wouldn't be able to recall the sound of their voices until they spoke to him. It was as if this was a dream, and he had woken up and was trying to pull the pieces together. *Blue, his eyes are blue.* Marion made sure to remember that about Jacob, though it had no importance, really; it might have been just to hold onto something true, something real, that wouldn't change, that wouldn't go away. Something human.

A part of Marion assumed his jumbled mind was an effect of the orb using him; though another part, a guiltier part, told him that he just hadn't been paying attention. That he had stumbled through this journey like a sleepwalker, only to awaken now- *but why*? He felt so awake, so knowing, like his eyes had been opened to see more than he had before. *Eye, Marion. You've only got one now.* There was a feeling this would wear as time went on, but once awake it was not so easy to return to sleep.

"Marion?" Jacob had looked up from their focused conversation and seen his friend standing confused in the entryway. Marion looked at him and saw that somehow his friend had changed. Perhaps it was how clean he was, or the strange clothing, but he acted stronger too. It was similar with Louis. His smile was the only good thing he'd seen since... he couldn't remember. They hadn't smiled genuinely since Amicus died, and Oliver had gone off on his own. *Why would you want to smile,* Marion thought, *when you have to watch your friends rot away before your eyes?*

"God, Marion, you must be starving. Why don't you-" Louis was cut off by one of the others, a woman that looked strangely familiar to him. She spoke in her own language, and one of the men beside her translated.

"He can eat later, she says. He needs to be here." The translator paused, listening to her additional statement. "She also thinks he won't have much of an appetite after-" The man grinned, amused. "His visit to the stables."

His friends looked confused for a moment, but shook it off.

"Very well." Jacob motioned for him to come over. "I'll catch you up."

In the moment of silence as he walked over, Marion could hear the pattering of rain and wind outside, and vaguely wondered in the back of his mind if the head above the door wanted to escape the rain. Then, a few moments after that, he wondered if he was going crazy. The others around the table resumed their small talk.

Jacob turned, embracing him tightly. "We're glad you're okay." He said, leaving Marion a little shocked. Louis hugged him too, the warmth very much welcome. He wasn't much used to such affection, but he found that he liked it.

Jacob started to explain. "These beasts have been terrorizing the village. At first it was only a few, and on rare occasions. Now the attacks come every night, and more are dying. They think it's the King." He lowered his voice so only Marion could hear. "They want the orb, Marion. They're worried that once we free it from the King they'll be forgotten. They want to leave the forest." His voice got even lower. *"They want to keep it. Tell me, how the hell would we tell Rendar we gave the Glass Shadow to a bunch savages instead of bringing it home?"*

Marion shook his head. Everyone wanted to get their damn hands on the orb, but he had a feeling the Glass Shadow wasn't as good as it was made out to be. Something with that amount of power was never good. It was always watching; there was something unnerving about that. At this point he just wanted to be rid of the King and the orb both, but he dared not voice so aloud.

Instead Marion whispered, *"We promise them the orb and get the hell out of here."* A voice in his head told him he was insane for wanting to leave so soon- here they had water, food, shelter, women and men both for entertainment. They might have had rough skin, but they were still people. It had been a long time since he had seen anyone but Louis and Jacob. Jesus, how long *had* it been? Weeks? Months? *Years?* He'd assumed fall was over. Seasons were tricky- they lasted however long it seemed fit to last, be it weeks or months or years. The past fall had lasted for three months before they left, and their journey so far must have been a year or more. Louis turned away from his conversation with the short man beside him and leaned in to theirs.

"We can't do that." Louis interrupted, seeming to have overheard them.

Marion rose his eyebrows. "Why, because it's immoral?"

"Because we need them. If we get the orb and somehow manage to destroy the King, we'll be on the verge of breaking down, mentally and physically- assuming there aren't any surprises that come our way. It's not as if all our problems will be solved. We'll never even make it to the border without their food and supplies, and they know it."

"So what do we do?" Jacob asked, looking at them with a hint of panic in his eyes. *One wrong move, and we could lose our chance for supplies, victory, and a way home with the orb in hand. We could lose everything.*

Louis grinned mischievously. "We gain their trust."

CHAPTER 32
LOUIS WILLSON
A GREY FOREST

He had an idea. Louis felt thrilled, better than anything he'd felt in a while because of it. He would have to explain the rest to them later, however, for the woman named Jaone Visir rose her voice and called to resume the meeting. At least, that was what he'd assumed. He didn't speak Marosi, and as far as he knew it was the only other language used in their world. He'd ask Jacob about it later. Louis turned to look at Jaone; he had learned much about her and her people that day, and was constantly intrigued. The head above the door had made him wary, though, and ever since then a strange feeling grew inside him. Maybe they weren't friends. Maybe they weren't even allies.

Jaone was otherwise known as she-wolf to most of the village, for her harsh behavior and unforgivingness. A few boys approaching manhood who had the mercy to bring himself and Jacob new clothes said that she may be rough, but the Taire had a liking for her. It was clear the boys did as well. She wasn't hard on the eyes, Louis had to admit, for a woman without hair and a gun at her side. Then again, she was one of the first women to speak to him with a hint of kindness other than his late mother and sister.

They had been isolated on a farm, and when Louis had visited the local town, his smiles were diminished by the stares and the looks of pity. No girl had ever really wanted him despite his rather rugged good looks (A man with one leg could not work) and it seemed to him now that he would never have one. Hell, Marion had probably slept around the whole of Calidor, men and women both, while he knew Jacob had been with a girl or two before his days on the streets. Louis? He was the weak farmer who still lived at home. He'd never even really had the chance. But now, in the midst of all this, that didn't seem to bother him that much. It was only an itch in the back of his mind, really. There were more important matters to focus on.

The translator's voice drew him from his saddening thoughts. "Jaone wishes for an answer. She reminds you that there is no need to be enemies, and that the Qasyies will be safer in our hands. She also offers to provide anything you need on our journey south when you return. We will insure you are well protected."

"*Our* journey south?" Marion asked, as Jacob opened his mouth. Louis frowned. They had not known. *He* hadn't known. Jaone snorted amusingly and muttered a few words to her translator.

"Of course. The Taire thinks it most wise to settle somewhere else, somewhere less... dangerous. Your lands are plentiful, and alive. We would like to see something green again."

Louis spoke up. "No offense, but you would not be welcome in Rendar. If you truly insist to make your way south, your best options are the marshes and possibly the grasslands. The most in your favor would be the Unventured Lands, but you would have to take the road through Malivia and Aleria, maybe even Calidor." He paused, thinking, and shook his head. "Go through Ekiliador and they'd throw you into The Pass, and going through Paerdan would be rather sneaky, and perhaps mistaken as some sort of ambush. You'd all be lynched in a matter of days. They're more than just farmers, they have one hell of a temper."

The sentence came out easily, but inside he felt shame. It was his land, his farms, his people. And every word was true. *Most all they said they wanted was a peaceful life and that was most what they got, but when the chance for blood came around the taste was always too good to resist.* It was a strange thought, but seemed to fit in his mind.

In times of war we desire peace, yet when we have it in our hands we find that there isn't enough blood, isn't enough vengeance, isn't enough purpose, isn't enough justice, isn't enough blame- and the realization comes to us that war was the twisted peace in ourselves we were looking for in the first place.

It made Louis wonder about the sanity of the world. It was simple, really. As long as people had an opponent to fight, to condemn, to complain about, they would not fight amongst themselves; as long as there was a problem that needed to be solved, there was harmony. Louis knew this wasn't the case for many, but it seemed to be the case in his life.

Then a voice spoke in his mind, clear and confident as the sun, almost amused, as if it had been reading his previous thoughts like a book and had some input on them. It was himself, Louis knew this for sure, but it wasn't. Not really. It was new, pounding in his head, like a memory.

When we have everything we want, what else is there to do but look for something else? When the fields turn dry and the skies yellow, what else is there to do but find new land? When a man lives in peace, what else is there to do but hope for war?

JACOB FORTEMER
A GREY FOREST

In the end, the Marosi agreed to take the safer road to the Unventured Lands, and the three travelers agreed to bring them the Glass Shadow. Jacob trusted Louis, but he was unsure of how this would all work out in their favor. Marion looked puzzled, almost worried, towards the final minutes, and that did nothing to reassure him. Louis seemed calm. Jacob was almost positive he had a plan.

He had little trust in these people, despite their newfound hospitality. As they left into the rain, the head above the door caught his glance, and he turned toward one of the Marosi.

"Who was he?" Jacob asked, and the man turned and looked at him grimly.

"He? That was the Taire's last wife. She... did not please him." The man quickly turned away, uncomfortable, and Jacob looked around worriedly. In a vague part of his mind he wondered where the Taire was now, and why he had not shown his face at such a meeting. As soon as the question arose, it was answered.

Luceir appeared out of the grim forest, a bleeding stag slung over his shoulder and five weary men behind him. *Hunting*. He presumed the Taire wasn't skilled in the art of negotiations and strategy, although he spoke english fairly well and, as Jacob remembered, highly arrogant.

Jacob took in a breath of wet cold air and prayed the next time they had such weather it would not bring them snow.

***

He slept soundly that night, but for one dream. Dreams came often now, but most often they were short and showed things that made little sense- a bridge, a running river, a tower in the sky, a bird with white eyes or even, once, the scene of a burning house on a hill. Now, however, the dream was clear and vivid.

In Jacob's mind he knew that these were just warnings the orb sent him, and that they were not to be taken seriously. Or so he hoped. He thought it was the orb, though at the same time the thought just didn't seem to fit. *What else could it be?* It just didn't feel right. There was something else going on here, Jacob was sure of it. Something about these visions was different.

Looking around, he found that he was standing on the street by which he had lived. From his view he could see his old home, and a sickening feeling came along with it. *Emilia.* What had become of her? It pained Jacob to think of the possibilities. But something in his mind drove him to forget about such things. He obeyed and instead waited for the dream to continue.

It was dead silent; no birds, no horses, no bikes or people or anything at all. It was eerie, and all of a sudden a tingling feeling crawled up his spine and he wanted nothing more than to leave. All of this was real. Too real. The wind was the only sound, rusting the few leaves left on the the the dying trees. The emptiness frightened him. A moment later Jacob wondered if anything were going to happen. This was a strange dream. A different dream. Perhaps *he* had to make something happen.

Jacob started to walk. And walk. And walk. He passed silent markets and dark windows that always seemed to hide something inside. He passed a dropped basket with oranges rolling out onto the street, rotten and brown, and a small, waning fire in an alley that had been left forgotten. Just as he thought he ought to wake up, a startling rumble shook the city. He fell on his knees, shocked. Of course. What else was he to expect? *In just a few moments it'll end, it'll stop, just as it always has.* But it didn't. It only got stronger.

Jacob's legs were frozen in place, unwilling to move away. There was nowhere to go. Stones fell around him, gaps and crevices forming along the street with ear splitting cracks, and his hands on the stones felt a deep rumbling under the earth.

Before he could blink the street exploded in a burst of dirt and stone and rocks ahead of him, and a darkness rushed out (*or just the darkness in the hole in his mind in the earth in the ground*) and what the hell was happening it was the endtheend of the world theendoftheworldtheendoftheworld *goddamnit what the hell is-*

And then he woke, sweaty and panting and scared oh so scared- and when he touched his hand to the cold hard ground he felt the deep rumbling under the earth, so far, far away.

***

He did not tell the others of his vision (*dream Jacob it was a dream only a dream just a dream of what could happen Jacob of what could*), and it was obvious to him they would not want to hear it. There were other problems to deal with, and so for the moment his vision (*dream*) left his mind. Today the Marosi sent them out, and with higher spirits since the border.

The rain had stopped and the clouds had dissipated, leaving them under a warming sun. There were four more dead beasts from last night and two more dead men, all the bones being buried by the shore. It was whispered that they were growing stronger. A wind whistled through the dead trees and through the wooden boards of the village, and the water left on the ground had frozen. Some Marosi children were sliding on it, hacking chunks away to throw or bite. Parts of the lake had frozen over as well, and most were out fetching the last of the fish for the winter.

People were at work, fires were blazing in the chilly dry air, and Jaone Visar, the Taire, and a scattered amount of unrecognized faces sent them off with good wishes, good mounts, and good food. Jacob's new mare was winter grey with spots of black, small but kindly and strong. Marion's was a chestnut color, the largest, and Louis's a beige-white with a scarred flank. He himself was ecstatic to be sitting upon a horse once again, and for once since the Barren, he felt almost normal. Almost enough to be confident. He could only imagine Louis's relief.

They were given furs and water, dried salted meats and fruits and nuts, a working lighter to start fires. There was rope and blankets, a pot and bandages, medicine and even some old world artifacts as a gift for their help. Jacob had shuffled through them was overjoyed to find a watch (though it didn't work), an engraved metal handle, a bag of rusted bottlecaps, and a cracked ball of glass that utterly fascinated him, (for glass was expensive, and no one was sure of how to make it anymore) with a liquid inside and flakes of white that floated around a little bronze statue of an eagle when he shook it. They were old and useless and fragile, but nonetheless they were meaningful gifts all the same.

It almost made Jacob feel guilty for what they would do, although of *that* plan he still did not know. He had told Louis that if they didn't come out of this alive with the orb in their hands they would have some talking to do. Louis had responded with saying that he would explain everything once they were away from listening ears. As he recalled this conversation he wrapped the little orb of snow in one of his blankets and stored it in his pack. Marion was left with the watch, and Louis with the handle and bottlecaps.

In his studies of history he had learned the names of many of the old world items, and was thrilled to have one of them in his possession. Jacob could not quite remember what it had been called, and promised to find out once he reached home. *If.* If he did. Somehow, in their stroke of good fortune, he had forgotten what little chance they had of succeeding. Jacob's thoughts turned to his daughter. Her face was already fading from his mind.

Emilia sat huddled in the alley, shivering, her grey eyes like sparks in the darkness. Rain poured down from the clouds above, running down in rivulets to the street; rain that was the only sound in the quiet night. The buildings surrounding them cast dim lights across her, and she pushed herself further into the brick wall, trying to escape something she couldn't see.

"Emilia," Jacob whispered, wrapping his arm around her slouched shoulders. "Honey, what's wrong?"

316

No response. Her gaze was fixated on a glowing window, blurred from the streaks of water running down it's glass. Inside a family ate dinner, smiles on their faces. Their laughter could be heard faintly, like an echo in his mind. Family. That was all she'd ever really wanted. All he'd ever wanted. Jacob sighed and hugged Emilia closer to himself, finding comfort in the warmth.

"Shhhhh. I know. I know." They sat like that the rest of the night, Emilia falling asleep in his arms.

Jacob remembered the stars, specifically. When the rain had ceased and the clouds had cleared, the stars had shone so bright that he had stared for hours. This memory was faint and far away, but he clung to it like a drowning man to a raft. Their odds of coming out of this alive were so slim, he wondered why they even continued to persevere. This was more of a curiosity than it was despair, and thought did not seems diminish his spirits.

So, Jacob gave his thanks to the Marosi, and followed his friends out into the woods once again.

MARION ARMAIS
A GREY FOREST

The forest was different, somehow. Perhaps it was because he was higher than before, stronger, ready for what was to come, or maybe it was only the sun peaking through the branches. Whatever it was, for once Marion felt hope where there had been none. He had fallen to the back and let Jacob lead- he wanted to keep an eye on them. They were quiet, waiting for Louis to give them reassurance in their future. They dared not ask him, though, until the sun started to set, the trees had thinned and they could see the edge of the forest.

"Louis." Marion called, trying to knock him out of his dazed expression. "*Louis.*"

"Hmm?"

"Would you care to tell us the plan?"

Louis paled a little, but otherwise remained silent.

"Do you not have one?" Marion asked, and he saw Jacob stiffen.

"Yes. I have one."

There was silence again and he began to worry. *What the hell is wrong with him?* "And?"

Louis looked into the distance, refusing to meet their eyes. "You won't like it."

Jacob scoffed. "There isn't much we like doing in the Barren, Louis. Spit it out."

Marion had a dreading feeling in his stomach, and a thought nagged at him. *What would he have us do to make him worry so much? What's he thinking?* He desperately hoped his friend was as smart as he thought.

"I had a vision." Louis started, scratching at his short beard.

318

(*no not a vision a dream a dream a dream*) A voice yelled out in the back of Marion's mind, but he tried his best to ignore it. (*we all have dreams they're just dreams of what could happen Marion of what could*)

Marion blinked. *Then how come I know what he's going to say?* He thought. *How come the vision I had last night was different, how come it seemed so real?*

(*It seemed real it seemed real but Marion it's just a dream we all have dreams*)

And then he saw it in his mind as Louis spoke, his vision, his clear vision, his *real* vision- *the stone the shattered shadow the tower the shattered glass-*

"We destroy the orb."

CHAPTER 33
LOUIS WILLSON
THE BARREN

His vision had been real. Louis knew it in his heart, and his previous plan of just following through and handing over the orb to the Marosi had been wiped from his mind.

There was a new goal now, there had to be.

In his vision he had been by *the ocean, fresh and blue and calming while small waves splashed up onto the shore. The King stood on the sand, though not too close to the water; he had no intention of getting wet. There was a castle ways behind him, and the wide sea ahead. The wind was soft and there was a salty smell in the air. It was the Barren, but it was not. It was Maros. It was flourishing, absent of the darkness that had taken hold.*

Here the King was simply a man, nothing more. He seemed young, with deep blue eyes and black hair absent of grey. He was far from the orb, far as he ever dared go now. It was the source of his power, wasn't it? Louis suspected that the time the King had spoken to them on the lake had been just an illusion; that this man had not gone past a mile from his kingdom in a very long while, perhaps even since the orb had been given to him. Louis did not know how he knew this, but it seemed he did and he was in no place to question the information his visions brought him.

After another moment or two, the King rose his arms and his eyes turned white. He was using the power of the Glass Shadow, it seemed, though Louis had no idea what for. There seemed to be no change, until Louis reached down, touched the sand, and felt a deep rumbling in the earth. Deep, very deep. The King seemed to have felt it too, and smiled.

Somehow this vision was from the past, Louis thought, but it was only a feeling. Like reading a book that was many years old, knowing everything in it had already happened, that the fate of the people in it had been decided long ago. Here it was the same, and Louis felt no reason not to believe it. What was hard for him to believe was that the Barren would look like this again someday, with trees and grass and flowers. It had changed so much.

Then, the white left the King's eyes, and with a small, arrogant grin he walked back towards the castle, his spiked silver crown atop his head and his black fur cape flowing behind in the wind. His dress shoes made imprints in the sand, and he smoothed his suit and tie as he passed. Louis tilted his head, smirking; the man had changed his style.

The King walked back to the castle, becoming a blur in the distance. And when Louis had had one last look at the ocean beyond, he felt he had a slight idea of what had just taken place, and it filled him with dread. He knew what they needed to do.

And he knew it now, as he said the few simple words at the edge of the forest. He had expected outrage, interruption, even glares or utterly confused looks. Anything but what he received. Louis saw Marion take a deep breath and nod, while Jacob did nothing but wait and listen. He supposed there was some shock on his friend's faces from the way they tensed, but Louis was riding behind and could not see. Trying to gauge their thoughts, he rode up beside them. He did not wait for any opinions, however, and started to explain. They would destroy the orb, and not just crack it like the King had wanted. No, they would shatter it.

"Have you ever wondered how the Barren became the way it is? This whole journey we thought just having the orb would solve everything, but it won't. The Glass Shadow is the reason for all of this. The King used it somehow to... bring something, control something, I'm not sure. But he brought the dark-radiation here." Louis paused, and a voice spoke in the back of his mind, almost laughing. He felt he was going insane. He supposed that was the price for having visions.

(but what about the darkness, it's the darkness in the dreams, you don't know yet but you will, yes you will very soon too soon) Louis chose to ignore it, for now. Something about it made him feel tingly. These were not his own thoughts.

"If the orb is destroyed, the King's power is gone, it's hold over the forest is broken and the Marosi will be able to leave- and the orb's control over the spreading of the Barren will be gone. We don't need to have it to set things right, we need to get rid of it."

Louis paused again, though not because of the strange voice. They had stopped at the edge of the forest, looking out to the land they were to face next. The landscape before them turned from soil to rock, though in the Barren that wasn't much of a difference. This rock was darker, and warm from the glare of the sun. Here there was no ice, no sign that winter was upon them- but Louis could feel it in the air, the dryness, the bitter, the cold. There were hills and fissures and caves and rising heaps of stone, and for once in their time in the Barren they spotted a faded cobbled path. With a glance in his companion's directions he took the lead, and heard Marion's voice behind him.

"That would be for the best, I think."

For a moment Louis had forgotten what their discussion had been concerning, and when he recalled it he was grateful he hadn't been opposed. There was no more talk of it, though it was on all of their minds. Louis highly suspected the others had been presented with visions as well; they had probably seen the same things he had.

Alongside the old road there lay a wooden cart, tilted to it's side, the wood dry and splintered. Skeletons lay beside it, of horse and human both. They did not halt to investigate, however. Louis was focused entirely on how they would obtain the Glass Shadow. It worried him. *We don't know anything we should. Where is the orb?*

(thetowerthetower)

Yes, but where's the tower? Where is the King, what does he do locked up in his castle day and night? How will we succeed, when the orb sees everything and the King has the orb?

(likehesaid, likehe said, the moments betweentime)

322

And then it hit him, hit him hard, and he stopped his horse and spoke aloud. "But how? How?"

The voices in the back of his mind spoke again. *(wesleptbut now we're awakeawake and starving, the orb theorb brought us but it takes it hurts our eyes oureyesoureyes)*

"Louis?" Marion asked, concerned. He rode up beside his friend. The voice spoke again, echoing louder in his mind.

(oureyes our eyes don't you see the white the light the cold)

"But-"

The voice interrupted again, and Louis's head had a cold hurt, not so different from when he used to chip ice from the ponds in younger winters and put them in his mouth.

(freeusfreeus we can give you time in time freeus at the gate at the gate time within time)

"Time within time?" He muttered, confused once again. Jacob grabbed his shoulder.

"Louis, what the hell is wrong with you?" Jacob's voice was annoyed, but his eyes were worried. Marion said something else but Louis didn't seem to hear.

"Time in time, at the gate, like the King..." Louis paused. "The eyes are the orb but what is it doing?" The voice had left him, and his mind felt hollow and empty. It was something, though.

It was something.

***

The fire that night was much welcomed, as was the meat. The light from the flames danced across the rocks, the ash and smoke and sparks rising up into the stars. It was a cold night but they were warm, and their stomachs full. Louis told them of the voices and there was no hesitation to believe him- they had heard them as well. All of them held the belief that whatever was speaking was also somehow sending them visions. It was not the Glass Shadow- no, that wasn't it. It was a different feeling, a different power. Why would the orb help orchestrate its own defeat? The voice was clearly trapped, trapped by the orb, perhaps possessed. And it was not only offering help, no, it was offering the chance to take down two birds with one stone.

At long last the choice was no longer between the King and the orb, there was another, another choice, and they were more than willing to take it. Something, or someone wanted the Glass Shadow gone- and who were they to stand it it's way?

JACOB FORTEMER
THE BARREN

The following morning they set off again, in the light of the rising sun. They passed old villages and roads and remains of the land it had once been. Ruins were all that was left, and yet there was a clear sense of something around them. This land might have been dead, but it was definitely not empty. Jacob knew that much, at least. In one ramshackled structure that used to be an inn, they scavenged a few dusty bottles still full of fine wine. As they left, Marion pointed out the sign on the ground, which had fallen from overhead. It was splattered with blood, the words letting them know they had just visited *The Poisoned Pint*.

Jacob hoped the name hadn't reflected on the content of the drinks. They drank as they rode, and to them no wine had ever tasted so good, although it was bitter and stale, drained of it's original full-bodied flavor. This did not bother Jacob. Better a last drink than no drink at all.

The wind tousled their hair, the sun retreated behind the clouds, and the dust rose up from the cobbled street as their horse's hooves made prints in the dirt and ash covering the road. Jacob licked his chapped lips and tasted blood in his mouth. It was soon washed away with another swig from his bottle, though, and he soon forgot about it. *Worrying about chapped lips? Ha.* There were more pressing matters to concern himself with, such as how to make this wine last longer than it should. Jacob was so wrapped up in his thoughts he almost missed what they were passing. Almost. He looked up only for a moment but stopped and stared, unbelieving. He almost felt as if he wanted to laugh. Up upon a hill to their west sat a house, charred and burnt by fire.

325

It looked the same as it had in his vision, though older and darker and no flames licking at the wood. He remembered the vision, the thought. *Dreams come often now, but most often they are short and show things that make little sense- a bridge, a running river, a tower in the sky, a bird with white eyes or even, once, the scene of a burning house on a hill.* The door swung on its hinges, the roof caving in on one side. It seemed to smile at him. There was no evil feeling about it, no sudden fear in his gut. Something about it was just... familiar. Lonely. A reminder of a childhood memory long gone. In response to the sight Jacob smiled back, shook his head, and continued on his way.

***

Days passed, nights passed. The sun rose, the sun set. Each day their bags got lighter and their horses wearier. Their mounts were so far safe from the touch of the Barren, it seemed, though they were tired. It might have been because of their species or something in their breed, but Jacob didn't put much thought into it.

Although the travelers had been healed slightly by their recent hospitality, they could still feel the sickness of the dark-radiation inside them. It had slowed, but it was still there. Twisting, growing, writhing. Biding it's time, Jacob liked to think, though it worried him to imagine it having a will of it's own. How they would survive it had slipped their minds, and Jacob prayed that whatever had enough power to send them visions would have enough power to heal them as well.

They heard no more from the voices, and received no visions, though he had not lost faith. *The gate,* Louis had said, and they all had assumed the gate of the castle. They were almost there. It was hard to believe it, that their quest would soon come to an end. Their lives might, too, if they weren't careful.

In the past Jacob had been sure they would fall gallantly, that they would be people to be sung in songs and told in stories. In the past he hadn't given the end much thought. None of them had. But now Jacob dared to hope for their survival. In fact, he yearned for it. They were so close. And yet the closer they moved to their fate, the more he wanted to complete their goal, reach their destination. He began to dream of it, plan it, picture it. Jacob could see himself at the end of it all, galloping home into the sunset like one of the old western heros in his books. He could see Emilia again. He was so close. But that wasn't the reality.

First off, home was south, not west. And he wasn't a hero. Not yet, anyway. So Jacob continued onward, the sick feeling in his stomach growing stronger and stronger. Perhaps it was the radiation, anxiety, or maybe even just hunger. The thought of food surprisingly became significantly less appetizing as they approached their likely deaths. If they lived, Jacob hoped they could have a feast afterward. A feast fit for kings. Hell, they deserved it. But for now, they were stuck with empty stomachs, and dreading hearts.

***

When they finally reached the bridge, Jacob was not filled with awe and excitement, pride or adrenaline. There was only the lowly defeated feeling that this was the day they would have to face the moment they'd been waiting for for over a year, maybe more. And if they made a mistake... there was no going back. And all their pain would be for nothing. Jacob could see the castle beyond, dark and in ruins. It rose up on it's hill of rock, foreboding and intimidating, surrounded by the ashes of the town around it.

The bridge itself was wood and stone, looking stable despite the cracks and crumbling rocks. The water below had an almost lazy current, moving slow and splashing against the shore. Jacob could not see the bottom, despite it being more of a stream than a river, only a swirling blackness. For a moment he thought he saw something moving in the depths, and a strange feeling that he was being watched swept over him. The others did not seem to notice, as they made to cross, so Jacob called out to them.

"Wait!" His voice was raspy, and after a few coughs he resumed. "Wait, wait, don't cross."

Jacob dismounted his horse and got as close to the stream as he dared, listening to the gurgling and splashing of the water. Upon a whim he started to walk alongside it, staring into the endless depths. One of the poems he had read in their handy guide echoed in his mind. Jacob had read it cover to cover, knew most of it by heart. It was this book of stories and riddles and and the thoughts of a dying old man that had entertained them on their journey. But this one, this verse, seemed to stand out the most.

Along the river, the river of black, when you go in you don't ever come back- Jacob spotted something ahead, something had caught his eye, so he moved faster, his boots sinking into the black sand. *When you follow it's path, you die of thirst, unless you drink and forever be cursed-* It was a body, half decomposed with showing bone and dried blood, rotting away under the pale sun. *So don't get close, don't go near, a darkness dwells forever here-* Jacob looked closer and saw the dark skin, the tattered clothes, the frozen face full of fear staring back at him.

He saw the hand clenched around the hilt of a dagger, the empty flaking holes where the crows had feasted on his eyes. And he knew who it was, he knew him, the rich man who had thought he could best the world alone.

Along the river, the river of black, when you go in you don't ever come back.

CHAPTER 34
MARION ARMAIS
A WINTER RIVER

Marion didn't believe it when he saw it, although he had told himself it was so when his friend had left. *Did you really think he would be alive?* He thought. *No, I hoped. God, I hoped.* When his companion had left Marion had been certain he would return, or wait, perhaps even circle back and go home. Never did he suspect that Oliver would go on without them, never did he think he would keep to his word. But he had, and ever since they had recovered his supplies at the lake by the beast, Marion had worried. He had mulled over what could have happened to his friend, if Oliver was still alive, struggling somewhere in the dark.

And now, as he faced what he knew to be true, he couldn't believe it; just as sometimes Marion thought Amicus had only left or stayed behind or gotten lost. He wasn't dead, just away for a while. That had been easier to accept than his sacrifice, though now when confronted with a body, there was no excuse. No way to push aside the reality and convince himself of something else. No. Oliver Monterose was here, and he was dead. What bothered Marion were the wounds, the bites, the missing bones and flesh of his friend. At first he had suspected the death to be caused by hunger or thirst; then he had wondered why he was halfway in the river, and why he was injured so gravely.

"There's something here." Marion said. It wasn't a question, it was a statement, bold and full of fear, and his companions did not question it.

"Where? In the river?" Louis wondered, adjusting himself on his crutches.

329

Marion nodded. *Where else, but the river of black?* The same dreadful poem had come into his mind as it had Jacob's, and it made him nervous. *Where else was there to go? Nowhere. There is nowhere to go, but the path that has been laid out for us.*

"Come on." Marion said, grabbing his horse's reins and leading his mare back over to the bridge. He tied the tether to a nearby rock, many feet from the river. *We'll be careful this time, and we'll all come out alive.* He did the same to the other horses, hoping they would be back to set them free. He then took their bags and walked back over to the shore.

"Marion, what-" Louis barely got the question out of his mouth before his friend threw one of their bags across the stream. It landed with a thump on the sand, and another soon landed beside it. The river was wide, but Marion was capable enough.

"Marion, what the hell? Why?" Jacob moved to stop him, but the last one was already across. "I mean- what-"

Marion shook his head. *They most likely think I'm going insane.* "When some ghosts or glass bats or something even worse comes out of that fucking river, I'm not losing anything. Come on." Marion stood at the foot of the bridge, motioning for them to join him. "We run at the same time. Oh, damn, Louis, I forgot. Here." He grabbed his friend's crutches and threw them across. They landed with a clatter, barely touching the water. Louis was left trying to balance himself, a little in shock.

"Marion, I could have damn well crossed that bridge on my own. There's nothing here, whatever got Oliver was in the river, the bridge is *safe.*"

But as he said it Marion knew he didn't believe it. There was something wrong here. It was too easy. Still, he did feel some sympathy for his friend. Who wanted to be carried like a child, risking other people's lives, not being able to carry their own weight? But it did not change the fact that it was the fastest way. Louis was safer in his arms anyway; Marion cared for the cripple greatly, and did not want to see him dead.

"Look, you're going to go across, get my crutches, and we'll all cross *with our horses* like rational people." Louis said, his face showing annoyance and frustration.

"This isn't a rational land." Marion responded, and with that he took a rock from the ground and swung it at Louis's head. It hit hard, perhaps harder than he meant, but it got the job done. Louis slumped into his arms, the hot dark red blood dripping down onto his clothes.

"What- *Marion*!" Jacob looked shocked. "What- why-"

"For God's sake, just listen!" Marion said, adjusting to Louis's weight. He was heavier than he had been before, though not by much. "He was never gonna cooperate, and I know there's something wrong here. I just... I don't want anyone dead today."

Jacob grimly shook his head, understanding but disapproving. He went along with it; Jacob seemed too tired to disagree. Marion prayed he had been overreacting, prayed that there really was nothing to be worried about- but prayers were not often answered in the Barren.

***

Despite wanting to run, neither of them did. For some strange reason it was all too quiet, and Marion felt that if they ran, if they made any more noise, something would wake from it's sleep. Perhaps if they were quiet, quiet as the wind and the water, they would go unnoticed.

Marion wanted to run, *knew* he should run, he was so close and if he didn't why the hell did he knock out his friend? If they weren't going to run Louis could have gone across on his own.

Now they would have to wait for him to wake. *God, what was I thinking?* It had seemed rational at the time, but now he was not so sure. He saw Jacob finger his dagger nervously. Marion wanted to run but he was tense, so tense and if anyone did anything else the standoff would end, the guns would go off, and someone would end up dead.

Halfway across, they were halfway across- then he froze. Marion halted in the middle of the bridge, Jacob beside him, Louis bleeding in his arms. The sound of the water had stopped. There was nothing. He was too afraid to look, too afraid to do anything but stand. The wind blew, blew through his hair and made him shiver to the bone. Silent.

When he finally mustered the courage to peek over the edge, his heart skipped a beat. The water was frozen, turned to ice, and Oliver's body had all but disappeared. *Perhaps he only rolled into the water, then froze.* But then the daunting image of Oliver's face under the surface staring up through the foggy glass that was ice chilled him, and he pushed the thought away.

The temperature had dropped significantly, and Marion's breath came out in a puff of cloud. Frost covered the bridge, slowly, creeping it's way towards the middle, towards *them.* He shivered. Jacob, with a warning glance, jolted him to the reality of their situation. With one last guilty look at Louis, he started to run.

However, before Marion could even hope to make it, the bridge burst out from under them and he was falling, falling, falling. It was not far to the ice, but the impact hurt, and his ears rang. Something warm and sticky ran down his face and arms, and he wiped it away from his eyes. Stones smashed into the river around him, cracking the ice below. One hit Marion's back, another his shoulder. He scampered to his feet, looking around. Louis lay beside him, a fresh wound on his chest and another on his arm. His head was still bleeding. Marion took him into his arms, held him tight, his face full of guilt and regret.

"Oh God, Louis, I'm so sorry-"

Marion was cut off by a hand on his shoulder. He whirled around to see Jacob, who seemed to be worse off than himself. He was bleeding less, but his arm was twisted in a strange angle.

"Jacob, your arm-"

"Shut up, I know. *We need to go.*" His voice was strained, impatient. "Damn you, Marion, get up! *You need to fucking run!*"

332

Jacob left him there, and for the first time he noticed the strange red glow beneath the ice. It was a dark, dark red, a bloody red, a red that made him think of dying roses and stained bandages and wine aged a hundred years.

Without hesitation he picked Louis up- this time it was much harder- and started to limp over to Jacob, who had gathered their bags and was yelling for him to hurry. But blood clotted his ears and the ringing was still there, so he did not hear. Marion had one foot sink into the sand when a burst came from the river behind him. Jacob let out a shout of warning, but had no time to react. A tentacle, dark red and thrashing, gripped Marion's ankle and pulled. It's hold was freezing, and felt dead on his skin. With a panicked, surprised shout he dropped Louis and grasped for something, anything. His fingers left trails in the night-black sand, stained with blood. The rest of the creature broke it's way through, and Jacob, half-dragging Louis, backed away in awe and fear.

It was a mass of tentacles, and in the center of it all, a neck and a head lined with spikes, and a maw with a thousand teeth. It's eyes were an icy, angry blizzard of snow.

White, and furious.

333

A KING IN A TOWER
VANDOR, THE BARREN

The Glass Shadow was, to say in the least, acrimonious. Beneath the glass a storm swirled, black and unforgiving. The King had come to ask the orb of any news, though it would have been easier for him to use the orb's power himself. He found it entertaining, and there was little other entertainment in the castle of Vandor. Just the past few evenings the Glass Shadow had been in a fine mood, until this morning when he had woken to a raging, thundering storm outside. However, the only storm that raged now was inside the glass, foul and bitter. The King grinned, for surely whatever put the Glass Shadow in such a destructive mood was all the better for himself. Now, upon the tower under the darkening sky, he dared to speak to it.

"So." The King said, hoping to receive good words. The insides of the orb froze in tension. Not nervous tension, mind you, but furious tension. It made the King very nervous.

"*So.*" The Glass Shadow said, in a horrible, horrible voice. It was holding in anger. *What happened?* The King thought, puzzled and fearful. *What the hell happened?* He was suddenly very sweaty, and very afraid. Fearfully, he opened his mouth, but no sound came out.

"*They mean to destroy me, did you know that?*" It said, in it's new, chilling voice. "*They happened to suddenly change their minds, after making a deal with my Marosi. Do you know why?*" The King slowly shook his head, holding in his breath. "*The travelers were getting visions. Did you know the creatures could send visions?*" It asked him, and this time he answered.

334

"No. I wasn't sure they could do much anything else other than... what they were called for." A feeling of guilt swept through him. *That was long ago, the past is the past.*

"No? Because the travelers have clearly been having dreams, and those dreams have somehow led them to believe such. The creatures have more power than you know. When you called them here, using my power, it was a grave mistake. They are growing hungry, growing restless, I can only keep them here, can only withhold them, for so long. They wish to leave, there is no more for them here, no more sustenance. Your plan for Rendar will not work. You should have used them when you had the chance."

"And? What're you going to do about that?" The King shouted, growing worried. Very worried. The Glass Shadow knew nothing of his interactions with *them,* and he intended to keep it that way.

"With their help... these men have grown into formidable opponents, even that I cannot deny. I should have killed them sooner. You should have. I cannot control them now, any of them, since they have decided to destroy me... your creatures are blocking me. But I can still control much more than they know."

With that it fell silent. He knew what he needed to do. Now was the time for Rendar to fall. The King stood for another moment, before turning towards the door.

A fear shot into him, hard and panicky. Should the orb be destroyed, he would die. Not of hunger or thirst, not of sickness, not even of valiant battle. The King would die of *age,* and the thought that such a thing would be the end of him was harder for him to accept than the day the creatures had come and wreaked destruction and chaos on his land.

MARION ARMAIS
A WINTER RIVER

The world around him disappeared, and the only thing was the creature, the creature and him- there was no ice, no sky, no Louis and Jacob. Marion neglected to feel the cold, the wind, the blood running down his face. All there was was the grip around his ankle, and the monster behind it.

The creature dragged him across the ice, slowly, painfully, and lifted him into the air, dangling him by his ankle. Panicked, Marion tried to wriggle his way free, though it did no good. It's grip was as hard as iron, unbreakable. The beast raised him above it's gaping maw, breathing a putrid scent, a dead scent, from inside. It admired Marion with it's swirling white eyes, seeing him somewhere in a tower far away where, it seemed to remind him, he could never reach. *The orb, the Glass Shadow, it knows it has to know-* he thought desperately. Marion spat at it, despite the dryness of his mouth. There seemed to be enough hate built up inside him to do so.

"Fuck you." Marion hissed spitefully. It was not directed at the beast; this was for the orb to hear. For the King. He grabbed the dagger from his sheath and slashed at the tentacle around his leg. The steel found it's mark, and the beast screamed in surprise. However, the grip only got tighter. A frightful thought came to him that maybe it couldn't feel pain. Marion stabbed at it again and again, but the dead do not let go. The thing thrashed and screamed, and at this point Marion felt as if his leg were about to fall off. The dagger dropped from his hands, and clattered on the ice. Now the beast was calm, and if it could have, it would've grinned. It lowered him towards the black, stinking hole that was it's mouth.

Suddenly, two gunshots rang in the air, then two more. The grip around Marion's leg was released, and he fell to the ice below.

His head hurt- hell, everything hurt, but nevertheless he turned to see the beast's eyes blown to bits, the sockets bleeding, staining the ice a dark red. That was when dizziness overtook him, and the world around him faded into black.

LOUIS WILLSON
THE BARREN

The world was cold. Very cold. Opening his eyes he saw only white. Only gray. The sky was absent of the sun, the wind absent of warmth. And there was snow. It melted on his skin, on his auburn hair, and made him blink when it landed in his eyes. His breaths came out in small puffs, and for a moment Louis felt at peace. He felt rested, he felt safe.

He would sit up and be in the fields, dry and harvested, the falling snow around him landing on the evergreens of the forest as evening approached. In the distance would be his house, the windows bright with the firelight from the hearth; and he would hear their voices and the smell of supper would fill his nose. Louis would hobble in and grab a blanket and huddle by the flickering flames, his family beside him, no worries, no fears, just... home. The memory faded when Louis remembered where he was, what had happened. When he felt the blood trickling down his face, when he tasted it, warm and metallic on his tongue. When his body cried out in pain as he tried to move, the rocks digging into his back, and when the voice he had listened to for what seemed like a lifetime penetrated his ears.

"Louis?" Jacob whispered, moving over to his friend. "Louis, are you there? Can you hear me?"

Louis took in a breath and tried to speak, but instead ended up coughing. The water canister was soon put to his mouth and he drank gratefully.

"Jacob-"

His companion cut him off. "I know what you're going to ask, I can explain." And he did, and after a few moments Louis's anger started to fade away. "Hey, hey, you're okay. Marion saved you. He saw it coming, he knew something was wrong, and we should have listened. It was quicker, and easier to… well, knock you out. I guess he knew you would resist. After the bridge collapsed… you might not have made it anyways if he hadn't carried you to the shore."

Louis nodded, his face now pleading. "Look, I know I'm a burden. Trust me, I know. And I'm sorry for that. Really. But if you only realize that I can help, there won't be a problem. If you'd told me your reasons I would've done what you asked me to. We *had* time, Jacob." Something in Louis's voice was calmer, more confident. Less ashamed. It was good. It *felt* good.

Jacob laughed, cracking a smile Louis hadn't seen in a while. "Yeah, well, tell it to the psycho who did it in the first place."

Speaking of what happened, where's Marion? Louis thought. He head throbbed painfully, and he wanted an apology.

"Jacob, where's-"

But Jacob had gone off to relieve himself on a nearby rock, and in his absence he saw his friend beside him, asleep. *Or dead, he could be dead, you don't know you don't know-*

"Marion?" Louis whispered, looking anxiously into his serene, motionless face. It was covered in so much dirt and blood that he was barely recognizable. Louis looked to see if his friend was breathing, but Jacob had done the kindness of covering them both with blankets, and with his own distorted vision it was hard to see. Louis wiped the filth from his eyes, though he still could not tell. "Marion? You son of bitch, if you're dead-."

His friend's eyes weakly fluttered open, and he breathed a sigh of relief.

"What did you call me?" Marion asked, his voice raspy and soft. He was smiling. Louis started to laugh, in gratitude, mostly, although it hurt. On the outside he chuckled, as if it were nothing, but inside he was thankful beyond thankfulness. *If he had been dead, God, if he had been dead.*

JACOB FORTEMER
THE BARREN

The river was still in their sight. The beast had gone howling down under the surface, it's eyes completely gone, the sockets bleeding empty holes. Jacob had shot it. He had, though he could barely remember doing it. Hell, he could hardly believe it. The gun had mostly been left forgotten after they'd found it… at least, until now. Jacob had one bullet left, and he knew exactly what he was going to do with it. There was a certain orb he'd absolutely love to shatter right about now.

The beast was gone, that they did not have to worry about. However, the cracked ice, the broken bridge, and the blood still remained. Jacob did not want to stay there any longer than he had to, though with two of his companions out cold it was hard to move anywhere. He had carried Marion first, come back for Louis, then for their supplies. It was full day before Louis woke, and although Marion had come to not long after, he had drifted off again into a deep sleep. The snow had come, along with the cold and the wet and the wind.

Their horses had crossed the ice willingly enough, with Jacob to lead them, though they clearly had the same sense of danger Marion had picked up on. They whinnied and neighed nervously, rearing back, their eyes wide.

The fucking thing is dead, he thought, *why so scared?* But as Jacob hurried them across the river, he had looked over his shoulder nonetheless. *Damn the Barren, damn the orb, damn the King.* They had finally gotten to their feet, only to be knocked down into the dirt once again.

Jacob thought these harsh thoughts as he tied their bags to their mounts once again, his hands numb and shaking. The wind was harsh today as well, and his showing skin was already flushed. The sky was gray overhead, the light of the sun shining dimly through the mass of clouds. His own grey, black speckled mare nuzzled him warmly when Jacob approached her.

It seemed the Marosi also favored riding their female horses over their males. The reason? Jacob had read on such topics, and liked to think himself highly educated (he had been a lawyer, after all), though there was really little to explain. The change in the world had affected many of the animals' hunting patterns, mating seasons, their behavior in general. He'd forgotten why- not many people now were interested in such things- but the mares were more active, kind, easier to handle, while the stallions were often too wild and did not care much for riding.

It was nice to avert his mind for a while, to think back on such things, but Jacob reminded himself that now was not the time. He looked back at Louis, who was curled up beside the motionless body of Marion on the snow-covered rocks. He had fallen into sleep again. All of them were freezing, covered in snow, and very, very frightened. They had not yet tended to their wounds; they dreaded even taking a piss it was so cold, much less removing most of their clothes to check on their injuries.

"Louis!" Jacob called, and his friend looked up. "We're riding today. We can't wait for him, and I- I don't wanna wake him. The horses'll die, and so will you."

Louis nodded grudgingly, took his crutches in hand, and wearily hobbled over to his horse. Their mounts were all different colors, though the beige-white of Louis's mare blended in well with the landscape.

Jacob walked over to Marion, heaved him up and lay him across his horse, thinking of no better way to do it. The mare would follow them, no doubt. She was smart enough to know there was nothing for her here. But for the sake of wariness, he tied his saddle to Marion's, so they could keep together. *God knows what'll happen if this storm gets any worse,* he thought, frowning. *The orb is not one to give up.* All they had to do was make it to the gate. At the gate, they would be saved. At least, he hoped. Hope was all they had left now.

Jacob then mounted his own horse, patted her neck, and moved towards the castle; though as of now they could barely see it. Hoofprints that were left in their stead were quickly covered, and all trace of them was gone. The river, the broken bridge, the cracked ice, the blood, the remains of the camp- all covered by a blanket of white. There were just rolling hills of snow, and no one would be able to tell whether it was grass underneath, or night-black rock.

Just white, in the sky and the earth and the cold winter air. The winds slowed, as did the fall of the snow, and soon it looked as if no one had been there at all.

***

Outside it was quiet, the last of the snow silently falling, the slight wind whistling through the boards. The air had cleared and they could see far through the window, to the castle and beyond. Inside it was warm, and a small fire burned in the hearth.

The travelers huddled close to the flickering light, staring into the flames. The home was but one room, small and in the open, but it was intact and it kept them safe from the winter outside. Marion had woken again, confused and worried, although there was no serious injury to his head.

"What do you remember?" Jacob asked him as he bandaged Marion's last wound. The blood soaked through quickly, though he was not worried. He had opened it, cleaned it, and wrapped it. Given him medicine from the Marosi and would now let him rest. There was nothing else he could do.

Marion ran his hands through his hair, and shook his head. "A bridge. Crashing, falling, stones. Red. Uh, lots of red. Gunshots? Louis, something... I remember... with a stone... and eyes. White eyes." He looked at Jacob again. "That's all. Well, there's more, but it's blurry. And... feeling betrayed. Or discovered, like we were hiding and someone found us. Exposed, maybe. *God,* I don't know."

Despite Marion being so unsure, Jacob was familiar with the feeling. The orb knew what they meant to do, and if that was the case, so did the King. They were not safe.

"The gate. We only have to make it to the gate." Jacob said reassuringly, though in truth he had no idea what the gate really meant, or what it looked like, even. But he did not disclose this to his companions. Instead Jacob turned to Louis, and started to tend to the wounds of his other friend. Then a thought came to his mind, and he asked Marion to check their bags.

"My, uh, old-world artifact, Marion, did it break? It was already cracked..." Jacob's voice was weak, as if he didn't really care what the answer would be. In the past it would have been much more important to him, but now he felt only little concern, a slight curiosity.

Marion shuffled through the duffel, and pulled out the little globe. It was wrapped in a blanket and still secure. Jacob was relived, but motioned for him to put it away. "I just wondered... you can put it back now."

Instead, Marion unwrapped it, shook it, and watched the little snowflakes fall down around the eagle with a mesmerized expression, like a child. Then his face grew concerned, and he set the globe aside.

"What'll we tell them?" Marion asked, his brow furrowed.

"Tell who?"

"The Marosi. How can we even tell them we betrayed them and destroyed the very thing they worship?"

There was no question that the travelers would have to confront the Marosi- they needed their food, their supplies, and most of all their protection.

Louis bit his lip, and fidgeted with a splinter of wood he had chipped from the wall. "When we go to them, *without* the orb, it's not as if we can lie. We'll them the truth, I guess. What does it matter if they're free to leave?"

Jacob sighed. "What does it matter? They've worshiped the damn thing for God knows how long. When they hear we destroyed

343

it… if we destroy it… I'm not sure what they'll do. You saw that…" He made a disgusted face. "… that head above the door. So, think what you want, but I'm not sure we can rely on them."

"Who else is there to trust?" Louis wondered aloud.

"*Them.*" Marion whispered, gazing out the window. There was a moment of silence. For a second the only sounds were the wind and the crackling of the fire.

"Them?" Jacob asked, not catching on. He was suddenly concerned for his friend's mental stability.

"The voices." Marion turned and looked at the others. "The ones who told us to go to the gate."

Jacob nodded, suddenly understanding. How had he forgotten? *Of course.* There was something else, something bigger. Perhaps it was these voices they could trust.

"Maybe. Yeah, maybe. For now… just rest." Jacob set aside the bandages and handed Louis the half-empty pill bottle. "Take those. I've got first watch."

His companions fell asleep easily enough, though Jacob was worried he wouldn't be able to. *What else is out there? What else is the Glass Shadow controlling, searching for us out in the endless white? What else will try and end us before the end can begin?*

CHAPTER 35
MARION ARMAIS
THE BARREN

Marion's watch was the last, and felt longer than it had the nights before. With only three of them now... there was less sleep and more huddling by the fire, staring out the window searching for something, anything. *Why?* Because they needed to be careful. They all did. It might not have helped them much beforehand, but had they not been more wary their horses would most likely be dead, their supplies gone, themselves even more injured and wandering in the cold. Being careful, well, it meant being alive.

Marion glanced out the window once again, but dawn was approaching, the sun shining on the fresh snow, and his watch was almost up; so he let down his guard and instead stared into the dwindling flames, which were fading into the glowing coals. The mornings were the moments he looked forward to. Each time they would wake up to the rising sun, sit around the dying fire and eat silently before mounting their horses and going on. The reason he enjoyed the mornings was simple. Marion felt at peace. There was no fear in the mornings, no falling into an exhausted sleep after a long day, no worry, no fights. That was for riding. That was for adventures, for their journey. *But not for the morning.* He suspected this was the last morning they would have together... if they didn't make it. The gate was close, and so was the orb.

***

The road had been covered, but it made no difference; their own path was clear. The horses trotted through the city of Vandor, though it looked little like the cities of home. The streets were wider, the building different, not as tall or clumped together. And although it was a dead city, Marion could tell it had been full of people with nothing better to do than talk and drink, for there were quite a lot of inns and bars. There were homes and markets and even a small stadium- there was still dried blood on the metal where the poor had fought for coins, with any weapon they happened to have on them. There was so much more, though all of it in ruins, cold and dark and desolate.

It once might have been a city of variety, though now everything looked the same. Snow had a way of doing that. It was quiet, and although Marion had never had a problem with silence before, he had the eerie feeling now that something wasn't right. Cities were not supposed to be quiet. No, not at all. It reminded Marion of the ghosts under the graveyard, and he shrunk back warily from the black, empty doorways and windows.

The snow started to fall again, and he heard Jacob sigh behind him. Louis was ahead, leading the way, though it did not take great skill to know where to go. The castle loomed ahead of them, and Marion kept his eyes locked on the tower. It was the tallest, and thought there were others just as impressive, he had a feeling in his gut that that was where the Glass Shadow lay. Marion feared in his mind that they would come yet again to be face-to-face with another abomination of the Barren, yet another enemy to fight- but somehow in his heart, in his dreading heart he knew that was not the case. *What here can the orb control? Nothing lives here.* The gate was close, and the gate meant answers. The gate meant a purpose, the gate meant hope.

"Marion!" Jacob called, his voice lowered. The orb and the King most likely knew of their presence, but they still didn't dare speak louder than they had too. "What about the horses?" He asked, and Marion furrowed his brow.

"What about the horses?"

"We can't bring them. And... we don't know what will happen at the gate."

346

Marion took his meaning and dismounted, leading his horse inside a nearby bar. The others did the same. Louis was not much in favor for it, but did not complain. He knew it was a smart decision, as did all of them. They had grown highly attached to their mares in the short time they'd had them, and Marion understood not wanting to leave them alone in such a place. Tied up, they couldn't run if something was out there. He pushed the thought from his mind. *There's nothing here, and you know it.* He did, and for the first time he was certain.

It was empty, deserted.

The only danger to them now was in the castle- or perhaps at the gate. They continued on foot, their boots sinking into the snow. It all seemed bigger now, all a little more real, when they weren't mounted on their strong steeds.

"Who do you think they are?" Marion asked, turning to Louis, who was having trouble hobbling through the snow on his crutches. He was asking about the voices, that much was clear.

"Who?" Louis said, shaking his head. "Not who. What." That was all the man said, and Marion gave up the attempt at conversation. They were all struggling on their own, now that they had come to face the most important moment of their lives. The silence was good, and within it they thought, they worried, and they gathered up the courage they could.

Marion, however, did not want to think; it made it all the harder to go onward. Nevertheless his mind wandered, and he found himself wondering of the life he had missed. There wasn't much to miss, really, and that filled him with regret. He didn't miss Calidor. Sure, he wished for the trees and the lakes and the pure sky again, the lights and sounds and the absence of fear, and the people. He missed the regular things, the peaceful things- but there were no people he loved there. There was only the old man at the markets of which he had forgotten his name, the blurred faces he had spent lonely nights with, and the criminals he every once and so often associated himself with. Everyone he'd loved was gone, buried in shallow graves. *How was I to know that life could be so short, and*

347

swept away so easily? He had been miserable, and hadn't had the mind to realize it.

Marion glanced over at a few skeletons lying on the porch of a home, at the fallen-in roof and the decomposing wood, at the darkness once filled with light, wondering how it had ended for them. Wondering, even though their lives had been cut short, if they had lived a better life than his. Was it so bad that the life he had now was in fact *better* than the one he'd had? He didn't know.

Marion had ones he loved now, even if they were only a cripple and a commoner who loved books. He had a purpose, one that meant more to him than stealing for others. He had a home, maybe one that wasn't in one place but it was more of a home than he'd ever had. Was it so bad to chose these things over everything he knew before? Marion didn't know. All he knew was that he was glad for once in his life, no matter how much pain he was in. Glad to be with people he loved, and glad to be doing what was right.

LOUIS WILLSON
THE BARREN

The snow fell, the wind blew, and everything around him faded. Faded into a blur of white and grey, of wood and sky. Louis walked though he put no thought to it, only to move forward alongside his companions, his friends, his brothers. This was it, this was the time, and though he was so relived to finally be here, he was terrified. Louis wanted nothing more than to keep going, to keep journeying on and on so they would never have to face what was to come. At the same time he knew there was no other way, he knew that at the end he would do what had to be done and that soon it would be over, it would all be over, and they could finally go home.

They could go back to Rendar. Somehow the thought of going to live at the farm again filled his stomach with a... wrongness. Like finishing a task and going back to do it over again. Like walking the same road over and over, like waking up and doing the exact same thing every day. He would visit them, his family, though now they were no more than people from the past. Louis had forgotten some of their names, and if not that then what they were like. What they did, what they wished, how much they trusted him and how much they cared for him. Except for May. Her, he would always remember.

Perhaps Louis would live in the Unventured Lands. Live in the forests and drink from the streams, see the lakes and the blue skies and the white puffy clouds. Somehow the thought of living in Rendar disgusted him, and for the first time he saw the reality of it. What he wanted was peace, and returning with a horde of savages and no Glass Shadow would not bring him such.

Maybe he would venture to the wilderness. *Maybe by the ocean and the salty breeze, or in the woods, the fields of wildflowers,*

349

the hills or the rocks or the lakes. Louis might even ask Jacob to come with, and Marion as well. After this... he knew none of them could return to their old lives. They were supposed dead, and he presumed that a great many people would not be glad to see them back. This did not bother him. He found he barely cared what anyone thought anymore.

However, if they didn't survive... Louis guessed it would be over soon either way. It surprised him how little he cared which fate it was. He wanted to live, though he thought that it wouldn't be so bad to die alongside his brothers, in a valiant fashion. It would be an honorable death.

And either way, it would all be over soon.

JACOB FORTEMER
VANDOR, THE BARREN

They were here. After all of the confusion and pain and suffering and loss- here they were. Jacob didn't feel any different, he didn't feel as if everything had become clear and he knew exactly what to do. Because he didn't. The world wasn't like that. The world wasn't black and white, it was gray. A gray world, always different shades- and it was up to him to decide on the darker and the lighter. *Sometimes, to obtain justice, we have to do things that may be unjust.*

They were going to kill a man. They were going to destroy the only thing that might be able to help them, if they had chosen wrong- they were going to stake thousands of lives on their decisions, on their choices. They had all committed crimes, done unjust things, and even now Jacob didn't know if what he was doing was right. If it was *just.*

Yet here he stood, among the ashes of mistakes and betrayal and failure, and he knew no matter what happened, they would try and bring a little more right into the world.

For the first time in a while, his mind wandered to Emilia. She would be eleven now, or twelve. Jacob had almost forgotten what she looked like. Blonde hair. He remembered that. Like gold, like the sun. *I'll find her,* he thought, *when I go back. If I go back.* Jacob was unsure of what he wanted to do, if he ever returned home. He would take Emilia somewhere, away from the city and his sister, though he did not know where. *Maybe find myself work.* And books. He would read and read, and perhaps write. Write of what had happened to him so someday someone would see the truth. So someone would know what the real history was.

However, he did not want to leave the company of Marion and Louis. They were brothers to him, more so than his sister had ever been, and had been by his side more than anyone he could remember. It was bliss to think about such things, so close to death. Their chance was small, though it was hard to tell what would happen. Should they have the help of whatever waited for them at the gate, the odds might just be in their favor. Whatever the case was, whether they would succeed or die, Jacob was glad he was not alone.

***

(hurryhurry before its toolate) The voice was there again, strong and powerful- urgent. All other thoughts vanished from his mind. *(hurry run to the gate tothegate tothe gate)* Jacob stopped in his tracks, listening. *(theorb the glassshadow it knows itknows, HURRYHURRY RUNTOTHEGATE)*

The others had stopped as well, and somehow he knew they all heard it. The voice was stronger. It was *panicked*. The travelers didn't move, despite the warning to run. It had come on so suddenly they needed a moment to take it in. They were so used to the silence that the first quake almost passed their notice... almost. It was subtle and faint, though it was the reality they needed to start running.

Louis hobbled along as fast he could, and was not left behind. Neither him nor Marion tried to help- somehow Jacob felt Louis would not appreciate being carried on the last walk before they met their fate. There was also the difficulty of hauling another man through the snow while he was trying to get through himself, and Jacob had a suspicion that carrying Louis would have been even slower.

The second quake was stronger, and sent them stumbling. Stones fell and wood cracked, snow shifted and the ruins of Vandor were disturbed for the first time in centuries. They continued onward, though it only got worse. At one point they were all on the ground, having fallen in the snow, praying the street wouldn't open up below them and send them plummeting down into the dark. Jacob was cold, cold all over, holding his ears to muffle the sound of destruction around him. Structures collapsed, cracks split the stone. Then it faded, and the rumblings of the earth quieted, and the travelers rose once again to face the gate.

Wearily they wondered of their horses, though most importantly they wondered what was coming. Adrenaline, mostly panic, rushed through him, and they soon came to the gate. When they arrived, Jacob expected to see someone, something, a clue or a gift or even a voice in their heads to tell them what to do. But there was nothing. Only stone pillars that rose, twisted, in an arch above them, engraved and elaborate.

A road led beyond, and Jacob almost thought he could see the doors of the castle. The steel black gates that had once been guarded and controlled the flooding of people had been broken, twisted, and thrown aside, now buried under the snow. The world was silent and gray, like an old black and white photo showing memories that could never reoccur, and the thought somehow made him very sad.

They walked closer to the gate, all urgency forgotten, unsure of what would happen. When they were close enough that another step would lead them past it, they stopped. Instead of going on, they waited. And waited. And waited. Jacob was about to voice his concern when suddenly he noticed the snowflakes were not falling. They were still in the air, granted, but they had just… stopped. The wind had as well, and the rumbling under the earth had fallen eerily silent. Everything was still. No matter how empty and motionless the city of Vandor had seemed before, somehow it was quieter. Somehow it was stiller. Somehow it was so empty he felt as if he were the only man in the world.

Jacob turned and looked at his brothers, who had noticed as well, and stared around the scene. It had happened to them once before, though that did not mean they were accustomed to it. *Time within time,* he thought. No voice came to them, but Jacob had an inkling of what they were supposed to do. It seemed the others did, too, for none of them spoke as they walked up the road towards the castle, through the frozen flecks of white- and Jacob suddenly felt as if he were in his own little glass orb, and that reality had been shaken and the storm had begun…

But their world was cracked and broken, and in the very paranoid back of his mind he feared the snowflakes would never reach the ground.

CHAPTER 36

MARION ARMAIS
VANDOR, THE BARREN

The large, foreboding doors were wooden, strong and solid and scarred. Bronze handles shone in the still light, and with almost trembling hands Marion reached forward and pulled. He had expected it to be locked, and the fact that it wasn't set fear in his heart. A trap? Though the travelers had the upper hand, and Marion knew it. Perhaps there was a trap, but not in the moments between time, not in the place where snow didn't fall and the wind didn't blow. For now, they were safe.

We'll find the orb, we'll find the King, and we'll kill them both before they even have a chance to see us. Before we even set foot beyond the gate... in their eyes. It was clever, though somehow it almost seemed too easy. Who, what had given them this advantage, and why? *Why?* But Marion did not complain nor turn back, he only kept an eye out for things unseen. No matter what the case was, their chance was here, their chance was now- and they would not miss it.

He pulled the door open and it creaked, loudly, sending echos through the halls ahead. Inside it was dark, the only light shining in through the open windows; a white, pale light that made it feel even more abandoned than it had before. When all was black, Marion didn't know what was hiding in the shadows. This lacked that haunted feel, that chill and fear. It was more like visiting a place of the past and knowing it could never be the same.

They did not talk, for every breath and every footstep seemed like thunder in their ears. The castle was stone, cold stone, the carpets on the floors having been reduced to little more than scraps and dust. Braziers lined the walls, though they were absent of any flames.

As Marion looked around, it was obvious that there had once been fine furnishings and art, music, books and riches and more within these walls. Once. Now all that remained were bones, dried wood and rags, ruins and an orb in a tower beneath the sky. *Too easy.* Marion thought again, as they walked slowly through the halls. *It's easy, too goddamn easy.* Perhaps that was how it was sometimes, and that after all the hard work there didn't need to be one last fight, one last stand. *Maybe there doesn't need to be an unbelievable, dramatic, suspenseful ending to my story. Maybe real adventures are different.*

But Marion didn't believe it. Not for one second. Because if there was one thing he was certain about, it was that the orb wouldn't go without a fight, that it wouldn't go without vengeance- and *that* would not be so easy.

***

They wandered for what felt like eternity. Marion's adrenaline had left him, and he was weary from roaming the endless halls. Always up, up the stairs, turning back and trying another way. He knew they were running out of time. Once, only for a moment, the snow had started to fall again. Another time he saw the pale light from outside shift slightly with the shadows, and a crow had landed on a windowsill before freezing again. Twice they had heard and felt the faint rumblings under the earth, and they knew whatever was helping them was losing it's grip on time.

"Marion?" Jacob asked, as they waited for Louis to ascend the stairs. His voice echoed. "Is this the last?"

It was. Every other staircase had been climbed and marked by scratches in the stone. Either this was it, or there was another way to the tower. Marion nodded, a tight feeling in his stomach. No adrenaline now- only fear. A deep, deep fear.

They continued up, the old smell of the castle replaced by a light one, of snow and breeze and height. The spiraling stairs went on and on, the air getting colder as they rose. As much as Marion urged himself to hurry, to do the deed, to rush because there wasn't much time- there was another part of him that only wanted to turn around and run, run and run and never come back.

He just wanted it to be over.

Finally, Marion turned to see a door, so harmless; yet it chilled him to the bone. He froze and it almost seemed as if time had a hold on him too, until his companions came beside him and motioned for him to open it. Marion was in no state of mind to argue, so instead he gripped the ice-cold doorknob and pulled. And pulled again. It didn't open, and Jacob cleared his throat. Marion turned to look at him.

"Ah..." Jacob walked up, turned the knob, and pushed lightly. It swung open, absent of any creaks or groans. For a moment there was an embarrassed silence, but it did not last long. Who could blame him, with what lay ahead? Marion took a deep breath, and with no further hesitation, he moved. Nervously they stepped out into the grey light, into the frozen snow, into the cold air and stared into the depths of the Glass Shadow.

JACOB FORTEMER
VANDOR, THE BARREN

White. It felt so familiar, yet so strange. Instead of eyes, the swirling storm was now inside the orb, frozen in the moments between time. The glass was untarnished, not a scratch to be found. A cage encircled it, though once Jacob reached out his hand to touch it, the steel crumbled to dust at his touch. It had been there for the King; in fact, the cage might not have been there at all, just an illusion the bond had formed, to keep the King and orb apart.

The travelers were high, very high, and though the wind was absent, the thin air was still cold and bitter, despite thier furs. The sky was pale and cloudy, no sun to be seen. Snow was everywhere, and the city stretching out below them was covered in it. They could see for miles around, and for a moment Jacob's breath was taken away. It was quiet, it was peaceful.

They did not know where the King was, most likely somewhere in the castle, and they preferred it to stay that way. Here he faced the Glass Shadow, Marion and Louis beside him. Jacob walked forward, carefully, his footsteps quiet. Just as his fingers brushed the smooth, cool surface of the orb, their moment between time fractured; their ally's grip slipped and to their devastation, the wind started to blow. The snow started to fall, the light and the clouds started to shift, the rumbles of the earth were felt again- and the white storm inside the orb pulsed a raging black, swirling fast and almost panickingly.

"Oh no, no no no..." Jacob muttered, pulling his hand back in fear. *Just smash it, just grab it and smash it-* but he couldn't, he couldn't. Jacob could feel it trying to get inside his mind, to his eyes, to control him. He could feel it and he fought it, fought it hard, and he assumed the others were doing the same. Then it stopped, and he heard laughing. Laughing of many voices, but it was only one. Jacob ran forward and grabbed it, but he could not lift it. His hands burned, but he could not take them away.

Marion came, as did Louis, and he tried to yell, to warn them, but they touched it and a second later they were torn away from the tower,

       away from the wind,

           away from the snow,

               to a city.

His brothers were beside him, and they stood in the middle of a road, though no one seemed to see them. There were people and animals and bars lit up with laughter and light and the clinking of glasses, there were homes and children running... and a castle. Vandor. It was Vandor, the city of the Lost War. The city of the King. There was some unrest, a few guards and wary looks, but the war had moved, and for now they were safe. A voice filled his head, demeaning and harsh, though at the same time amused.

"See it? Does it remind you of home?" It taunted, and Jacob took a step back. This wasn't real, it couldn't be, just a dream just a dream *just a dream-*

"But is it?" The voice said again. *"Watch."* Jacob did, for what other choice did he have? Then he felt it, the rumblings, but they were strong they were so strong- people glanced around worriedly, a child dropped her doll, a vendor selling fruit from his cart picked up a rolling apple. And then Jacob fell and stumbled, scraping his hands of the stone street. Chaos erupted, it was a quake, it was a quake but little did they know it was something much worse.

The road exploded in front of him, and he lapsed back to his vision, and Jacob knew it was the darkness coming from the depths of the earth; and it was, it was long and dark and filled the air with a putrid smell. It's body was that of a snake, with night-black scales and two swirling white eyes. Nostrils flared, and it's tail crushed both wood and stone. One man who got too close withered up and died, his cheeks sinking, his skin drying, his face in a frozen expression of terror.

When the creature opened it's mouth it revealed hundreds of teeth, sharp like talons and hard as steel. The thing thrashed and fought and wreaked destruction, everything around it poisoned. The child who'd dropped her doll started to cry, but no one heard. In only moments her innocent little self had turned into a corpse, dried and broken and reeking of sickness... of dark-radiation. The fruits in the carts shriveled into rotten clumps before splattering to the ground. The beast, could he even call it that, reared up and screeched, it was so loud it hurt oh God it hurt- and Jacob put his hands to his ears. When he took them away, he saw they were bleeding.

Then Jacob fell into darkness, and landed in an open field, with trees and crops and a small little farmhouse in the distance. Marion and Louis were once again by his side, and he moved closer, giving them nervous looks. He was grateful they were there.

"Jacob, the-" Marion stopped mid-sentence, and looked down at the dirt beneath his feet. It had turned black, and in some parts had hardened into rock. The crops started to wilt, the leaves fell from the trees, turning to dust as they withered. The trunk rotted, the branches twisting, and all around them everything started to die. A terribly sick feeling came onto him then, and Jacob could feel the radiation seeping into the land. One of them was close. He knew there was more than one of the creatures, just as he knew they were the reason for the radiation. The King had undoubtedly used the orb to summon them from their dormant states, in his lust for power. In doing so he had wreaked havoc on his own lands and doomed himself. Once again there was the rumblings, though nothing burst onto the surface.

"*These Vertem, the ones you've put so much trust in... see what they've done?*"

A shout escaped Jacob's throat. "It was you, you bastard! You controlled them, you brought them here, it was all you!"

The orb chuckled. "*Perhaps. I only did what the King bid of me, at the time. But now I see. They have more power than I thought, it seems. You lost your chance. You see what they can do? They were hungry, but there is nothing left for them here and I would not let*" *them leave. Combined with that and my own control over them... Do you know where they are right now?"* It asked, and Jacob shook his head, a panicked feeling filling his mind.

Where? Where are they? He had heard them, though it seemed like forever ago. Jacob had heard them under the ground, moving. The scene of the dying farm faded and now he was home, but this was not the past. He was in Viajar, Malivia, the city of the Castle, the city of his home... and everything was in ruin.

***

"No. No, no no no." Jacob shook his head, unwilling to believe it. Stones crumbled around him, a harsh air stung his lungs and old papers fluttered in the harsh wind. It was grey. A grey world, with gloomy clouds and the feeling no one was here but him, and that something was going to happen but he didn't know what. It was Viajar, his home. Buildings were collapsed and streets destroyed... the ones who had been in hiding, who had refused to leave- it was their bodies that were scattered along the streets, and to his despair there were much more than Jacob had imagined. They were bloodied and battered and most of them dead, while some had withered up and died and then he saw his daughter, alive, blood streaming down her face and she called for him- she called but he could not answer. Jacob knew what had done this but he did not blame them, no, he was too smart for that... he blamed the orb. In his fury the scene disappeared and they were back in the tower and the voice of the Glass Shadow echoed in their heads.

"These Vertem, fascinating creatures, aren't they? Their own bodies create a dark-radiation so strong, look what it did to Maros. But... enough. You have betrayed me, and sided with the very beasts that are at this moment wreaking havoc on your home. Free me. Take me from this cage to the ocean, and I will forget your foolish actions and let you live. I will cure you of dark-radiation, I will stop controlling the Vertem and I will never return."

There was something in that voice Jacob didn't like. He had no trust in the Glass Shadow, none at all. He had no trust in the King, and little trust in the Vertem. What Jacob did have trust in was himself, and at this moment he felt that the writhing demons from under the earth would be of much more help to them than the orb.

"What do you chose? Death or life? This is your last chance. The King is coming, I can see him now."

And it was not wrong. Jacob could hear him. Hear his footsteps up the stairs, fast, knowing something was wrong, that something was out of place. Jacob turned to Louis, who looked shaken up, worried, and he imagined that the poor fellow had a family back home. Or... he did. Who knew what had become of their homes? He glanced at Marion. Who knew what had become of Calidor? Of the Unventured Lands?

Then the door handle turned, and the King stepped through; he saw them and his face became one of surprise and fear, but most of all anger. A dark feeling was in the air, and the winds raged; the orb seemed displeased with how things were going.

The King rose his hand, his deep blue eyes filled with shock and betrayal and hate- and then he stopped. The wind stopped. The snow, the pulsing storm inside the orb, the light and the clouds and time, it all stopped. Jacob did not freeze with it- instead adrenaline filled him again, and a new voice in his mind...

(Do it Jacobdoit do it destroy it smash it BREAK IT) And in that moment he felt right, felt strong, and he stepped forward, without hesitation. Time was running out, though time was different here. Time was different now.

Jacob put his finger warily to the glass, but it did not burn him. It was only cold, ice-cold, like the air around him, like the storm inside. It was smooth, flawless, the mist inside still black like a thunderstorm but it would not be so much longer.

Jacob picked it up, and it was lighter than he had expected. Light as a feather, fragile, precious. With the face of his bleeding daughter stuck in his mind, with the faces of all the others who had died, Amicus, Oliver, the people of Rendar and Maros and the

362

travelers before him- he rose the orb into the shining sunlight one last time before smashing it hard against the grey stone.

Time resumed itself, and a feeling of peace filled his heart. Avenged. The Glass Shadow shattered into pieces, the smoke inside rising up, dissolving into the winter air. The glass remains shimmered in the pale sun, seeming so harmless, so clear.

The King gasped, staring around. He ran over to the broken shards, picking them up, muttering under his breath. He cut his fingers, but didn't seem to notice. When the King realized all hope was lost, he turned to the men behind him, furious. The King yelled, rising to meet them. He pulled a dagger from his sheath, and it gleamed in the sunlight.

They were speechless, and could not find the will to draw their own weapons. The orb was gone, the Glass Shadow dead- they had no resolution to dealing with the King. He came closer.

His voice was trembling, holding back furious anger. "If you think you've won, you're about to be sorely disappointed."

And to their shock he leapt forward and drove his dagger deep into Jacob's heart.

***

Now, here's a little something to know about Jacob Fortemer. When he was only ten, his sister abandoned him at an orphanage and went off to pursue her own dreams concerning the Castle. This not only angered him because of her desertion, but because she would be working for Rovas Mchenry; the man who was responsible for the death of their parents. However, that was a story for another time.

This led Jacob into the life of the street, stealing and hiding in dark alleyways. For a while he was able to pull himself out of poverty, rising up within the system. It took time, effort, and pure will to push himself through, but he made it. He got an education, became a lawyer. Eventually he was lucky enough to earn himself the position of prosecutor in a case against Mchenry himself. The trial was brutal, unending, the courtroom filled with tension; and then it was over, the decision made. Rovas Mchenry spent several years in prison for his involvement in the gangs of Rendar. All crimes he was responsible for, yet for not all was he deemed guilty. Still, it was enough for Jacob. He had avenged his family, in a sense, in the best way he could. He had done what he had set out to do. Jacob Fortemer was respected in Malivia. He was important. He made a difference.

Though even this could not last very long. A year after the trial, allies of the political leader he had condemned sent him spiraling down once again into poverty. But not all hope had vanished.

Emilia was lost, and Jacob Fortemer found her. Gave her a home. Gave her a family; which, frankly, was something they both needed at the time. He resolved issues with his sister, got another job, and continued reading his books. The future no longer looked as dark as the nights he had once slept under.

Then, inevitably, the bill came due. The past caught up to Jacob Fortemer, a man who had never wanted to remember his past in the first place. A certain political influence was released from captivity, and had an aim to settle his quarrels with those who had dared oppose him. Jacob was captured, met a group of men who became his brothers, and started the journey that would never bring him the money he was promised. The end of his story was approaching, whether he wanted it to or not.

If Jacob Fortemer had known then where his choices would lead him, he never would have walked into that courtroom.

Too little to late, I guess.

CHAPTER 37
MARION ARMAIS
VANDOR, THE BARREN

Marion stood in horror as the body collapsed, blood spilling, staining the stones and the snow. Jacob coughed, and coughed again. The wound was deep and clearly painful, and his friend gasped as blood streamed from his mouth.

For a moment Jacob convulsed, then lay still, the surprise still painted evidently on his face. His blue eyes glassed over, reflecting the pale sky and snow above, like little lifeless orbs.

Everything was quiet for a moment.

Marion felt as if something was wrong, dreadfully wrong. They had done it, they had destroyed the Glass Shadow, so why was his friend lying on the floor, unmoving, blood soaking his clothes? Why did the King have a bloodied dagger clutched in his hand, an insane, sickly grin of satisfaction on his face? Why, dear God why hadn't they done something? His gut filled with a sick, horrible feeling, and he could feel tears brimming in his one good eye.

But he was Marion, the hunter, the survivor, he couldn't cry he wouldn't- but it was Jacob, it was his brother, with a hole in his chest and they had done nothing *they had done nothing*- and he turned to the King, without really thinking, pulled out his own knife and felt a growl escape his throat.

Without hesitation, in a surge of anger, he forcefully gripped the King by his collar and pulled him close, snarling. Without a second thought, Marion flipped his knife and stabbed him in the eye, plunging it deep into his skull and twisting.

Marion's vision was consumed by red, white, furious flashes of anger. Panicked, the King let out a brutal scream that echoed in

365

his ears, but Marion didn't seem to notice. Everything had become a blur, a mess blinded by tears, by grief.

Marion drove his dagger into the other eye, and soon they were both covered in blood, the King clawing at his empty, mauled sockets, face streaming red. He stumbled back, but somehow only seemed stronger and angrier. Furiously the King moved towards them, slashing his knife into empty air. His breathing was heavy and labored.

"YOU - FUCKING - FILTHY - SONS OF-" The King suddenly gripped his throat and emitted a strangled noise, almost as if he were choking. "No, no, *no*." He stumbled backward, falling to the stone floor.

His hair started to fall out, the age working it's way up from the roots, going from black to gray to white. The King's cheeks sunk into his skull, and his body thinned and deteriorated. The black cloak and faded clothes he wore had became only rags. A strong gust of wind blew dust from his skin, which had turned gray as well, and soon they stood before a skeleton, who had chosen his last words to be insults and denial. For moments after the travelers stood there, silent among the calming wind and the fading snow.

Louis collapsed to his knee at Jacob's side, holding his head in his arms and mumbling, sobbing, but Jacob couldn't hear him, he knew he couldn't hear him. Marion, without really sure if he was in control of himself anymore, knelt at his friend's side and stared. Marion gently brushed a strand of black hair from Jacob's forehead, shutting his brother's eyes, unable to look at the glassy blue any longer. An emptiness filled his heart, overwhelming, and Marion leaned forward and pressed a gentle kiss at Jacob's hairline; a final farewell.

He didn't know quite how long he sat there, but the sun was to the west now. For some reason that was all his mind could comprehend, and so he repeated it in his mind, trying to make sense of it as he gazed, shocked, at the motionless body in front of him. After so much of this, Marion turned back to the lands of which he could see so far, and waited. Stared into the horizon, mind blank, body numb. For what he waited for, he was unsure of, but Louis did the same and had no objection. For the first time in years, perhaps his life, he saw the true beauty of the world.

Marion saw how even a desolate wasteland such as this could be redeemed. Not only that, but he enjoyed it. Enjoyed being alive, appreciated his ability to breathe in the chilly air and smell the scent of the winter cold, even if it was ruins he was looking over. The sea to the north was a frozen expanse of ice, with nothing to see but endless white and a dock with a few old boats.

He felt so at peace, strangely, and so serene. Like his mind had been emptied and calmness was all that was left. Marion was so relived that their task was done, but all the same he struggled to remember his dead friend's last words and could not. He looked down to see his bloodied hands shaking. Marion had lost the use of one eye on this wretched journey, and he felt it was right to rid the King of two before his death.

These Vertem were the only menace still out there that they knew of, and a part of his mind hoped that once they were free from the Glass Shadow, the creatures would be on their way, to the ocean, under it, wherever they wished. Wherever they had been called from. But somehow Marion knew that was not so. Not until after they had spoken with their victors.

And after hours of waiting, his legs growing numb, he felt them. The rumbling under the ground. It slowly grew stronger and stronger, closer and closer. He looked at Louis, and his friend nodded. It was time. There was no fear in him now.

Marion picked Jacob up in his arms; he seemed so light compared to the burden that had been removed from his shoulders. He tried his best not to notice the blood dripping from his friend as they walked. Louis had been clinging to Jacob's shirt, and reluctantly let it go. The travelers descended the tower, their footsteps echoing in their ears. It didn't seem so eerie anymore. The castle was as silent as is had been before, but… friendlier.

They walked through it in shock, as if not quite believing what had happened. It was a shorter journey, but they still found themselves lost at times. When they pushed open the wooden doors and emerged into snow and sunlight victorious, he felt his heart lift inside his chest. Neither of them had said a word after Jacob had died, but no words were needed. The body in Marion's arms was still warm, and his tears fell on the pale, lifeless skin. He sniffed, trying to gather his emotions and shove them deep, deep down. *It's what I've always done, isn't it?*

Marion stood, grateful that their nightmare was over, but saddened. Grateful that they were both alive and had someone to thank for it- but someone else was dead, bleeding in his arms, and there was nothing he could do to change that.

The ground started to shake once again.

They were here.

LOUIS WILLSON
VANDOR, THE BARREN

He stumbled back, and though he knew what came was no longer an enemy, his heart still raced. Louis could feel them, their power, and a sick feeling filled his stomach; their dark-radiation was stronger here than it had been in the visions the orb had shown them. Louis was reminded of the effects it was having on him, and had he had the chance to look at his reflection he most likely would not have recognized himself.

Louis Willson was weary, he could grant himself that, but he felt stronger now that the Glass Shadow was broken and the King was dead. He felt lighter, as if a huge weight of despair, fear, and exhaustion had been lifted off his chest. Their hardships were done, for now.

These... Vertem only had to leave them be, head off on their own, and they would be free of the darkness. Perhaps Maros would even grow again, if these creatures left; perhaps the radiation would fade without the beasts there to sustain it. The thought of living here did not appeal to him, but Louis assumed it would for others, if the freelanders brought word of it's revival.

If such did not happen, this would be a wasteland for as long as it was here, but it would be rid of the poison of the orb, the King, and the beasts beneath the earth. Either way, it was over; but one thing at a time. For now, they had to face the Vertem. *And the fate they bring to our lands,* Louis thought worriedly. Shifting on his battered crutches, he stared as the ground burst, darkness emerged, and a demon came to greet them.

It was large, and had surely grown since the rage on Maros, but the calm look in it's wide, sea-blue eyes made it seem all the less intimidating. Now it did not seem as much of a monster, but more of

369

a creature that had been trapped in a cage and, after a long while, set free. It's scales seemed more obsidian-jewel than night-black coal; almost beautiful. The only thing that wasn't different was the poison it emitted around itself, melting the nearby snow. Louis gazed up in awe, and somehow could not find the words to say... well, anything. Neither of them could. Instead the beast spoke first, in their minds- maybe the only way it was able.

At the same time it hissed in a slow tone, and it occurred to him that that was their language, and that it was being translated in their heads. Louis wasn't sure how, but... he wasn't really sure of anything anymore.

(We thank you. We can finally see, and we are glad. Once we are gone your lands will be safe. We won't return, if that is your wish.) It paused, tilted its head for moment as if it were thinking, then went on. Perhaps it was observing Jacob.

(There are other lands beyond your own, if it matters. We give you that knowledge, and this.)

It bent down to the stone and opened its mouth, revealing unchanged teeth, and a rolling dark blue tongue. It cracked one tooth on a rock, so it fell out into the snow.

(Crush it and spread it in a fire. The smoke will heal you.) There was another moment of silence. *(Again. Thank you.)*

And with that the beast disappeared into the ground, and they were left with nothing but a hole in the ground and a broken fang among the rubble. The rumblings under the earth soon faded, and the air was quiet and still.

***

They buried Jacob at the gate. Marion had no strength left to carry him, and it only made him regret what had happened. *It will grow to be a beautiful place,* Louis thought, looking around. *Just give it time.*

They left Jacob and their sorrows behind in the dirt, but the empty face of their dead friend was all he could think of as they walked. Louis suspected it would haunt their nightmares for a while yet. Their horses were safe enough, along with everything they carried, and that alone made Louis want to grin. Want to. He didn't. Couldn't. Whenever he started to feel good, he would glance over at Marion, at his arms still covered in Jacob's blood, and the feeling would be gone. The day seemed sunnier already, but his mind and soul were shrouded in mist and rain. The clouds had cleared, and the light shone on the snow. It might not have been a cheerful event for them, but it certainly was for the land. It was finally over, after all they had done. After all that had happened- here they were. Two of them, at least.

Louis stroked his horse's mane and vaguely wondered if he was obliged to return her to the Marosi. It depended on how pleased they were that their *Qasyies* was dead. It seemed this was on everyone's mind, for Marion, fang clutched in hand, voiced a thought.

"Do we... go back to them?" Marion asked. "The Marosi? To tell them they can leave the forest?"

Louis hadn't considered the thought of going home on their own, after their deal, but it seemed that now the Vertem were gone, the land was healing... it might be that they could just make it without the help of savages. Especially if they were healed.

So Louis shook his head. "No, I think not. They'll figure it out soon enough, when the grass turns green again and the flowers bloom. If we go, and they don't take the news well..."

Marion understood. They could be the next bleeding head mounted above that door. And all they had done would be not for them to see. It was better this way- they were healed of their sickness, and they could survive with what they had.

Marion slipped the tooth into his bag, tied Jacob's horse to his own, and lead both mares out into the open. Louis looked at him expectantly. *Why can't we use it now?* He thought questionably. Louis wanted to light a fire and throw the tooth as quickly as humanly possible. They could rid themselves of the disease that had been haunting them for over a year, maybe more, and now that they had a solution they would *wait?*

"Tonight." Marion said, mounting his horse and trotting down the road. "I want to get out this awful place first."

Grimly, Louis nodded. Though he did not quite agree, he understood the feeling, and respected it. He followed his friend out of the city of ruins, and back in the direction of home.

***

That night they lit a fire. It was a small fire, but warm, and that was all they really needed it to be. The orange flickering light hit their faces, and all around them was dark. Only their eyes shone, glassy like orbs floating in the air.

Marion took the fang from his pack, very carefully. Louis barely had time to wonder why he held it so gently before his question was answered. His friend passed it to him, and it was not heavy nor hard, and he would have thought it to be- but weak and fragile. It was like it had faded away in the time it had been separated from its owner.

Marion took it from him, and without any further hesitation he crushed it in his palm and sprinkled it over the fire. The flames instantly turned blue, and cast an eerie ocean-like light upon them. Louis leaned in and breathed in the smoke, and at first it made him cough. It made his mouth taste like ashes, burning his eyes. The next breath was somehow easier. Louis took another, and another. It filled him with… a feeling he could not describe, like falling fast or seeing a breathtaking sight. It was a good feeling, but only lasted so long.

The blue flames faded, leaving only burning coals that glowed when the wind blew. The last of the smoke drifted into the night air, and Louis suddenly felt a strong urge to sleep. He lay back on the rock and gave in. And just before he faded into darkness, just before he closed his eyes, he thought he could see the a twinkle of a star in the sky.

***

They did not return to the people of the forest. They did not return to the cave, the lake of the beast, the Crossing, the graveyard or even the village they had been captured in so long ago. They took a different path, by the shore of the sea, and walked along the beaches wondering of what was beyond the horizon. Wondering if they would *really* dare to venture out in search of other lands, of other people. Louis loved the thought of it. Exploring, making a difference in the world, but not taking a single step. With the reassurance that there *was* something out there, all they had to do was find it.

Louis found that he was a changed man. Marion was, as well. Before they had even left the Barren on their journey home, they had seen things, little things, that hadn't seemed to matter much before. A blade of green grass, a bright leaf on a tree, an animal that didn't look as if it had been dead and then rose again. The one thing that cheered them most of all was the absence of swirling white in the eyes of every living thing they saw. Each time they looked into someone or something's eyes, they were reminded of their victory, of their accomplishments. Of the people they had become. All of those little things touched Louis's heart, while beforehand he would barely have even noticed if it were a sunny or cloudy day.

Before, he had been no one. A cripple, a commoner, a face among hundreds. Thousands. But he had changed that, and now he was who he wanted, and no matter what anyone saw him as, that is what he would always be. Louis would never again live in blurred days, wondering if his life would get any better, his only joy the bed at night. He would never be that man again, and he felt he could see so clearly now. Louis knew what he wanted, he knew what he loved, he knew himself, and had accepted it.

Now he trotted along the beach, his horse's hooves sinking into the sand, his new brother riding beside him. The sun rose to the east, and he breathed the salty cold air. Much time had passed since they had been at the castle of Vandor, months possibly. Winter had come and gone quickly, and spring was close. He hoped it was a long one.

Louis's red hair fell in tangles at the base of his neck, his short beard growing longer. He had done his best to keep it clean, but now he hardly cared. His blisters, bruises, scratches and various injuries had faded, become scars and old memories not quite forgotten. His clothes were so worn it was impossible to tell what color they had been. When he looked at himself in streams, when he looked at Marion, he barely recognized the people he saw- Louis remembered what they had been like before, and perhaps had gotten used to the change, but he knew whoever remained for them in Rendar would not know them. They would be considered foreigners, strangers. But none of that mattered now. They could not change it, only face what it was. They were close. Very close. He could sense it, in the wind.

They were almost home.

"What do you think will be left?" Marion asked, as they headed inland. They were turning east now, making for the bridge.

Louis shook his head. "Will it matter to you?"

Marion didn't respond. He knew his friend had almost nothing to return to, and it may have been a little harsh to remind him of that, but Louis was much too concerned with worrying for his own family. It hurt to think of them. His sister, May... she was young. She had been ill the day he had left, and he prayed she was alive. She was strong. His brothers would be there, most likely. They had been cruel to him, though Henry and Kendrick were kind enough. The others, though... Faylon especially. He always had to be better at everything. *What they would think of me now,* he thought, shaking his head. *With a murderer at my side, a rough beard, a horse of my own and a dagger on my belt.* And despite still being a cripple, he knew he was someone that no one wanted to mess with. His scars were proof enough of that. He was a survivor now. A fighter. A part of him was proud of that.

Louis thought these strange thoughts as they rode through the grasslands, towards the river and towards home. Inside he still felt a little like the younger, weaker man from the farm in Paerdan- but too much had changed for him to be the same. Everyone changed, even if they didn't know it.

Marion had untied Jacob's mare and wanted to let it go, but it had followed them and refused to leave. Here it was still, at the end. For they were there, crossing the bridge, staring into the crushed city beyond it. He remembered Jacob saying he had a daughter, Emilia. An image flashed in his mind. It was the girl from the vision the orb had shown them, the little girl bleeding, wandering through the streets. The one Jacob had been so wreaked upon seeing.

"Marion, we have to try and find her."

"Find who?" The criminal asked, scanning the dusty ruins for any signs of life.

"Jacob's daughter." There was silence. "We owe him that much, don't you think?" Louis sighed, continuing. "You've been to Malivia, right? You've been here? Did you recognize the street in the vision?"

There was no more that needed to be said. Marion burst suddenly into a gallop, charging into the city of Viajar, dodging through ruins and crumbling stone structures. Louis charged in after him, following best he could. He could understand his friend's urgency- the least they could do for their dead brother was this, and the faster they found her the faster they would feel they had done all they could for him.

Louis could see the buildings of the Castle in the distance, many of them torn down, a lone flag waving in the breeze. The street they had seen in the vision, the one where they had seen the girl, came into view, and he frantically looked around. Marion had dismounted his horse, and he followed.

"*EMILIA!*" Louis shouted, unsure of what to do.

Marion gave him a warning look, but he ignored it. What were they going to do, search the entire city? He could hear his voice echoing in the emptiness.

"*EMILIA!*" Louis yelled again, grabbing his crutches and hobbling down the road. There was no response, only a clatter of stones somewhere far off, lost in the wind. He started to notice the bodies, skeletons now, and the rats that scampered by looking for nonexistent food. Then a knife was pressed to his throat, the metal cold and rusted.

"*Who are you*? How do you know that name?" The voice was a little girl's.

"What?" He asked, confused.

Marion was motionless, staring, not wanting to provoke anything. Louis knew his friend didn't want to chance losing everyone he cared about; everything he had left.

"Maybe I'm not making this clear enough for you." She pressed in harder, and flecks of blood started to drip down his neck. "*How do you know that name?*"

Louis let out a shaky breath. "We were looking for her, our friend Jacob-" She took the knife away.

"*Yes?*" She pushed. "Tell me!"

"Are you Emilia?"

"Not anymore, not really. What happened? How do you even..."

Louis's voice shook. So, here they were, and he had to be the one to tell a little girl her father was dead. "He... he's gone. I- I'm so sorry."

She took a deep breath and sighed. "Why would he leave? Where were you going?"

Louis turned to face her. She had tattered clothes and dirty blonde hair, pulled back. Some of her face seemed burned, as did various parts of her arms and neck- and there was barely anything covering it up. It truly made him realize how long it had been. She was young, with a pretty face, but her eyes were grey and ferocious. Jacob would not have known her, Louis realized. Then again, she might not have recognized Jacob either.

"It's a long story, Emi-"

"That's not my name."

"What am I supposed to call you then?"

"Does it matter?" She asked, and Louis nodded.

376

"To me."

She looked up at him, and cocked her head. "Aveiry."

"Any reason why?" He wondered aloud.

She pulled out a silver chain from under her shirt, attached to a strange looking seashell.

"It's what my friend called me. His name was Gabriel. He brought me this, when he left to the ocean. He never really went anywhere because of me, but I learned to survive without him. So he left. He always told me there was something better out there."

Aveiry glanced at the shell once again before she tucked it away. It was white, smooth, with a black marking on it- like a rune of some sort. Vaguely Louis wondered who this Gabriel was that had called her by her new name. And then, as he looked over at Jacob's mare, he knew he had found a use for it.

"We're going to the ocean." He said at once. Marion looked at him for a moment, before nodding respectively. They had never decided, but they had talked of it and had always been in the back of their minds. "And it's a long story."

Louis offered his hand, dirty as it was, holding it out under the setting sun. The girl seemed surprised at the sudden respect. She looked at it for a moment, her eyes bright, before she sheathed her knife and shook it.

CHAPTER 38

MARION ARMAIS
THE FARMLANDS, PAERDAN

Everything was different. The fields were empty, the air still. It was all just... abandoned. All the life and soul Marion had known about this land had gone, their only company the birds in the sky. Paerdan usually was crowded, the roads full of travelers and traders, rich and poor. Now there was no one. They trotted along the path that cut across Malivia, Aleria, and Paerdan to get to the ocean.

"Louis, this boat... when did you last see it?" He asked, his suspicions aroused. Louis had told them of a ship his father had found and repaired, though he did not know where it might be now.

"It was large, and strong, on the docks by the sea. My brother Henry took me there once, to watch our father work. He'd wanted to sail it one day." He didn't say more. They hadn't gotten much out of Louis concerning his family, but they had food and water and a chance for a boat, and that was more important than anything. *I can't wait to get away from here,* Marion thought, looking into the distance. Something about Rendar made him feel sick inside. Aveiry shrugged, and flipped her dagger in her hand.

"I would too, if I were him." She said. "Will any of your family be a problem?"

Louis looked surprised, then sad. "I couldn't tell you. Not anymore."

There was an awkward silence, but it was broken by voices in the trees to their right.

"This is all we have left, I'm telling you-" The voice was accompanied by a woman's.

"There's more in the towns, there always is, we're close now. Maggie told me they were heading just south of Wellburrow, we can-"

"Calidor is still far away, hell, Maggie is probably dead. You heard, didn't you? And I won't have you eating everything we have in just one night."

Two commoners pushed though the bushes, weary, the man with a graying beard stepping onto the road with the plump woman just behind him.

"Vince, wait, what about..." Her frighted brown eyes landed on them, and Marion smiled lightly. It seemed to only scare her more. The man came to notice them too, and stood in the center of the path. It was clear they hadn't seen many other people as of late. It was the same the other way round, so for a moment they all stood and stared. It was the older man who cleared his throat and spoke first.

"And who are you lot?" He asked, his eyes wavering for a moment on the little girl with a burned face and a knife in her hand. "Where... where're you off to?" He shifted his feet, nervous. When he reached Marion's face his eyes widened, and even more so when he saw Louis. It somehow made Marion feel a little more powerful, a little more intimidating. It made him feel in control.

"I'm Marion Armais. This is Louis and... Aveiry. We're headed to Paerdan, to whatever's left of it. You?"

The old man stuttered. "T-to The Unventured Lands, m-mister Armais. Everyone was in Calidor... but it wasn't far enough. Some may have escaped, o-or left, I-"

Louis interrupted him. "Your name?"

"My- my name?"

"Yes."

"Vince. Vince Dyer. Th-this is my w-wife, Lisa." The woman glanced around nervously.

"Well, Vince Dyer, why are you so afraid?" Louis asked them, confused. Something wasn't right about this.

The old man trembled. "Please... please don't hurt us, we don't have anything..."

"What do you mean?"

"You're wanted. You, and him. There were others, too, but I can't remember..." Vince fidgeted with the hem of his shirt. "When you all disappeared, goodness, it was so long ago... Mchenry p-put it in the papers. Everyone knew your names, your faces. He said you all had helped in the- in the murder of Paulen, that Denroe boy... that you were capturing men a-and women and children and... h-horrible things. K-killing farmers and stealing their crop, raiding villages and r-raping and torturing. That you were behind any bad thing that ever happened here, even if no one saw you. No one did, I-I don't think, but they put sightings in the p-papers anyway. Not the girl. You two, and two others."

Louis looked shocked, his breath stolen from him. Marion could feel the heat rising in his face.

Aveiry spoke up. "When was this? I never heard..." Her face grew slack. "All the times he wouldn't read it to me..." She seemed to finally understand something. Marion assumed her friend Gabriel had tried to shield her from all of the chaos.

"Where is he? Where's Mchenry?" Aveiry asked, her voice low and angry.

"Please, I-I d-on't know, please-"

The woman Lisa rose her high-pitched voice. "He fled to the ocean, he was scared, we all were-" She whispered something in Vince's ear before pulling him to the other side of the road. When Aveiry moved closer on her horse, they poor travelers started to run, and soon disappeared into the fields and trees.

Marion turned to Louis, furious. "What the hell just happened?"

Louis stared into the brush where the commoners had vanished. The man did not speak.

"I'm going to fucking rip that bastard's throat out myself, you know that?" Marion's voice was scarily quiet. "I'll cut him 'til the ocean turns red, then drown him in his own damn blood. That'll remind him. Sent the wrong people out to die."

Louis looked up, into the distance. Rovas *would* pay- that much he agreed with. "They think I'm a murderer, Marion. That I.. that I..." Louis shook his head. Marion couldn't believe it either. They hadn't done those things, but they looked just then as if they could have.

"The ocean, he said, right?" Aveiry noted. The others nodded, sensing their chance for revenge. She had all the reason to be angry with Rovas as well. He had taken her father from her, destined her to her fate, whatever that was. Because of him, Aveiry was without Jacob, without a home. Perhaps in some twisted way, they were all alive because of Rovas Mchenry, but that didn't stop any of them from hating him.

Marion's heart suddenly lifted. *The man fled to the ocean, did he? Well I hope you're ready, you son of a bitch.*

I hope you're ready.

***

Paerdan hadn't changed much. There hadn't been many people here in the first place. Only farmers, travelers who just wanted to say that they'd been, and those passing through to get to somewhere else. Not so different from what they were doing now. He had only visited a few times, and to be honest Marion hadn't much liked it.

Now they walked along an old dirt road, trees lining the sides and fields beyond. Louis led the way, growing tenser. They were close; they had gone off the main road, passed a village and now what was left but their destination?

"This is it." Louis stopped, taking a deep breath. "Alright, we pretend we don't know anything about what was said about us, agreed?"

The others nodded. It was easier that way. Marion was aware that his friend had a large family, and had prepared himself for such.

A bigger family meant more eyes, more suspicions, more opinions and more arguments. Had they not fled further south, they would have had to find a ship on their own- and that could take days. Weeks, maybe. This boat might be gone and they would be searching for a ghost. So it was for that reason that Marion hoped the farm would not be abandoned. They were finding a ship, no matter what happened.

"Louis?" Marion asked, trotting up beside him. "Are you alright?" *Of course he's not alright, what's wrong with you?* But Louis nodded silently and moved forward. Slowly, but forward nonetheless. They had faced the Barren, had been wounded and chased and frightened in a living hell; they could deal with a few siblings. There was nothing to be worried about.

But you're not in the Barren anymore, a voice told him. His own voice, thank God. *You can't run from your problems- not now. Now you've gotta be careful, like before. Cunning. Manipulative. Confident. Use your mind, not your sword. You face people now, not beasts, and that is the surest way to get what you want.* And Marion told himself he was right. This wasn't wasn't a battle, this was negotiation, and if what those travelers had said was true, they'd have to keep it that way. Louis was dead to his family; and from what he'd heard, not many of them had cared for him much anyway.

They arrived at a turn in the road, leading to a small wood house and fields of dying crops. A fire blazed outside, in a pit circled by stones. Three people sat on benches beside it, holding their hands out to the flames. There was light inside the home, and movement. No one worked in the fields. There was nothing to harvest. He shivered. *What do they eat?* Marion thought. There had been little to no one in the village, only an old man and a few eyes glittering in dark windows. There had been no food to buy, no supplies nor weapons. People were quiet, and worried. Those left didn't know the danger was over.

Louis, Marion, and Aveiry trotted down closer to the people, and one of them looked up. He immediately shouted to the ones beside him before picking up a rusted spear-like weapon and walking up to greet them; though not in a friendly manner.

"What do you want? We don't have anything for you here." The man wore a flannel shirt, torn jeans, and boots. His greying brown hair was smoothed back against his head. A beard grew dark and bushy, though short enough and neatly trimmed. Marion saw recognition flash in Louis's eyes, and waited for him to speak.

"Henry?" Louis asked, and Marion winced, waiting for a reaction. None came.

"How do you know me? Who are you?" Then Henry's eyes took in the missing leg, the crutches tied to the side of the horse, the slightly familiar eyes and hair. His eyes widened.

"Oh my God. It's you. It's really you." Henry looked too shocked to say much else. When Louis tried to dismount, his brother lifted the spear, warning in his eyes.

"Shit, Louis, you better stay back, you stay right where you fucking are." His voice was panicked. The poor man truly didn't know what to do.

"Henry, what's going on?" Louis asked.

Marion breathed a sigh of relief. Pretend, yes, pretend. It would all be better that way. *Calm him down.*

"What the hell do you think is going on?" Henry said. "You can't- you can't just show up like this after leaving, after everything you've done-"

"I didn't leave, they took me!" Louis yelled. Something in him seemed to have snapped. "They took me! And I haven't done anything but save your damned life! Don't you see what's happened to me?" Louis gestured to himself. "I traveled across the fucking Barren and lost the only real brothers I've actually ever cared for. Is this how you'll treat me, when I finally come home?"

Henry was silent, confused. "What're you talking about?" He lowered the spear. "In the papers, everyone said-"

"I don't give a damn about what everyone else said. That was Rovas, it was all Rovas."

"The leader of Malivia?"

"Who else? What did you think, that I really murdered innocent people? That I'd run away from my only family to become an outlaw, a raider? Jesus, I'm a cripple, Henry! A fucking cripple! *Use your senses!*"

His brother dropped the spear into the dust, brow furrowed. "Who are they?" Henry asked, looking at his companions.

Marion stiffened. *Please let us in let us explain God let us get out of here. Tell him I'm your traveling companion, tell him she's... she's....* He knew how it would look to the brother. A little girl, wounded, scarred. For all Henry knew, she could be with them against her will.

"A friend. Marion. And... his daughter, Aveiry."

Henry gave them a wary glance. "Throw down your weapons. All of them."

They did as they were bid. Henry watched them closely as he collected their cold steel, his hands slightly shaking. Marion saw that Aveiry had not given up her dagger. Henry did not notice.

"Leave your horses. Follow me."

They dismounted, and tied their mares to the nearest tree. Marion felt naked without his weapon, and it gave him a vulnerable feeling; he didn't much care for it. Henry gave Louis one last glance before turning his back to them and leading the way down the path. The two others who had been by the fire approached, and seemed not to recognize their brother either. One of them whispered in Henry's ear, but he did not respond. A girl looked out the window, her eyes widening, and she let out a cry of shock before reeling back into the house. He saw Louis look down at the ground, shamed.

Marion leaned over, whispering. "*You have nothing to be ashamed of, Louis Willson.*"

Louis's eyes widened, surprised, grateful. The cripple smiled and regained his senses, taking on a more confident look. It suited him. Henry opened the old wooden door and motioned for them to come inside.

CHAPTER 39

LOUIS WILLSON
THE FARMLANDS, PAERDAN

Louis sat at the table, picking at a splinter of wood with his nail. The room was quiet. It was just as he remembered it, if not for a few subtle changes. Then again, it had only been just over a year, maybe two. It felt like a decade.

Marion sat to his left, Aveiry to his right. She sat close to him, despite their unfamiliarity. The rest were on the other side. Henry. He looked so different. Worn, almost. May was sickly and tired, more so than ever. Caios and Wrenn glared at him from across the table. All of them presented hard stares. Faylon was not there, and neither was Kendrik. If they were, Louis most likely would have been lying dead on the front porch. There was quiet. Louis knew he needed to speak first.

Candles lit the room, rusted lights hanging from the ceiling. One of the bulbs was broken. A radio hummed static in the corner. A deer hung from the rafters, a fresh catch, he assumed. The air in here smelled stuffy, like dust and old wood.

"Where are our brothers?" Louis asked, his voice shaky. Henry answered him. No one else seemed willing to talk.

"Faylon left for Calidor. Kendrik's dead."

"How?"

His brother seemed reluctant to answer. "He went after you. He didn't believe what they were saying. Kendrik... he tried to figure out the truth. He was slaughtered in a raid in Leison. It was blamed on you, and the others you were with." Henry glanced at Marion distrustfully.

Caios rose his voice. "So why have you come here? To kill us too?"

The voice was unfamiliar to his own ears. Much had changed since he had left. Louis met May's eyes, but she turned away. He sighed, exhausted. He was sick of this. Sick of all the judgement. Sick of all the hate.

"I've been through so much since we've last seen each other, it seems almost silly that I have to sit here and justify myself." Wrenn's angered expression turned to one of confusion. "I was tormented, hell, injured in more ways than you can imagine, inside and out. There were five of us. We all faced nightmares you wouldn't believe, and yet here I am, a cripple, with one other survivor. You deserve an explanation, but not a justification. I wouldn't have come back if I didn't need something, but this should come first. You might not believe me. You won't. But listen. In the end you'll understand. Just bear with me for a while."

***

It was dark when he finished. Louis had left many parts out, but the story was still long and hard to remember. They stared at him, eyes wide, and for a moment he thought they believed him. That all would be well, that they could trust him again. Then they started to laugh. Wrenn, Caios. Their laughter filled his ears, and his heart sank. Henry and Maise stayed silent.

"You didn't really think we'd believe that, did you?" Caios chuckled, his face red. He turned to Henry. "Get this lying little shit out of my sight."

Aveiry stood up and drew her dagger, the steel shining dangerously in the dim light. She held it in front of her threateningly, and there was silence.

"*Shut up.*" She said, shifting nervously.

Then Caios smiled, and chuckled knowingly. "And this little girl is supposed to frighten me?" He stood from his seat and walked closer to her.

"*Shut up!*" She told him again. "You're going to give us what we want, and we're going to leave."

Caios laughed. Marion stood as well; he didn't want her to get hurt. Louis looked behind him, at the door.

Henry locked it, and slipped the key in his pocket. "You're not going anywhere, Louis."

Caios ignored Aveiry's warning and came closer yet, a confident smirk on his face. The fear in Aveiry's eyes dissipated, and was quickly replaced with something cold, inhuman. In a flash the dagger was lodged deep in his throat, hot blood pouring from the wound. Caios collapsed, gurgling, choking on his last insult. His body lay still on the dirty floor, blood draining into the cracks of the wood. Aveiry stumbled back, the fear returning to her eyes. She was breathing heavily, scared. Something about her... something was wrong. But Louis pushed it out of his mind. His brother had just been killed. And despite the cruelty the man had shown him, the fact hit him cold in the heart.

"I'm sorry, Louis, I'm sorry-" Aveiry looked like just a little girl again, scared and confused.

Marion stared at her, holding his breath. Louis was frozen, in shock. He couldn't seem to do anything. *God how had it come to this, why had it come to this-*

"You will tell us where your ship is." Marion said, turning back to the remaining family. His voice calm and intimidating. "You will return us our weapons, and you *will let us go.*"

Everyone was quiet.

May turned desperately to Louis, tears in her eyes. "You're leaving Rendar?" She asked. Marion responded for him. Louis couldn't seem to find the words to speak.

"Yes. We've gotten word of other lands."

Her eyes lit up. She leaned forward eagerly. "*Please,* please take me with you, take me with you-"

"Why?" Louis asked, confused. "Why would you want to? It's dangerous."

387

"We're dying." Her breathing was ragged. "All of us. The land. It's breaking apart, it's dying, something dark broke it and it's sick and it's dying…"

Henry shook his head, the shock and angered defeat clear in his eyes. "She's… delusional. We're fine. She's staying here. The boat's at the dock, where it always was. Just… leave. Now." Regret flickered in Henry's expresion.

Aveiry scampered over, pulled her bloodied dagger from the body, and sheathed it, hands trembling. Louis winced at the sound. Marion helped Louis from his seat; he couldn't seem to tear his eyes away from his dead brother. Blood stained the floor, and the girl who had killed him left footprints of it as she walked. Aveiry jumped out of the open window and into the dark. The moment she left Wrenn rushed to his brother's side, shaking the motionless body.

"Come on." Marion said quietly. "Let's go."

In moments they were outside, breathing in the cool night air and stumbling towards their horses. Aveiry was already there.

"Hurry." Her voice shook. Marion tried to talk to her, but she deflected it. "Just… let's just go."

They mounted their horses and rode off onto the path. It was only then did Louis realize that there were no insects. No mosquitoes or the chirping of crickets, no buzzing or the little green lights of the glowbugs. Nothing. It unnerved him, as there were always things biting at him and buzzing when he had played out here as a child. Now it was different. Perhaps his sister had been right. Perhaps the land was dying.

But it didn't matter now.

No, it didn't.

Not anymore.

Not to them.

CHAPTER 40
MARION ARMAIS
THE OCEAN

The sea was bright and blue, shimmering in the sunlight. The shore had faded far behind them, and now Marion walked along the worn deck of the ship. Planks creaked under his feet as he walked, but in his heart he knew it was a strong ship. Small, but strong. They'd left, for good. Left adventurous into the great blue waves of the world. Marion's heart felt empty without Jacob, as if something were missing. As if something wasn't quite right.

And yet weight seemed to have been lifted off his shoulders, a pain vanished, a sickness healed. The salty wind tousled his hair and filled his lungs, the smell of fish and ocean and wood becoming familiar to his nose. It was peaceful, and he loved it.

"Marion?"

He whirled around, drawing his dagger and looking frantically for the danger. It was a woman, twenty-five or so, pale and frightened. He shook his head.

"You're- you're Louis's sister. May? How the hell did you get on the ship?"

She just stood there, trembling, weak and afraid. The poor girl opened her mouth but no sound came out. She had most likely snuck in before they had sailed.

"Never mind that. Why'd you come?" Marion asked, returning his dagger to its sheath and taking a cautious step closer. In the fading light, she looked almost like a ghost. A drop of rain fell on his cheek, then another. They were in silence for a moment more before she rushed forward and clung to him sobbing. It was not what he had expected; something was wrong.

He asked her again. "Why did you come?"

She looked up at him, desperate. "I want to help. I want to see Louis. *I want to escape.*"

Marion shrugged, uncertain, assuming there had been a fight with her brothers. "Okay. Uh, well, lemme show you to a cot then. You look exhausted."

He wrapped his arm around her and led her to the cabins below, out of the rain. Belowdecks it was dank and dark, despite the glowing lanterns hanging from the walls. Aveiry was fast asleep, Louis on deck, steering. The rhythm of the sea swayed them back and forth, the sound of the water splashing against the hull filling his ears.

"This alright?" Marion asked, and she nodded. May's body was light, frail, clothed in clothes too big; most likely from one of her brothers. Her face was tired and confused, filled with fear. With a mumbled word of thanks, May Willson collapsed on one of the cots. She was quickly pulled into sleep; her eyes were closed, and Marion stood in the quiet listening to the splash of the waves and the creaking of the ship.

***

On the deck, Marion walked over to Louis, who was puzzling over a faded map in his hands. The breeze chilled his skin, whipping through his thin white shirt and jeans. His friend had already discovered the sudden appearance of his sister, and though concerned, he had almost seemed relived. Marion was glad; Louis deserved a break from the stress.

"So?" Marion asked, leaning over the cold metal railing and taking a breath of the salty ocean air. It was calming, serene. He could get used to this.

"So what?" Louis asked, his green eyes shining happily as he looked up. The wind tousled his auburn hair, and he pushed it behind his ear absentmindedly.

"Still thirsting for revenge?"

"It would seem so."

"Rovas is as good as dead, then. You, Mr. Willson, are cripple to be wary of."

Louis laughed, and Marion grinned at the reaction; he was glad he could still bring some joy to his friend, even after all that had happened to them.

"It's true!"

"I'm sure it is."

There was a moment of silence, and Marion sighed. "How are you, Louis?"

There was a soft intake of breath, then a grin. Louis walked over to his side, looking out over the endless waves, at the beautiful horizon beyond, lit by the rising sun.

"You know, I think I'm okay."

Marion smiled.

"Yeah, me too."

THE END

ALAYNA COOPER was born February 23rd, 2003, in Athens, Ohio. From there she moved to Connecticut, then to Chicago for thirteen years, where she grew up writing. After eighth grade she moved to Denver, Colorado, and attended ThunderRidge High School. This is her first novel to be published.

AFTERWORD

First of all, I would just like to say how thankful I am for everyone who's supported me throughout this process; I couldn't have done it without you. Writing this was hard, frustrating, and took forever, but I would do it again. In fact, I'll be doing it all again very soon. This was the first of a trilogy, so there's still a long way to go for these travelers.

This has really been a great experience and I've learned a lot, which hopefully means this next book will be done a lot quicker and a lot better. I sincerely hope you enjoyed reading this, and I hope you took something meaningful away from it. And, on a completely different topic, I'd also like encourage you all to follow your passions. Do whatever makes you happy. It's worth it! I'm doing what I love and nothing makes me happier.

Please forgive me for any plot holes or mistakes, there were a lot of firsts in this novel for me, and I still have a lot to learn about all this. So, if you don't mind, give me a pass on any chunks of bad writing you may have encountered while reading.

Anyhow, raise your glass! Here's to a lot of hard work, to bringing stories to life, and to following dreams.

I'll be back.

EXTENDED DEDICATION

Dad ~ Mom ~ Owen

Nana ~ Pap ~ Grandma ~ Grandpa

Aunt Kristy ~ Uncle Greg ~ Aunt Sara ~ Uncle Aaron

Seth ~ Ben ~ Leah ~ Molly

And to all the people I've left out;
You all are awesome people, and I really appreciate your support.
Thank you!

CREDITS

Author
Alayna Cooper

Editor
David Derby

22056027R00216

Made in the USA
Lexington, KY
12 December 2018